Helen Black grew up in Pontefract, West Yorkshire. At eighteen she went to Hull University and left three years later with a tattoo on her shoulder and a law degree. She became a lawyer in Peckham and soon had a loyal following of teenagers needing legal advice and bus fares. She ended up working in Luton, working predominantly for children going through the care system.

Helen is married to a long-suffering lawyer and is the mother of twins who take up 90 per cent of her waking hours.

Also by Helen Black

(published by HarperCollins)
Damaged Goods
A Place of Safety
Dishonour

(published by Constable)
Blood Rush
Twenty Twelve
Dark Spaces
Friendless Lane

Taking Liberties

LEABHARLANNA CHONTAE FHINE GALL
FINGAL COUNTY LIBRARIES

Items should be returned on or before the last date shown below. Items may be renewed by personal application, writing, telephone or by accessing the online Catalogue Service on Fingal Libraries' website. To renew give date due, borrower ticket number and PIN number if using online catalogue. Fines are charged on overdue items and will include postage incurred in recovery. Damage to, or loss of items will be charged to the borrower.

CONSTABLE

First published in Great Britain in 2017 by Constable

1 3 5 7 9 10 8 6 4 2

Copyright © Helen Black, 2017

A CIP catalogue record for this book
is available from the British Library.

ISBN: 978-1-47212-420-3

Typeset in Bembo by Photoprint, Torquay
Printed and bound in Great Britain by
CPI Group (UK) Ltd, Croydon CR0 4YY

Papers used by Constable are from well-managed forests and other
responsible sources.

Constable
An imprint of
Little, Brown Book Group
Carmelite House
50 Victoria Embankment
London EC4Y 0DZ

An Hachette UK Company
www.hachette.co.uk

www.littlebrown.co.uk

If you cannot get rid of the family skeleton,
you may as well make it dance.

George Bernard Shaw

Chapter 1

August 1984, West Yorkshire
I hover outside the front room, wondering if now's a good time to ask Dad if I can have some money for new school shoes. I've got my eye on some lace-ups from the indoor market. I usually avoid asking him for owt. We all do. I'd rather wait till he's passed out and rifle his pockets, but for some reason he's taking it steady tonight. Typical. I'll have to brave it. I'm starting at the high school in a couple of weeks and I can't go in my pumps, can I?

I stick my head in and find him in his usual spot, legged out on the settee, a brown saucer acting as an ashtray balanced on his belly, a can of Heineken on the floor by his side. He's watching the Olympics, shaking his head. 'Have you seen this, Elizabeth?' He points at the telly. 'Silly cow's not wearing any shoes. I mean, how's she supposed to run without any shoes on?'

I shrug. The girl on the screen seems to be doing all right so far.

'Zola fucking Budd,' Dad spits. 'She's not even English. Born and raised in South Africa. She can't just change because it suits her.'

I watch her careering round the track in her bare feet. You'd think it'd hurt, wouldn't you? That she'd cut her toes and that. When I look back at Dad, he's draining his can.

'Get us another, Lib.' He crushes it in his fist and lets it drop to the carpet. 'And a box of matches while you're up. My lighter's had it.'

I scuttle out of the room. In the hallway Jay and Crystal are playing

1

Operation. The batteries are dead so if they touch the side with the metal tweezers they have to shout, 'Buzz.' Jay hasn't worked out that Crystal cheats. Frankie watches them from the bottom step, sucking at a baby bottle full of pop. I can smell his shitty nappy from here.

In the kitchen, Mam's sat on the high stool doing her makeup in a mirror. She puts on some really pale lipstick, which does her no favours, to be honest, but I'm not going to tell her. Frankie Goes To Hollywood is playing on the radio and she sings along. 'Dad wants another can and some matches,' I say.

She opens a drawer, pulls out a box of matches, shakes it, then tosses it to me.

'Where are the cans?' I ask.

'There's none left,' she says.

My face must drop, because she tuts. 'Do you think I can magic them out of thin air?' She turns the music up. 'Maybe if he got off his arse and earned some money once in a while.'

I feel a little tickle of panic in my chest. 'Can't I run round to the shop?'

'And use what?' Mam's scowling now. 'Brass fucking buttons?'

I flap my hands, trying to get her to keep her voice down, but it's too late. Dad's already in the doorway. 'What's going on here?' he shouts above the music.

Mam doesn't answer. Sometimes that's a good thing. Sometimes it's better to keep quiet. But not tonight.

'Turn that down,' he yells.

When Mam doesn't move, he slaps at her makeup bag. Eyeshadows and pencils hit the radiator.

'What did you do that for?' Mam asks.

Dad's eyes are flashing, his jaw flexing. 'A man needs some peace in his own house at the end of a day. Is that too much to fucking ask?' He leans across the counter so he's right up in Mam's face. 'Well, is it?'

She shakes her head.

2

'Right, then.' His fists are clenched, knuckles white, like the bones are going to pop through the skin. 'Give me a drink and let me get back to the telly.'

Mam stares at him for a moment, then she looks away, the anger drained out of her. She flicks her head to the ceiling, letting me know to get out of there.

I don't need telling twice and bolt from the kitchen, stopping at the foot of the stairs to scoop up Frankie. 'Bedroom,' I hiss at Jay and Crystal. 'Now.'

They take the stairs two at a time and don't slow down until they're in my room, skinny bodies pressed against the far wall. I stick Frankie on the bed, shut my door and push the dressing-table against it for good measure.

Through the floorboards we can hear the music playing. 'When Two Tribes Go To War' . . .

Then we hear the screaming.

Present day

Liberty fiddled with the dials on the dashboard, trying to turn on the air-conditioning. She'd had the Porsche six months and had been waiting for the weather to turn so she could razz into work with the roof down. But as soon as the sun had got his hat on, so had every protester in London, congregating outside the banks, insurance companies and law firms in the Square Mile. If she didn't want a face full of abuse, spit or worse, she needed to keep the car vacuum-sealed.

She'd made the mistake of trying to reason with them during the week between Christmas and New Year. Most of her partners were spending time with their families. Most of the protesters too. Each morning, as she pulled into her firm's underground car park, the same guy had half-heartedly waved a banner at her from the quiet street. He looked miserable in his combat jacket and beanie,

3

shivering in the splintering cold. On the third day she wound down her window and handed him the coffee she'd bought on the way.

'Is it free trade?' he asked, a drop of rain shivering at the end of his nose ring.

'Absolutely,' Liberty lied.

He'd taken the offering, wrapping his fingerless gloves around the cup, his nails black half-moons against the white polystyrene.

The next morning she'd arrived with another coffee and a blueberry muffin, but as she offered them to him, with a small smile, a girl had sprung from the shadows, knocking the cup out of Liberty's hands. 'Capitalist scum.'

From the girl's accent and straight white teeth, Liberty had her pegged. Student. Middle class. Home counties. She'd met kids like that by the lorry-load at university. Their rooms all slogans and scented candles. 'Back from skiing, are we?' Liberty asked.

The girl's face contorted. 'People like you have sucked this country dry, raking in millions, evading tax, while ordinary decent families are forced out onto the street.'

Liberty couldn't contain a laugh. Kids like her wouldn't know an ordinary person if one bit them on the arse. The only contact they had with the working classes was Mummy's cleaner and the terribly nice man who came to service the Aga at the beginning of December.

'You should be made to pay for what you've done,' the girl shouted.

'Oh, grow up,' Liberty said.

Then it hit her. Warm and slimy. Running from her temple to her cheekbone.

Dog shit.

Since then she'd ignored them all. Kept her windows and doors locked. Today, despite the welcome sunshine, she did the same.

★   ★   ★

'Boss wants to see you,' said Tina.

Liberty hid her irritation. She couldn't remember the number of times she'd explained to her secretary that she was a partner at Howell and May. She was her own bloody boss.

Tina hovered over Liberty's desk. Stout and immovable as a tree. 'He says it's urgent.'

'Don't you have some filing to do?'

Tina put her hands on her hips, a ring on every finger. 'I'll tell him you're too busy, then, shall I?'

Liberty put down her pen. They both knew that wasn't going to happen. In theory, all partners were equal but in reality some were more equal than others. And nobody told Ronald Tate they were too busy to see him. 'I think your Facebook status needs updating,' she said. 'I'd suggest Pain In The Arse.'

'Ain't you the funny one,' said Tina.

Liberty spun round in her chair, using her palm to propel her from the desk. It wasn't just that she loathed being summoned, like a minion, though she did loathe it, with a passion she usually reserved for articles in the *Daily Mail* about asylum seekers. Or reality television. Or farmers' markets. Farmers' markets in particular made her froth. All middle-class self-righteousness and hand-crafted venison pasties. But what she really hated about meetings with Ronald was her own reaction. Two seconds in his company, and she felt a fraud. As if she had no business working there.

'There's no point putting it off,' said Tina.

'Are you still here?' Liberty pushed off for another 360-degree turn, but Tina grabbed the back of the chair and brought her to a halt. 'They made you up because you're bleedin' good at what you do,' she said. 'Don't ever forget that.'

Liberty felt exposed. A wound without a plaster.

'Get going, then,' snapped Tina. 'I ain't going to bleedin' well carry you.'

★ ★ ★

5

Ronald Tate gave Liberty one of his best cappuccino smiles. 'Come on in, darling.' He gestured to the seat on the opposite side of his desk. 'Do sit.'

Ronald had the corner office with views over the Thames, Tower Bridge and Canary Wharf to his left, the London Eye and the Houses of Parliament to his right. He often joked that he could sell tickets.

Liberty sat.

'I need you to do me a favour, darling,' said Ronald.

'I need you to stop calling me "darling",' Liberty replied. In her head.

Ronald splayed his hands on the empty expanse of his desk, his nails buffed and shiny. 'Have you heard of callme.com?'

Liberty nodded. The website was the biggest dating chat room in the world, its owner a perma-tanned seventy-year-old, standing at tit height to the glamour model who often accompanied him.

'They want to merge with their biggest competitor,' said Ronald.

'Will the Monopolies Commission let them?' Liberty asked.

'Depends who they instruct as their lawyer.'

Ronald held her gaze, and Liberty felt the fizz of excitement shimmy down her spine. A multi-million-pound transaction like that was big-league stuff.

'I don't need to tell you that a deal such as this would put Howell and May on the map,' said Ronald. 'Taking any lawyers associated with it along for the ride.' He leaned forward. 'Can I count on your support, darling?'

Hell, yes. 'I'll do whatever I can to help,' said Liberty. 'Other casework allowing.'

'I'm glad to hear that because we need to do the owner a small favour before the job is officially ours,' said Ronald.

'Go on,' said Liberty.

'He has a problem with his son.'

Liberty recalled a photo of him in the paper, spliff in one hand, *Big Brother* contestant in the other. 'What sort of problem?'

'He's been arrested.' Ronald opened his palms. 'He's being held up in your neck of the woods.'

'Hampstead?' Liberty asked.

'No, darling.' Ronald gave three small, tight laughs. Ha. Ha. Ha. 'Yorkshire.'

Liberty blinked. It was a lifetime since she'd been back to Yorkshire. 'I can't really recommend anyone, Ronald. I don't know the firms up there,' she said.

'That's not what's needed,' said Ronald. 'This has to be kept strictly under wraps, strictly *entre nous*.'

'I don't follow,' said Liberty.

'We need you to go up there and sort out this mess.'

The speedometer read seventy-four and she yawned.

London had been deserted at the start of Liberty's journey and the Porsche had flown down Hampstead High Street. It had been like a disaster movie when the hero wakes up to find everyone dead, steals the nearest super-car and heads off like a mad man. As a kid, Liberty had read a book like that. The main character had been all on his own, hot-wiring a TVR and helping himself to chocolate from the shelves of deserted supermarkets, then setting off to find other survivors. How had that book ended? Did the boy find anyone else?

The traffic slowed to sixty-eight. Wasn't this supposed to be a bloody motorway?

Her mobile rang and caller ID flashed up on the dashboard. 'Hello, Ronald.'

'Good morning, darling,' he said. 'Just checking you're still set for the old trip up north.'

She caught sight of a sign saying ten miles to Wakefield. 'I'll be at the prison in less than half an hour,' she said.

'Good grief.' Ronald let out a chuckle. 'Did you set off at five?'

'Something like that.' In fact, it had been ten past. Knowing she'd have trouble sleeping, Liberty had drunk half a bottle of Rioja before bed. Then she'd finished it around midnight. At half past four, accepting sleep wasn't on the cards, she'd swallowed three Anadin Extra and taken a hot shower.

'Glad to hear you're so eager,' said Ronald. 'The sooner you sort everything out, the sooner you can come back to the office.'

Liberty pressed the heel of her hand into her eye socket. How could she explain herself without sounding negative? 'The thing is, Ronald, I'm not sure what I'm meant to do when I arrive.'

'Oh, I'm certain someone will guide you through Security, darling,' he replied.

Liberty released her hand, leaving her vision Vaselined. 'I was thinking more of the legal stuff,' she said. 'You do know I have absolutely no experience of criminal law?'

There was a slight pause, which Liberty's headache felt compelled to fill.

'What about Dirty Deptford Days?' Ronald asked.

The trainee solicitors and young assistants at Howell and May were encouraged to offer their services to a law centre in southeast London. A three-line whip to atone for the supposedly morally dubious day-to-day job of making rich people richer. Liberty had always wondered what the law-centre staff had made of them, streaming from their black cabs in their cashmere overcoats.

'Didn't you represent a guy on Death Row in Jamaica?' Ronald asked.

Liberty sniffed. Her twenty-five-year-old self had grabbed the case, hoping for a free trip to the Caribbean, with little thought for Leroy Reid sweating it out in his bare jail cell, literally waiting to be hanged. 'I don't think I could class that as relevant experience,' she said. 'The whole thing was over before it started.'

'You got him off?'

'No,' she replied. 'He topped himself.' She opened the window a crack and a rush of cold air kissed her cheek. She lifted her chin to let it cool her throat.

'What other cases did you do at the law centre?' Ronald asked.

'A couple of eviction notices,' she answered. 'A speeding fine, if I remember correctly.'

What she did remember correctly was how she had found any excuse not to go, loathing the rubbish-filled gutters of Deptford High Road, where the office was, and the smell of the halal butcher's next door. Most of all she remembered the clients and their sad, bewildered faces.

'Oh, well, not to worry, darling,' said Ronald. 'How hard can it be?'

Liberty wasn't sure. That was the point.

'You'll pick it up,' he continued. 'I have every faith in you.'

They said their goodbyes and Liberty turned off the motorway. As she slowed at the roundabout, an orange Fiat Uno stalled in front of her. She pressed her hand to the horn and a flock of rooks rose as one from a telegraph pole. The glossy black birds immediately headed south. They passed overhead, like a thunderous cloud, then disappeared, leaving only the splat of a shit on Liberty's windscreen.

Sol Connolly stood in the hospital room, hands in his pockets, looking at the young woman, still and pale on the bed, each eyelid held shut with a piece of tape. Only the rhythmic sigh of the ventilator punctuated the silence as it forced air into useless lungs.

He shook his head sadly and went to the window. In the courtyard below, patients, nurses and visitors huddled together to smoke. One man was still in his theatre gown, attached to a drip, which he pulled along like a dog on a lead. In different circumstances Sol would have admired his commitment to the cause.

The door opened, and he turned to find a doctor in the room, a mop of wild curls held in a ponytail with an elastic band. He flashed her his warrant card.

She crossed the room, her Crocs making a polystyrene squeak, took the card, checked it carefully and handed it back to him. 'Detective Inspector Connolly,' she said. 'What can I do for you?'

'I'm just here for an update,' he said.

The doctor gave a cool smile. 'I'm afraid there's nothing much to tell you. We're keeping her under until the swelling in her brain reduces.' She held up both hands, palms towards him. 'And I don't know how long that will take.'

Sol let out a breath that rattled his lips. She'd been brought in three days ago and immediately placed in a medically induced coma. Who could guess when he'd finally get to speak to her?

'Do you know her?' the doctor asked.

Sol nodded. 'Kyla Anderson.' He'd first met her twenty years ago. She'd been six years old and he'd been in uniform, green as you like. Sol had gone to the Andersons' flat to nick Kyla's dad for supply of class A. The stupid bastard had been caught on CCTV openly dealing outside the railway station. The pictures had been grainy back in those days, but he could have picked out Dale Anderson anywhere, all five foot six of him and two front teeth missing. He might as well have worn a T-shirt with his name and address printed on it. Even then, Kyla had been a cheeky sod, one minute telling Sol to fuck off, the next asking for sweets. Over the years he'd tried to keep an eye out for her, but what could you do?

The doctor picked up the chart at the end of the bed. 'A prostitute, right?'

'Yeah,' said Sol. Kyla had never really stood a chance, had she? With the parents she had and the place she grew up, it was a done deal. 'How did you know?'

The doctor shrugged. 'Vaginal and anal fissures. Plus we had to cut her out of a red PVC cat suit.'

Sol laughed.

'Though she wasn't using,' said the doctor.

'Really?' asked Sol, his surprise genuine.

The doctor held out the chart to him, as if she expected him to understand the medical jargon scribbled across the page in illegible handwriting. 'Her bloods were clear and there are no injection sites – well, no fresh ones,' she told him.

Sol moved to the bed and looked at Kyla's arms, laid by her sides on top of the blue blanket. The crooks of both elbows were a mass of old needle marks and her wrists were liberally layered with long, thin scars from her various 'cries for help'. But the doc was right. No new tracks.

She scrawled something across the notes then scratched her scalp with the end of the biro. 'You weren't expecting her to be clean?' she asked.

'You could say that,' Sol replied. Kyla had started smoking weed at twelve, skag at fourteen. For the last five years she'd been living on four digs of brown a day and ice cream. 'Has anyone visited?' he asked.

The doctor shook her head.

He pulled out his card and pressed it into her hand. Her palm was hot but not sticky. 'If there's any change.'

'I'll call you,' said the doctor, pocketing the card.

'And if there's any chance of her waking up . . .'

'You'll be the first to know.' The doctor turned to leave. 'Frankly, there's no one else to tell.'

★ ★ ★

11

Liberty slowed to a halt in the car park at number five Love Lane. 'You have arrived,' the satnav informed her.

She exhaled audibly. If she'd been a smoker, now would have been exactly the right time to spark up. But she wasn't. Growing up, everyone around her had smoked. Dad endlessly puffing away on the Embassy Regal, Mum on the Benson & Hedges. Beagles had inhaled less nicotine than she had.

Liberty was way out of her depth, terrified, cursing Ronald for insisting she come here. Why the hell had she agreed? Why hadn't she just told him she couldn't do it? Why could she never admit to any form of weakness? She locked the car and looked up at the prison. Built in 1594 as a House of Corrections, HMP Wakefield was now a high-security unit, housing prisoners serving life, predominantly for sex offences. Known locally as Monster Mansion, the names of its inmates read like a Who's Who of the mad, the bad and the absolutely fucking sick. The concrete walls blocked out the sun and it was cold in the gloom.

Ten feet away, an ancient BMW pulled in. The private registration read RAJ 23S. The bolts on either side of the S made it look like a dollar sign. Almost. The driver's door flew open and a cheap slip-on shoe appeared, the edge of the plastic sole flapping away from the toe. It hovered in mid-air for at least a minute, making Liberty wonder if anyone was attached. At last, its owner followed, and Liberty saw a short fat man in a suit and turban. He dragged a briefcase after him, the clasp open, papers spilling out. He tried to shut the car door but the end of his seatbelt was caught outside, making the unmistakable crunch of metal on metal. The man swore. His words were in a language Liberty didn't understand, but the meaning was clear.

When he finally managed to lock his door, he looked over to her. 'Nice motor,' he said. His accent was pure West Yorkshire.

'Thanks.' Liberty gestured to his rust-eaten BMW. 'You too.'

'Can't beat German engineering.' He patted the roof of his car. 'You're new.'

It wasn't a question.

'Is it that obvious?' Liberty asked.

The man seesawed his hand. 'All the solicitors in these parts know one another.'

'What makes you so sure I'm a solicitor?'

The man laughed. His teeth were white, but a hint of gold flashed from a crown at the back of his mouth. 'Smart clothes, expensive wheels, you're not likely to be a wife or girlfriend to one of this lot.' He jerked his head towards the prison wall, topped with razor wire. 'Not that many of our friends in here have wives or girlfriends. Most of 'em have been abandoned by their own mothers.'

He turned to the main entrance and gestured for Liberty to join him. She fell in beside him and they walked together, the loose sole of the man's shoe giving a tap after each step. 'Raj Singh.' He held out his hand, a dull gold band sliding down his wrist and wobbling against the base of his thumb.

His palm was surprisingly smooth and cool. The sort of hand you'd want on your forehead if you felt under the weather. 'Liberty Chapman,' she said.

'And where are you from, Liberty?' he asked.

'London,' she said. 'Hampstead.'

Raj knitted his brow, making his turban bob. 'Really? I could swear I detect a local twang.'

Liberty took a deep breath in through her nose. All those years down south and all that cash spent on elocution lessons. 'I moved away a long time ago,' she said.

He nodded, as if he was satisfied. 'And who're you here to see?'

'I don't think I should say.'

Raj gave a bark of a laugh. 'You are new, aren't you?'

'Client confidentiality and all that,' Liberty replied, with a raised eyebrow.

Raj patted her arm, still chuckling. 'Quite right too, love.'

Christ, it was like the Wild West up here. She was relieved when they reached the door and were greeted by a prison officer slumped at a long counter behind a Perspex window, one buttock taking up his stool, the other oozing slowly down the side. 'Morning, Reg,' he said.

If Raj was offended by the Anglicizing of his name, he certainly didn't show it. 'Morning, John,' he said. 'How's the back?'

John put one hand to his spine. 'Killing me.' The other reached over to a family bag of Cheesy Wotsits. 'What can I do? It's my trial.'

Raj slid his visiting order into the security slot and nodded for Liberty to do the same. John shovelled a fistful of Wotsits into his mouth and checked the paperwork. When he was satisfied, he sent it back through, and Raj returned Liberty's visiting order to her. There was a dusty orange thumbprint in the left-hand corner, which she avoided touching.

'Time for the technology,' said John. 'Eyes on the prize, Miss Chapman.'

'Sorry?'

Raj pointed up at a camera mounted above the window. 'Retinal recognition,' he told her. 'It lets John here check that the person coming out of the nick is the same one who went in.'

Liberty could hardly contain her laughter. 'Don't you think someone might spot an inmate trying to pass himself off as a woman?'

'You'd be surprised, love,' said Raj, and moved her to a small black X marked on the floor. 'Say cheese.'

When they had both had their eyes recorded, he grinned at her. 'Now for the locker room. This way.'

Liberty followed him into a square, windowless room to the

14

left, the four walls banked by metal lockers, every door bearing the same notice:

Only approved paperwork, pens and pencils allowed beyond this point.

No other items may be taken into HMP Wakefield, including money, keys, mobile phones and other electronic equipment.

Persons found in possession of unacceptable items will be detained and charged. No exceptions.

'They don't exactly trust us, do they?' said Liberty.

'To be honest, it's as much for us as them,' said Raj, making for the nearest locker.

'How's that?' Liberty asked.

'You can make a real mess of someone's face with a paperclip, love.'

Liberty chose a locker on the other side of the room to hide her face, which she knew would show horror and panic in every pore. When she opened it, she found a ball of used tissue nestled at the back. Checking her gág reflex, she decided against removing it. Her bag might have cost the best part of two grand in Prada, but it couldn't contract hep C, could it?

'Ready?' Raj asked.

Liberty slammed the locker door and followed him out of the room, back to John.

'Sorted?' asked John.

Raj nodded and placed his hand on the entrance door. As a low buzzer sounded, he pushed it open and a smell unfurled around him. It moved towards Liberty. Sweat, urine and disinfectant. 'Welcome to the ninth circle of Hell,' said Raj.

Chapter 2

May 1985

I take the tray of buns out of the oven. A couple are a bit burned but not too bad.

'They're nice,' says Mam, not taking her eyes off the mirror.

She had a bubble perm yesterday and is trying to comb it over the bald spot above her ear. Frankie sits on the chair next to her, grizzling. 'Give him a bottle, would you, Lib?' she says.

I reach into the cupboard for a baby bottle and fill it with pop. 'He's too old for these, Mam. The health visitor says they'll ruin his teeth.'

'Yeah, well, that stuck-up bitch doesn't have to live with him, does she?' Mam replies.

I hold the drink out to Frankie and he grabs it, sucking at it for all he's worth, making these funny little noises in his throat.

Mam gives her hair a last spray with lacquer and smiles at me. 'You're pleased your dad's coming home, aren't you?'

'Yeah,' I say.

'So why the long face?'

I start turning the buns out of their tin. It's not that I don't want Dad to come home. He's my dad and that's that. I mean, when he first got sent down I was glad. The mess he made of Mam during that last hiding he gave her! Broken nose, two teeth knocked out and a gash on the side of her head where he smashed her against the wall. There's still a bit of plaster missing on that spot above the radiator and her hair's never grown back properly over the scar. He deserved to go to jail.

Then she met some bloke down the Turk's Head. 'Call me Uncle Alan,' he said, and brought us all chips and gravy whenever he came round. Mam seemed happy until she caught him helping to wash Jay's arse when he was in the bath. We never mentioned Uncle Alan again.

Next thing we know, Mam's had a letter from Dad saying he's sorry, he's changed. Can people change?

There's a loud knock at the door and Mam jumps off the stool. 'That'll be him,' she says. 'You stay here.'

She clacks down the hall and opens the door. There are muffled voices and the tinkling giggle I only ever hear when Dad's around. When he sticks his head round the kitchen door, I can see he's a lot thinner and his hair's cut close to his scalp. 'Something smells grand,' he says.

'I made you some buns,' I reply. 'Do you want one?'

He looks at them on the cooling rack. 'Where's Crystal and Jay?'

'Playing outside.' I jump up. 'Shall I get 'em?'

Dad shakes his head. 'I'm knackered, love. Think I'll get my head down for an hour or two.' He ruffles Frankie's hair. 'Round everyone up at teatime. How about a Chinese? With your buns for afters?'

A Chinese. I can't believe it. I bloody love sweet and sour, I do.

'Right, then.' Dad rubs his hands together. 'Why don't you come up with me, Mrs Greenwood? Show me what's changed around here.'

Mam laughs again, like a little bell ringing, and I think that maybe, just maybe, everything's going to be all right.

The inside of Monster Mansion was altogether different from the outside. Where the exterior had been a study in razor-wire-topped walls and retinal security checks, the inside was bland and quiet. Only the plastic farting of the loose sole of Raj's shoe punctured the silence as they walked down a windowless and hourless corridor of concrete and strip lighting.

'Where is everyone?' Liberty asked.

'On the wings,' Raj replied.

'Doing what?'

'Smoking, talking, staring at the ceiling.' Raj shrugged. 'Twenty-two hours' bang-up, most days.' He gave her a sideways glance, his gold filling winking cheekily at her. 'What were you expecting?'

Liberty didn't have an answer to that. Or not one she was willing to share with someone she'd met less than ten minutes ago. Her main points of reference were the episodes of *Porridge* her parents had loved.

They reached the end of the corridor and waited at a door. The words 'Legal Visits' had been painted in blue. At last it swung open.

'Here again, Reg?' said the guard, a minimal amount of hair attempting to cover the maximum amount of pink scalp.

'Where else would I be on a nice summer's day?' Raj said, with a smile.

'He's waiting for you.' The guard jerked his head over his shoulder, dislodging a well-greased strand of hair that fell over his face, like a thick black arrow pointing to the floor. 'Usual spot.'

'Must be my natural charm,' said Raj, and handed over his visiting order.

Liberty followed suit, pressing her own order into the guard's hand.

He checked it, then looked at her for longer than was necessary, the stray strand of hair billowing gently in the air from his nostrils. 'Take a seat, Miss,' he said. 'He'll be brought out in a tick.'

'Thank you,' she answered coolly.

When they passed through the doorway, Raj gave her a nudge. 'Don't mind the locals,' he said. 'They don't get out much.'

She was about to point out that the staff might behave with manners if people like Raj pulled them up from time to time, but she lost her train of thought as she found herself on a walkway overlooking what appeared to be a school gymnasium, filled with tables and chairs.

As Liberty and Raj made their way down the staircase, the impression of being in a school gym was completed by the lurid yellow bibs that the prisoners were wearing. Liberty half expected a game of netball to break out.

As if reading her mind, like a spirit guide, Raj once again filled her in: 'They make it easier for the guards to spot the inmates,' he said. 'Keep tabs on where everyone is.'

Liberty glanced behind her and saw that, up on the walkway, the guard who had let them in was scanning the hall.

'Some of these people . . .' Raj tailed off. 'It's not like other prisons.'

Liberty nodded, and cursed herself for agreeing to take on the case. Her bread and butter came from drafting contracts. Clauses, sub-clauses, definitions and criteria: these were her friends. 'Don't we get a private room to speak to our clients?' she asked.

Raj shook his head. 'That's only in the purpose-built prisons. The Mansion's ancient so there's not enough space for such luxuries.'

Liberty was horrified. How could anyone conduct a confidential conversation surrounded by all these people?

'To be honest, love, you don't want to be in a room on your own with any of this little lot,' he added.

They picked their way through the tables but Raj slowed as they approached one table where a man in a bib was already seated. He stared at them eagerly. He was small, almost child-like in stature, though his face was lined and pockmarked. He bore a silvery scar between lip and nose. Liberty gave a sharp intake of breath as recognition hit her, like a sucker punch, and the man clapped his hands together, as if delighted that she knew who he was.

'Don't say a word,' Raj hissed at her. 'Just keep walking.'

Liberty couldn't have spoken if she'd wanted to: her throat had suddenly constricted. What could anyone say to a man who had raped and killed three little girls on their way home from Brownies?

As they came alongside the table, the man jumped to his feet. He was a foot shorter than Liberty, but he stretched out his arms to block their way.

'I'll be with you in a second, Dave,' said Raj, pushing past him, his voice absurdly calm.

'Aren't you going to introduce me to your friend?' the man asked.

His voice was soft, with a feminine quality. Liberty remembered that the papers had called it 'camp', but that wasn't quite right. They'd also reported that the victims had been dismembered, their legs found in a chest freezer alongside numerous bags of peas and sweetcorn, by a constable who had been in the job only a week. Sadly, the papers had got that bit right.

'Where are your manners, Raj?' Each word distinct, clear, like a staccato note from a flute. 'This isn't like you at all.'

Raj steered Liberty to an empty table at the far side of the hall. 'Don't look back. Sit facing away from him.' He pressed her into a chair. 'You don't want someone like that messing with your head. All right?'

She smiled weakly and he winked at her.

'Oh, Ra-aj,' Dave's voice sang out.

'Another day in Paradise.' Raj squeezed her shoulder and headed back to his client.

Liberty concentrated on breathing and placed her paperwork in two piles on the table in front of her. She aligned them perfectly as she tried to steady the ragged edges of each lungful of air. In through the nose, out through the mouth. She laid her pen horizontally, two centimetres from the first pile, pen tip and top right-hand corner of the piece of paper in line. In through the nose, out through the mouth.

'Liberty Chapman?'

Liberty's head snapped up involuntarily at the sound of her name. Standing at the table was a man in his early twenties, gym-defined, hair artfully highlighted, skin a Riviera-yacht golden tan.

'Mr Rance?' Liberty jumped to her feet and held out her hand. 'How do you do?'

Rance's handshake was cold and limp. He sneered at her, exposing even teeth that clearly spent every night in a bleaching tray. She was about to suggest he take a seat, when Rance plonked himself down with a thud. He wiped his nose along the inside of his palm with long slow strokes from the base of his middle finger to his wrist.

'As you know I'm from—'

'I shouldn't be here.' Rance held up his palm to silence her. A thin slug trail of snot glistened at her. 'You know that, right?'

'I'm sure we can resolve this problem in a timely fashion,' Liberty replied.

'Do you know what sort of people are in here?' Rance demanded.

Liberty did know. She could hear them all around her. She could smell them. Hell, she could taste their livery sweetness at the back of her tongue.

'You need to go and find the silly cow that stitched me up,' said Rance. 'Do whatever it takes.' He leaned towards her. 'Pay whatever needs to be paid. Just get her to admit that she's lying.'

'I don't think it works—'

Rance thumped the table, knocking Liberty's pen out of place. 'Everything works like that. You're a lawyer – you charge enough to understand how things are. She's lying and you need to prove it.'

Liberty rearranged her pen at the head of her client's charge sheet.

Case Number : 1670A201
    Regina
    V
    Renton Rance

On 22 July 2015 the above-named person, Renton Rance, was charged with:

1. Indecent Assault contrary to s14(1) and s15(1) Sexual Offences Act 1956
2. Assault occasioning actual bodily harm contrary to s47 Offences Against the Person Act 1861.

A very rich boy had attacked a very poor girl and now he thought he could buy his way out of trouble.

'You have to get me out of here,' said Rance. 'Find the girl.'

As soon as Sol got out of the hospital, he pulled out his e-cig. The wife had bought him a load of flavoured cartridges for it and he was working his way through them. Today's offering was Red Berries and it was rank.

'Who pissed on your chips?'

Sol looked up and smiled. Daisy Clarke was a lap-dancer and prostitute he'd come across during half a dozen raids. Lots of his colleagues in the Vice Squad didn't have time for the girls, thought of them as little more than meat. But didn't that make them as bad as the men they were trying to put away? 'That's a nice shiner, you've got yourself,' Sol said.

Daisy's fingers gently tapped a black eye, the top lid twice its normal size, a purple and green bruise underneath. 'And look at this.' She pulled down the front of her top to reveal infected toothmarks. 'Bastard.'

'I hope you've made a statement,' said Sol.

'Yeah.' Daisy pulled out a packet of Marlboro and lit up. 'He's banged up.'

Sol watched her sucking at the fag, blowing grey smoke from the corner of her mouth. 'Give us one of those, Daisy, love.'

The girl cackled and handed him the packet. 'I thought it was meant to be us lot that ponced ciggies off you lot.'

'You probably earn more than I do,' he said. 'And I know I pay more tax.'

Daisy smacked him playfully on the shoulder, watching him with a smile as he lit up. 'Gotta go, Sol. I need some antibiotics or something for this.' She waved vaguely at the bite mark. 'It's fucking minging.'

He nodded at her and lifted his cigarette in thanks. A delicious cloud of heat and chemicals filled his lungs and, not for the first time, he thanked the god of nicotine. As he watched her go, he had a thought and called after her, 'Hey, Daisy, you know Kyla Anderson?'

'Course I do,' she said.

'Did you know she got clean?'

Daisy's one good eye opened wide. 'Fuck me, wonders will never cease.'

'She's in here.' Sol jerked his head back towards the hospital. 'It's pretty bad.'

Daisy was a lot less shocked to hear this news. Girls like them got beaten up every day of the week. By punters. By pimps. Part and parcel of their job.

'Do you know where she'd been working?' Sol asked.

Daisy sniffed. 'Not recently. We were both up the Cherry but she left a couple of months ago. Shame, really. There's hardly any English girls left there now.'

'Didn't she say where she was going?' he asked.

'Said she was packing it in full stop.' Daisy laughed. 'But we all say that, don't we?'

'There haven't been any whispers about what happened to her?'

Daisy shook her head.

'If you do hear, you've got my number,' Sol said.

He watched Daisy totter inside, pulling the back of her mini skirt down over her mottled thighs, and finished his fag. Time to start asking a few awkward questions.

Liberty let the satnav guide her to the address Rance had given and tried to swallow the nauseous feeling that was swelling in her stomach and rising through her chest. She hadn't been down these roads in a long time. More than twenty years ago, she had caught the ten fifteen from Leeds to King's Cross and never returned. Now here she was again. Everything looked different, yet everything looked the same.

'Your destination is ahead,' the satnav informed her as she drove past a Polish mini-market, a bookie's and the Sun Studio – 'Yorkshire's Premier Tanning Salon'.

'You have arrived,' said the satnav and Liberty pulled over.

The Black Cherry had been a pub back in the day. Her parents used to drink there, though Dad always moaned that the beer was watered down. Christ, Liberty couldn't remember when she'd last given the place a glancing thought. She'd trained herself not to.

What she wanted more than anything was to get back to her real life. A life she had built for herself on blood, sweat and tears. Coming back here, dredging up old memories, was not part of that life.

She grabbed her mobile and called Ronald.

'Darling. How are things *oop* north?' Ronald put on a ridiculous Yorkshire accent.

Liberty was in no mood to fanny about. 'Pretty crap, actually. I've been to see Rance.'

'How is he?'

'In the right place as far as I can see.'

'Innocent until proven guilty and all that jazz, darling,' Ronald replied.

A fly had made its way into the car. It dive-bombed Liberty, its drone close to her ear. She swatted at it in irritation. 'He asked me to find the victim,' she said. 'Which, let me tell you, feels all kinds of wrong.'

'There is no possession in a witness,' Ronald replied. 'Nothing to prevent the defence questioning the girl.'

The fly had found the windscreen and buzzed angrily against the glass.

'Even when she's the sort of girl who works in a lap-dancing club?' Liberty asked.

'Especially when she's the sort of girl who works in a lap-dancing club.'

'Oh, come on, Ronald.' Liberty opened her window and tried to shoo the fly outside. 'This place isn't Spearmint Rhino. The girls who end up here don't have too many choices in life.'

'Which is why they're likely to be pretty poor witnesses.'

Liberty sighed. Ronald was right. Chances were the victim would have a habit and a string of previous convictions as long as her arm.

'Listen, darling, you're not there to harass anyone,' said Ronald. 'Just to ask a few questions and assess the strength of the case against Rance.'

'And if she's not here or she won't speak to me?' Liberty asked.

'Then you come home.'

Liberty hung up, reached into her bag for the prosecution papers, rolled them into a cosh and smacked the fly.

★ ★ ★

The Black Cherry still had the same square red-brick façade but the windows were now blacked out, the tinted glass painted with the white silhouettes of nude women and pairs of cherries. The sign above the door read, 'Live Dancing Seven Days A Week'. The poor women working there didn't even get to keep their knickers on of a Sunday.

Liberty locked the car and went inside.

'Listen, Ted, you know the bloody rules, you come in here often enough.'

A birdlike woman in her early sixties was shouting, legs akimbo, hands on her hips. The man she was yelling at was twice her size, head shaved, the tattoo of a claw-mark etched across his neck.

'No. Free. Dances.' The woman punctuated each word with an exaggerated nod. 'Ever.'

'You know I'm good for it.' The man's tone was surprisingly meek. 'Just a bit short till payday, like.'

'Then go home, Ted. Watch the telly, read the paper, remind your wife what you bloody look like.' The woman flung open the door. 'But don't come back with an empty wallet.' The man sighed and turned to Liberty. 'I hope you're not expecting a warm welcome here, love, cos you'll not get it.'

'Out,' the woman bellowed.

He shuffled away, and when the door had swung shut, the woman smoothed down her leopard-print blouse. The top three buttons were undone, revealing a tangle of gold chains and a wrinkled cleavage. She went to the black velvet drape that separated the reception area from the club and adjusted it. 'I'm not made of stone, but this isn't a charity, is it? ' she said to Liberty, who shook her head. 'Now, what can I do for you?'

'I'm looking for a girl.'

'Oh, aye?' said the woman.

'I think she might work here,' said Liberty. 'Her name's Daisy Clarke.'

26

The woman pursed her lips. Behind the drape, music began to play, the deep throb of bass seeping through.

'Police?' the woman asked.

'No,' Liberty answered.

'Didn't think so.' The woman looked Liberty up and down. 'That rigout's too nice for the law.'

'Thanks.'

'Bet them shoes didn't come off the market,' the woman observed.

Liberty looked down at her Louboutins. They'd cost almost five hundred quid, and that was in the sale.

'So, what do you want?' the woman asked.

Liberty noted she had not denied that Daisy Clarke worked there. 'I'm not here to cause any problems,' she said. 'I just need to see her. I'll pay for her time.'

The woman raised an eyebrow, so thin it was more pencil than hair. 'And if she doesn't want to talk to you?'

'Then I'll leave immediately.'

The woman stared at her, absently fingering a sovereign attached to one of her chains, hot pink nail tracing the edge in an endless sweep. Then, as if she'd made up her mind, she tucked the coin back down her shirt. 'She's not in just yet.'

'Can I wait?'

'You'll have to buy a drink,' the woman said.

'And one for you too,' Liberty replied.

The woman chuckled and held open the drape. 'You'll do for me, love, whoever you are.'

Inside, the room was dominated by a stage that ran down the middle. A dancer was snaking around in a Day-Glo yellow bikini and white plastic high-heeled sandals. She looked as bored as the handful of men who sat alone at tables, nursing their pints.

'Bit quiet in the day,' the woman shouted over her shoulder, as she led Liberty to the bar. 'Starts to fill up at rush-hour.'

Liberty imagined men popping in on their way home from work, desperate for a cold beer and a glimpse of snatch. The mind could only boggle.

The bar was deserted, and a draught blew in from a door at the back, which was open to a yard.

'Len,' the woman screeched. 'Len, get in here.'

A man in his fifties, with a pot belly and all four front teeth missing, sloped inside.

'That door's meant to be locked,' the woman hissed.

'Fucked if I know where the key is,' said Len.

The woman rolled her eyes. 'Two gin and tonics.'

Liberty was about to say that she'd rather a Diet Coke. She never drank in the day: it made her too tired. But, frankly, she didn't know if she could stomach this place without it so she handed over a twenty-pound note and took the drink. The glass was warm and there was no ice or lemon. She sipped it regardless.

The woman leaned in to speak, her hair, hard with half a can of hair spray, scratched Liberty's cheek. The smell made her cough. 'Lithuanian.' She jerked her head towards the girl on the stage. 'We've got a lot of 'em. Don't smile much but they're reliable.'

The dancer continued to scowl as she undid her top with one hand and released a pair of breasts that defied gravity, nipples larger, harder and rounder than marbles.

'The local girls get pissed off,' the woman continued. 'But it's like the boss says, we can't have an empty stage. The punters come for titties and they don't much care where them titties come from.'

Liberty wondered who owned the place. Running a pub was one thing, but a lap-dancing club involved another layer of aggro.

'Talk of the devil,' said the woman, and waved at a man poking his head around the drape. 'People say he's a bastard but I've worked for a hell of a lot worse in my time.'

The man coming into the club wore a black shirt and sunglasses. His hair was pushed back from his face and he was sucking a lollipop. He made his way towards them with a relaxed swagger that made Liberty nervous. Something about him was wrong, all wrong. When he was ten feet from them, he stopped and took off his sunglasses. Liberty felt the air rush from her as if she'd been punched. She dropped her glass, which fell to the floor and smashed.

The man let his gaze drop to the shards at her feet, then lifted it back to Liberty's face. 'Fuck me.' He pulled the lolly from his mouth. 'Is it you?'

Liberty couldn't breathe. Her lungs were on fire, full of razor blades, carving her from the inside. She scratched her throat and closed her eyes, hoping that when she opened them, this would be a mistake – that she could walk out of there and drive straight home. But no. When she looked again, he was still in front of her. It was Jay. It was her brother.

Chapter 3

June 1985

It's nearly eleven in the morning when Mam finally surfaces. She plonks herself onto the stool, elbows on the counter, head in her hands. She and Dad have been 'celebrating' since he got out of jail and every rum and Coke shows on her face. She's still in her nightie, a big bruise coming out at the top of her arm. She catches my look. 'I fell over.'

I nod and put the kettle on. It's perfectly possible that she did fall over, seeing as how she's been pissed out of her head every night for weeks. I could understand it to begin with, but it's getting annoying now. There's a new James Bond film out and some of my mates are going to see it, but I expect I'll be lumbered with the kids again.

Mam reaches for her fags and lights up, but after the first drag she lets out a burp and stabs it out.

'Feeling rough?' I ask. 'Maybe you should lay off the booze. Have a night in.'

Mam pushes away the ashtray, spilling ash and dog ends everywhere. 'I'm pregnant, Lib.'

I go over to the sink, piled high with dishes. I'd do the washing-up but there's no Fairy Liquid. I reach under a tower of cereal bowls for a cloth and start clearing up the mess on the counter.

'Did you hear me?' Mam asks. 'I said I'm pregnant.'

I don't look at her. 'How far gone?'

She rubs her hand across her forehead and groans. 'I don't know exactly. Three or four months.'

I push the dog ends into the bin with all the other shit and make us both a cup of tea. The milk smells sour so we have to have it black. When Dad was away, money was tight. It's not like we're loaded when he's here. He's out of work more than he's in it but he does a bit of cash-in-hand now and then. Without him, we were completely reliant on the social. So Mam did what she needed to do.

'Uncle Alan?' I ask.

Mam nods. Under normal circumstances this might not be the end of the world. Babies come early all the time. Crystal was two months prem and she's the only one of us with ginger hair. But there's a big problem here: Uncle Alan was black.

'You'll have to get down to the doctor's,' I tell Mam. 'Say you want to get rid of it.'

'I don't know that I agree with abortions,' says Mam.

I sigh. 'Well, then, let's tell Dad all about it. I'm sure he'll take it in his stride.'

Mam drinks her tea and rubs the bruise at the top of her arm.

Jay pressed Liberty into a plastic chair in his office and put a glass of water in her hands. Gratefully, she drained it in one long gulp, forcing her throat to open.

'Another?' Jay held up a bottle of Evian.

'Please,' Liberty answered.

He refilled the glass and turned to the door. 'Give me a minute.'

As he slipped outside, Jay gave her another glance, forehead creased with questions. Liberty knew how he was feeling. How was this possible? How, after more than twenty years, could they meet like this? In a place like this? She looked around her brother's office, which was in the far corner of the club. In truth, it was more of a storeroom than an office. A desk, behind which a mammoth mirror, with a heavy wooden frame, hung on the wall. The other walls were covered with ceiling-to-floor shelves, groaning under the weight of magazines, DVDs, condoms and Christ knew what else. Liberty fingered the nearest box full of tubes of strawberry-flavoured lube. Was this Jay's life? Sex toys and wank mags?

When he came back into the room, Jay was still wearing a mask of bewilderment. 'Mel says you're not here to see me,' he said.

'I didn't know you worked here,' Liberty replied.

'I don't.' Jay stood tall. 'I own it.'

On the one hand it seemed an odd thing to be proud of. A shithole of a clip joint on the wrong side of Leeds. On the other hand, the last time Liberty had seen her brother he'd been a skinny sixteen-year-old, with a chin full of blackheads and a charge sheet full of words he couldn't spell.

'Mel says you came to see one of my girls.' Jay ran his hands through his hair. 'Daisy Clarke.'

Liberty nodded. 'I'm sorry, if I'd known you . . .' She let her words hang in the air between them, like a bubble about to burst.

'What? If you'd known this was my place, you wouldn't have come?' he asked.

Liberty let out a long breath. Put like that it sounded so cold, so blunt, and yet they both knew it was true. She'd made a new life for herself and put the past behind her. And, from Jay's tanned face and well-defined muscles, so had he.

'Come on, then,' he said. 'What gives with Daisy Clarke? I don't suppose it's her sparkling conversation you're after.'

Liberty smiled. Jay had always been a joker. Even when they were growing up, trying to swim through all those endless rivers of shit, he'd made them laugh. Like the time they were all called into the judge's chambers to say their piece and the judge had been sitting behind this huge mahogany desk, fingers steepled, a grave look on his face, and Jay had let rip with the biggest, smelliest fart, so loud it had reverberated off the walls, making the judge's glasses fall down his nose.

'I'm a lawyer,' said Liberty. 'I just want to ask her a few questions.'

'A lawyer?' Jay let out a low whistle. 'You always were the brainy one.'

Liberty rolled her eyes. She'd heard it a thousand times. She was the brainy one. Jay was the funny one. Crystal was the pretty one. And Frankie? Well, he was the baby, the one they all loved the best. 'How is everyone?' she asked. 'Did you keep in touch?'

Jay took a step back as if he'd been pushed. 'Course we did, Lib. Only you took off.'

Liberty's stomach clenched, the muscles pressing in on the guilt that pooled in there like toxic waste. She had left them here. Yes, she had had her reasons, a lot of them bloody good ones, but she had left them here all the same.

'Crystal and me run the business together,' Jay said. 'She's got a head for figures and she knows how to get a good deal.'

Liberty laughed. As a kid, Crystal had been a girly girl. All auburn curls and soft lips.

'I'm telling you,' said Jay. 'Since she came on board, we've opened four more clubs and a ton of other stuff. She's hard as nails is Crystal.'

'And what about Frankie?' Liberty asked.

Jay's smile faded. 'He's all right.' From the look on his face, their baby brother was clearly far from it. 'We look after him the best we can.' His eyes darted around the room. 'Look, Lib, shall we get out of here? Get something to eat? Then you can tell me why you're really here and why you want to talk to Daisy the fucking Dog.'

Sol pulled up outside the Black Cherry, just in time to see Jay Greenwood leaving with a woman. Not his wife and not one of

the dolly birds he usually had in tow. This one was smartly dressed
in a grey suit and heels, dark brown hair bouncing in glossy waves
to her shoulders. The sort of woman who made you look twice.
What was that about? He watched them walk up the road away
from the club, then made his way inside.

'Hello, Mel,' he said, to the woman sitting at the bar.

Mel looked up from the pile of twenties she'd been counting
and quickly pushed them towards Len the barman, who popped
them under the counter. 'Sol.' She got to her feet. She must be
over sixty now, and lined as a pickled walnut, but still dressed like
she might turn a trick if she needed to. 'The boss isn't here.'

'So I gather.' He jerked his thumb towards the door. 'Just seen
him with a new lady friend.'

Mel swung her hands onto her hips, making her leopard-print
blouse gape open. She was less than five two, even in her heels,
but gobby as they came. 'Do you want something, Sol?' She stared
at him. 'A bit of fun with one of our girls? A little loan, maybe?'

Sol grinned. Plenty of coppers had reciprocal relationships with
places like the Cherry. You scratch my back and I'll scratch yours.
But Sol didn't play that game and Mel knew it. 'Kyla Anderson,'
he said. 'Remember her?'

'Doesn't ring a bell,' Mel replied.

'Worked here a while ago.' Sol took a seat next to the one Mel
had vacated and waited for her to get back on her own.
'Sometimes used the name Kiki.'

'Oh, her,' said Mel. 'She didn't work here.'

A group of men arrived, laughing and shouting as they parted
the drape. One of the girls went over to greet them, flicking a
long plait down her bare back where it tickled a huge tattoo of
a snake wrapped around a crucifix, its mouth open, fangs drip-
ping with blood.

'I heard she did,' said Sol.

Mel didn't blink. 'Well, you heard wrong. She came here look-ing for work but I told her to sling her hook.'

'Why?'

'We don't use junkies,' said Mel.

Sol raised an eyebrow and tried not to laugh.

'I'm not saying the girls here are angels.' Mel glanced at the woman leading the men to a table. She was facing Sol now, dis-playing another tattoo on her thigh: a smoking pistol tucked into a lace garter. 'What they do in their own time is up to them. But we don't have the ones who can't go a couple of hours without a fix. Jay runs a tight ship.'

Junkies aside, Jay Greenwood did indeed run a tight ship. Until a couple of years ago, he'd been no one. A petty criminal who'd barely set off the radar. Then, out of nowhere, he'd bought the Cherry and a few other clubs. Soon enough he had websites set up, selling all sorts. Everything above board. Or so it seemed. There were rumours, of course. Some of the outlandish ones, Sol discounted. (Jay Greenwood might be many things. But a hitman? Nah.) He would not be surprised, though, if the clubs were being used to launder money made from running girls, guns or drugs. Probably all three. There'd been a few efforts to put a case together, but there'd never been the will from the top brass – or the budget to go with it – for a proper job. 'So you didn't even give her a try?' he asked.

'No point.' Mel slid off her stool. 'I could see what she was and Jay wouldn't thank me for having her round the place. Now, I've got to get back to work, Sol.'

He stood. His time was up. He'd get nothing more out of an old pro like Mel.

As he moved to leave, Mel called to him. 'Who was it told you she worked here?'

He smiled and shook his head. There was no way he was giving up Daisy's name. There was also no way that Daisy was wrong about Kyla working here. She'd been too sure. Which begged the question of why Mel was lying.

Frankie chopped out a line of ching with a Nectar points card. He didn't have a good enough credit history for a credit card, and Crystal wouldn't let him open a bank account – she'd had to bail him out with the last one – so he didn't even have a debit card. He snorted the white powder up from the toilet cistern and felt it burn the back of his throat. These days, it didn't give him the buzz it used to. That was the trouble with using rock – everything else seemed like shite in comparison.

There was a thump on the door.

'What?' he shouted.

'He's gone,' Mel yelled back.

Frankie pocketed the Nectar card and sniffed hard. He'd come over to the Cherry to tap up Jay for a bit of cash, but he'd just missed him apparently. Instead the frigging police had walked in so Frankie had made himself scarce. The worst they could do was nick him for a bit of personal, but who needed the aggro?

He opened the door and hawked up a throat full of gunge, spat it into the toilet bowl and walked out. Mel wrinkled her nose at him and flushed it.

'What did he want?' Frankie asked.

Mel folded her arms and screwed up her face. 'He wanted to know about Kiki.'

'What did you tell him?' Frankie asked, rubbing his bottom teeth.

'Have a guess.'

He wanted to smack that cockiness right out of her, but he couldn't. Jay loved the bones of the sour-faced bitch, looked out for her like she was his mother, instead of some poisonous old tom. If Frankie touched one hair on her head, Jay would go bat shit. He walked over to the bar as if he owned the place. Which he did, in a way. Jay was always banging on about how this was a family business and Frankie was most definitely family.

'Give us a beer, Len,' he said.

The barman gave a slow nod and pushed an opened bottle of Becks towards him. Frankie took a gulp and almost spat it out. Warm. Who could stomach warm frigging beer? Last summer, he'd spent a month in Marbella. Jay had sent him. Told him to lie low after a bit of trouble with some bird. He'd been a bit pissed off at being sent away like some naughty school kid, but when he got out there, well, he wasn't pissed off any more. The sun shone all day, beating down on the white sands. Not that he'd spent much time on the beach after he'd discovered the bars and clubs, where not only was the beer as cold as Christmas but it was poured into iced glasses. That's right. The glasses had been put in the freezer.

Night after night, he drank and danced. Did as much posh as he could lay his hands on, and drank and danced some more. He got a name for himself as a bad boy and made friends with some of the local faces. Lads from London who knew how to make a few quid and how to spend it. Cars, girls, clothes, drugs.

One night he'd ended up at a party in some massive villa. One of the lads, whom everybody called Brixton Dave, convinced a bird to let them snort lines off her thighs. At first she thought he was taking the piss, but soon she was lying on a sunbed by the pool, skirt hitched up, giggling, as Brixton Dave chopped up coke on her sun-kissed skin. 'That tickles,' she'd said, when he ran the edge of a rolled-up fifty across the inside of her leg. Top bloke, Brixton Dave.

Frankie wanted that life all the time. With the businesses doing so well he shouldn't have to come crawling to his brother for a fiver. It was time for Jay and Crystal to stop treating him like a kid and let him do the necessary. He needed to show them that he knew what he was doing, so he'd already started to put the wheels in motion to get together a sweet little deal. When his brother and sister saw the money coming in, they'd have to give him respect.

He smiled at the thought of it, and caught the eye of one of the girls arriving at the club. She wasn't as good-looking as the Lithuanians, a bit more battered around the edges.

'All right, Frankie.' She sidled over to him. 'How are you keeping?'

'Not so bad, Daisy,' he said. 'You?'

She pointed to a black eye she'd tried to cover up with makeup so thick it could have cemented bricks, then leaned in to him so close he could smell Juicy Fruit on her breath. 'I'm feeling a bit shit, to be honest,' she said.

She looked shit, if *he* was honest. Her hair needed a wash, her lips were chapped and her see-through top showed only bones and saggy tits.

One of the Lithuanians wandered past, all high cheekbones and smooth thighs. She winked at Frankie but he didn't wink back. She was a looker, all right, but she didn't have something that Daisy the Dog would have, no doubt, and that was a blue rock of crack burning a hole in her back pocket.

The sweet and sour prawns were beyond salty. Liberty was on her sixth glass of water. She pushed one of the battered balls across her plate. It left a smear of sauce so orange it would have made William Blake proud.

'You not hungry, then?' Jay asked her. 'You used to love a Chinese.'

She gave a nervous laugh. 'It's just all been such a shock.'

He nodded and helped himself to another spoonful of egg fried rice. For the last hour, they'd talked. Liberty had told him about the Rance case, and Jay had told her about a club he was hoping to buy in Sheffield, all the while shovelling down his food. He finally stopped chewing when his phone beeped. 'Fuck,' he muttered, as he checked the message. 'Fuck's sake.'

'Everything okay?' Liberty asked.

Jay's face had darkened and he pushed away his food. 'I'm sorry, Lib, but something's come up and I've got to go.'

They both stood, and the moment became awkward. How were they going to leave this?

'Well, you know where I am,' Jay said.

Liberty gave a tight smile. They could part now and never see one another again. She would go back to her old life as if none of this had happened. It was obvious that her brother was doing just fine without her. 'Bye, then,' she said. 'I'll get the bill.'

Jay waved a hand dismissively. 'I don't pay in here. Local businesses, you know?' He paused for a second. Liberty thought he might speak but he didn't. Instead he made for the door. This was it, then.

Suddenly Liberty grabbed her purse and ran after him. 'Jay, take this.'

He frowned at her. 'Behave yourself. I don't need any bloody money, Lib.'

'Are you daft or what?' she said, and handed him her card. 'These are my details. Phone number and whatnot.'

He took the card and read it. 'You changed your name, then?'

She shrugged. 'That's why we couldn't find you.'

Liberty gunned the engine and peeled away from the lights. What an unbelievable day! First the hell-hole of the prison and the interview with Rance. Then the meeting with Jay. In a strip club. It was like the Christmas edition of *EastEnders*.

She needed to lie down and would have given anything right there and then to be at home in bed. Penelope, the cleaner from Zimbabwe, changed the bedding religiously on Mondays and Fridays. Liberty could almost feel the crisp, clean cotton of the pillowcase against her cheek and smell the lavender water Penelope used in the iron. When she graduated next year, she'd get herself a better job, of course, and Liberty would miss her. Now she'd have to make do with the hotel room. Hopefully, the minibar would be well stocked. Maybe Jay's influence would stretch as far as the Radisson and she'd get room service on the house.

She frowned. Jay would have been well within his rights to refuse even to speak to her. She wouldn't have been surprised if he'd taken one look at her, turned on his heel and left the club or kicked her out on her arse with a few choice words for good measure. The fact that he hadn't done either of those things was testament to the sort of person he'd become. Over the Chinese banquet for three, it had dawned on her how much Jay looked like Dad. Not that she'd mentioned it – he probably wouldn't have thanked her but the thick dark hair and clear unlined skin brought back instant memories of Jimmy Greenwood, although Jay was far quicker to laugh.

Neither Liberty nor Jay had mentioned Dad. Well, what was there to say? The old bastard probably chased Jay around in his nightmares, just like he did Liberty. More than thirty years that man had been giving her sleepless nights.

A flash made Liberty jump. She looked in the rear-view mirror. Speed camera. For the love of God, could things get any worse?

Chapter 4

July 1985
Dr Peters is a dickhead. He keeps asking question after question, his head tilted to one side. To be honest, Mam's not helping matters with her hands patting her belly and her eyes full of tears. I sigh.

'Mrs Greenwood.' *Dr Peters leans forward in his chair.* 'Perhaps it might be better if your daughter waited outside.'

'I want our Lib to stay.' *Mam gulps.*

Dr Peters reaches across his desk to where he's got a box of tissues. Not one of them man-sized ones. No, this box is square and the cardboard is pale blue with flowers on. There's a tissue poking out and he offers it to Mam. It's a sort of lilac colour and I wonder if it smells nice. It looks like it should do. Mam takes it and gives her nose a snotty blow.

'It's just that this is a very sensitive matter,' *says Dr Peters.* 'I'm not sure a child . . .'

I've had enough now. We've been here all morning. 'She's got to have an abortion,' *I tell him.* 'It's not my dad's baby.'

The doctor goes pink.

'And there's no way she can pass it off cos the fella she was with is black,' *I say.*

'And is the father of the child aware of the situation?'

I shake my head, so he looks back at Mam.

'Are you still in contact with this person?' *he asks her, and she bursts into tears.*

41

'Listen, Doctor,' I say. 'I know you mean well but the bloke was a kiddie-fiddler. We're well shot. But Dad can't know anything about this lot.' I wave at the tray of notes on his desk. Buff-coloured envelopes with pages of card stuck inside. 'Check what it says about him and you'll see why.'

Dr Peters picks up an envelope with Mam's name on the front and starts to read. He coughs. I presume he's got to the bit about Mam getting battered. He doesn't look at her when he speaks. 'You've taken your husband back, Mrs Greenwood?'

'He's a changed man,' Mam says.

Dr Peters frowns at the notes. I know what he's thinking. If Dad's changed, how come she needs an abortion on the QT? I catch Mam's eye and nod at her. We talked about this last night. You can only get an abortion if you're in danger from having the baby, either physical (apparently having a bloke who'll hospitalize you when he finds out doesn't count) or mental.

'My head's a mess,' Mam blurts out, making the doctor look up from the notes. 'I can't sleep and I can't stop crying.'

To make her point, Mam rubs her nose again but the tissue's disintegrating and bits fall into her lap, like purple dandruff.

Dr Peters's face is hard to read. 'By law you have to see two doctors.'

Bloody hellfire. We have to go through all this rigmarole again?

'I'll make an appointment on my way out,' says Mam, and we both stand up.

'In the meantime, I'd very much like you to meet with social services, Mrs Greenwood.'

We stop dead in our tracks. Social services. Round our way, folk like social services about as much as they like the police. Everybody knows how they work: first, some social worker comes round pretending to be all nice, telling you to call them Michelle, next thing the kids are in care.

'Your husband is a violent man, Mrs Greenwood,' says Dr Peters.

'He's changed,' Mam says again.

'So you say.'

'He has.' Mam's voice goes up a notch. 'Tell him, Lib. Tell him what your dad's like since he got out of jail.'

I think about it. Since he got out he's been mostly pissed. And when he's not pissed he spends his time on the settee watching the telly.

Dr Peters puts up his hand as if what I might have to say on the matter doesn't concern him. 'I won't be moved on this, Mrs Greenwood. You'll get your abortion but I'm making a referral to social services.'

The tonic in the minibar wasn't slimline but it would have to do. After the terrible day she'd had, Liberty would have drunk the gin neat and from a shoe if necessary. She couldn't believe she'd been caught speeding. She already had six points on her licence. She'd have to go on one of those courses and spend two days in a room full of teenagers watching videos of fatal crashes on the motorway.

To top it all, she hadn't even got to speak to Daisy Clarke.

Fuck it, she was going home first thing tomorrow and Ronald would just have to give the case to someone else. If she lost the callme.com takeover then so be it.

She sat on the edge of the bed, took a good glug of gin and tonic and checked the room-service menu. What were the chances that the chicken chasseur wouldn't be out of a tin?

Her mobile rang. She didn't recognize the number. 'Hello. Liberty Chapman.'

A gravelly slurp of laughter came down the line.

'Who is this?' she snapped.

'It's me, Jay,' her brother said. 'Sorry, I just can't get used to your new name.'

'Hi.' Liberty tried to sound cheerful. 'What can I do for you?'

'More a case of what I can do for you,' he replied.

Liberty drained her glass.

'That girl you wanted to talk to, Daisy Clarke, I've managed to get hold of her,' he said.

'Yeah?'

'Turns out you just missed her, so I've set up a meet.'

Liberty sat up. 'She agreed to see me?'

'Course. Come round the Cherry at twelve tomorrow and she'll be there,' he said. 'I'd have made it earlier but you know what these girls are like.'

'No worries,' Liberty replied. 'And thanks.'

She gave the menu another once-over and decided she'd risk a club sandwich and fries. She poured a second gin and full fat tonic and smiled.

'Carrot and coriander.'

Sol looked from his wife to the bowl of soup she had placed in front of him. Natasha had insisted he give up smoking and it looked as if she meant for him to give up eating too. Christ, he remembered when soup was a starter. 'Lovely,' he said, and took a spoonful. To be fair, it was tasty. It was just that he felt his main meal of the day should at least involve some chewing.

Natasha brought her own spoon to her rosebud lips. The soup formed barely an orange coating on the metal but his wife lapped it down. 'Carrots are an excellent source of thiamine,' she told Sol. 'Important for the nervous system.'

The health-giving or harming properties of food was Natasha's specialist subject. Her outlook on life had been what had first attracted Sol, her lifestyle an antidote to his own. It was as if it could cleanse him of all the problems that came with his job and clogged his system, like snake venom, poisoning him from the inside.

His first wife, Angie, said he was just a low-down cheating dog, like every other man thinking with his dick, but that wasn't the truth. Or, at least, not the whole truth. Angie had been in the job, too, and she and Sol had been as toxic as each other, coming home from work their minds full of horrors they tried to erase with drinking, shouting, sex, then more drinking. Their marriage would have killed one if not both of them. Sol meeting Natasha had probably saved Angie as well as himself, not that his ex-wife would ever see it that way. Now, with Natasha's diet imposed on him, Sol might live for ever.

He sighed. Eternal life wasn't for everyone.

'Something wrong, baby?' Natasha asked.

He noticed her little frown. It wasn't an annoyed frown but a sad one. He shouldn't have sighed. Whatever his wife said, whatever she did, whatever she fed him, it all came from the same place: a good one. She loved him. It was as simple as that.

'Not a thing,' he answered, and finished his soup. He was clearing away their bowls when his mobile rang. 'Connolly,' he said.

'That you, Sol?' It was Daisy Clarke. Her voice edgy. 'I need to talk to you.'

Sol's pulse quickened. 'You've heard something about Kyla?'

'What?' Daisy was irritated. 'No.'

Sol's almost empty stomach flooded with disappointment. 'So what I can do for you?'

'It's about that punter I reported. Thing is, Sol, I don't wanna go through with it,' she said.

'Come on, Daisy, you know the score,' said Sol. 'I'm not the officer in the case.'

'Yeah, well, I tried to get hold of her, didn't I?' Daisy began to cry. 'But the bitch won't pick up her phone.'

Sol glanced at Natasha, who was carefully placing fruit on a platter for 'pudding'. Two plums, a nectarine – was that what you called those smooth peachy things? – and six cherries. His belly growled. 'Meet me at Scottish Tony's?' he asked.

Daisy sniffed. 'All right.'

★ ★ ★

Scottish Tony's was actually called the Carter Street Coffee Cup. Anthony and Aileen McEldry had bought it ten years previously, hoping to run a pleasant coffee and sandwich bar. Unfortunately, they had viewed the premises on a sunny Tuesday afternoon and agreed with the estate agent that there was a lot of potential. Of course, what they didn't see, back on the InterCity to Glasgow, were the legions of working girls who came out to play on Carter Street as soon as the sun went down. To be fair, the McEldrys did end up with a thriving business on their hands. Just not in daylight hours.

'Usual?' Tony called from behind the counter.

Sol patted his stomach. 'The missus would have my guts for garters.'

'Lucky for you she's no here, then, eh?'

Sol slid into a seat with his back against the wall. There was an unwritten rule that no beef went down in Scottish Tony's, but no cop liked to leave himself open in an area like Carter Street.

Two prostitutes were sitting at the table by the window. Sol didn't know the first but he'd had a couple of dealings with the second. Her name was Jadine, and under her leather mini skirt and fishnets she had a cock and balls Sol would have been proud of. The word was, Jadine was saving to go to America for an operation to remove her tackle. Ten grand was a figure often bandied about, although the numbers changed depending on who was telling the story.

Tony came over and slid a plate in front of Sol. Two slices of plastic white bread book-ended a fried egg, two sausages and three rashers of streaky bacon. A heart attack in a sandwich. 'You'll be the death of me, Tony,' Sol chuckled.

'No a bad way to go, though, eh? Tony replied, passing him a bottle of brown sauce.

Daisy arrived in the doorway of the café. She clocked Sol, scowled and stomped across to him.

'You want one of these?' Tony asked her.

Daisy shook her head and slumped into the chair opposite Sol. She'd had a habit so long now, solid food was a thing of the past.

'Drink?' Tony asked.

'Hot chocolate,' Daisy replied. 'With loads of that whippy cream.'

As they waited for Tony to make it, Sol carefully removed the top slice of bread from his sandwich and spread brown sauce across it. Then he replaced it and watched Daisy pick the scabs on her knuckles. A bead of blood rose to the surface of her skin and she sucked it.

When Tony brought over the hot chocolate she smiled weakly and began to spoon the swirl of aerosol cream into her mouth.

'What's up, then, Daisy?' Sol asked.

'It's like I told you. I don't want to go through with these charges,' she replied.

'Because?'

Daisy shrugged and took another mouthful of cream. 'You know how it is, Sol. I was off my tits, got confused like.'

Sol reached across and tugged at Daisy's collar to reveal the angry bite mark. 'Nothing confusing about that.'

She batted his hand away. 'I'm not going to court.'

Sol took a bite of his sandwich. The bacon was salty sweet, and the sausages had a little kick of pepper as the rich egg yolk coated them. He groaned in pleasure. 'The CPS can get an order,' he said. 'They can make you attend.'

The truth was that the CPS wouldn't bother – prostitutes were hardly top priority and they made legendarily poor witnesses – because it was better for the end-of-year figures that a case be withdrawn than the defendant get a not-guilty.

'I mean it, Sol.' Daisy looked him right in the eyes. 'I'm not giving evidence.'

'What's made you change your mind?'

Daisy shrugged.

'Has the punter got to you?' Sol asked.

'He's inside,' she replied.

'Someone on his behalf?'

Daisy stirred the hot chocolate, then licked the spoon. 'Listen, Sol, I'll do you a deal, all right? If you put in a word for me about this shite, I'll do something for you. Something you'll like.'

Sol frowned. There were coppers who accepted favours from the girls and boys of Carter Street. A blow-job here, a blind eye there. But he had never been that guy. Never.

'What?' Daisy asked. 'What are you looking at me like that for?' Suddenly she understood, laughed and pointed her spoon at him. 'Fucking hell, Sol! Not that. I'm not being funny but you're old enough to be my dad.'

Sol didn't point out that Daisy regularly shagged men old enough to be her granddad for the price of a rock.

'If you work this out for me, Sol, I'll find out what happened to Kyla Anderson,' she said.

A nerve at the base of Sol's spine began to buzz. 'I thought you didn't know anything about that.'

'I don't,' said Daisy. 'Nobody does. Which is weird, don't you think?' Daisy held Sol's gaze. 'And what's even weirder is that no one is even chatting about it.'

The buzz in Sol's spine turned into a pulse. Gossip was the number-one hobby of choice among sex workers. In lives blighted by violent customers and doses of the clap, hearing that someone somewhere was worse off was golden. The absence of gossip was usually deliberate. A collective decision.

'If no one's talking how can you find anything out?' Sol asked.

'You leave that to me.' Daisy fished into her pocket, pulled out a card and slid it across the table. 'This is the policewoman who

48

won't answer my calls.' She tapped the card with a dirty nail. 'You sort her and I'll sort the other.'

Liberty watched the younger woman suspiciously. She couldn't keep still, shifting in her seat, chewing an already bloody cuticle, while endlessly checking her phone.

They were in Jay's office and, although he'd cleared off his desk, there was now a pile of boxes stacked next to it each one bearing the words 'Supertight Pocket Pussy' with a picture of what looked like a silicone vagina.

'Thank you for agreeing to see me, Miss Clarke,' said Liberty.

'Call me Daisy.'

'That's good of you, but I want you to know that you're under no pressure to speak with me. If you want to leave at any time, you're free to do so.'

Daisy flapped a hand to show that there was no problem.

'I've got your statement here.' Liberty had it laid out in front of her. 'And I'd just like to ask a few questions, if I may?'

'Don't bother. It's a load of old bollocks,' said Daisy.

'I'm sorry?'

Daisy laughed. 'I were on a shedload of drugs, didn't know what I was saying.'

Liberty pressed her lips together. Daisy's agitation would certainly mark her out as an addict. And addicts got things wrong all the time, but there was no mistaking the black eye she was sporting.

As if reading Liberty's mind, Daisy said, 'It was someone else that did it. Another punter. I just got them mixed up.'

'Are you prepared to tell this to the police?' Liberty asked.

'Already done it, love.' Daisy scratched her cheek with ragged nails. 'Last night.' She pushed back her chair. 'Look, can I go now?'

Liberty stood. 'Absolutely.' She held out her hand and Daisy touched it with her own, though she didn't clasp. The skin of her palm was clammy. She withdrew it and checked her reflection in the huge mirror behind Liberty. She wrinkled her nose in disgust, then she was gone.

As Liberty cleared away her papers, Mel stuck her head around the door, lips painted bright red. 'Everything all right?' she asked.

'Yes. She's withdrawn her statement,' Liberty replied.

'Good result for you.'

Liberty frowned. It was indeed a good result, yet something about the whole episode didn't feel right. It was all just a little too convenient. She followed Mel out of the office and into the main body of the club. The lights were on and the barman was washing down tables, the air ripe with bleach. Two girls arrived in jeans and T-shirts, chatting in a language she didn't understand, presumably Lithuanian.

Mel tottered towards them in a pair of red patent mules that matched her lipstick. She leaned in to speak to the girls, who nodded and quickly disappeared through a side door. She eyed Liberty and fingered the coin at the end of her chain. 'You don't seem too happy, love.'

'I'm just surprised,' Liberty replied. 'It's quite a turnaround from Daisy.'

Mel let out a cackle. 'These girls change their minds more often than their knickers. Working here's like herding cats, I'm telling you. I'm as old as the hills and not a day goes by when this lot don't surprise me.' She put a bony finger on Liberty's arm. 'But if there's one thing I've learned, it's never to look a gift horse in the mouth.'

On her way back to the hotel, Liberty's stomach growled as loudly as the Porsche, and a wave of hunger hit her, like a breaker on

Blackpool sands. She pulled over near a baker's, garnering the attention of a group of boys, all snap caps and spotty necks. She double-checked the car doors were locked and trudged past them.

Outside the shop two young women were arguing. One waved a jumbo sausage roll, like an outstretched finger, at the other, who was sweating inside a hoodie pulled tight over the drum of her pregnant belly. 'I never said you was stupid.' Flaky pastry flew through the air. 'I said you was acting stupid.'

The pregnant girl bared urine-coloured teeth. 'It's the same thing.'

'No, it's not.' The sausage roll made another arc through the air. 'The one is saying you're a stupid person, the other is saying you've done a stupid thing. There's a difference, right?' The girl turned to Liberty. 'What are you staring at?'

'I'm not,' Liberty answered.

'Yeah, you are.' Flakes were caught in the girl's nylon hair extensions. 'You're staring right at me.'

Liberty sighed.

'You got something to say?' The girl moved towards her, her unkneaded-dough body blocking the path. 'I'm listening.'

'I just want something to eat,' Liberty said.

The girl threw her sausage roll at Liberty's feet. It landed with a slap. 'There you go.'

Liberty knew she should turn around and go back to her car. Hell, what was she even doing here? In London she never came into contact with people like this and their pay-day-loan lives. Her days simply didn't include them. Yet here she was, back in the north for two minutes, and she was craving meat pasties and wanting to give some random idiot a smack round the face.

'Aye-aye, what's all this about?'

Liberty looked up and saw Raj in the baker's doorway, an éclair poised at his mouth. 'Chantal?'

The girl pouted at him.

51

'You're on bloody bail, lass,' he said. 'Think about that when you started a fight in the street, did you?'

'She was looking at me funny, Raj,' said the girl, bobbing her head at Liberty.

Raj sighed and dropped his éclair back into its paper bag. 'According to you, the whole world looks at you funny. It's a wonder there aren't more car crashes and people falling down man holes, what with everyone not being able to take their eyes off you.'

'Now you're taking the piss,' said the girl.

'Maybe we should both piss off and be on our way?' he replied.

The girl grunted. 'It's a good thing you're such a top brief, Raj, or I'd have to kick your head in.'

'Yeah, yeah, tell it to the bloody judge.'

The girl gave an exaggerated eye roll and sloped away, her friend bringing up the rear.

'Her temper's going to bring some trouble,' said Liberty.

'That particular ship has already sailed and sunk,' Raj replied. 'She's got a trial coming up for glassing some bloke in Pizza Hut. She'll go down this time, I reckon. He's a nasty piece of work himself, but that won't help her.'

Liberty felt a twist in her guts and nudged the abandoned sausage roll with the toe of her shoe.

'So what are you doing here, Miss Chapman?' Raj flashed a grin. 'I thought you'd have legged it back to the big smoke at the first opportunity.'

Liberty smiled back. 'I had to question a witness this morning and now I'm starving.'

'Well, you could take your chances with a steak and onion slice, but I guarantee it will have been there since yesterday afternoon,' he said, and Liberty wrinkled her nose. 'Or I can offer you some of Mrs Singh's finest Ruby Murray.'

Liberty must have looked nonplussed because Raj took her by the elbow and spun her round so that she was facing the road. On the other side, next door to Vicky's Star Nails, was a solicitor's office. The windows were frosted and only the words Singh & Co were painted across them in gold lettering.

'*Mi casa, su casa,*' said Raj.

If the outside was a study in sparse, the inside was a cornucopia of clutter and chaos. The reception area was strewn with papers, files and empty Diet Coke cans. The bin was overflowing, a black banana skin hugging its base. 'Excuse the mess,' said Raj, cheerfully. 'The and-Co has called in sick today.'

They moved along a corridor, which housed more piles of paperwork, towards a small kitchen, the sink full of cups. Raj reached into the fridge and pulled out a Tupperware box, whipped off the lid and flashed the contents at Liberty. 'The missus packs me up last night's leftovers for lunch. Somehow they taste even better the next day.' He winked. 'Not that I mention that to her, of course. Want some?'

The contents of the box looked and smelt delicious. Liberty's stomach growled audibly.

'I'll take that as a yes,' said Raj, and flapped his hand back down the corridor. 'Second on the right is my office. Make yourself at home and I'll heat this up for you.'

Raj's office was worse than the reception area. There was barely a clear square centimetre on the floor or the desk. Liberty picked her way to a chair, moved the books piled on it and sat down. Her elbow brushed a potted plant that was slowly withering.

'Here you go.' Raj arrived with a steaming bowl, tiptoed through the obstacle course and plonked it in front of her. '*Bon appétit.*' He reached into his suit-jacket pocket and pulled out a spoon.

All thoughts about poor hygiene disappeared as the aromas

drifted up to Liberty and she dug in. The spices had a rave on her tongue. 'This is so good,' she said.

'Tell me about it,' said Raj, and jiggled his spare tyre. He sat in his own chair opposite and shook off his jacket. 'So, you went to see a witness, eh?'

'It was a bit of an eye-opener, really,' Liberty replied. 'She retracted her statement, said she'd made it under the influence.'

'Any other evidence?'

'Nothing much. Medical report, but that just proves the what, not the who,' said Liberty.

'Your boy say anything in interview?' Raj asked.

Liberty shook her head. 'No comment all the way.'

'Then you're home free.'

She smiled and scraped out the last of the food from the bowl. Soon she would be home. Soon she would be free.

Raj produced a paper bag and placed it between them. 'Éclair? I bought two, so you'd be doing me a favour.'

Why not? Today was working out very nicely indeed.

'Of course you'll need to hassle the CPS to get the case withdrawn.' Raj bit into his éclair, cream squirting through the edges. 'They can take bloody ages if you don't make a nuisance of yourself, which wouldn't be a big deal in the usual scheme of things, but seeing as how your boy's in the Mansion . . .'

Liberty felt the choux pastry melt on her tongue. Letting Rance stew in prison for a few more days seemed like a reasonable option.

'You might not like him,' said Raj, 'but he'll be shouting ten kinds of negligence if you don't get him out of there pronto.'

Rance was just the sort of little toerag to make a complaint, wasn't he? And his father had the money to see it through.

'My advice would be to put a rocket up the arse of the CPS.' Raj crammed the last of his éclair into his mouth so his already plump cheeks bulged. 'And in the meantime make an application for bail.' He rummaged under a pile of crime-scene photographs and pulled out a telephone. 'If you do it now, you might get listed first thing tomorrow.'

Tomorrow? Christ, that would mean she'd have to stay another night. Her heart sank. But what choice did she have? She reached for the phone, the receiver sticky from Raj's fingers.

Chapter 5

August 1985

'Ow.' Crystal screams. 'That hurts.'

'It wouldn't if you'd just sit chuffing still,' I tell her. I've spent the last twenty minutes trying to brush her hair into something that doesn't look like a wasps' nest. If she wriggles away from me one more time, I swear I'll bat her with the hairbrush.

'Shut up, the pair of you,' Mam shouts down the stairs. 'My nerves are already shattered.' She's tried on at least ten different outfits, wondering which one gives the best impression. She thinks her jeans are too casual, like she doesn't give a shit, but all her skirts are too short.

We managed to put off social services for a few weeks, telling them the kids were sick one after the other, but then we got a letter telling Mam that if she didn't keep the next appointment, the social worker would turn up unannounced. So here we are, buzzing around like blue-arsed flies getting the house cleaned up and making the kids presentable.

Dad comes into the kitchen, scowling. 'I don't know what all the fuss is about.' He's been saying that ever since Mam told him they were coming. 'These people want to keep their fucking noses out of other people's business.'

I look up at him and try to smile. 'Once they've seen we're all right, I bet they'll just leave us alone,' I say.

'But why do they need to see we're all right?' Dad looms over me. 'That's what I want to know. Who's been telling fucking tales?'

TAKING LIBERTIES

Mam hops in, trying to put her other court shoe on. White. To go with her white dropped-waist dress. A bit over the top, to be honest, especially with a pair of earrings the size of chandeliers. 'Come on, Jimmy, nobody here's said a word.'

Dad's eyes flash. 'They'd better not have done.'

Mam takes over with Crystal's hair, pulling the sides back and pinning them with glittery purple clips. She shows Crystal her reflection in the mirror. 'What a bobby dazzler.' Crystal grins back at herself. 'It was probably the old cow next door,' Mam says.

I know she's just trying to put Dad off the scent, but it's a bit unfair on Mrs Cooper, who's helped us out with teabags and ciggies many a time. Sometimes she asks me or Frankie to go to the shops for her and she always tells us to buy ourselves a bag of crisps for going.

'Well, she'd better stay out of my way if she knows what's good for her,' says Dad.

Mam rubs his arm. 'Come on, now, let's have a quick coffee and a fag before the social worker gets here. Put the kettle on, Lib.'

I do as I'm told.

'And let's give Frankie his bottle of pop now,' she says. 'I don't want anyone wagging their finger about that.'

I make up the bottle, call for Frankie and Jay arrives, carrying him. Mam's done both their hair in side partings and wet it down. They look like them evacuees we've seen pictures of in history class.

'I'm going to ask this social worker who's grassed us up,' says Dad. 'They don't just start something like this off their own bat, do they?'

Mam and I shoot each other a look.

'It's probably just standard procedure,' I say. 'When somebody gets out of jail.'

Dad narrows his eyes, mulling that one over.

'I bet she's right, Jim,' says Mam. 'I bet they have records of people when they're released. Paperwork and that.'

Dad lets out a snort but doesn't say anything else. It seems a fair enough scenario. Doesn't it?

I make a coffee for Mam and Dad and hand them the mugs. Dad blows over his rim, silently. When all this is over and the social worker is off on her way, Mam can get her abortion and we can go back to normal. There's even been talk of Dad being offered a job as a bouncer in one of the pubs up in town.

'I think I know why the social worker is coming today,' Crystal pipes up.

We all look at her. What the hell is she going on about?

'Hush now, Crystal,' Mam tells her.

'Let her speak,' Dad snaps.

Crystal's cheeks go pink and she drops her head.

'Come on lass.' Dad moves towards her. 'Spit it out.'

I step between them. 'Leave her, Dad. She's being daft.'

'Daft? I'll give her fucking daft.'

He tries to dodge round me, but I'm too quick and block his way. Behind me Crystal starts to cry.

'Not now, Dad,' I say. 'The social worker will be here any minute.'

He jabs a finger in Crystal's direction. 'Well, maybe that little bastard should have thought about that before she started creating.'

I shake my head at him. I mean, it's one thing to be mad at Crystal, and I do get mad at her a lot, because she's a law unto herself, like the frigging Queen of Sheba, basking in the admiring glances of all and sundry. But she's only five and, well, she's not actually the reason we're in this mess, is she?

'What?' Dad's right up in my face now. 'What?'

What? Is he really me asking me that? Does he not see for one second that the social worker is coming round because he put Mam in hospital?

'Nothing,' I say.

'Good.' He's so close to me that his spit flicks all over my face and I have to close my eyes. 'Because I'm not in the fucking mood for this.'

He pushes me. Hard. I fall to the side, clattering to the floor, banging my head on the radiator. Crystal screams. Mam jumps between her and Dad. 'For God's sake, Jimmy,' she shouts. 'Stop it.'

Dad goes wide-eyed. 'Me?' He points at himself with his thumb. 'You're blaming me?'

'I'm not blaming anyone.' Mam's gabbling now, tears pouring down her face, bringing electric blue mascara with them. She looks like Frankie's coloured her in with a felt tip. 'We're all on edge and no fucking wonder. So let's calm down.'

Dad lowers his voice. 'I'm perfectly calm.'

'Good.' Mam smiles and swipes at the makeup melting down her face. 'We can always rely on you in a crisis.' She holds out her hand to me and pulls me to my feet. 'Why don't you take Crystal upstairs and clean her up? Will you do that, Lib?'

'Yeah,' I reply.

'Good girl,' she says. 'And I'll make your dad a fresh coffee.' She moves to Dad's still full mug, left on the side. 'That one must be cold by now, Jim.'

Dad nods.

Mam reaches for the mug, empties it into the sink and flicks on the kettle.

'Paula,' says Dad, his voice soft.

Mam turns to him, jar of Nescafé in one hand, teaspoon in the other. 'Yes, love?'

They look at one another for a second, then Dad pulls back his right arm and punches her in the stomach. There's a horrible smacking sound and then a whoosh of air comes out of Mam's mouth and she doubles over, clutching her belly.

Dad watches her, flexing his knuckles. Mam lets out a low groan from somewhere deep inside her. 'For fuck's sake,' says Dad. 'Don't overreact.'

Mam is still bent at the waist, her hands clawing at her middle, gasping for air.

'Seriously, Paula, don't piss me off any more than you already have.'

Dad grabs Mam's chin and forces her upright. 'I barely touched you, woman.'

Mam's eyes are squeezed shut and her face has turned grey. Her lips are pulled tight over her lips. And she's making this awful noise. I wish she'd stop because it's just making Dad even madder, and if she's not careful he's going to kick ten bells of shit out of her.

'Mam,' I warn.

But it's like she can't hear me, like she's locked into herself.

'Mam!' I'm shouting now.

Then I see it. A river of blood pouring down Mam's leg, pooling in her best white court shoes.

The morning was hot and airless. The sort of weather that put everyone in a bad mood. Not that the people queuing outside the magistrates' court needed anything to put them in a bad mood. Their feelings were almost palpable, a constant grey bleakness that occasionally bubbled up into purple fury.

Liberty took her place in the line and pressed a hand to her cheek.

'Nice day for it.' Raj nudged her with his hip, arms brimming with files.

Liberty shook her head. 'How are you always so cheerful?'

'I grew up hearing stories about Partition.' They inched forward to the entrance. 'My grandparents lost everything. House, jobs, savings, the lot. When my dad was twenty-two he came to England with only sixteen quid in his pocket.'

'That must have been tough,' she said.

Raj nodded. 'He got a job in a biscuit factory. Quality control on the custard-cream line, not that he knew what a custard cream was until he got there.' He laughed. 'Worked his way up to Garibaldis.' Liberty slapped his arm and he laughed some more. 'I sometimes think that people are a lot happier in life if they haven't been handed everything on a plate,' he said.

She was about to tell him she'd been handed nothing. That her own plate had been completely empty and chipped into the bargain, when an argument broke out between the woman in front of them and the security guard operating a metal detector.

'I'm telling you now, you're not getting in with that.' The guard was over six foot and easily sixteen stone, with what looked like pure muscle straining the polyester of his uniform. 'Not a chance.'

His size didn't deter the woman in front, her eyes black slits in a jaundiced face, most of her teeth missing, and she took a step towards him. He didn't budge and rapped his left palm with his metal detector in rhythmic determination.

Liberty craned her neck to look into the tray to see what the fuss was about. There, beside a mobile phone with a smashed screen and a pile of coins, was a syringe.

'I'm registered disabled,' the woman snarled.

'You and every other junkie this side of Leeds,' the guard replied.

'If I was registered blind, would you say I couldn't bring a stick with me?' the woman demanded. 'Or a dog?' She pointed a finger at him, the nail bitten and black. 'No, you wouldn't do that, would you? Too scared of being done for discrimination.'

The guard looked like he might speak, but instead he let out a huge yawn.

'I know my rights,' said the woman. 'It's against the law, this is.'

The guard sniffed. 'Well, there's plenty of police around, if you think I'm breaking the law. Why don't we call an officer? And, while we're at it, maybe get them to give you a body search. See what you've got hidden away in your nooks and crannies.'

'Bastard.' The woman spat and snatched up her syringe. 'Complete fucking bastard.'

'Who told you my middle name?'

The woman scuttled away. 'You'll get yours,' she shouted, over her shoulder. 'I'll make sure of that.'

'I'm quaking in my boots, love,' the guard replied.

He was still chuckling as Liberty held out her arms and he waved the detector across her body, like a wand.

Once inside, she waited for Raj, fingering the bottom of a poster explaining that there was a weapon moratorium in operation and anyone minded to divest themselves of gun or a knife could do so in complete secrecy at the local nick. How the hell could he stand this place?

At last Raj waddled through, toothy grin intact. 'So have you ever been in a court like this?' he asked.

An image flashed though Liberty's mind. A waiting room with hard plastic seats and a witness liaison officer with a hard plastic smile. 'Do you think the case against my client will have been dropped?' she asked.

Raj began climbing a flight of stairs. 'Only one way to find out.'

At the top of the stairs was the CPS room, door flung open, the smell of strong perfume, possibly Angel, and the sound of expletives pouring out. Liberty knocked on the door and stepped inside, a smile plastered across her face. 'Hello, I'm Liberty Chapman, here for Mr Stephen Rance . . .'

Her words trailed away at the sight of a very large woman with a white-blonde bob standing at the far end of the room in a suit jacket and blouse but no skirt or trousers. The skin of her thighs was pink and dimpled and she was bellowing into her mobile phone. 'Listen, sunshine, I don't care how pissing busy you are. I've split my kecks and I need you down here with a fresh pair pronto.' She waved Liberty to approach. 'Go in my locker and bring whatever's in there. Understand?' She hung up and turned to Liberty.

'A shrinking violet I am not, but even I draw the line at facing the magistrate in my knickers.'

Liberty tore her eyes away from the red lace underwear.

'What can I do you for?' the woman asked, but was interrupted by someone else entering the room.

'Christ on a bike, Bucky,' Raj shrieked. 'My eyes are falling out here.'

The woman chuckled. 'Give us a sec, will you?'

Liberty heard Raj back out of the room, muttering, and shut the door behind him. 'I should wait outside too,' she said.

The woman checked her watch. 'Down to you, but if you need a word it's now or never. There's only one stipe here today, Acosta, in court one, and frankly, I'd rather keep Elton John waiting.'

Liberty gulped. She did need a word. 'My client's Rance. Stephen Rance.'

'Oh, him.' The woman ran fingers through her poker-straight hair. 'Forced a working girl to give him a blow-job, then battered her. Why these bastards don't just pay is beyond me.'

'The witness has retracted her statement,' Liberty said.

'What witness?'

'The girl in question. Daisy Clarke.'

The woman raised a pair of well-shaped eyebrows. 'The victim?'

Discomfort swept through Liberty, so she simply nodded.

The woman frowned and began to rifle through the files on her desk. Finding nothing she turned, revealing her arse cheeks, one bearing a tattoo of Bugs Bunny. Liberty averted her eyes as the woman bent to look through the pile of papers on the floor. 'Here we go.' She licked her finger and began flicking through the file. 'But there's nothing in here about any retraction.'

Liberty's heart sank. 'I can assure you it's true. Miss Clarke told me in person yesterday.'

'You've spoken with the victim?'

'There is no possession in a witness.' Liberty raised her chin. 'And I did absolutely nothing except listen.'

The woman nodded. 'I don't doubt it. It's just a bit unusual to bother on legal aid.' She looked Liberty up and down. 'Then again, you're not here on legal aid, are you?'

'I think my firm's fee arrangement is not a matter for discussion this morning,' said Liberty.

The woman gave a generous gurgle of laughter. 'Keep your hair on, I'm not mithered one way or the other.' She slammed the file shut. 'But there's still no retraction in here.'

Liberty clenched her teeth to try to stop the muscles of her jaw twitching. She'd hoped everything would be sorted. Case closed. The client would be over the moon and she would return to London, where his father would be waiting with gratitude and instructions for her to act for him on the merger.

The door opened again but this time an Asian man in his early twenties entered. 'Boss.' He unfurled a pair of black trousers like a carpet. 'These do you?'

If either was embarrassed by the situation, they didn't show it. Liberty tried to imagine any of her assistants catching her half dressed. They would die on the spot, or run from the building screaming at the very least.

The woman took the trousers, held them to her face and sniffed. 'They were better than the other pair, Bucky,' said the young man.

She shrugged, reached into her bag and retrieved a bottle of perfume. The air filled with the smell of chocolate and patchouli as she squirted Angel over the crotch. Then she pulled on the trousers and patted her arse with a smile.

'Ten o'clock, boss,' said the young man.

'Shit.' She grabbed her files and turned to Liberty. 'Gotta shift, sorry.' She marched from the room, sashaying her surprisingly pert buttocks, the assistant scampering after her.

Raj poked his head around the door. 'You met Bucky, then?'

'Yes,' Liberty replied.

'Force of nature that one.'

Daisy Clarke knew what people thought of her. Junkie, whore, skank. Daisy the Dog they called her behind her back. Well, mostly behind her back. She threw off the sheet and sat up in bed. A droplet of sweat ran from her throat, down her chest, pooling between her ribs. It wasn't the cold sweat that came when she was clucking, but the sweat you got from being too hot. Weird. She never felt hot, these days.

She got out of bed and peeped around the curtain. Everything looked yellow and still. Her mouth felt dry so she padded out to the kitchen, searched for a cup that wasn't filled with old fag butts, gave up and put her lips to the tap. She closed her eyes as she sucked down the water.

It hadn't always been like this. A lot of girls who worked the clubs and the surrounding streets couldn't remember a time when their lives weren't a pile of shite. They told stories about stepdads shagging them since they were seven or growing up in care homes. But not Daisy. She'd lived in a normal house on a normal street. Her dad worked on the bins and Mum did two days on the till in Asda. Daisy's nan used to come over for tea once a week. She'd bring a box of Milk Tray for afters and they'd all watch *Who Wants to Be a Millionaire?*. They'd shout out the answers, getting hardly any of them right.

Then one day Daisy's little brother had got ill and everything had fallen apart.

She finished drinking and splashed her face with cold water. Her cheeks burned even as she pressed her wet palms into them. She felt like she was coming down with flu or something. Then again it might be connected to the mother-load of rock she and Frankie had gone through last night.

Frankie Greenwood always spelled trouble. Nothing like his cunt of a brother, Jay, who had been on her case as soon as she'd stepped into the Cherry. Frankie just wanted a good time. Daisy liked him. He liked Daisy. And they both liked as much gear as they could lay their hands on. Last night he was bang on it, telling her about a job he was going to do with some lads from down south. The main bloke was somebody he'd met in Marbella. Brixton Dave he was called, or something else just as stupid. Apparently he was big in London and they were all going to make a mountain of cash.

Frankie had made her laugh going on about what he would buy her when he got his share. A skip full of bollocks, of course. A starter for ten: why would some big-time gangster want to hook up with Frankie fucking Greenwood?

She reached into an ashtray for a fag she'd left half smoked yesterday, lit it and took a deep drag. Where was her bag? Please let her have brought it back with her. She remembered leaving the Cherry with Frankie, then visiting a crack house up Kinsey Way. It had been full and loud. Lots of people, a sound system in the corner. Then there'd been a fight, glass smashed, blood spilled, and somebody said they should all calm down, have a bit of brown. So they had.

She looked in all the usual places. Kitchen worktops, behind the sofa, under her bed. She didn't have much stuff, so there weren't many options. 'Shit.' Daisy kicked a heap of dirty clothes on the floor. 'Shit.' Her life was in that bag: phone, with all her dealers' numbers, money, including last night's tips, a knife and mace spray she kept on her for protection. How had she let herself get so fucked up that she'd lost her bag? She sank to her knees, eyes stinging with tears. There wouldn't even be enough cash in her flat for the bus fare to the Cherry later.

Her misery was interrupted by a thump on the door. Who the hell would that be at this time of the morning? Not that she even knew the proper time without her phone. She hardly ever told anyone she lived here. Unlike a lot of users and working girls, she didn't run an open house. No parties. No punters back to hers. No people crashing on her sofa until they 'got themselves sorted'. To be honest, it made her unpopular with some of them, but that was a price worth paying to keep herself from falling completely off the edge of the cliff.

There was another volley of bangs on the door. Whoever it was, they wanted to see her big-time.

She poked her head around the bedroom door and saw a figure through the frosted glass. A man. Tall. Dark hair. Frankie? The man had Frankie's build and he did know where she lived. Oh, please, let it be Frankie so she could blag a few quid off him to get to work later. Maybe even a rock if he had one on him.

She slunk down the hallway, put on the chain and opened the door. Her heart leaped when she saw her bag being held out at arm's length. But it instantly sank when she saw who was holding it.

It wasn't Frankie.

'Nice place you've got here, Daisy.' Jay spread his arms wide to take in the worn sofa, carpetless floors and bare walls of Daisy's lounge. 'Minimalist.'

She gave her boss a thin smile. He thought he was a real funny man, but the only person who ever laughed at his jokes was Mel.

The bag was still in his hand, the strap wrapped around his wrist, a splash of red plastic against the black of his clothes. Black long-sleeved T-shirt that showed every muscle, black jeans tight across his thighs.

'You need to be more careful with your stuff.' Jay nodded at the bag.

'Where'd you find it?' Daisy asked.

Jay adjusted the sunglasses that he was wearing on top of his head, pushing them back slightly. 'Frankie had it.'

Daisy swallowed.

'He said he gave you a lift home from the club and you left it in the taxi. Lucky he spotted it, eh?' Jay leaned towards her and stared into her eyes. He didn't blink. Like some kind of fucking vampire. 'But I think we'd all be happier if you stayed away from my little brother.'

So that was it. Jay had come round to warn Daisy off Frankie. Ridiculous if you gave it a second's thought. Frankie was older than she was. But Crystal and Jay acted like he was some kid in need of protection. They didn't know the half of it.

'Do you understand me, Daisy?' asked Jay.

She nodded. No matter how much she wanted to tell Jay to go and fuck himself, she wanted to keep her job at the Cherry. Plus he had a reputation for losing the plot once in a while and she didn't want to be on the receiving end. Plenty of the girls at the Cherry had fallen foul of it. The only one who could ever handle Jay had been Kyla. And she still had to watch her mouth.

She looked longingly at her bag. She was pretty desperate for a rock and the only way to get one was to open that bag. Now Jay had said his piece, why couldn't he just do one?

Out of nowhere, Jay smiled. His teeth were white and shiny, like the bastard sprayed them with diamond dust each morning. 'But Frankie's not the reason I'm here,' he said.

Shit. If he hadn't come to warn Daisy off his brother, then what the hell was he doing here?

'I asked you to do something for me, Daisy,' Jay said.

'What?'

Jay moved even closer to Daisy, so that when he spoke his voice was a whisper in her ear. 'I asked you to withdraw the statement you made to the police about that punter.'

Daisy sprang back, relief flooding through her. 'I did, Jay. I saw that brief in your office and told her all about it.'

Jay took a step towards the window and threw open the curtains in one snap. The room filled with harsh light and Daisy had to shield her eyes. 'So why is the case still in court?' he asked.

'You know how it is, Jay, the police don't exactly make it easy. I left a ton of messages for the woman in charge, and when she wouldn't call me back, I talked to another copper I know, in Vice. We go way back.' Standing with his back against the window, light streaming around him, Jay looked more like a shadow than a man.

'And what did this copper in Vice say?' he asked.

'He said he'd sort it out for me,' she replied.

'Well, he hasn't.'

Sol had let her down. He'd promised to help. Well, not exactly promised, but he'd said he would do what he could. 'I'll call him,' Daisy said, her voice squeaky.

Jay raised an eyebrow and waited.

'My phone's in there.' Daisy gestured to her bag.

Slowly, Jay unwound the handle from his wrist, weighed the bag in his hand, then threw it at her. Daisy's hands shook as she opened the clasp and rummaged for her mobile. It had only fifteen per cent charge left, but that would be enough. She went into Contacts and dialled Sol's number.

Please let him pick up.

'Sol Connolly.'

Thank Christ. 'Sol, it's me, Daisy,' she said.

'What's up?' he asked.

'What's up? I'll tell you what's up, Sol. You said you'd sort that thing out for me and you haven't.'

Sol coughed into his phone. 'If I recall correctly, Daisy, you were supposed to get me some information. You help me and I help you.'

Daisy risked a look at Jay, who was cleaning his sunglasses, breathing on the lenses, then wiping them with the hem of his T-shirt. 'Meet me in Scottish Tony's in ten,' she said, and hung up.

Chapter 6

August 1985
Frankie's sat on my lap sucking his thumb. He's giving me a dead leg but I haven't got the heart to move him.

'I can't stand hospitals,' says Dad, marching up and down the corridor, like he's in the frigging army. 'There's something about them that does my head in.'

Does he honestly think there are folk who like hospitals? I mean, apart from doctors and nurses and that. Does he think people come here for the laugh? We've been waiting here for over an hour, jumping up every time somebody in a long white coat walks towards us. Mam's 'in theatre', which means she's having an operation. It's funny how they call it that. As if she's watching a show or something.

'I need a fag,' says Dad. 'I can't believe they don't let you smoke in here, what with all the stress. If they stopped people smoking in the nick, there'd be ructions.' He pulls out a packet of ten. 'Come and get me if there's any news. In the meantime say nothing to no one, understand?'

I nod and he walks off. When he's out of sight I feel the kids relax around me.

'What's going to happen?' Jay asks.

'I don't know,' I say.

'Is Mam going to die?' asks Crystal.

These are the first words to come out of her mouth since back at the flat when she said she knew why the social worker was coming to visit.

71

I wonder what happened to the social worker. Did she turn up and find the door locked? Did she just assume we were avoiding a visit? I bet she's writing her report now. 'Paula Greenwood remains uncooperative.'

'Well, is she?' Crystal repeats. 'Is Mam going to die?'

'No.' It's just a tiny word, so why is it choking me? 'No, she's not going to die.'

Tears well in Crystal's eyes and she lets them fall onto her tiny pink cheeks.

'Come on, now,' I say. 'I'm here, and I'm not going to let anything bad happen now, am I?'

She looks at me so solemn, as if she's a hundred years old. I try a smile but she doesn't smile back.

At last the ward door opens and a nurse comes out. She's got a blue smock thing on with a little watch attached to her pocket. She stands in front of us, her mouth tight. 'Are you Elizabeth Greenwood?' she asks.

I nod. The blood runs thick and hot in my brain, and I can't hear what she says next. It's like when you're under water and the noises around you are all foggy and wrong.

'Elizabeth?' The nurse's voice is sharper now. 'Did you hear what I just said?' I don't move and she looks puzzled. 'She's asked to see you,' the nurse says.

'Who?' I say.

The nurse laughs. 'Your mum, of course.'

So she's not dead, then. When I told Crystal Mam wouldn't die, I didn't have any idea if it was true. All that blood everywhere and Mam's face all still and blue.

'I'll stay here with the little ones for two minutes while you pop in,' says the nurse. 'She's groggy so straight in and out, okay?' When I don't get up, she puts her hands under Frankie's armpits and lifts him off my lap. He doesn't wriggle or cry, just puts his head on her chest. I push myself to my feet although I can't even feel them and wobble to Mam's room.

She's on the bed, all sorts of tubes attached to her arms, her hair pushed off her face so I can see her roots need doing. 'Mam,' I say.

72

She opens her eyes and tries to smile.

I walk over and sit on the chair next to her bed. Her nails are crusted with dried blood where she clutched herself. 'I thought you were a goner this time, Mam,' I say.

She blinks. 'I bet you were planning a party.'

'I've already baked the cake,' I say.

She laughs and puts her hand out to mine. Her fingers are cold. 'Listen, love, the police will start sniffing around soon.'

'Good,' I say. 'I hope they put him away for good this time.'

Mam shakes her head and squeezes my wrist. 'No, Lib, we can't talk to the police.'

I'm shocked and pull my hand away. She can't stand by him now. Not after what he's done. He'll never change. He might not have killed her this time, but one day he will. Or me. Or one of the kids. Surely she's not so bleeding soft she can't see it.

'I'm not messing about here, Lib.' Mam's voice goes hard. 'Once the law gets involved social services will have everything they need to put you lot in care. They're already gunning for me. They'll say I can't protect myself or you from your dad.'

I don't answer. It's pretty obvious that she can't.

'We say nothing. Convince them that this was an accident.' Mam narrows her eyes. 'Then as soon as things have calmed down we'll get your dad to sling his hook.'

'How?'

'Never you mind, love,' she says.

I shake my head. 'He's not scared of you, Mam. He's not scared of anything you can do to him.'

'Maybe not, but there are folk out there who do scare the shit out of him.'

Liberty sat at the back of court one and tried not to panic. The trouble was, panic was churning her guts, making her regret the scrambled eggs on toast she'd wolfed down for breakfast. 'What should I do now?' she hissed at Raj, who was seated next to her, coolly leafing through the five cases he would be juggling that morning. 'The prosecutor reckons she knows nothing about my witness retracting her statement. Can that be true?'

Raj crossed a foot over his knee and slid his finger under his sock to scratch a hairy ankle. 'Tessa Buckman is a bloody nightmare when she wants to be, but she's straight down the line. If she says this is news to her, you can be sure it is.'

Liberty watched Bucky, which was what everyone seemed to call her, take her place on the front row, a tower of files by her side. She leaned in towards the court clerk, who was perched on the end of his desk, and said something that made him erupt into laughter. Ease poured out of her. Unlike Liberty, who could feel her armpits prickle with sweat.

'My witness assured me she'd already informed the police,' said Liberty.

'Maybe she did, maybe she didn't—'

Raj was interrupted by the door to the magistrate's chambers opening.

'All rise,' shouted the clerk, sliding to his feet, and everyone got up.

The magistrate entered. He was pale and thin, glasses perched low on a pointed nose. He nodded to the clerk and stepped up to his seat at the large wooden desk.

'Mr Acosta,' Raj whispered. 'Not what you might call the patient type.'

Great. Liberty could only imagine how he was going to react to her special brand of inexperience.

'Just tell him what you know,' said Raj. 'Don't dress it up.'

She was about to ask what the hell he meant by that, when the first case was called and Raj lumbered away to the front row, managing simultaneously to bow to the magistrate and wink at

Chantal as she stomped into the dock, wearing so much makeup it looked as if the shelves of Superdrug had fallen from the sky and landed on her face.

Scottish Tony's was deserted. It always was in the mornings.

'I don't know why you still open up,' said Sol.

Tony slid a cup of mahogany tea onto the table, eyes red-rimmed, stubble covering both chins. 'Habit, I suppose.'

Sol took a sip and nodded. Natasha always said that if you did something twenty times it became a habit. He would only have to do his yoga stretches before breakfast twenty times for that to become the new normal – instead of his usual routine of fag, coffee, another fag. He believed her and had the best of intentions to make new healthy habits. Habits that would enhance his life. But the bad habits were both strong and seductive. A mistress with sharp nails and teeth.

His mobile rang but he didn't recognize the number. 'Sol Connolly.'

'Oh, hi.'

He didn't recognize the voice either. 'Who is this, please?'

'It's Dr Cohen,' said the woman. 'We met at the hospital in Kyla Anderson's room. You gave me your card and asked me to call you if there was any news.'

Sol's ears pricked. 'She's woken up?'

'Sadly, no,' Dr Cohen replied. 'The swelling on her brain is still extensive.'

'Shit.' The word slipped out before Sol could stop it.

'I know it must be frustrating,' said Dr Cohen, 'but if we bring her out of this coma, she may have a seizure and that could lead to brain damage in the longer term.'

'I'm sorry, I didn't mean to sound like such an arsehole,' he said.

The doctor laughed. 'You're just doing your job.'

He appreciated the fact that she didn't feel compelled to give him a lecture. 'So what news do you have, Doctor?'

'Ah, yes. Well, I had the day off yesterday, and when I checked Kyla's notes this morning I noticed she'd had a visitor.'

Now that put the cat among the pigeons.

'Actually, it was more of an attempted visit,' the doctor continued. 'It never in fact took place because the man in question refused to present any identification.'

Sol's heart dipped a smidge. 'So you don't know who he was.'

'No, we do.'

'I thought you just said he wouldn't give ID?'

'Indeed he wouldn't, but there was another officer here at the time.' The doctor paused and Sol could hear notes being rifled. 'An Officer Amira Hassani. Anyway, she recognized the man as someone known to the police.'

A smile crept around the corners of Sol's mouth. 'Do you have a name?'

'Yes.' More pages were turned. 'Jay Greenwood.'

Sol was still smiling when he said his thank-yous and hung up. Jay Greenwood had tried to visit Kyla. The same Jay Greenwood who had never employed Kyla at his club, according to his side-kick Mel.

'What are you looking so bleeding happy about?' Daisy had arrived and dumped herself unceremoniously in the chair opposite Sol. She looked very far from happy and didn't wait for his reply. 'Fucking hell, Sol, you said you'd sort this case out for me. Did you even speak to the bitch in charge?'

Sol knew the card Daisy had given him was still in his pocket, untouched since they had last met at the exact same table. 'Didn't she call you back?' he asked.

'No.' Daisy's face dropped as if she'd remembered something. She rummaged in her bag and pulled out her phone. 'Out of fucking charge.'

Sol shrugged. 'So she might have called you.'

Daisy groaned and let her head fall to the table, oblivious to the sugar and salt grains, the sticky cup rings and hardened smears of egg yolk. 'Can I use yours?' she asked.

Sol raised an eyebrow and Daisy groaned even louder. 'I asked around about Kyla, okay?' she said.

'And?'

'And no one knows anything. She left the Cherry and it's like she fell off the face of the earth. No one knows where she was working or where she was living.'

Sol folded his arms. Kyla had never been as far as the turn-off to the A1. She'd lived her whole life in a three-mile radius. 'What did she say when she left the Cherry?' he asked.

Daisy screwed up her face. 'That she weren't going to do it no more. No tricks, no dancing, nothing.'

'So how was she going to manage?'

'That's exactly what I asked her.' Daisy jabbed herself with her thumb, caught the now scabby bite mark and winced. '"What you gonna do for money?" I says.'

Sol picked up his cup and waited. His tea was cold but he took a sip all the same.

'She just laughed and said it was all sorted. "Had a bit of luck, have you?" I says, and she goes, "Nah, Daisy, you have to make your own luck in this life." But then she always did talk a lot of shit.' Daisy turned her phone over and over in her hands. 'I said she'd better not fuck with Jay cos luck has a way of running out and she wouldn't want to burn her boats, but she just said Jay wouldn't be a problem and gave a daft wink.' Daisy looked up at Sol.

Was that really all she knew about Kyla? 'Let's ring this policewoman now, shall we?' he said, fishing in his pocket for the card. When he pulled it out and read it, he frowned. The name of the officer dealing with Daisy's case was Amira Hassani.

★　★　★

Frankie looked at the KitKat. He felt sick but knew he needed to get something down him. As he snapped the bar in two and brought the first finger to his lips, the smell of the chocolate made him gag. He still had his head inside the toilet bowl when his mobile rang. Probably just Jay or Crystal calling to have a pop. He wiped his mouth with the back of his hand. He'd like to tell them where to go, but he needed some cash. As usual. When he checked caller ID, he saw it was Brixton Dave belling him. Shit. 'All right mate?' Frankie's voice wobbled.

'Fucking hell, bruv!' Brixton Dave's laugh was so loud, Frankie had to hold his mobile at arm's length. 'You sound like crap. Good party, was it?'

Frankie thought about the night before, spent in a crack house and then back at Daisy's empty flat. 'Top party,' he said.

'You are a proper animal, mate.' Brixton Dave laughed again, even harder. 'But listen up. I'm gonna be in your area in the next few days.'

'How come?' Frankie asked.

'Business, bruv, you know how it is.'

'Yeah.' Frankie used the edge of the slimy toilet bowl to push himself to his feet. 'I've got a lot on myself.'

'Gotta earn a pound, am I right?'

Frankie knew that he had less than three pounds left in the pocket of his jeans. 'Not wrong, Dave.'

'So can you spare me an hour, Frankie?' Brixton Dave asked. 'Fit me in to your busy schedule?'

'Course,' Frankie replied. 'Never too busy for a mate.'

'The Crown versus Stephen Rance,' the clerk called.

Liberty's mouth went dry as she made her way to the front. She knew she needed to introduce herself but her tongue was the texture of feta cheese. As she tried to work up enough saliva to clear things, the magistrate snapped up his head. 'Where is the defendant?'

Everyone turned to face the empty dock.

'Well?' Mr Acosta narrowed his eyes at Liberty. 'Where is your client, Miss . . . Sorry, I don't know your name.'

Liberty coughed. 'Liberty Chapman, sir.'

'Well, Miss Chapman, where is your client?'

Liberty willed herself to be calm. These were not difficult questions. No reason to be hyperventilating in the margarine lights. 'HMP Wakefield, sir.' She looked down and saw her hand was trembling, but she managed to keep her voice clear. 'He's in custody.'

The clerk tapped deftly on his keyboard, the tight pecking sound filling the court.

'He hasn't been produced,' the clerk told Mr Acosta.

'Why on earth not?'

'The case isn't listed until next week,' the clerk replied.

'Clearly the case is listed today, as here we all are.' Mr Acosta gave an I'm-surrounded-by-idiots shake of his head. 'Except, of course, the one person we need.'

'The hearing today is the result of an emergency application made by Miss Chapman,' said the clerk.

Immediately all eyes fell on Liberty who stuck up her chin.

'Did you tell the prison service that your client's presence was necessary this morning?' Acosta asked her.

She hadn't. Of course she hadn't. For fuck's sake, she hadn't even known she was meant to do that. Once again she cursed Ronald for sending her here. 'I'm afraid there wasn't time,' she answered.

Throughout law school, it had been impressed upon the young students that under no circumstances must any solicitor mislead a court. However, years of practice at the cutting edge of corporate law had taught Liberty that there were a million shades of grey.

Sure, the lack of time had not been the main reason for her not informing the prison, but even if she *had* understood that this was her responsibility, there wouldn't have been any time to do it. She had no idea what the process was to get a prisoner to court, but she suspected it entailed more than a quick call from their lawyer.

'My instructions were to move this issue along with all haste,' she added.

Acosta stared at Liberty for an elastic moment. 'Please do explain the urgency, Miss Chapman.'

'Well, sir, the main witness in the case, I think it's fair to describe her as the only material witness, has withdrawn her statement.' Liberty paused to emphasize the importance of this fact. 'She told me in person that she had made an error due to excessive drug use. She also informed the police of the situation. In the circumstances, it would have been utterly remiss of me not to bring this matter before the court as the earliest opportunity.'

Acosta raised an eyebrow, clearly interested. Yes, she had him.

'Given that my client is a man of impeccable character and is currently being held in a high-security prison more generally populated by convicted sex offenders, I hope you understand my desire to expedite matters.'

Acosta gave no indication that he understood anything of the sort but instead turned his gaze to Bucky, who pushed herself to a standing position. 'While I completely see where my friend for the defence is coming from, unfortunately I know nothing of this change of heart by the victim,' she said. 'Perhaps we could adjourn until tomorrow for me to look into it?'

No, no, no. Another day here was more than Liberty could bear. And what if Bucky still didn't have any more information tomorrow? It would be Friday, and the case might be postponed over the weekend. Saturday night in the bar of the Radisson Hotel might just finish her off. 'Sir.' Her voice was too loud, clanging around the courtroom. She corrected herself. 'Sir, I can see that my friend for the prosecution has an enormous caseload.' Liberty waved at Bucky's files. 'But my client cannot be expected to spend another night in an establishment often called Monster Mansion.' She made quotation marks in the air with her fingers. 'That would be a misuse of the authority to remand an innocent man in custody.'

More staring. Another moment. Not elastic like the last, but brittle and hard around the edges.

The magistrate got to his feet and barked, 'Both lawyers in my chambers now.'

Bucky and Liberty followed Mr Acosta through the door at the back of the court to the small ante-room beyond: his chambers. One wall was filled with shelves of leather-bound legal tomes. All years out of date. On the desk in the middle of the room there was a bottle of San Pellegrino and a glass beside it, rim down on the wood. Mr Acosta sat behind it, bony fingers steepled under his chin. 'How, then, to sort out this mess?' he asked.

There were two chairs in front of the desk. Bucky took one. 'I can't just drop the case, sir,' she said. 'Not without talking to the officer in charge of it.'

'So talk to him,' said Liberty.

'Her.'

'Okay, talk to her.' Liberty didn't sit, but hovered behind her own chair. 'Pick up the phone now.'

Acosta sighed. 'Miss Chapman, we are in the middle of a busy session. At least forty cases are listed this morning. I can't have my prosecutor wandering off to pursue one matter.' He enunciated his words carefully, taking ownership of the court. A middle-class white man, local but not local, who chose to spend his days judging the lives of others.

'A two-minute call right now might save a lot of time in the long run,' Liberty replied. 'And money.' She dropped that last word like a stink bomb. Delays cost money. And someone would have to pay.

'I've a lad here from the office,' said Bucky. 'I'll get him to make the call.'

Amira Hassani's day was going from bad to worse. The baby had been up half the night teething and she'd had to prowl around in the dark, jiggling him on her hip, rubbing his gums, hoping he wouldn't wake everyone else. When she'd finally got him back down in his cot and collapsed into bed herself, Dad's alarm had gone off, a shrill electronic blast followed by the breakfast show on Radio Arabique. 'Yalla habibi' rang out and Dad sang along at the top of his lungs. Amira had been grateful when her brother, Zaid, had pounded along the landing and snapped off the radio, screaming that pop music was *haram*. His current religious conversion was useful for some things. She'd been almost asleep when her mobile rang. 'Amira Hassani.'

'Sorry to bother you, I know you're not on shift today.' A man's voice. 'I called the nick and they told me to use this number.'

Amira groaned. Her mobile number was only supposed to be given out in emergencies. In reality, no one at the station could ever be arsed to do anything on anyone else's cases so all queries were directed to the officer's mobile.

'It's about Stephen Rance,' he continued.

The name didn't ring any bells. The constant sleepless nights were destroying her memory. Like someone using a scalpel on her brain, removing it slice by slice, each painful and bloody cut leaving less behind. 'Sorry?' she mumbled.

'Assault charge on a working girl up at Carter Street?' he said.

Now she remembered. A nasty attack, including a bite. The perp was some posh bloke from down south. 'What about it?' she asked.

'The case is up in court today.'

Amira sat bolt upright in bed. She was knackered, yes, forgetful, definitely, but miss a court date? No way. All hearings were triple logged. 'Are you sure?' she asked.

The man laughed. 'Don't panic. It was listed by the defence for a special mention, all last minute, like.'

Amira felt momentarily relieved before her spider senses began to tingle. 'Listed why?' she asked.

'The lawyer says the victim's retracted her statement. Apparently you know all about it.'

It was true that Daisy Clarke had left a long, garbled message on Amira's voicemail, but she wasn't going to take it at face value. Victims were warned off giving evidence all the time, especially by men like Rance. Amira had tried calling back but no one had picked up. 'There's not much to know as yet,' she said.

'Thing is, we're in front of Mr Acosta and things are getting a bit hot under the collar. The defence are threatening costs.'

Now that was out of order. What was Amira meant to do? She couldn't drop the charges without speaking to the victim in person. 'Give me twenty minutes,' she said. 'I'll meet you in court.'

Amira's shirt had a brown stain down the front, courtesy of last night's biryani. She usually changed before dinner, but she'd been starving and had intended to wash it today. She considered doing up her jacket but it was roasting out. Sweaty armpits were not going to improve her mood.

The guard waved her through Reception and she took the steps up to the courts two at a time, eager to tell Rance's solicitor where she could stuff her demand for costs. It never ceased to amaze her how quick some people were to condemn the police when most of her colleagues were decent folk. Not perfect, but fundamentally decent. Maybe they should try living in a place where the police really could not be trusted. A place where right and wrong were unimportant.

Bucky was waiting for her at the top of the stairs with a young bloke, presumably the one who had called her. He was Asian. Good-looking. He smiled at her with white teeth. '*As salaam alaikum*, sister.'

'*Wa alaikum salaam*,' she replied.

'Which I assume means "How do, cocker?" in Arabic.' Bucky grinned. 'Listen, love, thanks for coming, I know it's your day off.'

'No problem,' Amira replied automatically. Actually, it was a problem. There was no one to babysit Rahim. In the end, Zaid had agreed to drop him at his girlfriend's for an hour (his religious conversion not yet precluding sex with girls on his college course).

'So, what do you know about this Daisy Clarke business?' asked Bucky.

Amira shrugged. 'I was called out to something going off in Carter Street. It's not my usual area but a lot of units had got caught up in an arson attack on the Crosshills estate.' It had been a big deal. A plastic bottle of petrol through the window. Two houses up in flames, a family having to escape out of an upstairs window, including a couple of toddlers.

'I heard about that,' said Bucky.

'Like I say, I headed over to Carter Street, and when I got there Daisy was covered with blood and screaming blue murder,' said Amira.

'Happy to cooperate?' Bucky asked.

'Happy? She all but jumped in the squad car, telling me we had to drive around until we picked up the punter who'd done it.'

'And when you found him she made a statement? Without any nudging from you?' Bucky asked.

Amira laughed. She knew what Bucky was getting at, but Daisy had been calling Rance every cunt from here to Christmas and had needed no persuasion.

'And what about this retraction of hers? What do you know about that?' asked Bucky.

'I know she called me and left a message,' Amira replied. 'She was obviously off her head or stressed or both, talking in circles that she can't go through with it.' Amira put up a finger. 'Not that it wasn't true about Rance attacking her, but that she couldn't go through with coming to court. Not the same thing.'

'Have you spoken to her about it?'

Amira shook her head. 'I called but she didn't answer.'

Bucky smiled, clearly satisfied.

'So, where's this solicitor that's making all the fuss?' Amira asked.

Bucky looked around, her gaze resting on a woman in high heels with impossibly glossy hair, tapping on her iPhone. Amira pulled her jacket around her to cover the stain on her shirt.

Chapter Seven

September 1985
There's a riot going off in somewhere called Handsworth. It's on the telly now. Buildings on fire, lines of boys throwing stones and bottles at the police.

'What they doing that for?' Jay asks.

'Cos they're angry,' I say. 'And they don't know what else to do.'

Jay laughs. 'That's just daft.'

I watch him pull a face at Crystal, trying to get a rise out of her, but not managing it. Our Crystal's a quiet one at the best of times but since Mam's been in hospital she's settled into a sort of wary stillness. Jay gives up and pokes Frankie instead.

'Pack it in,' I shout.

One of the lads on the screen lights a rag that he's stuffed into a bottle. He throws it high into the air, like a shooting star. When it lands a couple of feet from the police, it explodes, making them move back. Some bloke is saying they'll have to send in the army to sort it all out. Another one tries to talk to the rioters, but they don't want to know. Eventually one pulls a woolly scarf round his face and moves towards the microphone.

'Why are you doing this?' the reporter asks. 'Why are you attacking the police?'

'We can't take no more.' The boy's voice is muffled by his scarf. 'We take it and take it, until we just can't do it no more.'

The reporter tries to ask him something else, but the boy's not listening, instead he picks up a brick and lobs it.

'Daft,' Jay says again.

I shake my head. I don't think it's daft at all.

There's the sound of the key in the door and three pairs of eyes look to me for what to do.

'Say hello, then go to bed,' I tell the kids.

Dad walks in. He's had a few but he's not drunk-drunk. 'Chips.' He waves a parcel wrapped in newspaper. 'And curry sauce.'

Jay and Crystal both hate curry sauce but I give them the dead eye and fetch some plates from the kitchen.

Good as gold, everybody scoffs their chips, Jay and Crystal avoiding the pool of yellow shite I made sure was right on the edge of their plates. Frankie, who's not got a fussy bone in his body, wolfs the lot, licking his plate for good measure. 'The kids had best be in bed now,' I say.

Dad nods. 'Aye. Me as well. Busy day tomorrow.'

Doing what? He stays in bed all morning, then spends the afternoons pinballing from the pub to the bookie's. If he backs a winner, the landlord of the Hope and Anchor will see him again. If not, he'll watch telly and shout at us.

Mam's promised that as soon as she gets out of hospital, she'll sort him out. I've asked a load of times what she's planning, but she just taps the side of her nose and says what I don't know won't hurt me. In the meantime, I've to keep him sweet. Make sure the kids don't drive him crackers so he does something stupid.

I pick up Frankie, feeling his damp bum where his nappy's leaked. He should be potty-trained by now. 'Night, Dad,' I say.

'Night, Lib.' I head upstairs, wishing I could stuff a rag into a bottle of petrol and set it alight.

Liberty checked through her email. She'd been away from her desk for two days now, and although Tina was keeping things under control, there were a number of things that needed her attention. There was also a message from Ronald.

To: Liberty Chapman
From: Ronald Tate
Re: callme.com
I had a little drink with Charlie Rance last night at the club. Seems the merger is going ahead. I assured him that his golden boy would soon be back in the bosom of his family, which pleased him no end. Call me with news, preferably of the good variety.
Ciao
Ronald

Liberty exhaled a long breath. She hated that Ronald was on little-drink terms with Charles Rance. How did he do that? Was there a club they all belonged to? When she did the work on this merger, would they let her join? It was all so unfair. She was smart. Smarter than most of the lawyers she knew. And she worked three times as hard. Yet her entry to the next level was dependent on securing the freedom of a man dogs wouldn't piss on.

She spotted Bucky watching her, saying something to a police-woman flanking her. She waved and Bucky waved back, but the policewoman just scowled. Liberty slid her phone into her bag and walked over.

'This is Amira Hassani,' said Bucky. 'The officer in the case.'

Liberty held out her hand. Hassani gazed upon it as if Liberty had offered a used tissue. Then she grabbed it, the skin of her own hand flawless, the colour of dark honey, gave one firm pump and removed it as quickly as possible. 'I hear you've been in contact with Daisy Clarke,' she said.

'That's right,' Liberty replied.

Hassani's stance was combative. Feet planted apart, shoulders squared. 'Why?'

'I wanted to ask her some questions about her statement,' Liberty replied.

'You shouldn't have done that,' said Hassani.

'I'm perfectly entitled to speak to any witness in the case.'

Hassani shook her head. She had long, thick hair − good hair − pulled into one rope of plait. 'No one is entitled to hound a victim to talk them out of giving evidence.'

Liberty raised an eyebrow. She liked the younger woman's style of giving no fucks, but she couldn't let the assertion lie. 'I didn't hound anyone. I simply went to Miss Clarke's . . . place of work, and I certainly did not talk her out of anything. Frankly, I didn't need to.'

Liberty thought she caught sight of a smirk loitering at the corner of Bucky's mouth. Enjoying the show, no doubt.

'So you turned up at the Black Cherry and then what happened?' Hassani demanded.

'Miss Clarke wasn't there,' Liberty replied. 'I left a message for her and her employer arranged for me to meet her the next morning.'

Hassani threw up her hands. 'Her employer? Do you mean Jay Greenwood?'

Liberty reddened at the tone Hassani used when stating her brother's name and gave a small nod.

'Jay Greenwood is not Daisy's employer. He's a pimp. A low-life. Living off girls who have no other means of supporting themselves than showing their tits to strangers.'

Liberty felt her blush deepen and prayed her makeup was doing its job.

'If Jay Greenwood had anything to do with this, then it's definitely dodgy,' Hassani added.

Liberty knew she had to close this down. Without realizing it, the policewoman was making the situation all too personal. She turned to Bucky. 'We can stand here all day, discussing the possible reasons for Miss Clarke's decision.' She put up her hands to restrain another onslaught from Hassani while still looking at Bucky. 'But that's going to waste a lot of precious time, which, given I'm paid by the hour, is a lot less worrying for me than for you, Miss Buckwood. Why don't we go straight to the horse's mouth and call Miss Clarke?'

'I'd rather discuss this with her in person,' said Hassani.

And I'd rather be in my office right now, asking Tina to bring me a caramel latte, thought Liberty. 'The clock's ticking,' she said to Bucky.

Out of nowhere, Bucky gave a hard and dirty chuckle. 'And Acosta's going to rip me a new arsehole when the alarm goes off.' She put a hand on Hassani's shoulder and squeezed.

'Fine,' said Hassani, and pulled out her mobile with a weary sigh. 'I tried yesterday but she's not answering.' She scrolled through her contacts and pressed. After a moment she smiled, triumphant. 'Voicemail.'

Liberty swallowed a groan. Now what? She tried desperately to remember Raj's advice. List the case to try to get it dismissed or at the very least secure her client's release from Monster Mansion. 'Bail,' she blurted out.

Hassani and Bucky stared at her.

'What?' Liberty asked. 'You can't get hold of Miss Clarke at the moment but in due course you will. In the meantime you must agree to bail.'

'No way.' Hassani crossed her arms. 'Absolutely no way.'

Liberty racked her brain for an ancient memory from law school. What were the grounds for objecting to bail? There was a vague recollection gathering dust at the back of her mind. Seriousness of the offence? Beating someone up certainly seemed serious to her, but was it in the great scheme of things? If there was a sliding scale with speeding at one end and double murder at the other, where did an assault like this sit?

'Hang on a mo. This is a bloody serious case,' Bucky stated, answering Liberty's question. 'Punching somebody in a bar fight is one thing, but taking a chunk out of a prostitute with your teeth? That's Jack the Ripper territory. And there's the small matter of your client being extremely rich.'

'That's not a crime,' Liberty said. 'Yet.'

Bucky laughed again. In a different set of circumstances, Liberty could imagine going for a drink with her. She looked like she could hold her beer and would tell a good tale.

'It gives the suspect a lot more options to abscond than your average punter,' said Bucky. 'He could book a ticket out of the country like that.' She snapped her fingers. 'There would be no point in offering any sort of surety. The family are so loaded they could afford to lose it without a second thought.'

Liberty thought that was wrong. She'd met a lot of filthily wealthy people and they didn't waste their money. Where the poor would spend their last farthing and roll the dice until next pay day, the rich were careful with their pretty green. 'He could hand in his passport,' she suggested. 'Maybe he could give a specific address where he would stay in this area and the police could check he was there. Just until you can verify the situation with Miss Clarke.'

Bucky patted Liberty's forearm. 'The coppers are a bit too busy round here to do personal house calls. But he could sign in at the local nick.' She put up a finger. 'Morning and night.'

'Agreed,' said Liberty.

Bucky turned to Hassani. 'I know it feels like a kick in the nads but we've no choice. Miss Chapman's going to walk straight out of here and head directly for the Crown Court.' Liberty had not even considered that but nodded vigorously as if the address were already in her satnav. 'Any judge is going to hear that her man's got no previous yet he's stuck up the Mansion and lose his shit. When it comes out our victim's been trying to drop the whole thing, we'll probably get stung for costs.'

'But we don't know that Daisy is going to drop the whole thing,' said Hassani. 'I smell a big old rat here.'

'And I smell a written warning for us both if my department has to hand over hard cash to someone like Rance,' Bucky replied.

Hassani let out a hiss, like the last breath of a deflating balloon.

Liberty had won. Sort of.

'Loser,' Brixton Dave sneered, at the old boy feeding the fruit machine.

Frankie liked to play them himself but he laughed along.

'It's easy to make money, mate.' Brixton Dave leaned back, arms stretched along the top of the booth. 'When the world is full of fucking mugs.'

His voice was too loud and some of the Butcher's Arms regulars looked over to see who was making all the noise. Brixton Dave either didn't notice or didn't give a shit. He was different from how Frankie remembered him. In Marbella, his tanned skin made him look like one of the players. Today he was a bit frigging orange, to be honest. And the teeth? What were they about?

'Like taking sweets from a fucking baby,' Brixton Dave added.

The barman banged down a pint glass at the sound of another 'fucking' filling the air, or 'fah-ckin', as Brixton Dave pronounced it.

'Keep it down, Dave,' Frankie said.

Brixton Dave eyeballed him, cockiness coming out of every pore. 'I thought you were the man round these parts, son. Thought your family were the people to know.'

Frankie squirmed inside. He'd probably given the impression that he was a face. Well, no probably about it. There'd been a lot of talk as they'd chopped out lines in the bogs of El Paradiso. 'I like to keep things on the low.' It was something Frankie had heard in an episode of *The Sopranos*. 'Don't want to attract the wrong sort of attention.'

Brixton Dave narrowed his eyes. He didn't seem suspicious, though he might have been, more like he was weighing up Frankie. 'Fair dos,' he said at last.

An old bird brought over the food Frankie had ordered. A couple of cheeseburgers and chips. Frankie had had to borrow from Jay and put up with his bitching, but he didn't want to look like a tight arse and make Brixton Dave pay for his own. He took the top off the burger bun and discarded the limp lettuce leaf. 'So, tell me the story,' he said.

Brixton Dave's eyes lit up and he rubbed his hands together. 'Me and the boys, we have a regular thing going with some Russians. Good product, good price.'

'Sweet,' Frankie said.

'Too right. Only now these fuckers have decided they ain't happy no more. They want us to take twice as much off their hands.' Brixton Dave dipped a chip in ketchup, ate it and took a swig from his bottle of Becks. 'We tell them we don't want no more. This is our area and we know exactly how much the market will bear.' He pointed at Frankie with his bottle. 'You know how it is, mate. Supply enough, but only just enough. Always keep the muppets wanting more and the price stays steady.'

Frankie nodded, but it didn't make that much sense to him. The more drugs you sold, the more money you made. Surely?

'We've tried reasoning with them but you know Russians.' Brixton Dave shrugged. 'They say that if we don't want the extra supply they know another crew that does. And that, my friend, ain't fucking on.'

Frankie drained his beer and ran his tongue across his top lip. He didn't want his burger and wished he hadn't ordered it. 'I take it you're going to get another supplier?'

'Already got one lined up,' Brixton Dave replied.

'But?'

'But that ain't the fucking end of it, know what I mean? We need to teach these lairy cunts a lesson. Make sure everybody's clear about who can and who can't be fucked with.'

Now that did make sense to Frankie. If you let people push you around, they did it more and more. Sometimes you had to make a stand. Look at how Jay and Crystal acted, cutting him out of the business, treating him like a car crash. It hadn't always been like that. When they were kids they'd stuck together through thick and thin, and there'd been some serious amounts of thin. It had felt good, though. Like they could get through it all so long as they had each other's backs. Frankie needed to show Crystal and Jay that they could go back to how it was. That they could be a unit together, if only they'd let him in. He needed to force them to see things differently.

'Put it this way,' said Brixton Dave. 'The next handover ain't gonna play out how the Russians expect it to go.'

'Where do I come in?'

Brixton Dave grinned, the shine from his teeth white and blinding. 'Fresh meat,' he said. 'If we ask anyone from our manor to help us, the word will get out, but no one's ever heard of you.' He opened his palms. 'No disrespect, Frankie.'

'None taken.'

'You can come in under the radar,' he said. 'Like a fucking ninja. Bam.' He slapped his hand on the table. 'Take the drugs from the Russians before they know what's fucking hit them.'

Frankie took a deep breath. A ninja. He liked the sound of that. A ninja couldn't be bossed off the ball. A ninja couldn't be ignored. Jay and Crystal would have to respect a ninja, then everyone else would follow. Oh, yeah, Frankie Greenwood was going to be everything he wanted to be. A ninja. A bat-shit frigging ninja.

Sol tried Amira Hassani's number for the tenth time.

Jay Greenwood was the key to finding out what had happened to Kyla Anderson. She'd been working for him, even if Mel had denied it, until she'd left in what seemed quite strange circumstances and fallen off the radar, and he was the only person who'd shown any interest in her since she'd turned up half dead.

'You've reached the mobile of Officer Amira Hassani. Please leave a message after the tone.'

Sol hung up. He'd already left at least three. Didn't anyone teach these rookies to check their phones regularly? Hassani sounded young on her voicemail message but that was no excuse for ignoring basic procedures.

He checked Hassani's card again. Underneath her number was the name and address of the nick where she was stationed. Fine. If the mountain wouldn't come to Muhammad . . .

Hyde Road nick was a twenty-minute drive from Carter Street and had bugger-all parking close by. There was a decent-sized car park for the officers who worked at the station but Sol didn't have the code to punch in at the automated gate. Instead, he had to go round in circles until someone outside an estate agent's finally moved. By the time he had bought a ticket from a machine on the other side of the road – the nearest one was broken – he was in a seriously foul mood. Hassani had better have a damn good reason for not returning his calls.

When he got to Reception and was told she was in court, he

could have kicked himself for not calling the nick rather than hightailing it over there. Who was the rookie here?

Back outside the nick, a gaggle of young lads were smoking. Sol reached for his e-cig, but was in the nearest newsagent buying a pack of twenty and a lighter before he could say Benson & Hedges. The smoke scratched as it went down, and his throat closed in protest. Sol carried on smoking anyway. He liked smoking. He wished he didn't but he did. He liked it in the same way that he liked black coffee and fry-ups and Jack Daniel's and difficult women. In fact he liked those things more than most others. The only thing that really came close was catching criminals. He laughed at himself. He knew it was the nicotine talking, as it crossed through the thin membranes in his body to his blood system and was transported at breakneck speed into each and every cell in his body.

When the fag was finished, he ground the butt under his heel, jumped into his car and set off for the Black Cherry.

'Seriously?' Mel bared her teeth at Sol. 'You think you can just come in here and demand to see Jay?'

'I think he'll want to talk to me,' said Sol.

'I doubt that.'

'Tell him it's about Kyla Anderson.' Sol took a seat at the bar. 'That girl who never worked here.'

Mel stared at him, the feel of her eyes like two razors ripping his skin. But in the end she stalked across the club to the back office.

Without a word, or even looking up, Len pushed an opened bottle of beer in front of Sol. He raised it to the man and took a warm mouthful.

Five minutes later, Jay Greenwood sauntered from his office to the bar. He was a big bloke. Tanned and handsome. Always well turned out, if a bit flash.

'I know you're busy, Mr Greenwood,' said Sol.

'I am.'

'Kyla Anderson.' Sol let the poor girl's name hang in the air. 'She sometimes went as Kiki. Ring any bells?'

Greenwood shrugged.

'She worked here for a while,' said Sol.

'You'd need to check with Mel,' said Greenwood. 'I don't keep a track of the girls.'

Clever. He hadn't denied she'd ever worked there. Palmed it all off on good old Mel.

'This one was a bit different from the others,' said Sol. 'Lovely-looking for a start. Bit of a handful.'

Greenwood chuckled. 'Aren't they all?'

Sol chuckled back and took another swig of beer. 'Unfortunately, she took a real pasting from a punter, ended up in hospital. We're looking at attempted murder. Worse, if she doesn't pull through.'

'Well, it didn't happen here, if that's what you think.' Greenwood glared. 'We don't let anyone touch the girls. They're safe in the Cherry, which is why they like working for me.'

Sol had spent a lot of his working life weighing people up, channelling out their noise, winkling out the truth. Something about Greenwood's demeanour told Sol he was telling the truth. Or, at least, what Jay Greenwood believed to be the truth.

'So why did you visit Kyla in hospital?' he asked.

Greenwood shook his head with a soft laugh. 'I didn't.'

Now that was a lie. Even without Hassani's say-so, Sol could read the dishonesty on the other man's face. 'Last Tuesday. You were seen.'

'I think you need to go back to whoever said they saw me and buy them some glasses.'

'And I think you need to do better than that, Mr Greenwood. I've got witnesses who say you knew Kyla pretty well. And I've got witnesses who can place you at the hospital.' Sol finished his drink and slid the empty bottle back towards Len. 'From where I'm standing that puts you right in the middle of things.'

'If you had anything concrete I'd already be under arrest.'

Sol stood to leave. 'There's time, Mr Greenwood. I'm a patient man. Obviously, I'll need to speak to the other family members.'

'Good luck trying to see Crystal without a warrant.'

Sol walked away. 'Crystal won't play ball, but Rebecca might be a bit more amenable, don't you think?'

Raj took a seat next to Liberty. 'By the look on your face, I take it things are going well.'

Liberty smiled. 'Bucky's agreed to bail while they track down the witness. She's putting something in writing now for Mr Acosta.'

'Round one to the new kid on the block.'

'I'd never have got this far without you,' she told him. 'I'm still not sure why you've been helping me out.'

'I can understand more than most what it feels like to be out of the loop,' he said.

'Let me take you to lunch,' she said. 'As a thank-you. It's a beautiful day – we could find somewhere to sit outside.'

Raj placed his hands on his belly and jiggled the flab. 'I'm not a man to turn down free food.'

Liberty's mobile rang. It was Jay. She mouthed, 'Excuse me,' to Raj and stepped away.

'Listen, Lib.' The old nickname made her heart flutter. A bird's wing against the cage of her ribs. 'I'll get straight to the point.'

'Go on.'

'I need a favour,' he said.

'Okay.'

'The police want to talk to me about something that happened last Tuesday,' said Jay. 'I need you to tell them we went to lunch at Jade Garden.'

'Well, we did,' answered Liberty.

There was a pause.

'Jay?' Liberty prompted.

'I need you to say we stayed there until after four.'

'I'm a solicitor, Jay,' Liberty hissed.

'I know, I know, but just hear me out. The police – you know how they are, they get an idea and they won't let up. They're saying I'm involved in something.'

Liberty pictured her brother shoving sweet and sour into his mouth. A phone call. A hasty retreat. 'And are you?' she asked.

'No.'

'So why did you leave the restaurant?'

Jay let out a long sigh. 'Promise you won't hate me?'

Liberty laughed. He was asking her to give a false alibi, yet he was more worried that something else would make her judge him.

'I went to see a bird.' His voice lost all its bluster. 'Not the missus.'

'So get her to talk to the police.'

'I can't. She's not in a position to help me out,' he said. 'In the meantime the police are threatening to talk to Becca about it.'

'Why would they talk to your wife?'

Jay's laugh was bitter. 'To cause me as much aggro as possible. Oh, they're looking for ways to bring me down, don't you worry about that. As far as they're concerned, I'm still that little scrote in care, got ideas above my station and due a very big fall.'

Liberty didn't know what to say.

'Stupid thing is, it's over between me and this woman,' said Jay.

'I only went to see her because I felt bad and she's not well. Will you at least think about it?'

'I don't know,' she replied.

'It's a big ask. But I'm really struggling here, Lib.'

'Okay, I'll think about it,' she said. She hung up as her biggest fan made her way over. 'Officer Hassani.'

Behind Hassani was a man. Tall, over six foot, and well built. Hair just the wrong side of scruffy, but only just. 'Miss Chapman,' said Hassani, face like thunder. 'This is DI Connolly.'

Liberty got to her feet and shook the man's hand. Unlike Hassani he took it in one smooth motion, grip firm but not tight, looking Liberty squarely in the eye from behind his choppy fringe. Totally in control. Had he come to kick up a fuss about bail? Surely he couldn't overrule Bucky. 'I'm afraid Miss Buckman is already drafting the paperwork.' said Liberty.

Connolly waved a hand as if that was of no concern. There was a small pink scar in the shape of a half-moon that began at the knuckle of his little finger.

'My client will hand over his passport and sign in at the local police station,' she added.

Connolly looked amused. 'I'm sure that will be very nice for him.'

Liberty narrowed her eyes. If he had something to say about bail, he needed to say it, not play stupid games. And she would fight him. He need make no mistake about that. No doubt he was used to getting his own way. He was wrong if he thought that would happen today. A deal had been struck with Bucky and the deal would stay.

'I understand that you had lunch with Jay Greenwood on Tuesday,' said Connolly, taking out his card and handing it to her.

Liberty felt the air escape through her lips. This had nothing to do with bail or Rance.

'At the Jade Garden restaurant?' Connolly asked.

Liberty nodded and checked the card.

'Can I ask how long you were there?' he asked.

She swallowed hard. She had told Jay she needed some time to think about this. What the hell was he playing at? 'We arrived at around one,' she said.

Connolly smiled with one half of his mouth. 'And what time did you leave?'

Liberty's head was swimming. She was a solicitor. She couldn't lie to the police. 'I don't think I know the exact time,' she answered.

'Ballpark,' said Connolly. 'Two, three, four, five?'

Liberty touched her top lip. It felt slick. She couldn't lie. Of course she couldn't lie.

'It's a simple question,' said Connolly.

But it wasn't simple. Not at all. Nothing about coming back here and seeing Jay again was simple. Nausea welled from the pit of her stomach to her throat. 'I'm sorry,' said Liberty. 'Do you mind if I sit down?'

Hassani jutted out her chin. 'I think you need to answer DI Connolly.'

Liberty ignored her and stepped back, flopping into one of the metal seats. Suddenly she was transported back to another time when she had sat outside a courtroom waiting to see if they were going to send Jay away to a young offenders' institution for nicking a van from outside the post office. Short sharp shock. As if he hadn't had enough fucking sharp shocks in his short life.

'Miss Chapman.' Hassani's voice was cold. 'If you don't want to talk to us here, we can continue at the station.'

Liberty looked at her. So young, yet so full of anger. Convinced she knew the truth about Liberty and Jay, when even Liberty and Jay didn't understand it. And Connolly. Enjoying himself. Enjoying the game. She heard her own voice, not even realizing she was going to speak. 'I was with Mr Greenwood until after four o'clock.'

Chapter 8

September 1985
I'm so knackered I feel like I'd fall over if I got off the end of the hospital bed. Mam's faffing around, packing her stuff into a holdall I brought with me, fussing about whether she should put her slippers at the bottom of the bag or on top of her clothes. I watch her and scratch my scalp. The itching's getting worse. Last night I felt like cutting all my hair off.

'Pack it in, Lib,' says Mam. 'You'll have it turning bad-ways.'

I don't show her the yellow scab I've picked off.

'Now, shall I wear this?' She holds up a white blouse with puffed sleeves. 'Or this?' She waves a stretchy black top covered with sequins.

'Is that new?' I ask her.

She shrugs. 'Your dad brought it for me yesterday.' She chooses the white blouse, tucking the new top away with her slippers.

I wipe the scab on the edge of the bed sheet. 'You need to do what you said.'

'Oh, aye?'

It's all right for her. She's been holed up in here. Three nice meals a day. Safe.

'Getting somebody to scare him off,' I say. 'You need to do it as soon as you're back.'

Mam snaps up her head. 'Why? Has he been laying his hands on the kids?'

I don't answer. He hasn't. Only because I make sure they don't wind

102

him up. But I can't stop that happening for ever. Eventually one of them will do something that pisses him off, or he'll wake up feeling that way out.

'I'm off to put my face on.' Mam grabs her makeup bag. 'Check I've got everything, will you, Lib?'

She totters away and leaves me to it. The curtains are still pulled around the bed. It's like being in a tent. The air's all hot and still, the sounds outside a bit muffled. I lay my head down and close my eyes.

'Elizabeth?'

I jerk upright and see a head peeking through the join in the curtains. It's the nurse from that morning when Mam was brought in. The one who put Frankie on her knee.

'You all right, love?' *she asks.*

'Tired,' *I say.*

She comes inside, letting the curtains shut behind her so we're alone, in our own little world. She pours some water from the jug on the bedside cabinet and hands it to me. I take a drink but it's warm. 'Your mum had a lucky escape,' *she says.* 'She could have died.'

She's got a mole on her chin with a whisker growing out of it. I didn't notice that before.

'If someone did that to her . . .'

'She fell down the stairs,' *I say.*

'Let me finish, love, and then I'll get out of your hair.' *She takes the plastic cup from me and sets it down.* 'If someone did that to your mum they need to be punished for it. They need to be put away somewhere where they can't hurt anyone else. How old are you? Eleven?' *I nod.* 'Too young to have that sort of responsibility sitting on your shoulders.'

I look down at the floor and the nurse's shoes. They're black lace-ups, a bit like a pair I've had my eye on for school in Freeman Hardy & Willis. They look like they'd be comfy.

'Elizabeth?' *The nurse says.* 'Do you hear what I'm telling you?'

'She fell down the stairs,' *I reply.*

★ ★ ★

Liberty made her excuses to Raj about lunch. He was obviously disappointed but didn't make a fuss. 'Trouble at mill?' he wondered.

'Don't ask,' she replied. And he didn't, which made her like him all the more.

By the time she got back to the hotel, she felt an uncontrollable urge to throw up and hadn't managed to close her door behind her when a torrent of bile came out of her mouth. She tried to catch it in her hand as she raced to the bathroom and flung herself to the floor at the base of the toilet. She heaved five or six times until she was purged, then let herself fall sideways into the side of the bath, her cheek against the cool porcelain of the lip.

She couldn't quite believe what she'd done. She, who weighed, measured and analysed every aspect of her life. She, who never acted on her gut. She, whom the assistants at work called the Ice Queen. She, who didn't mind the nickname one bit. Why the hell had she lied to the police? What had she been thinking?

There was a green slimy patch down the front of her white shirt. Disgusting. She ripped at the buttons, clawed it off and slung it over her head into the tub. Then she sat in her skirt and bra and tried to control her jagged breathing.

At last, when the pounding in her ears had subsided, Liberty pulled herself to her feet and leaned against the washbasin. Her reflection in the mirror on the wall confirmed that she looked every bit as crap as she felt. Plus there was also a green mark on her bra where the bile must have soaked through. She unhooked it and threw it on top of the shirt. She'd send them to be cleaned by Housekeeping. Nah. Screw that. She'd chuck them. Buy new.

She turned on the cold tap, let it run, then put her lips to it, taking a mouthful and spitting. Rinse and repeat. She wiped her mouth on the back of her hand and staggered into the bedroom, flopping backwards onto the bed, arms out as if she'd been crucified.

She had no responsibility to look out for Jay. Not now. She never had, or at least she shouldn't have. What she'd done all those years before, well, there'd been no choice. Now there *was* a choice. She'd just made the wrong one. She'd allowed her feelings – old feelings – to overrule logic. But she could put things right. She could tell Connolly she'd made a mistake. She rolled over onto her stomach and leaned into her handbag, searching for his card. There it was. DI Sol Connolly. Vice Squad.

Liberty pulled out her mobile. She was going to have to play this very cool indeed. Make like she'd made a simple error, apologize, but not too profusely. Hang up. She punched the numbers into the phone. It rang once, then went to voicemail. Damn. Should she leave a message? Or would that make her look guilty? She hung up. Better to speak directly to Connolly.

It was cool in the room, with the air-conditioning set to low. Liberty scooted under the covers and put her cheek on the pillow, but as she closed her eyes, the silence was pierced by the loud *brr* of the hotel phone. She snaked out her hand and answered. 'Yes.'

'Lib, it's Jay.' Oh, God. 'I just wanted to say thank you.' She should tell him right now that she wasn't going through with the lie. 'You've saved my bacon.' He laughed but Liberty couldn't join in. 'Listen, I'm having everyone round for dinner tonight. You should come.'

'Everyone?'

'The wife, kids, Crystal and her husband,' he said.

Liberty sat up. 'Crystal's married?'

'Yup. Nice bloke as it happens. Sound.'

Liberty rubbed her face.

'Frankie might even make an appearance,' said Jay.

Liberty tried to speak. She opened her mouth but no sound came out. Just a horrible rasp.

'Pick you up at seven?' Jay asked.

Dinner with Jay, Crystal and Frankie. The thought made Liberty shiver. Jay, Crystal and Frankie. Her family.

'So, what do you reckon?' he asked.

'Okay,' she said.

Jay's home was not what Liberty had expected. What had she expected? Not this farmhouse built of York stone, nestling at the end of a winding drive. The tyres crunched on gravel as Jay pulled up outside. 'The missus chose it,' he said.

Liberty smiled. 'It's lovely.'

Jay beamed. He'd always needed approval. Didn't everyone? She needed to tell him that she'd changed her mind about the alibi, but didn't have the heart right now. She'd let him show off tonight: his home, his life, his family. Then she'd text him. Better to do it that way. Or was she just being a coward?

Rebecca met them at the door. Another surprise. A solid woman in sensible clothes. Jeans, long-sleeved Breton top, loafers. Her hair was short, well cut, but remained a defiantly undyed mousy blonde. The wife of a middle-aged businessman. She smiled warmly at Liberty and spoke in a deep voice, the accent local but nowhere near as pronounced as Jay's. 'I can't believe it,' she said. 'After all these years, Jay's found you.'

Liberty winced. Rebecca had made it sound as though Jay had been looking for her. Surely that wasn't right. Not after all this time. 'Weird, huh?' she said.

'Of all the gin joints in all the towns,' Jay did an exaggerated Bogart, 'and she walks into mine.'

Rebecca rolled her eyes at Jay and led Liberty through the hall-way to an enormous kitchen with views on to the garden beyond. Two little boys somersaulted on a trampoline, screaming and whooping.

'Liam and Ben,' said Jay.

'Should I call them in?' Rebecca asked.

Liberty shook her head. The night was still warm, the children happy. 'Let them play.'

Rebecca laughed. 'You're as bad as Jay. He'd leave them out there all night if they were having fun.'

Liberty caught his eye and, for a second, was transported back in time. Little kids in a damp flat, hiding in a bedroom with the dressing-table pushed against the door for protection. A whoosh of warm air touched her cheek as her sister-in-law opened the oven. 'I hope you're hungry,' she said, and pulled out a tray lined with roasted tomatoes, each topped with a blackened leaf of basil.

'I am now,' Liberty replied.

'Something smells good,' came a voice from the hall.

And three people stepped into the kitchen. Two men, one woman. The first man was unfamiliar. Tall, blond, an easy smile. But the other two were unmistakable. The second man, dark, a younger version of Jay. The woman, beautiful with creamy skin and a mane of auburn curls. Frankie and Crystal.

'Is it really you?' Frankie asked.

Liberty didn't trust herself to speak so she nodded.

Frankie looked to his older brother, as if he needed further confirmation. When Jay nodded, Frankie laughed. 'Total headfuck.'

'Language,' Rebecca admonished. 'The little ones are around.'

'They'd need bionic hearing from out there,' Jay said.

Frankie laughed again, moved to Liberty and, before she knew what he was going to do, he hugged her. The feel of him was overwhelming. Her baby brother. His hair tickling her mouth, the smell of him in her nose. Aftershave, fags, something acrid yet minty. He stepped back, still laughing.

'He's still not the full ticket,' said Jay.

Next, the blond man moved, his hand held out. 'Harry,' he said. 'Crystal's other half.'

Liberty shook it, embarrassed because she knew hers was

sweating. Over his shoulder she could see Crystal staring. Her eyes were impossible to read.

'Lib,' she said.

Liberty had a word ready on her tongue but it dissolved. Her blood was pounding so hard that her chest physically hurt. The room swam dangerously.

'Any chance of a drink, Jay?' Harry asked.

'Yes, Jay, drinks all round,' said Rebecca, her voice spilling into shrill. 'There are three bottles of bubbly in the fridge.'

Sol brought the thick green liquid to his lips. It had the texture of milk of magnesia – did people still use that stuff? – and the taste of rotting grass.

'You don't look like you're enjoying that,' Hassani said.

He looked down at the smoothie his wife had decanted for him into an old water bottle. He'd returned home to the threatening sound of the liquidizer turning things you wouldn't want to eat whole into things you still didn't want to eat but liquid. Natasha had smiled up at him, a bunch of spinach in her hand.

He'd been grateful to receive a call from Hassani suggesting they meet, but Natasha wasn't going to let him off the hook that easily.

'I don't think enjoying it is the point,' Sol replied.

They were outside the security office in the hospital, waiting for the man on duty to locate CCTV footage from Tuesday. It had already been forty-five minutes and Sol was losing the will to live.

'What's in it? Hassani asked.

Sol held the bottle up to the strip light. 'The secret of life.'

Hassani laughed and Sol noticed her teeth: small, even, sharp. Despite the long hair and dramatic black eye-liner, there was something distinctly boyish about her.

'Are you sure it was Jay Greenwood you saw?' Sol asked, for the tenth time.

She nodded.

'But you were busy on another job,' Sol pointed out. 'How much attention were you paying?'

'Daisy was being patched up,' Hassani replied. 'Her bite had got infected. I came to hold her hand but she didn't need it.'

'You weren't distracted?' Sol asked.

'Not really. I sat around, waiting, just like we are now.'

Sol took another swig of his smoothie, winced and placed the still full bottle in a bin without a sound. 'What happened when he came on to the ward?'

Hassani sighed.

'Humour me,' said Sol.

'He spoke to the sister at the desk,' Hassani replied. 'I didn't hear exactly what was said, but soon there were raised voices so I moseyed my way over.'

'Did you say anything to him?'

She shook her head. 'By the time I got there, he was leaving. But I got a proper look at him. It was definitely Jay Greenwood.'

'And you know him how?'

'Is there a copper round here that doesn't know who Jay Greenwood is?' Hassani asked, with a laugh.

Sol narrowed his eyes.

Hassani rolled hers. 'I've been in the Black Cherry several times when he's been in there. I'm telling you it was him.'

So why would the solicitor lie? Sure, Sol had met bent ones in his time. Just like bent coppers, they usually did it for the money. Chapman didn't seem like she needed the money, though. A few phone calls had confirmed she worked for some smart outfit in London. Rance had instructed the big boys. Or his daddy had at any rate. Chapman was at the top of her game and it radiated from her. But Jay Greenwood? What the hell was Chapman doing having lunch with him? Greenwood's business had grown in recent times, but enough to afford legal rep like that?

It didn't make sense.

'We're going to question the family, right?' Hassani asked.

'We'll get zilch from Crystal,' Sol replied.

'Then we target the wife,' said Hassani. 'She might be interested to know that her loving husband is visiting his lap-dancers in hospital.'

Sol put up his hand. 'We need to tread carefully. At the moment the alibi is cast iron. Talking to his wife could be seen as harassment.'

'I keep telling you that his alibi is bullshit,' said Hassani. 'You'll see for yourself.'

The door to the security office opened and the manager emerged, smelling suspiciously of skunk. He gestured them inside towards a monitor. 'I've isolated the date, time and ward,' he said.

He sat in front of the monitor, Sol and Hassani standing behind him. Together they watched the screen. A grainy image of the desk appeared, a figure moving behind it.

'That's the ward sister,' said Hassani.

A moment later, another figure came into shot: A tall, well-built man, with his back to the camera.

'It's Greenwood,' said Hassani.

Another moment passed and a third figure came into shot. The man turned to it briefly, then moved away.

'Don't tell me,' said Sol. 'That's you.'

Back in the car park, Sol pulled out his e-cig. He took two drags, waiting for the scratch, but these things didn't work like that. What could you expect?

'Problem?' Hassani asked.

Sol blew water vapour at her. 'Total waste of time.'

'It proves I'm right,' said Hassani.

'No, it doesn't,' Sol replied. 'It proves someone came to the hospital to see Kyla Anderson. It doesn't prove who it was.'

'I can say who it was.' Hassani pressed her palm to her chest. 'I say it was Jay Greenwood.'

'And a solicitor says it wasn't.'

Hassani crossed her arms. 'She's lying.'

Sol raised an eyebrow.

'I've had two dealings with that woman and they both reeked like an over-full bin bag,' said Hassani. 'On my case she convinces Daisy not to testify. On yours she alibis a person of interest. The only real person of interest. Something's going on with her and we both know it.'

Sol nodded. Something *was* going on, and Miss Liberty Chapman seemed to be up to her pretty neck in it.

'We should go to the Chinese,' said Hassani.

Sol's stomach growled in response. He could murder some crispy duck.

'Greenwood and Chapman say they were eating in the Jade Garden,' said Hassani. 'So let's ask the manager if they're telling porkies.'

The smell of hot fat hung low and thick in the air of the restaurant. Amira ran her top teeth over her tongue, surprised not to find a solidified layer coating it. Dad was forever deep-frying *kibbeh* at home, even though she had told him you could bake it in the oven, which wouldn't make their clothes smell or clog their arteries, but this was way worse. As if the oil hadn't been changed in decades.

A woman with a smooth round face greeted them with a huge grin. 'I help you?' she asked, in broken English.

Her grin dropped when Connolly produced his warrant card and her eyes flicked nervously towards the kitchen. 'We're not Immigration,' he said.

'I get manager,' said the woman, and scuttled away, shouting something in Chinese.

Amira and Connolly waited in the reception area, watching fish swim round and round and round in their tank, ignoring the plastic shipwreck at the bottom. At last a man appeared, the smile on his lips not making it to his eyes. 'Come through,' he said, and led them to a large round table set for eight. 'Take a seat.' He waited for them to sit, before taking a chair himself, then called behind him in Chinese. Almost instantly the receptionist re-appeared with a tray containing two glasses of water and a plate of prawn crackers, which she placed in front of Amira and Connolly without a word.

'Thank you,' said Amira

The woman nodded but did not look at her.

'Now, what can I do for you?' the man asked.

'You're the manager?' Connolly asked in reply.

'For my sins.'

'And your name?'

'Song Chen.'

Amira took a prawn cracker and bit into it. Stale. She forced it down with a gulp of tepid water.

'Mr Chen, I'd like to ask you about last Tuesday,' said Connolly 'You were open?'

Chen nodded. 'We're open seven days a week.'

'Lunchtimes and evenings?' asked Connolly

'People must eat.'

Amira opened her notebook and took out a pen. So far Chen hadn't said anything noteworthy but the point was to show that she was listening attentively. She'd learned early on that a lot of police work was about perception.

'Do you know a man called Jay Greenwood?' Connolly asked.

'Of course,' said Chen. 'He owns the Black Cherry.'

'Does he ever come in here?'

'All the time.' Chen was still offering his cold smile. 'Our food is very good.'

'And was he here on Tuesday lunchtime?' Sol asked.

Chen didn't miss a beat. 'Yes. He had lunch with a lady friend.'

Amira looked up from her notebook. Chen hadn't even paused to think about it. Either he had a fantastic memory or he had been expecting this question.

'Do you recall when they arrived?' Sol asked.

'Around one.'

'And when they left?'

'Around four, I believe,' Chen replied. 'Perhaps a little later.'

Too slick. No ums or ahs. No 'Let me think.'

'You seem very sure,' said Sol.

Chen bowed his head slightly and Amira glanced at Connolly who gave her a little frown. This was bullshit and they both knew it.

'If that's all . . .' said Chen.

He was too clever by half, but Amira was about to knock the stupid smile off his face.

'You keep a record of each meal served?' she asked. 'Each bill paid?'

'The taxman would not have it otherwise,' Chen replied.

'So you'll have a record of what Mr Greenwood and his companion ordered,' she said.

'Of course.'

'And you'll have the bill going through the till, presumably with the time recorded on it?'

She and Sol exchanged a mental high five.

'I'm afraid not,' said Chen.

Amira put down her notebook. 'Mr Chen, this is something we can easily check. We can get a warrant if necessary.'

'I'm afraid a warrant won't assist you,' Chen replied.

'Because?'

'Because I did not charge Mr Greenwood for his meal on Tuesday.' Chen stood. The meeting was clearly at an end. 'I never charge Mr Greenwood.'

Dinner passed in a blur. The food looked and smelt delicious. A huge leg of lamb, studded with sprigs of rosemary, sliced into thick pink ribbons. Hot cubes of potato, their skins crisp. The roasted tomatoes and bowls of oily olives. All served on pristine white plates in the dining room, patio doors flung open to let in the warm night air.

But Liberty could barely eat. She felt panicked and overwhelmed. The air was hot, the children endlessly jumping down from their seats. Frankie's laugh was loud and there was a sheen of sweat on his upper lip. Her mouth was dry so she glugged down some wine. That calmed her enough to force down some food. It tasted of nothing. A mouthful of cardboard.

Frankie took several pictures of Liberty on his phone, then grabbed hers and took one of them both. Her smile looked wild.

When everyone had finished, Jay and Rebecca began to ferry the plates back to the kitchen and Frankie went outside to smoke. Harry smiled at Liberty and put a hand on hers. 'We know what you're doing for Jay and we appreciate it.'

Liberty gulped.

'The police,' Harry continued. 'They want to ruin Jay. They don't care how hard he's had it. How far he's had to come.'

Liberty picked up her glass, drained it and reached for the bottle. She was drinking too much, eating too little. Her head was spinning. The sound of Jay and Rebecca's laughter filtered from the kitchen.

'I know you're probably wondering why he'd get involved with another woman when he's got such a good thing going here,' said Harry.

Liberty shrugged. People had affairs all the time at work. It wasn't her business.

'He's a good bloke,' said Harry. 'A bloody great brother-in-law, but he's got a self-destruct button.' He flicked a glance to the open patio doors. 'Frankie as well.'

Liberty looked at Crystal. They had said very little to one another. Then again, Crystal hadn't said very much to anyone.

'I don't suppose you can live through the things that you lot did and come out of it untouched,' said Harry.

Liberty didn't break eye contact with Crystal as she wondered how much her sister had told Harry. If she knew Crystal, it would be very far from the whole truth. More the edited highlights. As kids, they'd got very good at that, cutting and pasting, depending on who was doing the asking. But Harry was right about one thing. What had happened had marked them all. 'I don't really understand why I have to give the alibi,' said Liberty. 'Jay should be asking his . . . friend.'

'He can't do that,' said Harry. 'For one thing, she's not the sort of person the police are likely to believe.'

'A girl from the club?' Liberty asked.

Harry nodded, at least having the decency to look embarrassed.

Liberty sighed.

'We'd really rather keep her out of it,' said Harry. 'For every-one's sake, especially Becca's. If she found out . . .'

Liberty groaned. If Rebecca found out that her husband was having it away with one of his lap-dancers, what might she do?

'Anyway.' Harry gave a cough. 'We really appreciate it.' He turned to his wife. 'Don't we, babe?'

Crystal's eyes flashed at Liberty. 'Yeah.' Her voice was even. 'Really appreciate it.'

And, in that second, Liberty knew she was not going to call Sol Connolly to tell him she had made a mistake.

Chapter Nine

September 1985
She's dead.

Gone.

I feel like I ought to cry, but I can't.

'Good riddance to bad rubbish,' says Dad.

I can't believe he just said that. Then again, I can't believe anything he says or does. It's like somebody made a bet with him to be the biggest arsehole in the world and every day he does his best to win the prize fund.

I sit with Crystal watching the hearse pull up outside. The coffin's in the back, covered with white flowers. 'Pretty,' she whispers to me. I nod and put my arm around her tiny waist. She hardly eats, these days.

I wonder what the funeral will be like. I've only ever been to one. There were prayers and singing and that. Afterwards we all went to the hall at the back of the church and had cups of tea and meat-paste sandwiches. I don't really like meat paste as it goes.

'What did she die of?' Jay asks.

'Spite,' Dad replies, and flicks on the telly.

I push Jay's fringe out of his eyes. He needs a haircut. 'Heart attack,' I say. 'She were very old.' To be honest, I don't know how old Mrs Cooper was. It's like she's been that age all my life. Grey hair, pinny, mouth permanently tucked around a cig.

Dad turns up the sound. Mr Cooper will be able to hear every word through the wall. I wonder how he'll get on now his wife's gone. He's a martyr to his knees and hardly leaves the flat. Maybe the council will put him in an old folks' home.

Mam comes into the room dressed head to toe in black. Black sequined top, tight black skirt and black fishnets.

'Why the hell are you done up like that?' Dad asks her.

'I just thought . . .'

'Well, think again,' says Dad.

A man gets out of the hearse. Like Mam, he's dressed all in black, but unlike Mam, he doesn't look like he's out on the pull.

'What's that?' asks Crystal, tapping her head.

'A top hat,' I say.

'Come away from that window,' Dad shouts.

We do as we're told and turn to the telly. The horse-racing's on and Dad's bobbing his head along as if he was riding one of them nags himself. When the winner goes past the post in a blur of green and yellow stripes, Dad snaps off the telly. 'Back to school tomorrow, then?' he asks.

I'm shocked he's remembered.

'I bet you need new shoes,' he says.

I'm even more shocked by that so I just nod.

Dad rubs his hands together. 'Right, then, we're off into town. New school shoes for the lot of you.'

'Jim,' says Mam. 'We haven't the money, love.'

Dad shakes his head and points to the blank screen on the telly. 'Arthur's Boy, ten to bloody one.' He laughs. 'So new shoes all round.' He turns to Mam. 'But get changed first, for fuck's sake, woman.'

Liberty wiggled her toes under the table. The heat coupled with a hangover had made her head throb and her feet swell. She needed some breakfast.

'Can I get you some tea or coffee?' asked the waitress. She was young and fresh and pretty. Blonde hair impervious to the humidity that was building in the room.

'Earl Grey,' Liberty replied. 'And iced water, please.'

The girl scribbled on a pad with a red stump of pencil. 'Glass of iced water.'

'Not a glass,' said Liberty. 'A jug.' She squeezed her shoes back on and headed to the buffet, lifting the lid of a hot tray. The fried eggs underneath looked like they had been parted from their pan some hours ago, yolks hard and orange. She replaced the lid and helped herself to a croissant and an individual box of Crunchy Nut Corn Flakes. When she turned to go back to her table, she saw a man sitting there. 'Excuse me,' she said. 'I think you've made a mistake.'

The man looked at her over his shoulder and scowled. 'No mistake.'

Liberty almost dropped her plate. It was Rance.

'You don't look pleased to see me,' he said.

Liberty pulled on her poker face and sat down. 'Surprised, that's all, Mr Rance.'

'You knew I'd got out,' he said.

'I did.'

'And you knew I had to stay local.'

'I did,' she said again.

'So where exactly did you think I'd go?' He snapped a finger at the waitress, who came over. 'Get me coffee and a full English.'

'I'm afraid it's a buffet, sir,' said the waitress.

Rance stared at her, letting his eyes move from her face, down her body to her feet, then back up again. 'And I'm afraid I don't do buffets.'

'I'm sure I can sort something out,' said Liberty, smiling apologetically. She went back to the buffet and loaded a plate with eggs, bacon, sausages and an unyielding slice of black pudding. Then she dumped a spoonful of beans on the side. 'Here,' she said, and slid the plate in front of Rance.

'Jesus,' he said. 'Is this what passes for food around here?'

'I'm sure it's better than you've had in the last few days,' she replied.

Rance didn't answer but picked up one of the sausages, rolled it around between thumb and forefinger, then bit off the end. Liberty felt an acid lurch of nausea. 'So how long have I got to stay here?' he asked, pieces of pink meat caught in his teeth.

'Just until Miss Clarke confirms her intention to drop the case.'

Rance pushed the rest of the sausage into his mouth. 'And how long will that take?'

'I'm sure the police are chasing matters.'

'Let's hope so.' Rance sucked the grease from his fingers. 'In the meantime we're both stuck in this shithole.'

In the hotel car park the pretty waitress was having a fag. Liberty pressed her car key and the Porsche beeped. 'Nice motor,' said the waitress.

Liberty smiled. 'Sorry about him in there. He's a dick.'

'Yes, he is.' She took a last deep lungful and flicked the still-lit butt away. It landed on the tarmac in a spray of red sparks. 'I'm only working here to save for an air ticket,' she said. 'That's what I think about when I have to deal with wankers.'

'Where are you off to?'

'Anywhere but here.'

Liberty watched the girl go back inside and promised herself she'd leave a big tip tomorrow. In the meantime, she needed to find Daisy Clarke so she pulled out her mobile and sent a text to Jay, asking for her address. He pinged it straight back.

★ ★ ★

The Crosshills estate was even worse than Liberty remembered. When she'd lived there, more than thirty years ago, it had been a rough old place. Not that she'd thought too much about it. As a kid, she'd just accepted that lifts always smelt of piss and vomit, and gas sniffers sometimes collapsed in the walkways, their aerosols of choice peeping out of their dirty sleeves. Today it seemed like somewhere left to rot. Windows and doors kicked off, leaving gaps like missing teeth in a long-dead skull. She checked the address again and began to climb the stairs. By the third-floor landing, she was sweating.

Briskly, she made her way along the walkway outside the flats, looking straight ahead. To her left was the barrier, and beyond that a long drop to the concrete below, but she didn't let her eyes wander. Number 32A had a pale blue door, the lower half dented and scratched by what looked like shoes. Someone had kicked the door open and left it ajar. 'Daisy,' Liberty called, and pushed the door gently. 'Daisy, are you in there?'

No answer.

She pushed the door fully open and peered inside. 'It's Liberty Chapman here. We met the other day at the Black Cherry.'

The air inside was hot, still and silent. Dust motes danced in the columns of light. Liberty stepped inside. 'I'm the solicitor, remember? I just want to ask you a couple more things.' She padded quietly down the hallway and opened the door at the end. 'I know you're very keen to get this court case sorted.'

It was a bedroom. Empty apart from a double bed and a pile of clothes on the floor. Liberty was now sweating so profusely she could smell herself.

'Daisy?' She left the bedroom and headed into what turned out to be a sitting room. 'I'm just here to help make this whole thing go away.'

'I bet you are.'

Liberty's heart leaped into her mouth and she spun round on her heels.

Frankie never got up this early. The light hurt his eyes even though he couldn't open them properly and he was wearing shades. He had to stop caning it with Daisy. Last night, though, he'd needed to get out of it. Meeting Lib like that had been a complete headfuck. After all these years, there she was, standing in Jay's kitchen, chatting with that boring wife of his like it was perfectly normal.

'Is she staying around, then?' Daisy had asked.

'Dunno.'

'Do you want her to?'

Frankie was too busy setting up another pipe to answer.

That morning, he called a cab, got into the back and closed his eyes. A long time ago, he and Lib had been a 'we'. Everything they did was based on it. It had seen them through. If Lib was back for good, could they be a 'we' again? Frankie lifted his sunglasses onto his forehead, thought better of it, put them back down. Jay had been happy to see Lib, cracking shit jokes, showing off. Crystal had said virtually fuck-all. But Crystal was sour and silent at the best of times. You couldn't read anything into it.

The cab pulled up beside a burned-out house, brickwork still blackened, metal plates affixed to the windows and doors. Why the fuck did people do business in places like this? What was the point? When this deal with Brixton Dave came off and people started coming to Frankie, he'd do the necessary out of one of the clubs. Beer and snatch on tap.

The plan was simple. So simple that Frankie had to agree with Brixton Dave: absolute genius.

Every Friday night, the Russians came to do the handover. Brixton Dave changed the location each time, texting them a couple of hours beforehand. 'The Old Bill mostly leave us to it,' he told Frankie. 'But you never know when some new cunt'll decide to make a name for himself by bringing down a player.' He'd jerked a thumb at himself. 'Well, not this one, son.'

You had to hand it to him: he knew exactly what he was doing.

'The Russians bring the gear and we bring the cash,' said Dave. 'Everyone goes on their way happy, or they did do until this crew started thinking they can call the shots. They know I ain't none too pleased with what's occurring so they'll be watching us in case we make a move.' He'd clapped Frankie on the back. 'And while they're watching us, they ain't watching you.'

Element of surprise was what was needed to get the job done. And those Russians were in for one massive surprise.

Frankie got out of the cab and walked up the path to the house. The grass on either side was knee high, littered with dog shit and needles. As soon as he was at the door, a panel in the metal plate slid open. 'What d'you want?' asked a voice from inside.

'I'm here to see Earl,' Frankie replied. 'He's expecting me.'

The metal panel swung shut with a clang, leaving Frankie standing out front in the heat. At last it opened again. 'Come round the back,' said the voice.

Frankie walked around the side of the house, stepping over a used condom. When he was bang on it, he went to crack houses in worse states than this and literally gave no fucks. He had to stop doing that. First thing he needed to do was avoid Daisy the fucking Dog.

The back door was also boarded up, but someone had swung it open and a boy of about fourteen stood in front of it, thinking he was the man in his box-fresh trainers. 'Where's Earl?' Frankie asked.

The lad looked at him like he was just another punter come to buy gear. Somebody needed to teach the kid a lesson or three, but before Frankie could get into it, Earl stuck his head out. 'Frankie Greenwood,' he said. 'What brings you onto my patch?'

'Business,' Frankie replied.

'Step into my office.'

The inside of the house hadn't been cleaned up much. The walls were still coated with soot, the acrid smell of burned plastic hanging over everything. Earl's boys were in the old kitchen at the front, cooking up, serving up as and when, playing cards in between.

Earl used the old lounge at the back. An armchair set up in the middle of the room, facing a flat screen and a stack of DVDs. A slasher movie was playing.

'How's it going, then, Frankie?' Behind Earl on the telly, someone was peeling the skin off a skull, like it was a fucking banana. 'I hear you've opened up a new club.'

'Yeah,' Frankie replied. 'Can't complain.'

Earl went to the corner of the room and dragged a metal stool across the floor, placing it next to the armchair. Frankie sat on it, and Earl flopped into his armchair. They watched a doctor slice open someone's stomach and put in both hands up to his wrists. 'So, what do you want, Frankie?' Earl asked. 'I'm assuming you didn't come up here for the shits and giggles.'

'I need a couple of guns,' said Frankie.

'Why don't you just ask Jay?'

Frankie growled and Earl laughed. 'Fine. When do you need them?

'Later today.'

'It's gonna cost you.'

'I know.'

Liberty's heart slowed a little when she saw it was Hassani who had followed her into Daisy Clarke's house.

'What the hell are you doing here?' Hassani demanded.

'I came to speak to Miss Clarke.' Liberty opened her arms wide. 'But evidently she's not here.'

'Why did you kick the door off?'

'I didn't,' Liberty replied. 'That wasn't me.'

Hassani snorted, clearly not believing a word of it.

'Oh, come on.' Liberty lifted a foot and waggled the six-inch heel on her patent peep-toe shoe. 'Do I look like I could have managed that?'

Hassani stared hard. 'Why are you so desperate for Daisy to drop this?'

'I'm not desperate.' Liberty swallowed. Every fibre of her being was desperate. Desperate to finish this job. Desperate to get Rance out of her hotel, out of her life. 'I'm simply doing what's right for my client.'

Hassani shook her head. 'And that includes coming to the victim's home? Kicking her door down?'

'That wasn't me.'

'Of course it wasn't.' Hassani took a step towards Liberty. 'I suggest you stop trying to track down this vulnerable young woman and go back to your swanky office in London where you belong.'

A bubble of anger burst in Liberty's chest. Who the hell did this copper think she was? 'Are you threatening me?' Liberty's voice was cold.

Hassani took another step. 'Not a threat, a promise. If you don't leave Daisy Clarke alone I will nick you.'

'Don't be bloody ridiculous,' Liberty said.

Hassani moved so quickly, she was little more than a blur. Then each of Liberty's arms were wrenched behind her, the pain in her shoulder-blades blinding. Hassani's mouth was so close to Liberty's ear, she could feel air and spit as she spoke. 'Liberty Chapman, I am arresting you on suspicion of perverting the course of justice. You do not have to say anything but it may harm your defence if you do not mention now something you later wish to rely on in court.' Hassani squeezed Liberty's shoulder, sending a juddering pain through her body. 'Do you understand?'

Tears were streaming down Liberty's face and her words came out through gritted teeth. 'I want to call my lawyer.'

'Does somebody want to tell me what the buggering hell's going off here?' asked Raj.

Liberty had never been so glad to see anyone in her life. 'Thanks for coming.'

Raj entered the interview room where Liberty had been placed by the custody sergeant and grinned. 'My new bezzie mate got herself nicked for perverting the course of justice. How could I resist?' When he caught sight of the red welts circling Liberty's wrists, his smile faded. 'They never cuffed you?'

Liberty rubbed the marks. The skin was sore, but nowhere near as painful as her shoulder-blades. 'It was the policewoman from court,' she said. 'Hassani. She has seriously got it in for me.'

Raj nodded. 'That much is obvious, but I've got to ask what you were thinking of, going to Daisy Clarke's house.'

'I wanted to bring her to the station to make a statement,' Liberty replied. 'How is offering someone a lift perverting the course of justice?'

Raj leaned back in his chair. His tie, an electric blue polyester monstrosity, fell to one side, following the curve of his ample belly. He fixed Liberty with rich brown eyes, but then the door opened and a young police officer came in. He was so young that the hair on his upper lip was still a fuzzy layer of down. 'Custody sarge sent these,' he said, putting two mugs of tea on the table.

'Grand,' Raj said.

'Thank you,' said Liberty.

The young man went pink, hovered for a second, then departed.

Liberty picked up the mug and brought it to her lips. The tea was scalding, the steam rising to sting her face. She didn't move it away.

'Tea is a good sign,' said Raj.

'Really?'

'Oh, aye.' Raj picked up his mug. 'Most people get slung in a cell and left there until interview. This room, the tea, that's special treatment right there.'

Liberty took a sip of tea. It burned her tongue. She blew over the top of the mug and tried again. The tea was strong and milky and sugarless. Right now, this did not feel like special treatment. She put it down.

'Of course, Hassani's probably peed in it,' said Raj.

Liberty snorted a laugh and knocked her mug, spilling tea on the table. Raj laughed too, tea sloshing over the side of his. He rubbed ineffectually at the leg of his trousers, but a dark patch was already spreading.

'I know I probably shouldn't have gone to Daisy's house,' said Liberty. 'But I'm used to getting things done, you know?'

Raj laughed again. 'No messing about with you, eh?'

Liberty ran her finger through the splash of tea and wrote the letter L across the plastic. A long time ago she'd changed from being a person who had things done to her to a person who got things done. A line had been drawn, dividing her life into before and after.

'Think of this as a new experience.' Raj opened his arms. 'Life-enhancing.'

Liberty had been in enough police stations to know that the experience rarely enhanced anyone's life. 'So, can you get me out of here?' she asked. 'Or do I have to do my time up at the Mansion?'

Raj hauled himself out of his chair. 'Let me talk to a few people.' He looked down at the dark patch on his thigh. 'Tell me the truth. Do I look like I've wet myself?'

'No,' Liberty lied.

Sol balled a fist and pressed it to his mouth, tapped his lips three times. 'Tell me this is a joke.'

Hassani leaned against the bonnet of his car, arms crossed. 'If it is, then I don't know the punch line.'

When she'd called Sol to tell him she'd arrested the lawyer in Daisy's flat, he hadn't known whether to laugh or cry. Instead, he'd driven straight over, told her to meet him in the station car park. 'This is going to get you into a whole world of trouble,' he said.

'Me?' Hassani was incredulous. 'I'm not the one giving false alibis. I'm not the one trying to pressurize a witness.'

'You don't have any evidence that Chapman's done either of those things.'

'I know what I know,' said Hassani.

'Then you know that this is not how the game is played.' Hassani thumped the roof of his car. Sol ignored it. 'You know that you cannot arrest a solicitor, drag her back to the nick in handcuffs and expect there to be no come-back. That woman is not some two-bit paper-shifter.'

Hassani glared at him, anger white-hot in her eyes. He knew how she felt and had been there a thousand times. All she wanted to do was stop bad people doing bad things. When you couldn't do that it burned and you did stupid things. On the scale of one to ten of stupid things, Sol had spent a lot of time clocking up elevens. 'You say the door was kicked off?' Sol asked.

Hassani nodded.

'And Chapman was in the flat?'

'Yeah.'

'Right. We say you thought Daisy was in danger, it all happened too fast. You made a mistake.' Hassani opened a mouth to speak but Sol cut her off. 'And you let me do all the talking. Okay?'

Hassani looked at the ground, scuffed the tarmac with her shoe.

'Okay?' Sol repeated.

'Fine.'

Chapter Ten

October 1985

Mrs Simons is a right laugh. Not all the time. She keeps everybody in line when she needs to, especially Carl Fitzpatrick, who can get a bit bonkers. Some of the lads say it's because his brother, Keith, was killed in a car accident. Well, Keith wasn't in a car, actually. He was in a shopping trolley, riding it down the A1 off his head on glue. But a car hit him.

'I've marked last week's homework,' she says. 'Read 'em and weep.'

Everybody groans as she hands back our books. The girl I sit next to, Anne-Marie Harrington, gets a C minus. She frowns, but it's not that bad, considering she's virtually backward.

I open my own book and take a peek. An A stares back at me, with one of them little smiley faces that Mrs Simons sometimes draws on our work. I shut my book before Anne-Marie can see. I like getting good marks but it's best if no one else here knows. They don't like swots and show-offs.

'Elizabeth Greenwood,' Mrs Simons calls.

'Yes, miss.'

'Can you stay behind after class, please?'

Anne-Marie pulls a face at my book. 'Bad, were it?'

I just nod.

When the bell goes, everyone files out and I stay in my seat, packing my bag slowly. I don't know what I'm meant to have done. She liked my homework and I've not been messing around at all. I mean, I did jab Carl's hand with a compass yesterday, but he'd never grass.

Mrs Simons comes over to me and sits on the end of another desk. She's wearing brown corduroy trousers tucked into suede ankle boots. I can just make out the top of her socks. 'Do you know what I want to talk to you about, Elizabeth?' Mrs Simons asks.

'Is it because of that compass?'

Mrs Simons frowns.

'Cos it wasn't very hard,' I say. 'Didn't even break the skin. Or not much anyway.'

Mrs Simons reaches over and puts her hand on my shoulder. 'I don't know anything about a compass and I'm pretty sure I don't want to know, do I?' I shake my head. 'No, it's about your work.'

'I'm sorry,' I say.

She frowns even harder. 'Why are you sorry?'

I've no idea. I just know that when you're in trouble for anything, it's best to get in first with a sorry.

'Actually, Elizabeth, it's excellent,' says Mrs Simons. 'It's always excellent.'

I feel myself going all hot and pink.

'I think you're a very promising pupil,' says Mrs Simons, 'and I was wondering if you'd like to go on a special course at half-term.' She slides off the desk and walks back to her own, reaches into a drawer and pulls out a leaflet. 'This is some information about it.' She places it in front of her. 'Take it and show it to your parents. See what they think.'

As I'm leaving, I take the leaflet and stuff it into my blazer pocket. A month ago I would have just put it in the bin so as not to set off Dad. But things seem a lot calmer now. He seems a lot calmer. I think Mam nearly dying might have scared him – or he was scared that he nearly got done for it. If I get him in the right mood, he might let me go.

By the time I get home, I've decided I'll hide the leaflet in my room for now. Then I'll see how the land lies. Wait until he's had a win on the *horses. He's having a lucky run at the minute. I let myself in and go to the kitchen to find Mam, her back turned, doing the washing-up.*

'Guess what?' I ask her. 'Guess what Mrs Simons has said I should do in half-term?'

When Mam turns, my smile falls. Mam's lip is thick, a ragged slice right through it. Here we go again.

Raj Singh was a surprise. Sol had been expecting Chapman to summon someone from her own firm back in London, or at least one of the bigger firms in Leeds. The ones who regularly sued the police and won six-figure settlements for their scrote clients. Instead, she'd called a tin-pot one-man band from down the road. And here he was, all tatty cuffs and wet patch on his trousers. Sol led him to a table in the canteen and held out a chair. 'Can I get you a drink?'

Singh looked around at the tables full of uniform, shovelling down their sausage and beans, and took a seat.

'Tea?' asked Sol.

'Just had a cup upstairs,' he replied. 'And, frankly, I wouldn't give it to my plants.'

Sol gave a tight nod and sat down. Somewhere on the other side of the canteen a group of coppers burst into raucous laughter. 'A cold drink, Mr Singh?'

'I'll be honest, Detective Inspector Connolly.' Singh leaned forward. 'I should be in court this morning so I'd rather we didn't piss about.'

More surprises. 'I'm sure we both want to sort this out as quickly as possible,' Sol replied.

A PC passed by their table carrying a tray laden with bacon sandwiches. The cheers that greeted her made Sol think it must be the end of a shift. He used to enjoy that. The sense of camaraderie when the team finished a night's work and decompressed in the canteen.

'Ball's in your court,' said Singh.

The two men stared at one another. It would have been a whole lot easier to deal with tirades about police harassment and threats to bring litigation, but Raj Singh just sat in silence, forcing Sol to make a move. 'What does your client want?' he asked.

Singh smiled. His lips were fleshy, outlined by skin a shade darker. 'She'd like to go back to her hotel,' he said.

'What else?' Sol asked.

Singh shrugged. 'We haven't talked about that.'

Bullshit.

He didn't want to, but Sol had to ask the question. 'Is she going to make a complaint about Hassani?'

'Like I said, we haven't talked about it.'

'Hassani's a good copper.'

Singh was still smiling. 'We both know she was way out of line to arrest my client.'

'And we both know your client was way out of line going to Daisy Clarke's home.'

Stalemate. The two men continued staring at one another.

Liberty rubbed her wrists. There was a recording machine on the table in the interview room and a camera on the wall, angled in her direction. She felt her pulse begin to race at the thought of Hassani turning on both machines to question her.

She tried to calm herself. Raj would sort this out. There would be no interview.

When he bounced back into the room she gave an involuntary shiver.

'The good news is the powers-that-be are shitting themselves that you'll make a complaint against Hassani,' he said.

'I bloody well am going to make a complaint,' Liberty replied.

'You sure about that?'

Liberty held out her arms to display the deep red welts in her skin. 'Very sure.'

'Understandable in the circumstances.' He seesawed his hand. 'But if you do that, they'll feel backed into a corner.'

Liberty gave a small growl of satisfaction. Right now the thought of backing Hassani into a corner was appealing.

'People with no options tend to come out fighting,' said Raj. 'They'll probably defend Hassani by throwing the book at you.'

'But I haven't done anything wrong.'

Raj cocked his head to one side and Liberty reddened. 'They can make a lot of trouble for you,' he said. 'Drag out this charge for one thing.'

That would mean she'd have to tell Ronald. She'd be suspended from work at the very least. And she could kiss goodbye to the merger.

'Even if they can't make this charge stick in the long run, they'd pick at you like a dirty scab,' said Raj.

Liberty sighed, suddenly desperate for a shower. She couldn't have the police poking around, as much for Jay as for herself. 'If I agree not to make a complaint?' she asked.

'You'll walk out of here and we'll all shake hands like gentlemen.'

'It's blackmail,' she said.

'It's life.'

Sol could tell by the look on Hassani's face that this was going to be the sort of conversation he would rather have over a drink. He checked his watch. The pubs had just opened. They'd taken a corner table in the Three Feathers. Given its proximity to the nick, there were very few times of the day when you wouldn't find any police in there. Consequently, the locals steered clear. 'If we let her go they won't kick up a fuss about you,' he told her.

'I'm not dropping this,' Hassani hissed.

Sol put a half of lager in front of her. 'I know it's early,' he drank from his own half, more head than body, 'and I know we're on duty, but get it down you.'

She pushed her glass across the table to Sol, leaving a long, wet smear between them.

He pushed it back. 'You need to calm down.'

'I'm a Muslim,' she answered.

'Right.' He leaned over and picked up her drink, placed it next to his. 'If Chapman doesn't get to leave the station in the next hour, I guarantee Singh will make a formal complaint against you.'

'So what?'

Sol took another drink. Licked the froth from his upper lip. 'You'll be suspended pending outcome, and when someone at the CPS gets hold of the case against Chapman, they'll drop it like a piece of shit on fire anyway.'

Hassani picked up a beer mat and began shredding it.

'Let her go now and we all live to fight another day,' said Sol.

Hassani looked down at the pile of cardboard confetti she'd made. 'What about talking to Rebecca Greenwood?'

'Not a chance.'

'Sometimes this job is really, really crap.'

'You'll hear no arguments coming from me,' Sol replied.

Liberty collected her belongings from the custody sergeant. Her handbag, purse, keys. The belt they'd taken from her trousers, presumably to stop her hanging herself. Hassani stood back, rage radiating from her in waves, frantically chewing the inside of her cheek. Connolly stood by her side, face devoid of expression. Raj watched intently as Liberty took a Bic biro from the sergeant, the end chewed white, and signed where directed.

'Right, then,' said Raj. 'We'll be off.'

When they got out of the station, Liberty took a deep gulp of midday sunshine. Delicious. 'Thanks for that, Raj,' she said.

He winked. 'Never a dull day with you around, eh?'

Liberty thought about her life back home in London. How she got up each morning and drove to the office. How twelve-hour working days were not uncommon. Her days were full, yes, but not especially exciting. Even weekends had a pattern: a visit to the gym, the occasional catch-up with friends for drinks and dinner. Everything ordered and scheduled and diarized.

'Walk with me to court?' he asked. 'I instructed a good bloke I know to cover my caseload, but I might just see if he needs a hand.'

Realization dawned on Liberty. Raj's work life was also diarized in advance, but her arrest had thrown him a curve ball. 'I'm so sorry I put you to all this trouble, Raj,' she said.

He waved her away. 'Trouble, my backside. What's the point of the journey if we can't make little excursions?'

The magistrates' court was quiet when they arrived as most cases had already been dealt with. Raj toddled off to find his representative, leaving Liberty on one of the benches.

'Don't tell me you've listed another case without telling me?'

Liberty looked up to see a grinning Bucky standing a few feet from her. 'No, no, no.'

'Just here for the atmosphere?'

Liberty laughed, and Bucky sat next to her, resting a pile of files on her lap. She stretched out her feet in front of her, displaying wedge sandals and immaculately painted red toenails. 'Busy?' Liberty asked.

'Non-stop since first thing,' replied Bucky. 'Court three. Traffic.' She wrinkled her nose. 'I was owed a day off in lieu today but

Don, who usually covers me, had to rush to hospital. His wife's having triplets.'

'Triplets!'

'The poor bastard's fifty-two,' said Bucky. 'God knows how he'll cope. Should have kept it in his trousers and stayed with his first wife.' She let out a belly laugh that sent some of her files flying to the ground. Liberty bent to help pick them up. She handed back the first, then scooped up some photographs that had skidded away from another. They were black-and-white, of people driving cars.

Bucky sighed and wagged a finger at them. 'That's how I've spent my morning. Speeding cases. Is it any wonder I turn to Pinot Grigio and online shopping?'

Liberty looked again at the photographs.

Bucky was still speaking but her words were smears on glass. The world stopped turning. The photographs were grainy and the faces of the drivers not always clear, but the registration plates were perfectly decipherable. As were the time and date stamps recorded in the corner. She tried to pass them to Bucky, but they fell from her hand, scattering even further across the floor. Her fingers were suddenly slick with sweat and she couldn't get a grasp on them.

Bucky put down her files and crouched next to Liberty. 'Bloody things.'

Liberty tried to give what she hoped looked like a smile but the muscles in her face seemed paralysed. The speed camera. She had forgotten the speed camera.

Chapter 11

October 1985
Everything's black. I try to open my eyes, but they're already open. I think.
I must be lying down, because my feet don't feel like they're touching
anything, but there's something hard under my cheek. There's a smell of fag
ash and something sour.

Why am I like this?

I remember coming home from school, stuffing the letter about the half-
term trip in my pocket. I remember opening the door, seeing Mam's face.
Then nothing. Why can't I remember anything else?

It feels like there's something spiky inside my head. Like a cactus. Like
it's growing and pricking me from the inside. I don't like this.

I try to shout for Mam, but the words come out like a scratchy cough.
My throat feels dry and sore. I want to cry but I can tell there won't be
enough water inside me to make any tears.

I push myself up, taking my weight on my forearms then onto my
hands. I can see where I am now. I'm in the front room. No one's drawn
the curtains, even though it's dark outside and no one's put the lamp on.

When did it get to be night time? Why can't I remember?

I'm kneeling up now, my head fizzing and buzzing and hurting.
Between my legs feels damp. I know what that smell is. I've wet myself.
I should probably be embarrassed but I'm too scared. Like the time I fell
from the top of the climbing frame in the rec, smacking my head on one
the bars on the way down. When the ambulance men put me on a stretcher

I did a huge fart. But I didn't care because I was too worried about the blood and Mam screaming blue murder.

I use the settee to pull myself to my feet and lurch towards the door, like Dad after a bender. I need to get to the kitchen and drink some water. Maybe then I can work out what the chuffing hell's going off.

The walls of the hallway feel all spongy, which I know they're not. They're not even wallpapered. Mam's always threatening to do it, but the peeling yellow paint has stayed the same for as long as I can remember. Once in the kitchen I rush to the sink and drink straight from the tap. Then I throw up. Long strands of stuff coming up, covering the mucky pots. Mixing with this morning's Ricicles. I rinse my mouth, spitting out the water.

I leave the kitchen, go back down the hall and stop at the bottom of the stairs. The Operation game is open on the third step. Where are the kids? 'Jay?' My voice is still hoarse but better than before. 'Crystal?'

I listen but there's nothing. Where are the kids? Oh, my God, where are the kids?

I need to call the police. Something's not right.

We don't have a phone. We got one once but Dad ripped it out of the wall when it woke him up one too many times. When we've occasionally needed to use one, we've asked the lady next door. What's her name? I rub the side of my head. Why can't I remember her name? And what is the dried stuff on my forehead, flaking off under my nails?

I open the door and go outside, the walkway balcony cold under my fingers. I look out at all the lights that zoom towards me, then rush away just as quickly. I think I might be sick again.

I push myself in the direction of next door and realize that I'm not wearing any shoes. The walkway feels rough through my school socks. Mam will go mad later and tell me that she can never get the grime out.

I bang on the neighbour's door. I can picture the woman. All iron perm and wrinkled upper lip. She wears those massive clip-on earrings but she's always taking them off and rubbing the pinch marks they leave on her lobes. I once asked her why she didn't just get them pierced.

'I did once, love,' she said. 'Went septic. I were on antibiotics for weeks.'

I bang again but no one comes so I bend down and open the letterbox.

'Can you come to the door?' I can hear the telly from inside. 'It's me from next door, Mrs . . .' What's her name? Why can't I remember her bloody name?

No one comes to the door but the corner of the curtain twitches from inside.

'Please help me.' I bang on the window. 'I need to use the phone.'

A face peers around the curtain edge. It's not the woman but an old man. Her husband. His white hair is so thin I can see his pink scalp.

'Please!' I shout. 'I need to call the police.'

Weirdly, he smiles at me showing his gums but he doesn't move to open the door.

'The police!' I shout again. 'I need to call the police.'

He's still smiling and gives me a thumbs-up before dropping the curtain and disappearing. I thump again but he doesn't come back. What the hell is wrong with him? Turns out I was wrong about the tears. They've come now, streaking down my cheeks. I turn away from the window, lean against the balcony, putting both hands out as wide as they can go, pressing my head into the railing.

I've got to do something. I can't just stand here.

Through my tears, I look down below. There's a phone box.

I haven't got any money, but 999 calls are free, aren't they? I start to run down the walkway towards the stairwell, past the flat. The door's still wide open and anyone could get in. But what have we got to steal? A telly on the never-never and a plastic settee covered with cig burns.

I keep running when I get to the stairs, taking them two at a time in my socks. I can feel all sorts of rubbish getting stuck to them but I don't care. Mam can shout and bawl all she likes. When I get to the bottom, I'm out of breath, but I don't stop. I sprint to the phone box like I'm the last leg of the relay team.

When I get there, I can see that most of the windows are smashed. No one hardly ever uses it, or at least not to make phone calls. I yank *open the door and pray the receiver hasn't been vandalized. The stink of glue comes up at me and I heave. Someone's left a used bag in the corner and mounds of toilet roll covered with what looks like blood.*

I reach over and grab the receiver. Please let it be working. When I put it to my ear, there's no sound so I bang the receiver. On the wall above someone has drawn a cock and bollocks in marker pen. They've even added hair. I bang the receiver again. Dialling tone at last. Panting, I dial the numbers and wait.

'Police, Fire Brigade or Ambulance?' asks a woman. 'Which do you require?'

'Police,' I reply.

'What's your name, please?'

'Lib,' I say, then add, 'Elizabeth Greenwood.'

'Right, then, Elizabeth.' The woman's voice is all calm and that. 'Can you tell me the problem?'

'I don't know.' My voice sounds shrill compared to hers. 'I don't know. I woke up in the dark and everyone's gone. Mam and the kids, they've all gone.'

'So you're on your own, Elizabeth?'

'Yeah.'

'And how old are you?'

'Eleven,' I tell her.

She says something else but I don't catch it. Instead, I watch the receiver falling out of my hand and then I feel myself falling after it.

Liberty stared at her phone. She was sitting on a bench outside court, breathing in pollution and feeling the sweat trickle down her back. Images of those grainy photographs pushed and shoved their way to the front of her mind.

She had lied to the police and now they were going to find out. Her career was over, and without her career, her life was over.

The flat with views of the Heath, the Porsche, the health-club membership. All gone.

The traffic on the road ahead had come to a standstill. Drum and bass music blasted out from the open window of a red BMW, the low notes making Liberty's bowels curdle. She took a breath and punched in Jay's number.

'Hiya.' He sounded chirpy. 'Everything all right?'

'No.'

'Sorry to hear that,' His voice had lost none of its sunshine.

'I've got a problem,' said Liberty. 'We've got a problem.'

'Go on.'

'The alibi I gave to the police isn't going to stack up,' she said.

There was a breathy noise down the phone, which might have been a sigh. 'Course it'll stack up, Lib. You're a solicitor. Word is your bond and all that.'

The passenger of the red BMW let his arm trail out of the window and the smell of a fat spliff floated towards Liberty.

'I was caught by a speed camera on the way home from the restaurant,' she blurted out.

'What?'

'I forgot about it until just now,' she said.

'Are you sure?' Jay asked.

'Yes, I'm sure.' Liberty tried to swallow her irritation. 'I was flashed on the road to my hotel. It's only a matter of time before I get a summons.'

There was a pause on the line as Jay processed what he was being told. More frustration welled in Liberty. Jay was the funny one, never the clever one. 'I doubt anyone will put two and two together,' he said at last.

Liberty jumped up from the bench. 'That's not a chance I can take, Jay. I'll lose my job over this. I could bloody well go to prison.'

'Hold up, Lib. Don't get carried away.'

'Carried away?' she hissed. 'I lied to the police. I lied to protect you.'

'I know,' he said.

The red BMW began to crawl away and the passenger flicked his roach into the gutter.

'I'm going to have to tell the police I made a mistake,' she said.

'You can't do that.'

'I've got to,' she said. 'I know it will land you in the shit, and I'm sorry about that, honestly I am, Jay, but this is my life we're talking about here.'

His voice dropped. 'It won't be just me in the shit, though, will it?'

'What do you mean?'

'Think about it, Lib. There's no way the police are just going to accept a U-turn from you. The coppers involved are complete bastards. They'll do you for wasting police time at the very least.'

Liberty thought about Connolly and Hassani and slumped back onto the bench. 'Fuck.'

'You need to speak to Crystal,' said Jay.

'What for?'

'If anyone can help us out with this, it's Crystal.'

The portable air-conditioning unit in Jay's office rattled, a dribble of water pooling below it. An endless throb of music from the main stage in the Black Cherry bled through the closed door and Crystal tapped her foot in time. She was sitting on the desk, a box of love eggs at her side. She was wearing skinny black jeans and a scowl. Her hair had been tamed, curls glossed and separated. 'So, this is a complete and utter fuck-up,' she said.

Liberty nodded. Of that there could be no doubt. 'I should never have come back here,' she said.

Crystal reached over for a packet of Juicy Fruit laid on the desk, took out a stick and pointed it at her. 'Yeah, well, you did.' She unwrapped the gum, bit it in half and chewed, then pushed in the remaining half. The sweet plastic smell of childhood travelled across the room to Liberty. Crystal didn't offer her a stick.

'Jay said you would be able to help,' said Liberty.

'I bet he did.' Crystal looked away, staring at the wall, her jaw moving as she chewed.

'Can you?' Liberty asked. 'Help?'

Crystal snapped her head back towards Liberty, eyebrows raised. 'Yes.'

'How?'

Crystal narrowed her eyes at Liberty, reached into her mouth and pulled at her gum, forming a long string. Then she shoved it back into her mouth.

'Tell me how, Crystal,' Liberty pressed.

'Pay people.' She waved a hand. 'Lift the photograph. Without that the whole thing goes away.'

'What people?'

'Police, CPS, DVLA,' Crystal replied. 'Depends what stage it's reached. Hopefully we can intercept it before it's been through too many hands.'

Liberty took a deep breath. Crystal was suggesting they pay corrupt officials to remove evidence. 'That's a crime,' she said.

'So is providing a false alibi.'

They stared at one another for a long moment. Crystal's eyes were grey as flint. Liberty, Jay and Frankie had eyes the colour of melted chocolate. A window to their souls. Crystal's had always been hard and sharp.

'I don't think there's much choice.' Crystal let herself slide from the desk to her feet and reached down for her bag. 'Do you?'

Liberty blinked rapidly. Her eyes felt dry and sore. Was there a choice? Another way out of this? If there was, she couldn't think

143

of one. She felt like she was letting herself be pulled out of the way of a car directly into the path of a ten-ton truck.

Crystal nodded and made for the door.

'How do you even know the sort of people who can do this?' Liberty asked.

Crystal stopped, cocked her head to one side, lips pressed together. 'Do you want this to happen or not?'

'Okay,' Liberty said. 'And thanks.'

'I'm not doing this for you.' Crystal shut the door behind her, leaving Liberty alone with the love eggs.

Amira Hassani stamped down Carter Street. The girls didn't usually come out until the evening, but things always got started earlier than usual on Fridays. Maybe someone would know something. She was still furious about the morning. Having to let the solicitor go had felt like an icicle being plunged into her chest. Those people made her sick. Who did they think they were? Above the law? Safe and protected? Their whole lives easy, a smooth passage from good to better.

Well, she might not be able to nail Chapman for perverting the course of justice but she wasn't going to just roll over. No way. She was going to find Daisy Clarke and make sure she testified against Rance. Sol had told her to stay well clear but screw that for a game of soldiers. She checked her watch. Three thirty. She'd need to go home soon so that Dad and Zaid could go to mosque.

The door of Scottish Tony's opened and a working girl called Jadine came out, platinum blonde wig puffed out like a synthetic halo. Amira crossed over to her. 'Can I have a quick word, Jadine?' she asked.

'Course you can, love.'

Jadine was a regular down the nick but Amira always treated her with respect. A lifetime of not knowing who you really were would mess with anyone's mind. You could hardly blame them for turning to drugs and drink. 'Have you seen anything of Daisy?' she asked.

Jadine batted false eyelashes. 'Daisy the Dog?'

Amira nodded.

'Not for a bit,' said Jadine. 'She's not down here so much now she's got a spot at the Cherry.' She reached into a pink fur handbag, extracted a packet of cigarettes and offered it to Amira, who refused. 'Rather her than me.'

'Why do you say that?'

Jadine lit a brass Zippo, the gas making a small whoosh. Amira worried for the wig.

'The Greenwoods.' Jadine pulled a face. 'Who needs them in their life?'

A car pulled down the street and Jadine dipped to look inside. She was six foot yet still wore high heels. When the driver caught sight of Amira he quickly went on his way.

'Is that it?' Jadine asked. 'I don't want to be rude but I really need to earn some cash. I'm clucking like a turkey on Christmas Eve.'

'Have you got any idea where I might find Daisy? She's not at the Cherry and she's not at home.'

Jadine took a drag of her cigarette, her lipstick leaving a ring on the filter. 'She's been spending a lot of time with the youngest Greenwood, Frankie. They're both a bit too fond of the rocks.' She gave a little shrug. 'Not that I've got much room to talk.' As another car came down the street, Jadine raised heavily pencilled eyebrows and Amira melted into the shadows, leaving her to pick up her first punter of the day. The passenger window lowered and Jadine leaned in with a breathy laugh. 'Looking for business, love?'

A part of Amira wanted to pull Jadine away, tell her that she didn't have to do this, that she needed to make a life for herself that didn't involve getting into cars to give blow-jobs to strangers. But realistically what sort of life would that be? She was a forty-year-old trans woman with hepatitis B and a heroin addiction. The world was not exactly her oyster.

Frankie liked London. There was a buzz about it, as if everybody had somewhere proper interesting to go, rushing out of the station, chatting shit into their phone. When this deal set him up back home, maybe he could talk Jay and Crystal into expanding down here. Crystal would give him the death stare, tell him they needed to stick to what they knew. But Jay would probably be up for it.

'Frankie.' Daisy elbowed him in the side. 'I need the toilet.'

Frankie sighed. They'd decided, or at least he'd decided, that they needed to keep clear heads. No brown. No rocks. A couple of lines of ching just to keep them going. A couple had turned into one every half an hour, with Daisy spending the whole train journey in the frigging toilets. He watched her waddle off towards the Ladies in King's Cross station and began to regret bringing her.

It had seemed a good idea. Who was going to suspect some bird of anything dodgy? She could blend in, innocent like. In the cold light of day she didn't look anything other than what she was: a skanky tart who took too many drugs.

His shades were making the bridge of his nose sweat. The strap of the bag on his shoulder was digging in. Guns were a lot heavier than they looked.

They took the tube to Brixton and emerged on Brixton Road among a sea of people trying to get outside. A man in a pair of shorts so tight they would have done for the 1972 Brazil team tutted at Daisy as he banged past her.

'There's too many folk here,' she whined.

She'd been whining all morning about one thing or another. She kept going on about not understanding why they were going to London. No matter how many times he repeated himself, she just kept muttering away. 'Something doesn't feel right, Frankie,' she said, over and over, as if she'd have the first clue about putting together something like this. All she knew about in life was taking drugs and giving blow-jobs.

Frankie growled. She was starting to get on his tits. Obviously, she'd never been anywhere or done anything, but she didn't need to act so retarded. When this job got done, he was going to pay her off and kick her to the kerb. He walked up the street, keeping an eye out for a cab. Brixton Dave had given him an address but Frankie didn't have a clue how to find it. He'd just hand the bit of paper to the driver and let him take them there.

The pavement soon got blocked off by some tables outside a bar, each seat taken by someone smoking and drinking. The beer looked fucking shot, so cloudy they wouldn't get away with it back in Yorkshire. The sign above the bar's door said 'Micro Brewery'. No wonder it was 'micro', selling that shite.

'I need the toilet,' said Daisy.

Frankie bit his knuckle. He so badly wanted to give her a slap. 'Fine,' he snapped. 'Go in this bar.'

When she was gone, he thought about getting a drink but wasn't about to risk stomach rot from the mardy-looking ale they were selling. Instead he went into the newsagent next door and bought a bottle of Lucozade. The sweetness on his tongue made him think about Lib. How she used to give them all Lucozade when they were poorly. Crystal would argue that she'd never done anything like that and that Frankie had been too young to remember what had gone on. But she was wrong. He did remember.

Daisy appeared by his side, a sheen of sweat thick on her forehead. 'Give us a swig.'

He handed it to her and watched as she brought it to her lips. There was a whitehead in the corner of her mouth that made him feel sick. What person looked at themselves in the mirror and thought, Nah, not popping that? Then again, it wouldn't surprise him if Daisy never looked in a mirror, except when she was dancing down at the Cherry or snorting coke off one. She held the bottle out to him. 'Keep it,' he said.

Back in her hotel room, Liberty poured a miniature bottle of gin into a glass, topped it with tonic water then poured in a second bottle of gin. She drank almost half off the bat. The panic that had paralysed her earlier had disappeared, allowing the cold, hard truth of what she'd done to look her in the eye. She didn't flinch.

There was a rap at the door, which she ignored. Then it came again. If it was Rance, she would send him packing without any saccharine. She opened the door.

'Hello.' Jay nodded at his sister's glass. 'Bit early for the hard stuff.'

Liberty jerked her head for him to come in and shut the door behind him with her foot. Then she opened the minibar with a flourish. 'Help yourself.'

Jay took a bottle of beer. The top came off with a soft *pfft* and he sat next to her at the foot of the bed. They didn't look at one another and they didn't speak. They just stared straight ahead at the television, which wasn't turned on, and gulped their drinks.

'Tell me about this girl you were visiting,' said Liberty.

'Kyla?' Jay asked. 'Not much to tell.'

Liberty cocked her head at her brother.

'Fit bird,' he said. 'Bit of a laugh.'

'You got yourself into this mess for a "bit of a laugh"?'

Jay groaned and rubbed his head. 'Okay, okay. She's a dancer and a junkie, a complete fuck-up, and she's not the first by a long shot. I don't know why I do it. Well, I do, but I don't know why I can't not do it.'

'Do you ever wish you could just press rewind?' Liberty asked.

'I used to,' Jay answered.

'And now?'

Jay blew across the top of his bottle. 'And now I just try to concentrate on the here and now.'

'Do you hate me for what I did?'

Jay frowned. 'What would be the point of that?'

'It's what I deserve,' she said. 'The world was ending and I left.' Tears stung her eyes. 'I left and I didn't look back.'

Jay finished his beer, placed the empty bottle on the carpet and reached over to put his hand on Liberty's knee. 'You're here now.'

Liberty laid her hand on his. 'Do you think that doing bad things makes you a bad person, Jay?'

'Nah,' he said. 'Just makes you human.'

Amira Hassani was glad to find the station relatively quiet. No one around to ask awkward questions about what she was doing. She logged on to the system and tapped in a search for Frankie Greenwood. The screen immediately sprang into life with a long list of previous convictions dating back to when he was a minor. A quick scan confirmed they were mostly for shop-lifting and possession of drugs. No custodial sentences.

She extended the search and found a couple of cases against him that had been dropped. The first was another drugs charge. He'd been searched outside a nightclub and an officer had found a couple of grams of coke down his trousers. Unfortunately, the lab test had confirmed that the baggie of white powder had been sweetener and Greenwood had walked.

Amira found the details of the second charge infinitely more interesting. Assault occasioning actual bodily harm, contrary to section 47 of the Offences Against the Person Act 1861. She scrolled to the victim's statement and her jaw fell slack.

My name is Magdalena Aleksas and I live at an address known to the police. My date of birth is eighth April 1995. I am a Lithuanian national but have been living in the UK for almost two years.

For the last four months I have been working as a dancer at a club known as the Black Cherry. I found the job through other Lithuanian girls that I know who introduced me to the manager, a woman called Mel. I do not know her surname. I used to work every day, arriving at around four p.m. with the other girls I know. The club is nearly always busy.

The owner of the club is a man named Jay and he is often present. Sometimes another woman, who I believe is called Christine, visits the club with him. By the way Mel and the bar staff treat her, I assume that she, too, is a boss.

Another man who regularly visits is Frankie. Although he does not have to pay for anything at the Black Cherry, it is obvious that he is not in charge. When Frankie comes into the Black Cherry he likes to drink beer at the bar and chat with the girls who work in the club. I have spoken to him lots of times, although only briefly because I am not fluent in English.

Yesterday the club was very busy. There were a lot of customers. Frankie was sitting on a stool at the bar. He seemed like he was a little drunk. When I walked past he said something to me and his voice sounded slurred. I didn't understand what he said and I was in a rush to get changed for my next dance, so I just smiled at him and carried on walking.

As I walked away he shouted at me but I didn't reply.

When I got as far as the door to the girls' changing room, I could feel someone very close behind me. I turned and saw it

150

was Frankie. He was sweating heavily and seemed very angry. I tried to explain that I was in a hurry but he held an arm across the doorway. Eventually I ducked under his arm and tried to get through the door, but Frankie pushed me hard and I fell forward banging my face against it and falling to the floor. My nose began to bleed and my right cheek began to swell.

Fortunately Mel quickly arrived and led Frankie away, otherwise I think he may have continued to assault me.

Amira's mobile rang and she screwed up her face when she saw her brother's number. 'Zaid.'

'Where are you?' he snapped.

'Just finishing up at work.' She checked her watch. Damn. 'Literally just leaving.'

'Seriously, Amira, you are way out of line. We're going to be late for prayers. You can't just keep dumping Rahim on us like this.'

Amira was stung. 'He's your nephew, not some random stranger. I thought family was the most important thing in Islam.'

'Don't even try to lecture me about my religion, sister.'

Amira sent the last document to print. 'Look, I'm doing my best, Zaid. I'm just trying to do my job and build a future for me and Rahim. It's not easy.' She scooped up the pages and ran for the door. 'Why can't you just support me?'

Zaid didn't answer immediately but when he did his voice had softened. 'Just get here as quickly as you can.'

Amira hung up and smiled. Zaid might be a pain in the arse, but he was her pain-in-the-arse brother.

Daisy knew that Frankie was getting pissed off with her. It didn't help that he wouldn't let her have any gear. He said they needed to keep a clear head, but Daisy couldn't function on just a couple of lines of Charlie. And shit Charlie at that. The tightness in her stomach had turned into a stabbing pain, like there was a lit cigarette inside. And the sweat was unreal. It was rolling off her. Even though it was a scorching day and the other passengers on the train had been huffing and puffing, fanning themselves with magazines and books, people had still stared at her as she melted into a salty pool. The stupid thing was she still felt cold.

But even in this state Daisy knew there was something off about the whole deal. According to Frankie, Brixton Dave was a face around these parts, but if that was true, why was he coming to Frankie with his problems? Surely he'd have a lorry-load of his own people to sort the Russians. And, anyway, what was he dreaming of, thinking this was the best way to do that? Everyone knew you had to do things properly with them. You couldn't mess with them and expect to keep your bollocks. Jay and Crystal never did business with them.

Brixton Road was heaving as they picked their way to a mini-cab office. Inside, the woman behind the counter had obviously just sprayed air-freshener. It hung in the air so thickly that Daisy could taste it. There was nowhere to sit, so she leaned against the wall, the back of her head pressed against the concrete, eyes and throat closing.

Frankie gave her a look filled with disgust.

If she wasn't feeling so sick, she'd have told him to do one. He wasn't so fucking squeaky clean. She wiped her hands down the front of her jeans. The legs inside felt brittle and bruised, an ache seeping right into the marrow of her bones. She'd started taking drugs when her little brother had his second round of radiotherapy. His hair had already fallen out and he was in ex-cruciating pain. The irony wasn't lost on Daisy.

Frankie handed over the address to the woman and she told them to wait outside.

'What's going to happen after?' she asked.

'What are you talking about now?' Frankie snapped.

'After we've taken the stuff,' she said. 'This Brixton Dave must be expecting some come-back.'

'He can handle himself.'

'So why isn't he handling *this* himself?'

'Shut the fuck up, Daisy,' said Frankie.

Soon they were in the back of a cab, on their way.

'You know what you've got to do?' Frankie hissed at her.

Daisy nodded. There was no point saying anything else.

'You can't fuck around,' he said. 'We go in quickly. We leave. End of.'

Daisy forced a smile. The quicker they got this over with the better. Then at last she could have what she needed.

Chapter 12

October 1985

'You all right love?' the nurse mouths.

Since I still can't hear too well, she's made this big song and dance of it, her lips doing all these weird shapes, her eyes open wide like a fish's. They say my ear drum's perforated, from where Dad hit me or where my head bounced off the wall. I still can't remember much. Either way, they say it'll get better, that I'm not to worry. So I'm not. 'I'm fine,' I tell her, hoping I'm not speaking too loudly.

She holds my wrist in one hand and checks her watch with the other. What's that about? Whatever it is, she writes it all down on a chart at the end of my bed. Then she hands me a little plastic cup. It's so small it's more like a bottle top. My pills, one pink, one white, rattle around at the bottom. 'Get them down,' she says.

I do as I'm told, throwing them into my mouth and accepting a glass of squash to wash them down.

'Mr Reid will be along soon,' she tells me.

Mr Reid's a doctor, but because he's important he gets to use 'Mr'. How funny is that? You'd think a doctor would be higher up than a normal person. He's got quite a kind face, and he's the only one who doesn't make a pantomime of speaking to me. He just talks up a bit and looks straight at me, which is all anyone needs to do, really. He says he's a child psychologist and he was the one who told me what happened.

'How are you today, Elizabeth?' He arrives and sits on the edge of my bed.

'Fine.'

He rests his right foot on his left knee so I get a good view of his trainer. I always used to assume that doctors wouldn't wear things like trainers because they were too posh. Mr Reid seems posh. He talks all posh. But he always wears trainers. Maybe it's different for psychologists.

'I saw your brothers and sister earlier today,' he says.

My heart gives a little flutter at the thought of the kids. 'Are they . . .'

'They're absolutely fine.' Mr Reid puts his hand on mine. 'They send their love and they'll come and see you soon.'

'You said that last week.'

Mr Reid nods. 'I know I did, Elizabeth. The trouble is, they had to be put in a placement quite a distance from here until things are resolved.'

'You mean until they catch Dad.'

'Exactly that.'

Dad's been on the run since that night. The police are looking everywhere for him. It's been on the news and everything.

'You're perfectly safe here in the meantime,' says Mr Reid.

I glance at the copper on duty at the end of the ward. They change all the time. This one's about fifty and is having a cuppa with one of the nurses. He wouldn't stand a chance if Dad was set on getting in here. But I don't think he will. He's away on his toes, probably in Ireland by now. He wouldn't come here and risk getting banged up again.

'I understand that you don't enjoy speaking about it, Elizabeth,' says Mr Reid.

I know what's coming and he's right, I don't bloody well like talking about it. I don't bloody well like thinking about it.

'Your mum,' he says.

I give a little cringe at the mention of her. I don't mean to but it's like someone has poked me in my bad ear. 'What about her?' I ask.

'It must have been a terrific shock,' he says.

'Not really.'

He gives a small smile to show that he doesn't believe me.

'It were only a matter of time,' I say. He looks away. There are some things even he doesn't like to face head on. 'If you'd been there you'd get it.'

He slips off the bed and sits in the chair next to it, so his face is at the same level as mine, then looks deep into my eyes. This is the serious bit. The bit where he tells me something really important. 'You're allowed to be shocked, Elizabeth. Or sad or angry. Or all three.'

'I know,' I tell him.

'And you're allowed to express those emotions,' he says. 'You don't have to keep them all in.'

I look at him with his floppy haircut and scruffy trainers. In his world you get to say what's in your heart. You get to let it run out, then throw it away like bog roll. But I know I can't start that game. Paula Greenwood was my mother. Sometimes she was lovely, but a lot of the time she was rubbish. She didn't read to us or make us nice things for our tea. She didn't put plasters on our knees or tuck us in at night. She spent a lifetime as Dad's punch-bag, seeing the inside of A and E more times than any of us want to remember. Then one night she tried to put an end to the violence and got herself killed.

Now she's gone.

'I'm tired,' I tell Mr Reid.

He nods. 'It's the meds.'

I close my eyes, like they're too heavy for me to resist, then I wait for him to leave me alone.

The bar in the Radisson was empty. Liberty took a stool and ordered a gin and tonic that she most definitely did not need.

'Ice and lemon?' asked the bartender.

'Does it come any other way?' Liberty asked.

He smiled, mixed the drink and placed it in front of her on a paper circle. Then he put a small bowl of olives next to it. Liberty popped one into her mouth, then took a slurp of her drink.

'Shouldn't you be out looking for Daisy Clarke?'

Liberty spun in her seat to find Rance standing in front of her, arms crossed. Maybe it was the alcohol coursing through her. Maybe it was the fact that she had committed two criminal acts that day. Either way, Rance seemed small and spoiled and pathetic.

'I have looked,' she said. 'I went to her flat, I asked her employer. No one knows where she is, not even the police.'

Rance stuck out his bottom lip. A twelve-year-old boy in a man's body.

She cupped her ear. 'If you've any other ideas where she might be, then do let me know.'

'What if she doesn't turn up?' he asked.

Liberty drank some gin and let an ice cube slip into her mouth. She crunched it, letting the noise fill the bar. 'I suspect that that is exactly what will happen,' she said. 'And you'll have to be patient, Mr Rance.'

'I'm not staying here.'

She shrugged. 'That's up to you. But if you leave, they'll have you back in the Mansion before you can say lap-dancer and there won't be a thing I can do about it.'

'And what are you going to do while I'm being patient?' asked Rance.

'Me?' Liberty smiled at him and raised her glass. 'I'm going back to London.' As soon as she said it, she knew that was exactly what she was going to do and laughed at the prospect. 'When Daisy is still a no-show in a week's time, I'll list your case again and it will be thrown out. I might not even have to come back.'

Rance was a thin sliver of spite, glaring at her. 'You've got it all figured out,' he said.

Liberty finished her drink and signalled for the bartender to fill her up again. 'No, Mr Rance, I don't have it all figured out. I'm just working with what's been thrown at me.'

Sol almost laughed out loud. The way Chapman dealt with Rance was class. He watched the man leave the bar, puce with rage, and slid into the stool next to the lawyer. She radiated heat, expensive perfume and alcohol. She was just the right side of pissed. God, how Sol loved that point of the evening. The point where everything was funny and everyone looked good. The point before the fights and the hangovers kicked in. 'Miss Chapman,' he said.

She turned, still smiling. In another situation that smile would have had him. No question. As soon as she clocked it was him, the smile retreated. Not fully, though, she was too drunk for that.

'Detective Inspector Connolly.' She didn't sound as well-spoken as she had in court or at the station. Her vowels were blunted by the booze. 'To what do I owe this unexpected pleasure?'

He gestured at the barman to give him a beer. 'I've been speaking to my colleague PC Hassani.'

'I bet she had only good things to say about me,' Chapman answered.

'She told me something rather interesting as it goes.'

Chapman put an elbow on the bar and placed her chin in the palm of her hand. 'I'm all ears.' Her dark hair fell across her face and he checked the impulse to push it to the side. In the end she did it herself and Sol took a quick, distracting drink of beer. 'She was doing a bit of digging on the Greenwood family back at the station.' He took another sip. 'I mean, there's quite a lot of stuff there. These aren't people who've made much effort to stay clean over the years.' Chapman blinked slowly, but otherwise didn't react. 'An intriguing but little known fact, though, is that there are four Greenwoods. Jay, Crystal and Frankie have an older sister.'

TAKING LIBERTIES

When Hassani had called Sol to tell him about Frankie's dropped assault charge, she'd asked for clearance to access the confidential files in the database. He'd been reluctant. The kid was too hot-headed by far, yet he had to admire her doggedness. He'd given her the password and told her to mail him with anything juicy.

'I think your name is Elizabeth Greenwood,' he said. 'Known by her family as Lib Greenwood.'

She pushed herself up and gave him a slow hand-clap. Sol could see the family resemblance now and he wondered how he'd missed it so far. 'Why don't you use your real name?' he asked.

'Liberty Chapman is my real name.' She didn't miss a beat. 'I changed it over twenty years ago.'

Sol nodded. The historical files Hassani had found evidenced a torrid tale of the father murdering the mother. The kids all placed in care. Who could blame Chapman for wanting to start afresh? It was quite a feat that none of the Greenwood kids had ended up doing serious time, given their childhood, and it was utterly astonishing that one of them had gone away to become a successful brief.

'You gave your brother Jay an alibi,' said Sol.

'I did.'

'That's very different from a solicitor giving their client an alibi.'

'I never said he was my client,' she replied.

Sol had already checked his notes about that. Chapman had never even hinted that this was the case. He had added two and two and made five.

'You think I lied because he's my brother,' she said.

'I think the Greenwoods are tight knit,' replied Sol.

'Yes, they are, but I'm a Chapman.'

Sol smiled. Even drunk, this woman was sharper than most. 'What's in a name?'

'Everything and nothing.' She pushed her glass towards the bartender for another. 'But that's not why you shouldn't consider me a part of their family.'

He waited until the next gin and tonic was in front of her, watched her pick out the slice of lemon, suck it once, then drop it back into the liquid.

'I'm no longer part of the Greenwoods.' Her voice was getting hoarse. 'I haven't been from the time I changed my name, actually.' She raised the glass to her lips, but replaced it on the bar without taking a sip. 'In fact, I hadn't seen any of my family since I was eighteen years old.' She raised a playful eyebrow. 'What do you think of that? Our Chinese meal together was the first time Jay and I had clapped eyes on each other since 1994.'

Sol exhaled. 1994. A lifetime ago. No one would ever believe that an upstanding person like Chapman would lie for a brother she hadn't seen in more than twenty years. And no one would believe she'd made a mistake on timings, given how unusual the circumstances were for their meeting. The alibi was solid. He wouldn't be able to shift it and they both knew it. 'You're a very good liar, Miss Chapman,' he said. 'What I don't understand is why you're doing it.'

She looked deeply into her drink. 'In life, the what is the easy bit, Detective. The why is always much more complicated. Don't you think?'

Frankie looked at Daisy in the back seat of the taxi, slowly unravelling. He'd wanted them both to stay straight, but he hadn't realized how far gone she was. She was clucking, talking rubbish, doing his head in. She was going to create a problem if he wasn't careful.

Fine.

'Listen, mate,' Frankie leaned forward to the driver, 'can you pull over at that McDonald's?'

Daisy looked at him, bewildered, but as he pushed a rock into her hand, her face changed to gratitude. When the cab pulled up, she dived out. The girl who had barely been able to put one foot in front of the other all day was gone in a whirl of anticipation. He knew the appeal. The whoosh of the gear when you lit the pipe was electric, like a firestorm running from lungs, to brain, to limbs, until every molecule in your body was alive and crackling.

Fuck it.

Frankie got out of the cab and followed Daisy to the toilets.

Liberty leaned over the washbasin in the hotel room. The porcelain was cool under her fingers. She considered making herself sick to avoid tomorrow's hangover. Nah, she wasn't that drunk. Instead she brushed her teeth, drank three glasses of water and lay on her bed fully clothed. She thought about Connolly. He knew full well that she'd lied but he also knew that the alibi would stick. The only thing that might have helped him was the speeding ticket, but now he'd never know about that. Interestingly, he hadn't been angry. Not like Hassani, who seemed like she was constantly battling with herself not to punch Liberty in the face. No, Connolly had appeared almost amused. Like this was all a big game and he was just biding his time to make his next move.

He was an attractive bloke. Not handsome exactly. Watchful, predatory almost. Liberty had known he was weighing her up during their encounter, though not why. She rarely met any men who piqued her interest as much as he had.

A knock at the door interrupted her thoughts. For a second she thought it might be Connolly and a flicker of excitement ran through her, but when she checked the spy-hole she saw it was Crystal. She opened the door. 'Come in.'

Crystal strode inside, past the bed and leaned against the table, chin jutted. 'I sorted the ticket.'

'Thanks. How much do I owe you?'

Crystal shook her head.

'I can't let you pay for that, Crystal,' Liberty said. 'I have plenty of money.'

Crystal sniffed. 'I'm sure you do.'

'Then tell me how much I owe.'

Crystal stared at Liberty, taking in the melting mascara, the untucked shirt. 'If ever it came to light that a piece of evidence had gone missing, who do you think they'd look at first?' she asked.

'Me I guess,' Liberty replied.

'And if they checked your bank account only to find several grand missing at exactly the same time as the evidence went walkabout?'

Crystal was right.

'For someone with a lot of qualifications, you really can be very stupid,' said Crystal.

Liberty didn't deny it and just watched as her sister reached into her back pocket for her Juicy Fruit. Crystal took out two sticks this time and threw one at Liberty.

'I'm going back to London tomorrow morning,' said Liberty.

Crystal unwrapped her gum and nodded.

'If you're ever down there, you should come over,' said Liberty.

'Maybe we could get cocktails and dinner.' Crystal's voice dripped sarcasm. 'Catch a musical in the West End.'

'I hate musicals.' Liberty turned her gum over in her hand, rubbing the silver paper with her thumb. When Crystal had been six or seven, Liberty had shown her how to worry a wobbly tooth with her tongue to hasten its departure, and she'd comforted her when the Tooth Fairy had forgotten to turn up with a ten-pence piece. She wanted to hold that little girl again and kiss away her tears.

Crystal's mobile rang and she fished in her bag for it, rolling her eyes when she checked caller ID. 'Frankie, where the hell have you been?' she demanded. 'Jay's been looking for you all frigging day.' She paused, her face rigid. 'Who is this?'

Chapter 13

November 1985

I'm that excited I can't sleep. The night nurse tucks me in again and tuts. 'You need your rest if you're going to get better.'

Thing is I am getting better. The swelling's all gone down and my hearing's almost back to normal. Mr Reid says I'm doing so well that I can go and see the kids tomorrow. Which is why I can't sleep. The social worker is going to pick me up in her car and drive me to the foster placement, which is in a place called Bramhope. I've never heard of it, but I think it sounds nice. I keep imagining a big house with a garden and everything. There'll be a shed at the back, and when I press the bell it'll play a tune. The foster-parents will bring me into the kitchen and give me a drink of squash, then I'll play with the kids. Outside if it's not raining.

I'll be on my best behaviour, minding my Ps and Qs, then hopefully I can go and live there too when the doctors say I can be discharged. I won't call the foster-parents Mam and Dad; I'm too old for that. But the kids might, especially Frankie.

The nurse wanders back to the end of the ward and starts chatting to the copper on duty. This pair flirt like mad. She doesn't seem too bothered about the hairs that poke out of his nostrils. While they're busy getting lovey-dovey, I sneak out of bed and down the corridor to the toilet. I'm meant to get somebody to come with me in case I fall, or stay in bed and use one of them cardboard pans. No chance. Last time I tried that, I ended up with wee all over my hands and my nightie. I creep away, my bare feet pattering on the tiles.

The toilets are empty so I choose the middle one. While I'm in there, I hear the door go. I hope it's not the nurse come to look for me. She might be all smiles for the copper, but she'll give me a right ear-bashing if she finds me in here on my own. I hold my breath and lift up my feet. Hopefully she won't try any of the doors. I wait for a few minutes, bum getting cold on the seat, thighs starting to ache with the effort of holding my feet off the floor. I can't hear anything. Maybe she went back to her post.

I lower my feet and gently open the door. No one's there.

Smiling, I set back off to my bed, not bothering to wash my hands, which I know is minging, but I need to be quick. As I'm passing the last cubicle, the door flies open and an arm reaches out and grabs me. I try to scream, but there's a big hand over my mouth.

'Sssh.' Dad has a finger to his lips. 'Not a word, Lib.'

I nod behind his hand and he lets me go.

I'm shaking as he steps back and lets himself flop onto the toilet seat. He looks terrible. Big dark circles under his eyes and his hair is as greasy as a bag of chips. He doesn't look like he's had a bath in weeks.

'Lib.' His voice is rough, like he's spent all day crying and smoking. He smells like that's what he's been doing too. 'Lib, you've got to help me.'

I don't know what he's on about, so I just stand there shivering, goose bumps coming up on my arms.

'You were there,' he says. 'You know what happened.'

I can't remember how many people have asked me what happened to Mam. Policemen and women, social workers, doctors, nurses. Mr Reid asks me every other day. And I've always said the same: I don't know.

'You can tell them.' Dad's voice cracks. 'You can tell them how it went down.'

I could as well. After the first few days when my head felt like it was filled with candy floss, my memory came back. I know exactly what happened and how it went down. I came home from school and Mam

165

had a split lip. Dad had lost his temper over an accumulator, she told me, but not to worry myself, she'd called someone, a friend of her brother's, and he was coming to 'sort it'.

A few minutes later a big bloke arrived with a crown tattooed across his neck. He held out a fiver to her. 'Take the kids out for some chips,' he said.

Mam took the money. 'Don't go in too heavy, Joe. I just want him to leave. You don't need to knock him to kingdom come.'

Joe laughed and shook his head. 'Get out of here, Paula.'

I was helping Crystal to put on her shoes, looking forward to them chips, when Dad came back. He looked at Joe. Joe looked at him.

'What's going off here?' asked Dad.

'You need to leave, Jim,' said Mam.

Dad growled. 'Leave?'

'I can't have you hitting me no more.' Mam started to cry. 'If you put me in hospital again, they'll take the kids away.'

I remember her words exactly because she didn't once say Dad shouldn't hit her because it was wrong, or that it hurt, or that she was scared. Her main worry was that we'd be put into care. Which is ironic, considering.

'And who's this twat?' Dad cocked his thumb at Joe.

Joe took a step towards him. 'I'm just a twat who doesn't like it when a man smacks about his woman.'

Dad laughed, then lunged at Joe, cracking him a good one on his jaw. Joe recovered fast and punched Dad three times in the stomach. Then they were battering each other, Joe bouncing Dad off the walls, but Dad not giving in.

Mam screamed at the kids to get out of the house. Jay picked up Frankie and ran outside, Crystal still in one shoe, shot after them. I was about to follow when Dad and Joe crashed into me, knocking the side of my head into the wall so hard I saw stars and fell to my knees.

Mam tried to get to me, but Joe and Dad were a blur of fists and knees. The door was open and they careered through it as if they were joined together, taking Mam with them, propelling her backwards, outside, lifting her off her feet like she didn't weigh anything.

I scrambled to get up but I couldn't. All I could do was watch as she went over the balcony.

I stare at Dad sitting on the toilet seat, head in his hands. His stinking breath coming out in rasps. I could help him. 'Who moved her body?' I ask.

He looks up as if it's a weird question, but I don't think it is. Someone must have done it because they didn't find her at the bottom of the balcony. They found her body in a skip half a mile away. 'We both did.' He shakes his head. 'Joe and me. We didn't know what to do, we just thought . . .' He rakes his cheek with his nails. 'It were an accident, Lib. You know it was. You can tell the police.'

I stand there for a second, my body convulsing. I can tell everyone what happened. I can tell the truth. I turn and run. Dad tries to grab me but I'm too fast for him. I sprint from the toilet back down to the nurses' station, where the policeman's sitting with a brew.

'It's my dad!' I scream. 'He's here!'

They'd put something over her head. If Daisy looked forward, she couldn't see a thing, but if she looked down she could just about make out her shoes. 'Don't piss about,' said a voice. 'Just do as you're told and no one gets hurt.'

She tried to keep her breathing even, taking in the smell of whatever it was covering her head, like it'd been freshly washed, but that still hadn't got everything out and a tang of metal lingered behind the detergent. If she concentrated on taking long, slow breaths she wouldn't panic and, right now, she definitely needed not to panic.

There was the sound of a big bunch of keys jangling, then a bolt snapping and the long creak of a door opening. 'Move,' said the voice.

Daisy moved.

Under her feet, the feel of concrete was replaced by sticky

carpet. She was going inside now. Keeping calm in bad situations wasn't new to Daisy. In her line of work, shit often hit the fan. Same with the gear. She often found herself in places where things were getting out of hand. She knew how to handle herself. To be honest, she'd been half expecting something to go wrong. Nah, scratch that, she'd been fully expecting something to go wrong. Hadn't she been trying to tell Frankie so? But that boy never was the sharpest knife in the cutlery drawer, was he?

She'd done as she was told. She'd gone to the flat. She'd chatted to the boys in there, laughed about some show on Sky, even though she didn't actually have Sky, didn't even have a telly.

Then the Russians arrived. Two of them. Ugly fuckers, with their shaved heads and skulls peppered with pink scars. And, man, did they have ink. Every finger, every thumb, every inch of skin on their necks was covered with tattoos. One of the Lithuanian girls back at the Cherry had once shown Daisy a picture of her boyfriend. He was Russian and doing time for GBH.

'These here.' Leja had pointed to the tattoos on her boyfriend's knees, each a four-pointed star. 'They mean he will kneel to no man.'

The Russians ignored Daisy and the other boys were all over them, like flies on shit, which was about the only part of the plan that had gone how it was meant to, giving her a chance to let Frankie in. He'd pressed a gun into her hand. 'Point at them and take the drugs.'

Daisy had racked her brain. Where were the drugs? She hadn't seen any. She hadn't even seen a bag. 'I don't think . . . '

But Frankie was too wired to listen and pushed past her, waving his piece like a bloody cowboy. When the Russians didn't react, he screamed at them, 'Drugs.' Spit was flying. 'Give us the drugs. Now.'

No one moved. It was like a game of musical statues. Then one of the lads laughed. Then another. Then the Russians both smiled and one said, in on accent more south London than east Moscow, 'Fuck off, mate.' That was when they'd covered her face and brought her here.

'Sit down,' the voice commanded, and hands pressed on each of her shoulders, forcing her knees to bend until she fell awkwardly to the floor. The sound of gaffer-tape being pulled off a roll jagged towards Daisy. Then her hands were pulled in front of her and bound together. Another scream of tape, and her ankles were strapped.

'Right,' said the voice, and its owner's footsteps moved away until a door opened and closed and Daisy knew she was alone.

The blood drained from Crystal's face as she listened intently to her mobile.

'Is everything okay?' Liberty whispered.

Crystal held up a hand to silence her. Clearly things were far from okay. 'I'm going to ask again who this is,' Crystal said, her face now a grey mask, even her lips colourless, the skin shocking against the red of her hair. When she spoke again her voice was ice. 'Are you sure you want to do this?' She listened again, then hung up.

'Jesus, Crystal, what's wrong?' Liberty asked.

When Crystal didn't answer, Liberty stepped forward and touched her sister's arm. Crystal looked at Liberty's hand as if she had never seen it before, then into her face. 'Someone's got Frankie,' she said.

Liberty let her hand drop. 'What do you mean? Got him as in what? Kidnapped him or something?'

She'd meant it as a joke but Crystal shrugged.

'That's ridiculous,' said Liberty. 'Who on earth would do that?'

'They didn't say.'

'Hold on.' Liberty threw her arms out to the side, then let them drop with a slap against her thighs. 'Someone called you to say they've kidnapped our brother?' Crystal blinked yes. 'It's a piss-take surely? One of his mates?'

'They called from his phone,' said Crystal. She checked hers again, then picked up her bag, made for the door. 'I need to speak to Jay.'

Liberty grabbed her upper arm to stop her. 'Come on, Crystal, you can't think this is real?'

The look on Crystal's face told Liberty that Crystal thought this was very real indeed. 'I haven't got time to convince you, Lib.' Crystal opened the door. 'I need to get a cab over to Jay's.'

Liberty snatched up her car keys and held them up. 'I'll take you.'

'You've been drinking.'

Liberty reddened. 'You drive.'

Crystal opened her hand and Liberty let the keys fall into her palm. Crystal clocked the Porsche badge. 'Nice.'

Daisy waited. She breathed in and out and waited. The room itself felt empty. Obviously she couldn't be certain, but her legs and feet didn't touch anything, no matter which way she moved them. And something about the place *felt* empty, as if the air was running freely, the sounds coming from outside, circulating. Her own flat often had the same feel. Not when she'd first moved in and had all the usual stuff, but after she'd sold it and was down to the bare minimum. She'd lie there stoned, staring at the ceiling, listening to the streets outside. Sirens, car alarms, people shouting in the court-yard below. Just normal life.

She thought the thing on her head might be a bag because, although her face was completely covered, the bottom was open all the way round. She could bring her hands to her mouth easily enough. She could start chewing her way through the tape if she wanted, but what if the man came back halfway through? So far he hadn't done anything to hurt her, but if he caught her trying something like that he might lose the plot.

She just had to wait a bit longer, listen as hard as she could, assure herself that he wasn't in the flat. She'd once had the same thing happen with a punter. A girl she knew vouched for him, said he was a bit weird but harmless, that he liked it a bit rough but never actually hurt anyone. Not properly. Happy to pay double. That sealed the deal.

After only a few minutes in, Daisy had had him pegged as a wrong 'un, but she already owed her dealer fifty quid. There'd be no chance of anything else on tick, not even a taste. He'd tied her up, pulled out a knife and started chatting shit. 'I'm going to cut off your tits and make you eat them,' he'd said, along with a whole string of snuff-movie staples. She'd waited him out until eventually he got bored and let her go.

That was one of the good things about working at the Cherry. The punters were regulars more often than not and even the one-offs were given a proper once-over by the girls before anyone offered services. It kept them safe. Mostly. It wasn't a hundred per cent, though. Sometimes a nutter slipped through the net, like that bastard Rance.

The creak of the door opening made her jump. Thank God she hadn't tried to get through the tape. Footsteps came towards her until she could see a pair of white Nike Air Max. Then there was a whoosh of air. She coughed and blinked, suddenly dazzled by sunlight.

'All right, Daisy?'

The man towering above her came into focus, smiling down on her, fag behind his ear, all south-London-cheeky-chappie. He held a rucksack, which she realized must have been over her head. He grabbed her by the chin and yanked her head so that she had to look him in the eye. 'I said all right, Daisy?' When she nodded, he seemed satisfied and let her go. 'Glad to hear it. Like to look after my guests. Only good manners, you get me?'

Daisy nodded again.

'That's my girl,' he said. 'Now, I need you to do something for me, okay?'

Daisy nodded a third time.

'Come on now, girl,' he said. 'Cat got your tongue? I need to know if you can do something for me.'

'Yes,' Daisy replied.

'Now that's what I like to hear.' The man wagged a finger at her. 'Positive thinking. Gonna get you a long way in life, Daisy.' He plucked the cigarette from behind his ear and lit it, leaving it in the corner of his mouth. 'Wanna fag?'

'Yes.'

The man made a mock-frown. 'I'm disappointed, Daisy. Manners are a two-way street, don't you think?'

'Yes, please,' said Daisy.

The smile returned to his face and he bent down so that he was at her level, took the fag from his mouth and held it to her lips. She took a grateful drag.

'I need you to make a phone call for me, Daisy,' he said. 'But I need you to say exactly what I tell you, word for word. Can you do that?'

'Yes.'

He let her take another pull on the fag before tossing it to the carpet, grinding it out with his heel and pulling a mobile from his back pocket. From the screensaver she knew instantly that it was Frankie's.

Jay paced back and forth on his patio, flicking a front tooth with his thumbnail. The sound of his boys' squeals floated through an

172

open upstairs window, followed by their mother's laughter. Liberty couldn't remember their own mother laughing. Not real laughter. Not unless she'd been drunk. She checked Jay and Crystal's faces to see if they were thinking the same thing, but their serious expressions told her that Paula Greenwood was far from their thoughts.

Crystal's mobile rang and Jay stopped dead.

Crystal slid the unlock button, pressed answer and held it six inches from her chin. 'Frankie?'

'No.'

Crystal had the phone on speaker so they could all hear. Jay and Liberty stepped closer. The person calling was female. She had a local accent and Liberty recognized the voice, though she couldn't immediately place it.

'Who, then?' Crystal asked.

'It's Daisy,' the woman replied. 'Daisy Clarke.'

'Daisy the Dog?' Jay said. 'What the actual fuck?'

Crystal slapped her hand over his mouth. 'Where's the man who called earlier, Daisy?'

There was a muffled sound, as if Daisy was saying something but away from the phone. Then she came back on the line. 'You need to listen,' she said. 'I'm only going to get to say this once, okay?'

'Okay,' Crystal replied.

'I'm with Frankie.'

'What?' Crystal barked.

'If you want to see him again, you've got to pay. If you don't pay, he'll get hurt. It's as simple as that.'

'How do we know Frankie's not already hurt?' Crystal asked.

'I'll call again soon to tell you how much you've got to pay,' said Daisy.

'Is Frankie . . .'

The line was already dead.

Jay hit his forehead with his knuckle. 'I told that girl to stay away from him. I told her that. What the hell has she got him into?'

Liberty thought about Daisy in the back room of the Black Cherry, fidgeting and scratching as she retracted her statement. 'I can't imagine her as a key player here.'

Jay's eyes flashed.

'I doubt she'd even know how to get to London,' Liberty said, 'let alone manage to lure Frankie down there for God knows what.'

'She's a junkie. And a whore,' said Jay.

The words 'like your mistress' formed on Liberty's tongue.

'Frankie's just a kid,' Jay continued.

'He's thirty-four,' Liberty said.

Jay tapped the side of his head. 'Not up here he's not.'

Liberty sighed. Maybe Jay was right. She didn't know Daisy or Frankie, did she? And, anyway, what did it matter? The important thing was what was going to happen now.

The lights in the kitchen came on, flooding the patio. Someone had dropped half a sandwich, the bread bearing the perfect imprints of a child's teeth. A long line of ants marched steadily towards it, more and more pouring out of a small hole in the edge of the lawn.

Jay gestured for them to move away from the house into the shadows.

'What now?' Liberty asked.

'She said she'd call back,' Jay answered.

'We can't just stand here and wait,' said Liberty. 'It might be hours.'

Jay shrugged.

Liberty had a suggestion. It was exactly what she would have done if you'd asked her yesterday. Her first response. 'We could call the police.'

Jay and Crystal looked at her as if she'd suggested calling the pope. She understood. She was now the sort of person who provided false alibis, the sort of person who paid for evidence to go missing. She was no longer the sort of person who called the police.

'She's right about not hanging around, though,' said Crystal. 'We've no idea when Daisy will call again. We might as well try to find out what we can.'

'I'll go to the Cherry,' said Jay. 'See if Mel or any of the girls know what Daisy the fucking Dog might be doing in London.'

'I'll ask around and see if Frankie's said anything to anybody,' Crystal added. 'He's not good at keeping secrets.'

They moved back towards the house away from Liberty. A breeze lifted, bringing with it the scent of jasmine from a pot by the kitchen door. Liberty assumed Rebecca had planted it, or perhaps a gardener. 'I can help,' she called after her brother and sister.

They turned to her, their faces saying it all.

'I can go to Daisy's flat,' she said. 'I know where it is. I can have a poke around, see if there's something that might help.'

Jay and Crystal glanced at one another, then replied as one: 'Fine.'

Chapter 14

'Are you absolutely certain you can't remember, Elizabeth?' The policeman puts his elbows on his knees and shoves his face up against mine. His breath smells of cigs and mints.

Mr Reid sighs, like he's getting pissed off now. We've been in his office for what seems like hours going over and over the same stuff. 'I've explained the nature of my patient's memory loss to you, Officer,' he says. 'These endless questions are not going to change anything.' He pushes a plate of biscuits towards me.

Not long ago his secretary brought us all a cuppa and the biscuits. I'm the only one who's eaten any so far. I've had a Jammie Dodger, a custard cream and a chocolate finger. There's just a ginger nut and a pink wafer left. I go for the wafer, sucking it, letting it dissolve on my tongue. I shouldn't have had that many, really. When I see the kids later, the foster-parents are bound to ask me if I'd like anything to eat and I don't want to look fussy or stuck-up, do I? I'll just have to force down whatever they offer me.

The copper sits up. 'Jimmy Greenwood is saying there was another man present at the scene, that he fought with this man and that together they accidentally pushed his wife over the balcony.'

Mr Reid sniffs. 'To paraphrase Mandy Rice-Davies, he would say that, wouldn't he?'

I have no idea who Mandy Whatsherface is so I just lick my fingers.

176

I'll leave the ginger nut because I don't want to look greedy. And, anyway, I don't like them much.

'Greenwood says his daughter can confirm his version of events,' the copper continues.

Mr Reid folds his arms across his chest. 'Well, she can't.'

The copper rubs the back of his head and lets out a long, faggy, minty breath. 'I don't want him getting off.' He gives me look. 'I don't think you want that either, Elizabeth.'

'Right.' Mr Reid claps his hands making me jump. 'That's quite enough. This line of questioning is becoming abusive. I know you have your job to do, Officer, but so do I and I am calling a halt to this right now.'

The policeman says something under his breath, stands up and leaves the room. Mr Reid follows him. I can hear them rowing outside the door. Not shouting and that. More sort of clipped. I swipe the ginger nut, but as soon as I bite into it I regret it. It makes my tongue fizz. I need a drink now and there's only a bit of cold tea left in my cup. I swallow it but it's not enough.

Eventually Mr Reid comes back in on his own. 'He's gone,' he says, and I smile back at him. 'We'd better get you back to your ward.'

'I'm going to Bramhope,' I say. 'To see the kids.'

He frowns at me. 'Not today, Elizabeth.'

'Yes, today,' I say. 'Four o'clock, remember?'

'You've had a terrible ordeal,' he says. 'Your dad coming to the hospital. The police arresting him like that.'

My heart plunges in my chest. 'I'm all right.'

Mr Reid shakes his head. 'No, you're not. You're already suffering from memory loss and now this on top. A long car journey followed by what is bound to be an emotional reunion with your brothers and sister? I simply can't countenance it.'

I let my head hang. What can I do? I can't let on my memory's just fine, can I? They'd probably put me in the same cell as Dad.

★ ★ ★

Liberty tried not to notice that her sister was pushing seventy-five as they sped across town. 'Do you like it?' she asked.

Crystal shrugged and floored the accelerator.

'I bought it a couple of months ago,' Liberty went on. 'Spur-of-the-moment thing, really.'

Crystal raised an eyebrow.

'What?' Liberty asked, but Crystal didn't respond, keeping her eyes on the road as she slowed only fractionally to take a sharp bend. 'You don't think I'm a spur-of-the-moment sort of person?'

'I have no idea what sort of person you are.'

As they entered the Crosshills estate, a man was pulling down the metal shutters over the doors and windows of the Happy Shopper. On the first shutter someone had sprayed the words 'Police Free Streets'. On the second there was a picture of a giant pair of boobs. 'It's over there on the left,' said Liberty, pointing at the stairs to Daisy's block.

Crystal pulled up with a screech, making Liberty's head lurch forward, then smack back against the head rest. Crystal scowled. 'You sure you wanna do this?'

'Yeah,' said Liberty.

'This isn't a nice part of town, Lib.'

'Crystal, we grew up not five minutes away.'

'A lot's changed since then.'

Liberty laughed. 'Don't tell me all the posh people moved out?' Crystal turned her head, presumably so Liberty wouldn't catch her smiling. 'It's fine. You go and do what you need to, come back for me in an hour.' She opened the door, got out and watched her sister roar away. Only then did she drop the act. Coming back to the Crosshills was a very bad idea indeed. If the police caught her, Hassani would throw the book at her, and Connolly probably wouldn't try to stop her. Even Raj would most likely leave her to her fate.

TAKING LIBERTIES

She looked over her shoulder at the graffiti on the first shutter and prayed it was true. The stairs were steep and she breathed hard as she climbed to the third floor and Daisy's flat. She paused in the stairwell on the first floor. It smelt of the chips that were liberally scattered around. She prayed that the yellow stain up the wall was curry sauce. The third floor stank but Liberty didn't hurry on. Instead she paused, watching the walkway in front of the flats. No one came in or out. Most of the flats were in complete darkness, the residents either out or in bed.

She waited another second or two, then strode along the walkway, head down. When she reached Daisy's flat, she could see that although someone had shut the door it wasn't completely flush with the jamb, presumably jarred out of position by being kicked open. In one deft movement, she pushed it wide and bobbed under the yellow police tape. Once inside she pressed the door as near to closed as it would go.

Her hand automatically hovered to the light switch, but she snatched it back just in time. She needed to be as discreet as possible and draw no attention from anyone. She pulled out her iPhone and turned on the torch setting, keeping it low.

The hallway was empty again. No bags, no shoes. Just an old radiator that looked like it had been painted a million times. The first door on the left to the kitchen was open and Liberty stepped inside. She swung the beam of light across the worktops. What should she be looking for? Post? A phone? A laptop? A diary? The surfaces were covered with crockery and old food cartons, cigarette butts clinging to every plate, bowl and cup. The tap at the sink dripped relentlessly onto a mound of teabags and a smashed glass.

To the right of the cooker was a small fridge. Liberty opened it, but the light didn't come on. It was broken and empty, except for a bag of unused syringes. On top of the fridge there were more cups, but as Liberty arced the torch beam across it, she also made

179

out a pile of letters. She reached over, picked them up and rifled through. The first was a demand from an electrician, urging Daisy to send a cheque, or telephone with credit-card details to avoid damage to her credit rating. The second was from her GP, requesting that she make an appointment for a blood test as a matter of urgency. The rest were flyers for pizza, curry and kebabs.

Liberty moved out of the kitchen and down the hall to the living room, though there was little evidence that any living was done there. She felt a pang of sadness for Daisy. Something had led her to this dog-end existence. Whatever it was must have been bleak. She scanned the room, realizing that this was a fool's errand. She wasn't going to find any clue here in the detritus as to Daisy and Frankie's whereabouts. Nothing but overflowing ashtrays and anything that could be turned into a crack pipe. Empty Coke cans, crushed and pricked, water bottles topped with foil. Even a blue asthma inhaler had been converted.

Just as she was about to give up and call Crystal, she spotted something on the floor by the side of the sofa. A piece of paper scrunched into a ball. Liberty reached over, picked it up and smoothed it out. It was a receipt for two meals at a pub called the Butcher's Arms with yesterday's date. At least they now knew one place where Daisy had been.

Suddenly, through the darkness, she heard a creak. Someone was opening the door.

Surely it couldn't be Hassani again. How could she even know Liberty was here? Of course she couldn't, not unless she'd been following her. Would Hassani do that? Liberty recalled the look on the young policewoman's face when she had walked out of the station. She wouldn't put anything past her.

She heard footsteps. If it was Hassani, she was already inside the flat. A spike of adrenalin rushed through her, clearing any residual panic. She snapped off the torch on her phone and ducked quickly behind the sofa. Then she held her breath. The footsteps moved from the hall into the kitchen, pausing, presumably to check it was empty. Then they came down to the doorway of the living room. A beam of light pierced the room, brighter than that made by Liberty's phone. It swept along the sofa, illuminating the stains and rips. Liberty remained stock still, squeezed her eyes and mouth shut.

At last the light and the footsteps moved away, heading to the bedroom.

Liberty knew she had only seconds to get out of there. Checking the bedroom would be a distraction but only a brief one.

She crept from behind the sofa to the door and listened. No footsteps, only breathing.

Then the smallest sound as Hassani, or whoever it was, stepped out of the hall into the bedroom. Knowing it was now or never, Liberty bolted from the living room to the front door, yanked it open and burst through the police tape, like a sprinter winning a race. She sprang onto the walkway and ran along it to the stairwell. Behind her, she heard something or someone but didn't break her stride. She took the steps two at a time, then three, using the wall to push her ever forward. Her breath came in jagged bursts, her heart breaking out of her chest.

At the stairwell of the first floor, her foot slipped on the discarded chips and she fell awkwardly, banging her shoulder against the metal rail. She yelped in pain, but bit down on her lip when she caught the sound of feet clattering down the stairs behind her. She thrust herself forward again and half ran, half fell down the last staircase.

Outside, she looked wildly around. Where now?

Then came a familiar sound she had never been so glad to hear in her life. The beautiful roar of a 911 coming round the corner. Liberty threw herself into the road in front of it as it careered to a stop. Crystal jumped out, eyes wide. 'What on earth do you think you're doing?'

'Just drive!' Liberty screamed, and staggered to the passenger door.

Crystal got back inside. 'I could have killed you.'

'Drive.'

Crystal gunned the engine and they leaped away just as a dark figure emerged from the entrance to the stairs.

Daisy let her head roll forward. She'd been sitting in the same position for so long that her shoulders and back were killing her. Mr Nike Air Max sat in a similar position at the other side of the room. 'Are you Brixton Dave?' she asked.

He didn't answer but flicked his lighter on and off, the flame roaring into life, then disappearing again.

'You'll use up all the gas,' she told him.

He patted his pockets and pulled out another lighter, then a third. Daisy almost laughed. 'You won't get any money out of them for me,' she said. 'The Greenwoods don't give a shit about me.'

'They care about Frankie, though, don't they?' He sparked up his lighter again and this time held the flame against a string of cotton hanging from his hoodie. 'Way I heard it, they do a lot to keep little bro out of trouble.'

And wasn't that the truth.

He gave a smile. 'I can tell by the look on your face that you don't think too much of that, Daisy.' He tossed the lighter into the air and caught it in his other hand. 'Am I right?'

Daisy shrugged.

Nan had been religious, went to church of a Sunday and all that, and she used to like to quote the Bible. One of her favourites had been from Corinthians. 'When I was a child, I spoke as a child, I understood as a child, I thought as a child; but when I became a man, I put away childish things.' Yeah, she used to wheel that one out a lot. Like the time Daisy had first got arrested at fifteen.

He stood up now, still tossing the lighter. He introduced the second, then the third, so that he was juggling. Eventually he caught all three in turn with his left hand and bowed. He was pleased with himself. And why wouldn't he be? He'd played a blinder, got a pair of silly twats to think they were going to make some easy money. Got them to walk right into this mess.

'Why don't you just call Crystal and tell them how much?' Daisy asked.

'Don't tell me I'm boring you, Daisy.'

'I just don't understand what you're waiting for,' she said.

Out of nowhere he threw a lighter at her and it bounced off her chest. Then he threw the second, a little harder. The third hit harder still so that it stung on contact. Finally he knelt at her feet to collect them back up. 'Never be predictable, Daisy, that's my motto,' he said. 'Keep the audience guessing.'

Liberty breathed deeply as Crystal sped away from the Crosshills estate.

'Want to tell me what's going on?'

Liberty put her hand on her chest. 'Someone came into the flat behind me. I ran but they chased me.'

'Kids?' Crystal asked. 'They'll rob anything round here.'

'There's nothing in there to rob.'

Crystal shook her head. 'They don't know that.'

Liberty considered. It was possible, of course. A bunch of road-men taking their chances when they saw a door already kicked off its hinges? 'I don't think it was kids,' she said. In fact, she was pretty sure it had been Hassani. If she'd been caught, she'd have been in serious trouble. But she could really do without a lecture from Crystal right now so she said no more.

They travelled on in silence, the streets almost empty now. Liberty pulled the receipt out of her pocket. 'I found this,' she said.

Crystal took it from her, steered the Porsche with her right hand, examining it in her left. Unimpressed, she dropped it into Liberty's lap.

'At least we know one of the things Daisy did yesterday,' said Liberty. 'Someone might have seen her and noticed who she was with.' Crystal's silence rankled. 'Did you come up with a better lead?' No reply. 'Did Jay?'

The hotel was right in front of them and Crystal parked at the entrance. She got out without a word and tossed the keys to Liberty.

'Suit yourself,' said Liberty. 'I'll go over there at opening time tomorrow on my own.'

'It's worked well for you so far.'

Liberty sighed. 'I was eleven years old when Mam died, Crystal. Eleven.'

Crystal fished in her bag, pulled out her phone and called a cab.

Chapter 15

December 1985

'Why can't you stay here?' Jay asks. 'We don't like it here without you.'

'Shush,' I tell him, checking that Mrs Cole isn't earwigging. I shake the dice and get a three. Then I move my counter along and pass the dice and little plastic cup to Crystal. She shakes it over and over again. 'Come on,' I say. 'You need a four to land on that ladder.'

She lets the dice spill out. It's a two.

'Never mind,' I say.

Crystal hands the cup and dice to Frankie. He can't count or anything but the rattling sound makes him giggle and he lets the dice fly up in the air and land on the other side of the rug.

'Frankie.' Mrs Cole comes into the room, her face scrunched up. 'We play nicely in this house.'

'He's only a baby,' says Jay.

'We all have to learn,' says Mrs Cole.

I lean over and look for the dice. 'I bet it's a six.'

'Maybe you should pack the game away now,' says Mrs Cole. 'The social worker will soon be here to pick you up, Elizabeth. I'll go and get your things.'

She leaves the room and Jay's face falls. Crystal throws her little arms around my neck.

'Come on, you lot,' I say. 'It's nice here.'

*And it is. Everything's clean and tidy and smells of polish. Mrs Cole
even folds the end of the toilet roll into a little point.*

'Why can't we come home with you?' Jay asks.

'I'm not at home any more,' I say.

'Where are you living, then?' Jay asks.

*'White Flower Lodge.' When he looks baffled, I add, 'A children's
home.'*

*Mrs Cole comes back in, holding out my coat. I take it from her, put
it on and do the zip up all the way to the top.*

*'I think that must be her now.' Mrs Cole scurries to the window like
a beetle and lifts the net curtain. 'Yes, it's the social worker.'*

*I kneel down and give each of the kids a kiss and a hug. 'Be good for
Mrs Cole and your new teachers.'*

'Best not to make too much fuss,' says Mrs Cole.

*'I'm not.' I shouldn't have said that, but she's starting to annoy me
now. I give them all another kiss, feeling Mrs Cole's eyes burning into me
from behind.*

*On the way back, I stare out of the car window watching the world
pass by. Postboxes, lampposts, bins. People walking their dogs, people
carrying shopping, people pushing prams. The social worker turns on the
radio and sings along with Shakin' Stevens.*

Hassani and Sol were the only customers in Scottish Tony's. She
adjusted a bright blue hijab as she slid into the seat opposite. 'Close
your mouth.'

'Aren't you hot in that?' Sol asked.

'Allah's love keeps me cool,' she said.

He wasn't sure whether she was joking until she gave a wink.
'So what did you want to talk about?' he asked.

She accepted a cup of tea from Scottish Tony and stirred in a
heaped teaspoon of sugar. Then another. 'I've looked everywhere
for Daisy. Been to all the usual spots. I even went back to her flat

late last night.' For a moment she looked like she might have something more to say, but instead she sank back in her chair.

Sol nodded. He'd put out a few feelers himself and everything had come back blank.

'The Greenwoods are involved, I'm sure of it,' she said. 'Kyla Anderson, Daisy Clarke, all of it. Up to their necks, especially the solicitor.'

Sol stirred his own tea, wincing at the sight of Hassani adding yet another sugar to her own – he'd given up sugar in tea and coffee when he'd moved in with Natasha. His teeth ached in solidarity.

'I think we should watch them,' she said.

Sol sighed. 'We won't get anyone to agree to that.'

'I don't mean phone taps and surveillance. I just mean watch what they do today,' she said. 'See where they go. I bet they'd lead us right to Daisy.'

'It's Saturday,' said Sol. 'Won't your husband have something to say about that?'

Hassani took a sip of tea. 'I'd be surprised if he did – I haven't seen him for over a year.'

'Sorry.'

'Don't be. He was a dickhead.'

Sol remembered that his own mother had been none too bothered when his dad walked out for good, taking the smell of beer and other women with him. She'd brought Sol up to be a man, take responsibility, know right from wrong. Thank God she wasn't alive to see how things were working out on that score.

'You take Jay and I'll do the lawyer,' said Hassani.

'No way,' Sol replied. 'You're not to go within half a mile of Chapman.'

Something flitted across Hassani's face. 'Fine.' She adjusted the pin on her headscarf, securing it. 'You do the lawyer.'

★ ★ ★

HELEN BLACK

Sol parked not five hundred yards from the Radisson Hotel.

Hassani was about to find out that surveillance was nothing like cop shows on the telly. You waited. You drank cans of Diet Coke. You waited some more. More often than not you left having not set eyes on the target. It was more than likely that Liberty Chapman would stay in her room all day and Sol would slowly braise inside his car until his temper or his bladder exploded.

He was surprised when, in less than ten minutes, she left the hotel and headed to her car.

There was no chance that Liberty was going to risk being accosted by Rance over breakfast. Instead, she'd marched through Reception without even looking into the dining room. If he'd caught her eye, she'd have felt duty-bound to speak to him. Eyes on the door, she drank the Diet Coke she'd grabbed from the minibar in two long, grateful draughts and ignored the smell of bacon wafting towards her. She'd eat in the Butcher's Arms but, first, she needed clothes. Her suit was crumpled and smelt.

She drove straight to a shopping centre. The pickings were slim. Not one shop was somewhere she'd usually walk into, but she didn't care. She grabbed jeans, a T-shirt, trainers, and slapped her credit card on the counter. She did a quick change in the toilets and headed off to the Butcher's Arms.

The pub was old school, all swirling carpets and dark brown tables that wobbled like drunks. Liberty went straight up to the bar and flashed a smile at the barman. 'Are you serving food yet?' she asked.

He didn't smile back but slid a menu towards her. It declared that today was Spicy Saturday and the special, Chicken Biryani, came with a free drink (choice of half a lager, a small white wine or a glass of Tango or Lilt). 'Anything else on offer?' she asked.

The barman thrust his stomach towards her. He was wearing a T-shirt emblazoned with the words 'Keep Naan and Curry On',

'Fine,' said Liberty. 'Chicken Biryani will be marvellous.'

'Lager, wine, Tango or Lilt?' he said.

'Lilt.' She took a seat at the nearest table and tried to rectify the mismatched legs with a beer mat. The only other customer was an old boy, studiously working his way through the *Racing Times*, licking the end of a green felt tip, then marking one of his dead certs. His eyes were watery and the end of his tongue stained.

Ten minutes later a woman came out of the kitchen with a tray and set various dishes in front of Liberty. Biryani, chapati, mango chutney and lime pickle. It didn't look half bad. 'There you go, love,' she said, with a grin. She, too, was sporting the comedy curry T-shirt, stretched over a double D chest.

'Can I ask you something?' said Liberty.

'Course you can,' said the woman. 'Though I'm not promising an answer.'

'I'm looking for someone,' said Liberty. 'And I think she might have come in here yesterday.'

'Oh, aye?'

'Daisy Clarke? Do you know her?'

The woman nodded. She was still smiling. 'Yeah, I know Daisy. She went to school with my eldest, before all the . . . well, before the crap she's got herself into.' She touched her earring, a silver heart with a pink stone in the middle and twisted it. 'But she weren't in here yesterday.'

'Are you sure?' Liberty asked.

'Definite.'

'It's just I thought she ate in here yesterday.'

The woman laughed. 'Two things. First, Daisy don't really eat no more, if you know what I mean. Second, when she does come here it's not for the curry.'

Liberty frowned. The woman seemed very sure that Daisy hadn't been in. 'What about Frankie Greenwood?' she asked.

The woman's smile melted. 'He another friend of yours, is he?'

'Not exactly.'

'Not mine either, and certainly no friend to Daisy, of that I'm very sure.'

'But he was in here yesterday?' Liberty asked.

The woman nodded. 'Yeah, him and some cocky little shit from London. All the patter.' She mimed a mouth opening and closing with her hand. 'Some people need to learn when to shut the fuck up, don't you think?'

Liberty knew precisely what she meant, and she should probably take the advice herself, but she needed the information. 'I don't suppose you know the cocky shit's name?'

'Dave,' said the woman. 'Brixton Dave, he called himself. Acted like he owned the place.'

'Thank you,' said Liberty.

The woman moved towards the kitchen, then stopped and turned back. 'Listen, love, I'm going to give you some advice and you can take it or bin it, your choice.'

'Go on.'

'Eat your curry – I made it myself from scratch – then bugger off and forget all about Daisy the Dog and Frankie Greenwood. That pair are going to bring you nothing but grief.' She didn't wait for Liberty's reply but went on her way having said her piece.

Amira parked just up the road from the Black Cherry and watched Jay Greenwood unlock the front entrance and let himself in. She hadn't told Sol that she'd seen the lawyer at Daisy's flat, or was damned sure she had. It had been dark and she'd been taken by surprise, but as she chased the figure down the stairs, she was convinced it was Liberty Chapman. Connolly would have said there was no way she could be so certain, that she was turning this into A Thing. He'd have refused her plan to watch the Greenwoods and ordered her to go home.

Then she watched and she watched and she watched as absolutely no one else arrived.

Sighing, she picked up her phone and dialled.

'Sol Connolly.'

'Anything?' she asked.

'Chapman left the hotel at ten thirty and went over to the Butcher's Arms. She's still in there now.'

'Alone?'

'Yup. I'm watching her through the window and she's having a meal all on her tod,' said Connolly. 'What's happening at your end?'

'Absolutely bugger-all. Jay arrived at the Cherry at just before eleven and he's been in there on his own ever since. No sign of Daisy or anyone else, come to that.' Amira wondered how long they should give it, but this had been her idea so she didn't want to be the one to bring it up.

'Hold up,' said Connolly. 'Chapman's coming out. I'll call you back when I see where she heads next.'

He hung up and Amira groaned. She should be the one following the lawyer.

Twenty minutes later a silver Porsche pulled into the Black Cherry's car park and Chapman got out. Clearly being a lawyer paid better than being a copper. Then Connolly's car pulled in behind Amira's. She looked in her rear-view mirror and he gave her the thumbs-up.

When Chapman was safely inside the club, Amira slipped out of her car and into Connolly's. 'This is like having an affair,' she said.

'You'd know all about that, would you?'

'I watch telly,' she said.

HELEN BLACK

Connolly gave a short snap of laughter.

'Of course, Daisy could already be in there,' said Amira.

Connolly looked at his watch. 'If she got into work this early, it'd be the first time ever.'

'Maybe she's been in there all night,' said Amira. 'Maybe they've kept her in there. Thought of that?'

Connolly laughed again. 'Now I know you've been watching too much shite on the box. I'm pretty certain that Daisy Clarke is holed up in a crack house somewhere, trying to talk her dealer into taking a blow-job in lieu of hard cash.'

Daisy was shaking so hard her head banged against the wall behind her. The bones in her skull felt like they were being smashed by a lump hammer, but she couldn't stop herself.

'You clucking?' asked Brixton Dave.

Daisy had spent a lifetime making excuses. A touch of flu. Food poisoning. Migraine. 'Like a fucking chicken,' she replied.

He nodded, fished in his pocket and pulled out a baggie of brown. 'Is this what you're after?'

'Yeah.'

'What have we said about manners, Daisy?'

'Yes, please,' she said.

'I haven't got any needles.'

'I'll chase it,' she said.

He brought out a rectangle of tin foil and sprinkled the powder on to it. 'I've never seen the point of this stuff, if I'm being honest, Daisy.' He pushed a metal tube into her mouth and flicked his lighter. Daisy's heart jolted with longing. 'The few times I've tried it, I've just fallen asleep, you get me?'

'So what do you use for the come-down?' she asked, her eyes on the powder, which was beginning to bubble and release its delicious smoke.

'Lucozade and will-power,' he answered, with a laugh. 'Brown's a mug's game,' he said. 'But I ain't sitting here with you in a pool of shit, piss and vomit, that's for sure, so get on with it.'

She brought the tube to the smoke and inhaled, letting the duvet close around her. She felt it reheating her to the very core until she liquefied.

As her head began to drop, he pulled the foil away. 'More,' she mumbled, the tube falling out of her mouth into her lap.

'Nah.' He took the foil to the window ledge and placed it next to the roll of tape. 'I need you firing on all cylinders.' He cocked his head to one side. 'Or a couple anyway.' He rubbed his hands together. 'Phone calls to make.'

Daisy tried to lift her head but her neck was molten. 'The Greenwoods?'

'Yup.' He came back over to her, knelt down and grabbed her chin. 'We've let 'em sweat all night over what's happened to poor little Frankie.'

Daisy's eyelids began to droop until she felt them being forcibly dragged open.

'Ten minutes and we're going to make the call,' he said. 'Get yourself together.'

Jay's hair was a mess and there was a white mark on the collar of his wrinkled black shirt. 'Did you go to bed last night?' Liberty asked.

Jay shrugged, and walked across the room to the bar, picking up a pair of discarded leopard-print stilettos that had been left on the stage. At the bar, he slung them into the corner and poured himself a glass of tomato juice. 'Want one?' He didn't wait for her to answer but reached for another bottle of juice, held the top against the edge of the bar and brought his hand down with a smack, sending the bottle top skidding across the floor.

Liberty took the drink, watched as Jay poured a slug of vodka into his own. 'I've just come from the Butcher's Arms,' she said. 'Frankie was in there yesterday with some bloke going by the name of Brixton Dave.'

'What sort of name is that when it's at home?' asked Jay.

'I imagine it's someone called Dave, who comes from Brixton,' Liberty replied. 'Not especially imaginative but there you go.'

'Who the fuck does our Frankie know from Brixton?'

'I was hoping you might be able to tell me that.'

The sound of the door opening and the click-clack of heels made them both look up. 'Any more calls?' asked Mel, resplendent in a skin tight black leather skirt.

Liberty raised an eyebrow at Jay. 'I trust her with my life,' he said.

Mel sashayed towards them, her eyes on Jay's glass. She took it from him, sniffed and put it down on the bar with a loud clink. 'You need to keep a clear head, sunshine.'

Jay pressed a thumb into the dark circles under each eye. 'Have you ever heard of a Brixton Dave?'

'Are you taking the piss?' Mel asked.

'Some bloke from London that Frankie met up with yesterday,' said Jay. 'Calls himself Brixton Dave.'

Mel's skirt creaked as she walked around to the back of the bar, flicking on the pumps with one hand, jettisoning a plastic plate full of dried lemon segments into the sink with the other. Aggressively, she turned on the tap, stepping deftly out of the path of the spray. 'The only folk Frankie knows from London are her,' said Mel, with a jerk of the head at Liberty, 'and that lot he met in Spain.' She snapped off the tap and pressed the waste-disposal unit, setting in motion a gurgling and burping noise as the lemons disappeared. 'He didn't shut up about them for months, remember?'

Jay shook his head.

'Trouble is, you and Crystal never bleeding listen to him,' said Mel.

'He talks too much shite,' Jay replied.

'Don't I know it.' Mel picked up Jay's now abandoned Bloody Mary and took a drink, pulled a face and searched around until she found a bottle of Lea & Perrins. Two good shakes later she took another sip and licked her lips. 'I'd make a few calls to Marbella if I were you,' she said.

Chapter 16

January 1986
I should never have got lippy with Mrs Cole, should I? The old cow's only
gone and said she doesn't want me to go to her house. Apparently, I make
her feel 'uncomfortable'. So, now I have to see the kids at a contact centre,
a.k.a. a church hall where the heating's on the blink.

We're all sitting here in our coats, staring into our pop. It's that watery
I can see the bottom of my cup. 'Did you get some nice Christmas pres-
ents?' I ask.

Jay does the zip of his anorak right up to the top so that his mouth
and nose are hidden. I know it's cold in here, but he's just making a point.
It's my fault and we all know it.

'Some gloves and some pyjamas,' says Crystal.

I nod and smile. I'm pretty sure they need stuff like that, but you'd
think Mrs Cole would get them a game or something as well. 'I've got
you a present each,' I say. At that all three of them perk up. Even Jay.
Out of my rucksack I pull three cardboard and plastic boxes, each with a
blue-bodied Smurf inside. Papa Smurf for Jay, with his red legs and hat,
white beard down to his chest. Jokey Smurf for Frankie, his tongue lolling
out of the corner of his grin. And Smurfette for Crystal, high heels and
blonde hair running down her back. They rip open the packaging, even
Jay, who says he's too old for stuff like this, but secretly bloody loves it
and will play for hours with his little figurine, talking to it and listening
to its reply.

196

TAKING LIBERTIES

The social worker comes over from the corner of the hall where she was reading the Sun. *'What's this?' she asks.*

'Christmas presents,' I say. 'Late but still . . .'

She gives me a funny look and I worry she thinks I nicked them.

'Mr Reid gave me a gift voucher,' I tell her. 'I used it to buy these.'

The social worker nods and goes to pick up Papa Smurf, whom Jay is balancing on the top of his hand. Jay snatches him away before she can touch him. 'I'm just not sure Mrs Cole will be too happy,' she says. 'She and her husband have strong feelings about commercial merchandise.'

I don't even know what that is. 'They're just Smurfs,' I say.

'It might have been better to check with me first, Elizabeth.'

I think of all the things I could have bought in Smiths with that voucher. The new LP by Sade. A book called Lucky *that everybody at school says is ace and has loads of sex in it. Even though the lady at the till might not have sold it to me because I'm not eighteen (are books like films at the pictures?) I could have tried. Worst case, I could have bought loads of sweets and comics with my voucher. 'I can't take them back.' I wave the ripped packaging at her. 'They won't let me.'*

'Perhaps you could keep them,' she says. 'Bring them with you when the next visit is arranged.'

'And when will that be?'

She goes pink. She knows full well that I've hardly seen anything of the kids even though I've been asking and asking. 'I'm not the person you need to talk to about that,' she says.

I jump up, making my chair scrape against the floor behind me. 'So who is?' My shouting echoes around the hall. 'Who gets to decide this stuff?'

She flaps her hands up and down, like she's patting a dog with each one. 'Calm down, Elizabeth.'

'I am calm,' I say.

Frankie starts to snivel in the way that used to drive Mam doolally-tap. 'Look now,' she says to me. 'The little ones are upset.'

197

See, this is what they do. They try to blame you. Even when it's them who cause all the ructions.

Suddenly Papa Smurf flies through the air and hits the social worker on the arm. Startled, her mouth makes an O. Then Jokey hits her other arm and she takes a step back, but not before Smurfette whistles towards her and pings her right on the forehead.

'*Look now,*' *I say to her.* '*The kids are upset.*'

Crystal arrived at the Black Cherry and crossed towards them, hair bouncing, mobile in hand. If she'd had the same trouble sleeping as Jay, she didn't look it. She was wearing fresh clothes and her eyes were bright.

'Well, look at you three,' said Mel, with a wry smile. 'I'd take a bet that you were a right bloody handful as kids.'

Liberty ignored her. There was no way she could know how good they'd tried to be. How quiet. How invisible. Instead she filled Crystal in on the Brixton connection.

'Might be them blokes he met in Marbella,' said Mel.

'We should never have sent him there,' said Crystal.

Jay shook his head tiredly. 'You know why we did it.'

Liberty was about to ask, when Crystal's mobile rang. She held it up and nodded. 'Yeah?'

'Crystal?' It was Daisy, but her voice was slurred. 'Is that you?'

'Yes.'

'I've got the instruc . . .' Daisy's voice trailed away.

'Daisy?' Crystal snapped. 'Daisy?'

'Yeah.' Her words were heavy and dull. 'I've got the instructions. You need to bring five hundred grand in cash, okay?'

'Where?' asked Crystal. 'Where do we need to bring it?'

'I'll let you know.' The line went dead.

They looked at one another. If it hadn't felt real before, it certainly did now. Whoever had Frankie and Daisy had just demanded half a million pounds.

'We should go to Brixton,' said Liberty.

Crystal rolled her eyes. 'Brixton's a big place, I hear. We can't just turn up and ask around for a man called Dave.'

'She's right,' said Jay. 'We don't need to be getting off on some wild-goose chase.'

'Just hear me out,' said Liberty. 'Our best guess right now is that Frankie's in Brixton so the chances are we're going to get a call later, telling us to get the money down there. Whoever has him will control this. But if we're already there, we might be able to find out where they're keeping him, and even if we can't, we can be at the drop-off point well before they're expecting us.' She took a breath. 'We might even get there before they do.'

Crystal shook her head. 'It's a long shot, given this Brixton thing could be nothing to do with it. And even if it is, we've got to get the cash together. Unless you've got half a bar sitting around.'

Liberty had some cash reserves, but nowhere near that amount. She'd need to sell investments, probably her flat, to get her hands on that amount of money.

'Thought not,' said Crystal.

Mel put down her Bloody Mary. The tomato juice clung to the sides of the glass in thick red patches that made Liberty's stomach flip. 'Going to Brixton's the smart play,' she said.

'It's not,' Crystal replied.

'Of course it is, just not for all three of you.' She pointed an acrylic nail at Liberty. 'This one should go with Crystal.' She turned to Jay. 'You sort the money.'

Liberty glanced at her sister. If she had to go with one sibling, Jay would have been the easier option. The face on Crystal spelled out that she wasn't best pleased either.

'If it turns out to be bollocks, you can come straight back home,' said Mel to Crystal. 'No harm done.'

'It just feels like we shouldn't be going our separate ways at a time like this,' said Jay.

Mel shrugged. 'Sometimes it makes more sense.'

Sol sucked on his e-cig. The cartridge was redcurrant flavour, or that was what he'd guessed from the picture of little red balls. It was like taking a toke on burning Ribena. He switched it off in disgust and pulled out a packet of Marlboro Lights. He supposed he should ask Hassani if she minded, but what was the point? He was going to smoke one anyway.

'You think I should let this go, don't you?' she asked.

He opened the car window a crack and flicked his ash. It would be a hell of a lot easier to let this thing with the Greenwoods go, a lot wiser in the long run too, no doubt. But who was he to lecture?

'I just think that sometimes you have to commit,' she said. 'Do the right thing, you know?'

Sol blew smoke out of the side of his mouth. 'As long as that's what this is about.'

'What else?'

'Ego,' he said.

Hassani stretched her feet into the footwell. She was wearing black Converse, the white laces clean and new. 'What about you?' she asked. 'You strike me as someone who knows when you're right.'

Sol laughed. 'A long time ago another copper told me that this job was like any other addiction, that the buzz was right up there with sex and drink and drugs.'

'Well, those three things are entirely missing from my daily life,' Hassani replied.

He was about to make a crack about violins when the door to the Black Cherry opened outwards and all three Greenwoods stepped into the sunshine and put on shades. 'Hang on,' said Hassani. 'It's the Reservoir Dogs.'

The two sisters were speaking to Jay Greenwood who was nodding profusely. He hugged them both and stepped back inside the club.

'Looks like we're splitting up again,' Sol told Hassani.

'Can I please take the solicitor?' she begged. 'I don't know how much longer I can stand it out here.'

'Not a chance,' Sol replied. 'Now sneak back to your own car while that pair have their backs turned.'

Hassani groaned, but did as she was told, taking her chance to jump from Sol's car and dive back into her own, leaving him alone, as Liberty Chapman and Crystal Greenwood walked towards the silver Porsche.

It looked like he was getting two for the price of one, Sol thought.

As Liberty pulled out of the car park, a Muslim woman in hijab turned away from her in an almost aggressive motion. The body language was mirrored by Crystal who leaned on her left shoulder, her head facing the window. 'You know you don't have to come,' Liberty said. 'You could stay here with Jay.'

Crystal snapped her head around. 'I bet you'd love that.'

'Excuse me?'

'Arrive in town in your big posh car.' Crystal patted the leather seat. 'Save the day single-handed.'

Liberty sighed. 'First of all, I bet you have a perfectly nice car of your own, and if you don't, it's not because you can't afford one. Second, you said inside the club that going to

Brixton was a total waste of time so how on earth am I meant to save the day?'

'Tell me it hasn't crossed your mind.'

Liberty turned on the radio. There was no point in trying to reason with her sister. Neither spoke as they made their way through streets filled with people enjoying the weekend sunshine abandoned tops revealing soon-to-be-pink shoulders and backs. Liberty's mobile rang and the Bluetooth picked it up, flashing Ronald's number on the caller ID. 'I have to take this,' she said to Crystal.

'Liberty, darling.' Ronald's voice filled the car. 'How are you?'

'Fine, thanks,' she said.

'Any news on the Rance case?' Ronald asked. 'The old man's been on the blower saying he's less than happy with the current state of affairs.'

Liberty snorted. 'He ought to be over the moon. His nasty little son got bail, which is more than he deserves.'

There was a pause. She'd gone too far. 'I'm doing everything I can to find the victim,' she said. 'I'm on my way to a tip-off now. Hopefully she'll be there and I can get her to formally retract her statement.'

'Then the prosecution will drop their case?' Ronald asked tersely.

'Absolutely.'

'Good,' said Ronald. 'Call me when it's done.' He hung up without a goodbye.

She glanced at Crystal and spotted a smirk playing around those rosebud lips. 'What?' she demanded, but Crystal just shook her head. 'Something funny, is it?'

'I just never had you down as playing anyone's bitch.'

Liberty slammed her foot on the brake, bringing the car to a juddering halt that sent Crystal flying forward as far as her seat-belt would stretch.

'What the fuck?' she shouted.

'Just get out,' Liberty shouted back.

'What?'

'I said get out.'

When Crystal didn't move, Liberty unfastened her own belt, threw open her door and stalked around the bonnet of the car. She'd had a gutful. Crystal, Rance, Ronald, they could all go to Hell. She was done with people taking the piss. She yanked open the passenger door. 'Out.'

A group of kids who were chasing each other with Super Soakers, looked round, nudging each other at the exciting prospect of a bit of street-side argy-bargy. Liberty gave them her best nothing-to-see-here look, but they weren't going to be so easily dismissed.

'Come on, Lib,' said Crystal, smiling.

Liberty was incandescent with rage. Which of them had been itching for a row from the start? Was she the one calling Crystal someone's bitch?

'You gonna crack her?' asked one of the boys, his Leeds United shirt dark with wet patches.

'Yeah, Lib.' Crystal was laughing now. 'You gonna crack me one?'

'It's not funny,' said Liberty.

'It's not not funny,' Crystal replied.

Oh, God. This was what having a family was like. Constantly interrupted. Never getting the last word. Being mercilessly ridiculed. Liberty had forgotten how that felt. She held out the car key to Crystal. 'You'd better drive or I might be tempted to toss you out on the motorway.'

Brixton Dave was over the moon with himself. He danced across the room, playing the air drums, probably thinking about all the ways he was going to drop his five hundred grand. Daisy, on the other hand, was thinking about all the ways this could go wrong. Brixton Dave was no big player, whatever Frankie thought. He was a chancer. He'd met a crack head from a rich family and seen an opportunity. And, like all chancers, he hadn't thought things through.

What if the Greenwoods couldn't get their hands on the money or, more likely, what if they wouldn't? What if they had other ideas about how to end this? They'd do what they needed to for Frankie, but her? Jay wouldn't piss on Daisy if she were on fire. And what would a loose cannon like Brixton Dave do then?

'Why the long face, Daisy?' he asked.

'Just aching,' she said. 'Sitting here all night like this.'

'Would it be better if I cut your ties?' he asked. 'Let you move about a bit?'

She looked up at him. He couldn't be serious.

He stared at her for a moment, then burst out laughing. 'You should see your mug.' He bent from the waist, slapping his thighs. 'What a picture.'

Daisy had clients like him sometimes. They'd say something they thought was funny, more often than not at her expense, then collapse into hysterics. They wanted her to laugh, too. Like it wasn't enough that she was in the back of a car going down on them for thirty quid, they needed her to understand just how little they thought of her. She didn't give a fuck. She hated them too.

'Good one,' she told him.

He did another little jig, his arms going like windmills. 'Don't know about you but I'm Marvin Haggler,' he said. 'I could well go for a burger and chips.'

Daisy's stomach churned at the thought. These days, she lived mostly on the individual pots of chocolate mousse she bought on her way to work. On days when she was trying to take herself in hand, she'd buy milk and Coco Pops, or maybe heat up a tin of beans and hot dogs, but she usually left most of it. 'Chips would be good,' she said.

He gave a deep bow. 'What the lady wants, the lady gets.' Then he skipped over to her and pushed his face into hers. 'It goes without saying that if you try anything at all I will rip you a new one.' He waited for Daisy to nod. 'Like you say, Frankie's family don't give a shit about you so the only reason I'm keeping you in one piece is because my old mum gets the hump if I get blood on my clothes.' He reached for the roll of masking tape on the window ledge, tore off a strip and placed it over her mouth. 'Good girl,' he said, and patted the top of her head.

As soon as he'd left the room, Daisy opened her knees, which she had been keeping tightly together. There, trapped between her thighs, was the metal piece of tube, one end still blackened from the smoke.

Chapter 17

March 1986

The new social worker's got flashes in her hair. I wonder if she had them done on student night at the local tech because they look like someone did them with one eye and a knitting needle. As she drives me to my new placement, she talks non-stop. She tells me all about her new cat and how she's called it Snowdrop. She tells me how when she first brought it home, it hid under a bookcase, did a shit and stayed there. Eventually her husband had to roll up his newspaper and whack the poor thing on the arse until it ran out and she could catch it.

The last social worker left after what happened at the contact centre. Apparently she was 'very upset' and put in for a transfer to the Living with Disabilities team. This one doesn't want to dwell on what went on before but says we all need to use our energy to 'look forward'. I'm trying, honestly I am, but it's hard when I don't know where I'm going to be living, if I'll be going to a different school or when I'll next see the kids.

'I think you're going to like this new placement,' she says.

'Is it a care home?' I ask.

'A residential unit,' she corrects me. 'No.'

'But it's not with a foster-family?'

'Not as such.' She pushes her stripy fringe out of her eyes. 'There's just one foster-mother, who specializes in looking after teens.'

'I'm nearly twelve,' I say.

'Let's not split hairs, Elizabeth,' she replies.

I certainly wouldn't want to split hers. With the amount of bleach put in it, a clump would probably come off in my hand. And then I bet they'd accuse me of pulling it out.

We turn off the main road on to a country lane full of pot holes. We bounce our way down it until we meet another car, when the social worker huffs and puffs as she has to reverse back a bit. We carry on like this, back and forth, back and forth, until we get to a gate. Well, when I say gate, I mean a hole where a gate should be. The actual gate has been torn off its hinges and is lying on the grass.

'Here we are.' The social worker drives through the hole. 'Langton Manor.'

When we get up to the house, my jaw drops open. Perched up on a grass verge is a grey brick mansion about a thousand years old. The roof is a huge white zigzag of rotting wood. One of the three chimneys (three!) has collapsed and the broken bricks are scattered on the ground near the door. It's like something from Hammer House of Horror. *'Geraldine is a very good person,' the social worker says, with a firm nod. 'Very good indeed to do what she does. Try to remember that, Elizabeth.'*

We get out of the car, and as we walk up to the door, it opens with the loudest creak I've ever heard and a woman steps out. She's about sixty and is wearing a donkey jacket, the lapels covered with badges.

The social worker gives such a wide smile, I worry her cheeks will split. 'Geraldine, this is Elizabeth,' she says, but unfortunately she trips on the crazy paving and falls over.

'Careful there,' Geraldine roars. 'The bloody thing is full of cracks.' She puts out a hand to help the social worker back to her feet. 'I ought to get it fixed but it's too damn expensive.'

The social worker says something but Geraldine isn't listening. Instead, she turns to me. 'So what do they call you, Elizabeth? Lizzie? Beth?'

'Lib,' I answer.

'Lib? Never heard that one before.'

'It was my brother's first word,' I tell her. 'Mam assumed he was try-ing for Liz, but he couldn't manage it.'

'Could be worse. Are you hungry?' she asks.

I'm about to be polite and say I'm fine but she's already heading back inside.

'Of course you are. Eat me out of house and home you lot will.'

The hallway is dark and cold and enormous. Like a cave. There's a bucket parked right in the middle of it and Geraldine taps it with her foot. 'Careful as you go. Bloody roof's leaking again.' She throws open a door at the end of the hallway and we're in the kitchen but Geraldine doesn't take her coat off. I don't blame her. It's just as cold in here as outside. And there are two more buckets catching steady drips from the ceiling. 'Sit,' she barks at us, so we plonk ourselves down at the square wooden table, with eight different chairs to choose from.

On one of the counters there's a glass dome, which she lifts to reveal a fruit loaf. She cuts a slice, chucks it on a plate and passes it to me. It looks a bit dry and burned at the edges but I know I've got to eat it anyway. I start nibbling and read some of the badges on Geraldine's jacket. Nuclear Power, No Thanks. Free Nelson Mandela. *Some are just symbols. Like an upside-down trident and a circle with a cross stuck to it. Not much point to them if only she knows what they mean, is there?*

'I'll be honest with you, Lib,' she says. 'I'm not actually very good at being dishonest. If you bugger me about I'll send you packing, but if you don't, I'm sure we'll get along like a house on fire.'

I glance around the kitchen, taking in the chipped tiles, the missing cupboard doors, the damp patches. A fire is all this house is good for.

It was a busy Saturday afternoon in Brixton when Liberty and Crystal arrived. They'd made brilliant time, due in one part to a clear motorway, and in another thanks to Crystal topping a hundred most of the way, flashing any car that dared to get in front of her.

'There might be cameras on the bridge,' Liberty had warned, as they passed junction twenty six.

'We don't bother with speeding tickets in this family.' Crystal laughed until she caught Liberty's withering glance. 'Joking obviously.'

She pulled into a Tesco car park, hoping to find a spot, driving around a group of boys crowded around an ancient Peugeot 106 with its sound system blaring, laughing and shouting at one another, smoking weed. That was the thing about Brixton: although the property developers had moved in and slaved their arses off trying to gentrify the area, it remained, at heart, a vibrant working-class neighbourhood made up of many races. The middle classes might have moved there because they could no longer afford Clapham but they had not driven away the old guard.

Crystal found a space and nudged the Porsche into it. 'So, what's the plan?'

'Call Jay and see if he got anything from the people in Spain,' Liberty replied.

'And if he didn't?'

'For fuck's sake, just call him.'

Crystal reached for her mobile and dialled.

'I was just about to bell you,' said Jay.

'Tell me we haven't come all this way for nothing,' said Crystal.

A couple of girls had joined the Peugeot crowd, all gold hoops and twerking butts. One had braids interlaced with red and orange strands of PVC. She grabbed a joint from the lips of one of the boys, took a draw and pushed it back between his teeth.

'No one can tell me anything concrete,' said Jay.

'Naturally,' said Crystal.

'But they do remember Frankie hanging around with some lads from south London when he was over there.'

'Did the name Brixton Dave ring any bells?' Crystal asked.

'Not the Brixton bit, but they did think one of them was called Dave. Bit of an arsehole, by all accounts. Cocky, mouthy, a bit too fond of the Bolivian marching powder.'

'Sounds like exactly the kind of twat our Frankie would take up with,' said Crystal, with a sigh. 'Any ideas on where to find him?'

'Like I say, nothing concrete, but I'm waiting on a call from Danny Macdonald.'

'I thought he was doing a five stretch.'

'Nah,' said Jay. 'That was his brother, Declan. Danny's out in Marbella running a bar. If anyone knows anything it'll be Danny.'

Sol breathed a sigh of relief when the Greenwood sisters finally turned off their engine. His petrol gauge had been winking red and angrily empty for several miles. Natasha never let her car go below the halfway mark, a habit Sol had intended to copy but had never managed. It would have been typical if he had lost them in order to refill the car when he'd managed to tail them all this way, despite their best bat-out-of-hell impression. But Brixton! Where did that come from?

Hassani called him on the mobile. She sounded pissed off. 'He hasn't moved,' she grumbled.

Sol kept his eye on the Porsche. Liberty and Crystal had parked up but were still inside. 'What?'

'Jay Greenwood,' said Hassani. 'He's still inside the Black Cherry. I've been waiting out here for hours now.'

'I told you surveillance was boring.'

'I'm gonna have to leave before I kill myself,' said Hassani. 'Or wet myself. Where are you?'

'Brixton,' he replied.

'Brixton? In London?'

'Yup.'

'Is that where Chapman lives, then?' Hassani sounded shocked. 'I'd have expected a swankier part of town.' Sol heard papers rustle at the other end of the phone. 'I've got her custody record here and the address she gave the sergeant was in Hampstead.'

'You have her custody record?' asked Sol.

Hassani gave a small cough. 'I photocopied it.'

Sol shook his head. Hassani was on self-destruct.

'No one saw me,' she told him. 'I waited until the sergeant was away from his desk.'

God, that was even worse. When he got back to Yorkshire he was going to have a really long chat with Hassani, try to make her see that she couldn't open herself up like this. 'I don't think they're here on a social visit,' he said. 'We're parked outside Tesco's.'

Hassani let out a long breath. 'I can't believe you're getting all the excitement and my backside's numb.'

'Get over it,' he said, and hung up.

Daisy wanted to scream as she dropped the metal tube for the tenth time. Once again, she had to pick it up with the tips of her third and fourth fingers, then move it towards her index fingers. The first time, she'd been too hasty and the tube had pinged away from her, bouncing from her leg to the floor, where it rolled away. She'd had to bum-shuffle to retrieve it, then bum-shuffle back in case Brixton Dave came in.

By the fourth attempt, the sweat had been pouring off her, but she'd worked out that she needed to use a gentle rolling motion to get the tube where she wanted it. The trouble was, even when she had the thing between her index fingers, it wasn't anywhere near the tape binding her wrists. She needed to bend it around, so that the end of the tube was touching the end of the tape, but by now her hands were slick and the tube kept slipping away.

Sunlight flooded through the window, the glass making the heat unbearable as it smacked Daisy in the face. Outside people would be doing all the things that people did. Daisy had to think for a second what those things might be. For a long time now all she had ever done was work to get money to buy drugs. Take the

211

drugs. Work to get money for more drugs. Ordinary people, though, they did other stuff, didn't they? They went to the shops, mowed their lawns, watched the telly. She used to feel sorry for people like that, with their stupid boring lives.

She held the tube as firmly as she could between her index fingers, then slowly spun it towards her, rotating it 180 degrees until it was now millimetres from the tape. All she needed to do was swing it back and forth a few times and connect. The edge of the tube would then hopefully nick her bindings.

She was so close. She just needed not to drop the damn thing again.

The sound of a door slamming reverberated around the walls. He was back. Shit. In panic Daisy let go of the tube, watching as once again it rolled away.

The Nike Air Max thundered up the stairs.

She tried to scoot towards the tube, but fell to the side, banging her shoulder.

The door was flung open. 'What the fuck?' he shouted.

Daisy closed her eyes and played dead. What else could she do?

He grabbed a handful of her hair and pulled her upright. She wanted to scream, but kept her face immobile, her eyes shut. The tape came off her mouth in an agonizing rip.

'Wake up!' he shouted. There was a fierce sting as he slapped her hard across the cheek.

'For fuck's sake.' He shook her hard. 'Wake up, you silly bitch.'

Daisy fluttered her eyelids as if desperately trying to open them.

Brixton Dave let go of her and laughed. 'Thought you'd gone and died on me there, Daisy.'

She opened her mouth slightly, then let it fall shut. 'I think . . .' She tried to sound as groggy as possible. 'I think I fainted.' He hadn't noticed the tube, lying next to her. 'It's so hot.'

'You wanna drink?'

Daisy nodded and watched him leave the room, muttering to himself.

As soon as he was through the door, she leaned over and tried to grab the tube. On the third attempt she had it in her grasp then quickly dropped it between her legs and clapped them shut.

Liberty got out of the car and frowned into the heat. Dad had always said that the south was 'two coats warmer'. That London was hotter still because of the pollution. Lord knew where he got it all from. As far as she could remember, he'd only ever been to London once on a coach trip to see a rugby match. He'd got so pissed he'd missed the game and managed to lose his shoes.

'Christ on a bike,' said Crystal. 'Let's get out of this lot, shall we?'

Liberty smiled at her sister. Her pale skin didn't like the sun and Crystal didn't like the freckles it sent out in defence. 'There are plenty of bars and cafés up by the tube station on Brixton Road,' she said. 'We can get a cold drink there, while we wait for Jay to call back.'

They fell in step, side by side.

'I wouldn't have thought this part of town would be your cup of tea,' said Crystal.

It wasn't. Liberty stuck mostly to the north side of the river. 'I've been to a few gigs.' She put on her shades. 'At the Academy.' In fact she'd been to one with a man called Alex, whom she'd dated briefly. He was an accountant and recently divorced, keen to relive the youth he vaguely remembered, before marriage and tax returns had ground down his soul. When he'd suggested they go to see Morrissey, she'd assumed it was a joke. It wasn't. Alex had worn a flower-print shirt and jumped around to the music, spilling lager from his plastic pint glass.

As Liberty and Crystal arrived at a packed bar close to the tube station, a couple got up to leave a pavement table. 'Grab those seats,' Liberty instructed her sister.

'Can't we go inside?'

'It'll be even hotter than out here and there'll be nowhere to sit.' She pushed Crystal towards the table. 'Don't worry, I'll angle the umbrella over you, Snow White.'

Crystal sat down with a 'humph' and checked every inch of her was in the shade as Liberty fiddled with the giant parasol. She then headed inside and bought two Diet Cokes. As they sipped their drinks, watching the crowds pass by, Crystal asked, 'Are you happy down here, Lib?'

'I've got a good job and a nice flat,' Liberty replied.

'That's not what I asked.'

Liberty was glad she'd brought the sunglasses. 'What about you? Harry seems like a good bloke.'

'He's the best. He knows all about this family, what a beautiful bunch of fuck-ups we are, and he married me anyway.'

'So you *are* happy, then?'

Crystal licked the moisture from her lips. 'I'm a Greenwood. Does any of us do happy?' Her mobile vibrated against the wooden slats of the table and she grabbed it to answer, putting it on speaker phone. 'Jay? What do you know?'

'I'm still waiting on Danny to call,' Jay replied.

Crystal groaned. 'What's he playing at? We can't just sit around here much longer.'

'He's probably sleeping it off somewhere. Siesta and all that.'

Liberty zoned out the rest of their conversation. Crystal's endless bitching was annoying, but she was spot on: they couldn't just wait around. There had to be something they could do. She imagined Frankie and Daisy arriving in London. What did they do? She turned her head towards the station. They'd have taken the tube from King's Cross, wouldn't they? But then what?

214

Maybe someone met them. Maybe Brixton Dave was there when they arrived.

Or maybe they'd had an address. Somewhere to meet him. How would they do that? Brixton was a big place and they wouldn't have had the smallest clue where they were going. A pair of hopeless cases stumbling along Brixton Road. Liberty looked up the street as if she could actually see Daisy and Frankie. Then she did see something and it made her smile. She stood up and walked away from the table.

'What the hell?' Crystal shouted.

Liberty pointed to the cab office just a few hundred yards away.

The woman at the desk wore a diamanté pendant in the shape of a seahorse and a black net bow in her hair.

'Were you working in here yesterday?' Liberty asked.

The woman narrowed her eyes. 'Why?'

'I'm looking for someone and I think he might have taken a taxi from here.'

The woman sat back in her chair. 'You police?'

Liberty shook her head and scrolled through the photographs on her phone until she found the one of Frankie and herself taken at Jay's house. She winced at the sight of them both. Herself grinning inanely, dead behind the eyes, Frankie corpse-white and sweating. 'This is my brother.' She held up her phone for the woman to see. 'I really need to find him.'

The woman checked out the photograph but said nothing. Liberty had anticipated this and extracted a twenty-pound note from her back pocket. She placed it on the desk, keeping her fingers on top of it. 'If you were here yesterday, can you just tell me if he came in?'

The woman stared at Liberty, but Liberty felt the note slide away from under her hand. 'Yeah, I seen him,' she said. 'Him and some girl, right?'

Liberty nodded.

'We don't usually take them kind if we can help it,' said the woman.

'Them kind?'

The woman kissed her teeth. 'Junkies. Too often they try to run off without paying. But things was quiet yesterday and the drivers was gettin' vexed.' She touched the bow in her hair. 'Better when it rains and nobody wants to walk.'

Carefully, Liberty pulled out another twenty-pound note and placed it in the same spot as before, this time applying more pressure with her fingertips. 'I don't suppose you could look up where the driver took them?' Again, she felt a tug on the note, but she wasn't about to let it go until she had what she wanted. The woman kissed her teeth once more and tapped on her computer. Then she scribbled on a receipt with a pencil.

Liberty released the money and took the receipt. 'It's been a pleasure doing business with you.'

Chapter 18

April 1986

Outside, you might get away without wearing a coat, but not here in the kitchen. We can see our breath.

'Is this a castle?' Crystal asks.

'No,' I tell her. 'Just a big house.'

'Is it haunted?' Jay asks.

I laugh, but I don't know why. I didn't sleep a wink the first week I was here, and not just because the mattress on my bed is lumpier than Mam's mash. I smile at all three of them and ruffle Frankie's hair as he picks at a brick of Geraldine's homemade banana bread.

The fact that I've finally got to see them is down to Snowy. She's one of Geraldine's mates. There's a gang of 'em come over to Langton Manor every Tuesday night. They're all dead posh but dead scruffy. They don't seem to mind the cold, and laugh about how much worse it was when they were at Greenham Common.

One night a woman with pink hair and yellow waterproof trousers asked me if I had brothers and sisters. When I told her I did but I'd not been allowed to see them for months she looked shocked and got me to tell the rest. Snowy, who's the one that never takes her Benny hat off, said she knew some of the top brass at social services and would 'make a nuisance' of herself. Bingo, a contact visit.

'I've got something for you lot,' I tell the kids. They sit there, all excited, little white clouds puffing from their mouths. I go to the cupboard and

217

pull out three Jelly Tots Easter eggs. Easter has been and gone, but none of us is going to mither about a detail like that.

'We're not meant to have chocolate,' says Jay.

'Which is why we're gonna eat the whole bloody lot now and tell nobody,' I say.

Crystal mimes zipping up her mouth. I do the same and add in throwing the key over my shoulder for good measure.

We open up the boxes and get stuck in. When everybody's face is smeared brown, Jay wiggles his hand deep into the pocket of his jeans. 'We got you something,' he says. He goes a bit solemn as he tries to reach whatever it is in his pocket. At last he gives a little grunt and shows me.

It's a bangle. Gold. I take it from him and check the hallmark. Real gold. 'Where did you get this, Jay?'

'A shop.' There's no way he got this in a shop. Who would let an eight-year-old buy a gold bangle? And where would he get the money? 'Don't you like it?'

'It's lovely,' I tell him. 'But where's the box?'

'What box?'

'The box it came in,' I say. 'Something as pretty as this must have come in a box to keep it safe.'

'I lost it,' says Jay.

The phone rings. Geraldine keeps it on a table in the hallway at the foot of the stairs. When she answers it her voice comes booming into the kitchen. 'Oh dear,' she says. 'Oh, Lord.'

I panic. Is it the social worker? Or the kids' foster-mother? Have they found out that Jay's nicked the bangle? 'Say nothing,' I instruct him. 'Do you hear me?'

He nods and I shove it into my own pocket.

When Geraldine comes into the kitchen, she looks serious. I mean, she never looks like she's having a laugh, but this is worse than normal. 'Lib, can I have a word?' she asks. 'In private?' I follow her out of the kitchen and she closes the door. We stand by the bucket, half full of water. 'No easy way to say this, Lib, so I'll just come out with it, shall I?'

I nod, but my heart is beating so fast and I want to tell her 'No. Please don't say Jay's in trouble. That he'll have to leave his placement. That I'll have to leave this placement. That we'll all have to start again somewhere else.'

'It's your dad,' she says.

'What about him?'

She puts her finger into her ear and wiggles it about.

'Is he okay?' I ask.

Geraldine puts a hand on my shoulder and I try not to think about the wax she must be smearing on my coat. 'He wants to see you,' she tells me.

I breathe out. I already know this. He's been banging on about it since he got nicked at the hospital.

'Thing is, Lib, he's got himself a decent solicitor and has made an application to the court,' says Geraldine. 'I'm afraid you're going to have to speak to a judge.'

Liberty raced across the road and narrowly missed getting splattered by a cycle rickshaw. When had they become a thing in England, never mind Brixton?

'Where did you go running off to?' Crystal asked.

'Cab office.'

'We don't need a cab, Lib, we've got a frigging car,' said Crystal. 'And, anyway, where the hell are we meant to be going?'

Liberty brandished the receipt, large childish handwriting scrawled across it.

'You're really starting to annoy me now,' said Crystal.

As they drove from the vibrancy of Brixton centre to the Goldfarm estate, it was as if they had crossed an invisible threshold. Few people were out on the streets, despite the warm weather, and those who were out and about had no Saturday amble to them, but strode purposefully. Occasional groups of boys sat on railings, all in black, hoods up, heads turned from the CCTV cameras mounted high on poles with anti-climb paint and spikes.

'Has there been an apocalypse someone forgot to mention?' Liberty asked.

Crystal shook her head as she took in the boarded-up shops. 'Christ knows what people round here do when they need a pint of milk.'

The strange thing was that the area itself wasn't run-down. The pavements were clean, the walls well-pointed and graffiti-free for the most part. A world away from Crosshills with its litter-strewn yards and dilapidated fences, recs full of kids at its grubby beating heart.

'Maybe they're all dairy-free,' Liberty replied.

They rounded a corner and found another group of boys sitting on the pavement, several bikes laid down beside them. The boys looked up at the Porsche, seemed puzzled, muttered to each other.

The address on the receipt was up ahead. A block of flats, not high-rise but three floors. Neat white windows, blue panels. Patch of grass in front.

'Now what?' Crystal asked.

'Let's just take a minute,' Liberty replied. 'See if there's anything to see.'

Keeping the two women in sight had been relatively easy in the centre of Brixton. Lots of people, lots of noise. Even when Chapman and her sister had stopped for a drink, Sol had ducked into a shop doorway, able to keep eyes on them without being spotted himself. When they'd gone back to their car, his heart had begun to sink. He really was going to run out of petrol any second. He turned off the air-con, even though he was sweating, to preserve fuel. When the women drove to the Goldfarm estate, he groaned. Groups of youngsters on the street immediately clocked him. A couple flipped him the finger, more made their thumb and forefinger into the shape of a C. Telling him they knew exactly what he was: a cop and, of course, the other C-word. No doubt they'd be on their phones alerting their brethren to the appearance of an undie.

Sol sighed. He didn't give a shit about the drug deals going on round here, but the kids didn't know that.

When Chapman's car pulled over, he did the same a few hundred yards away, hoping that the boys wouldn't draw attention to him, relieved when they evaporated into an alleyway. He knew that this was pretty much the end of the line today. The car was running on fumes and would soon refuse to start. Getting stuck there with zero back-up was the last thing on his to-do list. He called Hassani. 'You wet yourself yet?'

'Very funny,' she replied. 'Where are you?'

'The dark side of the moon.' Someone whizzed past on a bike, so close he could hear the spokes whir. 'The Goldfarm estate. What about you?'

'I gave up on Jay. I think he must have died or something,' said Hassani. 'I went back to the pub you saw Chapman go in earlier.'

'And?'

'And they don't talk to the police.'

Sol chuckled. 'What did you expect?'

'A bit of cooperation, maybe. A bit of community cohesion to keep people like the Greenwoods from running the place like the Wild West.'

He laughed some more. 'You're assuming people are unhappy with the status quo.'

'Yeah, well, they needn't come crying to me when it's their daughter getting her head kicked in, like Kyla and Daisy.'

The passenger door of the Porsche opened and Chapman got out, bending to speak to her sister, who was still in the driver's seat. 'Gotta go,' he told Hassani, and hung up.

Chapman carried on speaking through the door. She was dressed down, in jeans and T-shirt, hair in a ponytail, sunglasses on top of her head, but she still carried herself with the assurance of someone used to being in control. Sol could imagine Crystal losing the plot, throwing a glass or a punch. When Chapman was angry with you, she would simmer and make you feel ridiculous. He couldn't say which would be worse.

At last Chapman closed the car door, leaving her sister inside. They were splitting up.

Now what? It would be easier, and safer, to stay in his car and watch Crystal. The likelihood was that Chapman would be back soon. But he'd never been one for easy or safe, had he?

Shafted. Royally, totally shafted. Frankie slumped in the corner of the room and felt tears sting his eyes. It was pathetic to cry, and what good would it do? He couldn't help himself. This was supposed to be it, the deal that would set him up, make Crystal and Jay begin to trust him. Instead it had just confirmed all their views of him: an idiot, a waste of space, a liability.

Daisy had tried to warn him. She'd said it didn't feel right, but Frankie wouldn't listen, would he? Not Frankie. In any storm he was the one trying to catch the lightning bolt. It had been a set-up from the start, and Frankie had walked right into it, trusting Brixton Dave because of a couple of weeks in the sun. Stupid, stupid, stupid. He'd opened himself up to this and, worse, he'd opened Daisy up to it because, truth be told, Jay and Crystal would probably get him out of this, but Daisy? Not a chance. Poor Daisy, who had just been trying to please Frankie, like the dog she was.

TAKING LIBERTIES

Back in Marbella there'd been a girl, well, there'd been a lot of girls, but this one in particular had been around all the time, sniffing out what she wanted. Someone always ended up with her if they didn't pull a decent bird. Frankie couldn't remember her name. She was pretty but thin, with eyes dark in her sockets, up for whatever, even if whatever left her with bruises. One night he'd ended up lying next to her on a sun bed, smoking a fat one, trying to soften the come-down. He'd asked why she stayed out there. No friends and no family. Just Dave and his crew laughing at her, fucking her, hurting her. She'd told Frankie that she had no friends and family back home so she might as well let herself get ruined in the sun.

Tears streamed down his cheeks now as he looked around the empty room. He dragged a breath through his snotty nose. What was that girl's name? And what had happened to her?

The grass was surprisingly lush under Liberty's feet. No bald patches worn away by a thousand footballs or ruts from the endless push of buggies. She opened the gate in front of the flats and briefly looked over her shoulder to the Porsche, giving Crystal a wave. Sitting and watching had produced nothing useful so they'd agreed that one of them should do a walk-past of the flats.

Liberty said that it should be her. If the people who had Frankie had done their homework they might recognize Crystal, but there was no way they could know about Liberty. Crystal had argued — didn't she always? — but Liberty had won. As she reached the row of ground-floor doors and windows, she wondered if it wasn't a hollow triumph. Yes, Frankie might be in one of these flats, but that would mean whoever had taken him would be in there too. Liberty's blood pumped a little harder at the thought.

The trick would be to walk with enough speed not to be mistaken for a snooper, while actually doing some snooping. She

223

pressed a hand to her chest and set off. Unfortunately the first flat had blinds; the second had nets. Which was obvious, now she thought about it. Anyone with a ground-floor flat and an ounce of sense would put up something between themselves and potential nosy-parkers. She slowed her pace slightly as she passed, pricking her ears for any clues, and heard the sounds of a television and a baby crying. One window was open a crack, the smell of onions and garlic wafting through.

When she reached the end of the row, Liberty was no wiser than when she'd started. If Frankie was inside one of these flats, there was no way for her to discover that from the outside. She looked up to the first and second floors. Was there any point in going up there?

A plume of white smoke rose above the block, carrying the scent of charred meat. Someone was having a barbecue round the back. Liberty stopped. That meant there were gardens round the back, or terraces. Doors might be open. She'd promised Crystal she wouldn't move from her sight line, but she'd be quick, just a brief look-see. She pointed to where she was headed but couldn't see Crystal's reaction. Probably for the best.

As she passed around the side of the end flat, the smell of sausages and burgers became stronger and her stomach rumbled. She was imagining the taste of ketchup when she caught sight of a figure in her peripheral vision. She snapped her head around, but whoever it was had darted away, making her scalp prickle. She retraced her steps, searching for a glimpse. No one. The street was empty, the muffled sound of the baby's cries louder now.

Liberty was nervous and her mind was playing tricks. She needed to do a swift check around the back, then return to Crystal so they could plan their next move. Her feet moved with a confidence she didn't feel, and soon she was behind the flats, looking into a row of small gardens. The smoke from the barbecue billowed towards her, stinging her eyes. She stumbled through it, wafting it from her face.

When she was upwind she could see that a number of flats had their back doors and windows open. The vantage-point was further away than at the front of the block, but she might catch a glimpse of something. Or at least narrow down which flats definitely did not contain her younger brother. She moved along until she was looking at the end flat. Unlike the others, the garden was overgrown, the paint on the door dirty and scuffed. She was considering how different it looked from the other flats, when the door opened and a young lad emerged, dressed in black, hood up. He closed the door behind him and jumped onto a bike that was leaning against the wall, then disappeared in a whir of spokes.

A drugs house. 'Bingo,' Liberty whispered under her breath.

Chapter 19

June 1986

It's funny to see Geraldine all dressed up. I mean, she's not wearing a skirt or anything, but she's ditched the donkey jacket for a sort of raincoat with a belt. She's even polished her shoes. We decided that I'd be best off sticking with my school uniform. Though I've put tights on rather than socks because I don't want to seem like some daft kid.

She drives like someone who detests it, the gears grinding and screeching, Geraldine swearing and shouting. I'm glad when we get to the courthouse. It's not what I was expecting, though I'm not sure what I was expecting. This is like a new doctor's surgery or something. A square building with red bricks. The car park's empty except for two cars.

Just inside the door there's a reception desk with a man sitting behind it. He's in a black uniform, but he's not a copper. He's on the phone and Geraldine stares at him impatiently. She hates to be kept waiting. 'I fail to see what can be more pressing than getting you before the judge, Lib,' she says, with a huff.

At last a bloke comes off the phone and smiles. 'Can I help you?' he asks.

'We have an appointment at three,' Geraldine replies, showing him the face of her watch. 'To see His Honour Judge Monkton.'

'Let me look at the list,' says the man.

Geraldine rolls her eyes as if she's never met such an imbecile. I've seen her give that look to everyone from the plumber who said she needed a new boiler to the social worker who said it might be better for me not to do this. I've been on the receiving end of it a few times. The only person who escapes it is Snowy. 'There's a hearing and we're going to be late,' she says, moving past the reception desk.

'Right.' The man's flustered but he doesn't want to let us past. 'Is it the Greenwood application?'

'Yes.'

The man goes bright pink. 'They're running a bit late.'

'Well, that's bloody unfortunate,' says Geraldine. 'Because it took us a good hour to get here and Elizabeth had to take the afternoon off school.'

I flash him my uniform to underline her point.

'Right. It's just that I don't have anything to do with the timings,' he says.

'Oh dear,' says Geraldine, as if she couldn't give a shit.

'Could you wait here, please?' He almost runs through a door behind him, leaving us standing. There's a little table and three chairs at the other side of the room so I go and sit down, but Geraldine leans over the man's now empty desk and rummages through the papers that are scattered over it. That's another thing about Geraldine: wherever she goes she acts like she owns the place. Mam would have called her la-di-da, and she is a bit, but she's not stuck-up.

At last the man comes back. 'The judge says he's not quite ready, but since there's a child involved he'll expedite matters.'

'Good grief, man, we weren't expecting to find him in makeup and a ra-ra skirt.'

The man gives a thin laugh. 'Right. Well, if you want to come this way.' He opens the door to a corridor and lets us in, holding it open. We walk to the end where there's a door with a sign on it saying 'Chambers'. The man gives one loud rap and lets us in. 'Judge Monkton,' says the man. 'This is Elizabeth Greenwood and . . .' He looks at Geraldine but she's already pushed past him, her hand outstretched towards the judge.

'Geraldine Miller,' she announces. 'Elizabeth's foster-parent.'

The judge takes Geraldine's hand and gets his arm pumped for his trouble. When she lets go, he flexes his fingers as if he needs to get some feeling back into them. 'Do sit down, ladies,' he says, with a smile, and waves at some chairs. 'Now, Elizabeth, how are you feeling today?'

I've been asked that question like a million times by a million different people. To be honest, it's pissing me off. 'Fine.' I sit down. 'Completely fine.'

'And you know what you're doing here?'

I nod. I understand perfectly well. Dad wants to see me. He says it's because he loves me and misses me. And the judge wants to know what I think about that. I cross my legs and feel a trickle of sweat running down the back of my knee. I wish I'd worn socks and not a pair of tights.

Brixton Dave wasn't smiling any more. Daisy watched him carefully and could see the step-change. He was checking his phone, making phlegmy noises in the back of his throat. Something was wrong. 'What's up?' she asked.

'Police on the estate,' he replied. 'The Greenwoods wouldn't be that fucking stupid, would they?'

Daisy gave a snort. She was absolutely certain that neither Jay nor Crystal would have called the police.

'How can you be sure?' he demanded.

'I know them,' Daisy replied. 'The police are the last people they want sniffing about their business. And, anyway, how the hell would they know where we are? I don't even know where we are.'

That seemed to pacify him. Just. But he kept checking his phone, muttering under his breath. Daisy needed to distract him before he lost the plot. 'Can I get a drink?' she asked him.

He looked up from his phone like he'd only just noticed that he was sharing the room with a piece of shit. It made Daisy shiver. 'What?' he asked.

'A drink.' She nodded towards a bottle of Tango at his feet. 'Can I have some, please?'

His face was something between a sneer and a snarl but he scooped up the bottle of pop and brought it over to her. 'Thirsty, are ya?'

Daisy nodded.

His eyes locked on to hers, he shook the bottle, took off the top and sprayed her with the fizzy orange liquid. 'There you go,' he said, emptying the rest of the bottle over her head.

Daisy had had men pouring various liquids over her. The trick was to shut your eyes and mouth tight. As she battened down the hatches, she knew that she was running out of time.

Liberty watched the flat. More lads arrived on bikes, brakes screaming as they came to a halt outside, then disappeared inside for a few minutes before pedalling away again. There was no mistake. It was a drugs house.

Her mobile rang and she turned her back to the flat to answer.

'Crystal?'

'Where are you?' her sister demanded. 'You were meant to stay where I could see you.'

'I'm round the back of the block,' Liberty replied. 'You can get a better view here.' Another wave of smoke from a barbecue floated by, the smell making her stomach growl. She realized she was starving.

'And have you seen anything?' Crystal asked.

'I think so, yeah.'

'What?' Crystal shouted down the phone. 'You've seen Frankie?'

Liberty took a nervous look over her shoulder. 'No. But I've found somewhere he might be.'

'What are you talking about, Lib?'

Another boy, maybe thirteen or fourteen, rode up to the door of the flat. He caught Liberty looking and raised his left hand, made the shape of a gun and pulled the trigger. Liberty whipped her head away from him. 'Our Frankie's got a drug problem, right?' she asked.

Crystal sighed.

'Well, I'm standing very near to a flat where they're serving up,' said Liberty.

'And you'd know that how?' Crystal asked.

'For fuck's sake, I grew up on the Crosshills. I know a drugs house when I see one, same as you do.'

'So what are you going to do?'

Liberty checked the flat again. The boy had ditched his bike and was now inside. What was she going to do? She couldn't just knock on the door and ask to have a look around. The boy came out, tucking something into his waistband, but he didn't get back on his bike. Instead he walked away from the flat towards Liberty.

'I said what are you going to do, Lib?'

Liberty's heart thumped as the boy neared. He was running his bottom teeth over his top lip, making a small piercing in the skin above bob up and down. 'I'll call you back,' she whispered, and hung up.

The boy stopped a few feet from Liberty and jerked his head up, part threat, part question. What are you doing here? What do you want? 'What you looking for?' he said. His voice hadn't broken.

She was about to explain that she was looking for her brother, when she realized his question was not a general one. He wanted to know what she was looking for that might be found in his waistband. She almost laughed. Did she really look like she wanted to buy some drugs? Clearly this boy thought so. Still, maybe it was a way to get inside the flat to see if Frankie was there. 'I want some coke,' she said.

'Powder or rock?' the boy asked.

'Powder,' Liberty replied. 'Two grams.'

The boy nodded and held out his hand. 'Ninety.'

Liberty reached into her bag and took out her purse. For a second, she wondered if he might steal it and run off, but he just waited, hand outstretched, until she placed the notes on his palm. Presumably there was more money in drug-dealing than in street robbery.

'Wait around that corner,' the boy said, flapping his hand around the side of the flat. 'Another younger will come.'

'Can't I wait in the flat?' Liberty asked.

The boy let out a *pffft*. 'Shut up.'

'How do I know I'll get what I paid for?'

He gave her the once-over. 'You ain't from this area, is it?'

Liberty shook her head. 'North of the river.'

He nodded, as if that made perfect sense, and turned to move away, their conversation over.

Crystal was already calling Liberty's mobile when Liberty made her way around the corner as she'd been instructed.

'What's happening, Lib?'

'I'm buying some coke,' Liberty replied.

'What?' Crystal shrieked down the phone. 'Have you completely lost the plot?'

Liberty leaned against the wall, keeping her eye on the flat. 'I'm trying to get inside, remember.'

'And buying drugs is going to help how exactly?'

Liberty sighed. 'I don't know *exactly*, do I? I need to get inside somehow. Look, have you got a better idea?' She paused and listened to Crystal breathing heavily. 'Thought not. Look, we know Frankie and Daisy came to this block and, yeah, they

231

might not have been coming to the place where baby drug-runners are in and out every two seconds, it might just be a fat coincidence . . .'

'Fine,' said Crystal, and hung up.

Sol watched Chapman from a safe distance, barely able to believe his eyes. She was buying drugs. He tried to think of any other rational explanation for what he'd just seen, but there simply wasn't one. The lawyer had handed over several banknotes to a younger and was now waiting for her stash. It just didn't make any sense. Not the buying-drugs part. He had long ago stopped being shocked by who used. Coppers, lawyers, judges. He'd seen it all over the years. Hell, he wasn't so lily white himself.

But why come here? It had been obvious from Chapman's faltering stroll across the front of the flats, then the same routine at the back, that she hadn't known where she was heading. It was almost as if she'd stumbled across the flat in question and decided to buy some drugs on the spur of the moment.

At last, the flat door opened and Chapman, who hadn't taken her eyes from it, pushed a stray lock of hair from her face and secured it behind her ear. When another younger came out and picked up his bike, Sol caught her taking a few deep breaths, the only sign to confirm that inside she was probably bricking it.

The lad cycled the few steps to her, then stopped, steadying himself with one hand on the wall. He reached into his waistband for something Sol couldn't see, but knew perfectly well what it was, and pressed it into Liberty's hand. As he pushed his pedals to move off, Chapman spoke. Her voice clear, all trace of anxiety banished. 'What's this?' The boy turned to her and sniffed. 'I paid for four grams,' said Chapman.

The boy shook his head. 'Two.'

'No way, sunshine. I paid for four.'

The boy stared hard and Chapman did a very decent job of holding her own, arms crossed, one eyebrow raised. Miss Liberty Chapman was a bloody good actress. But he already knew that, didn't he? 'Don't piss me about,' she said. 'Give.'

'The mandem said two grams.'

Chapman laughed. 'I don't care if the Queen herself said two. I paid for four.' She took a step towards the younger and pointed at the flat. 'Let's go in there and sort this out.'

The boy flapped his hand at her. 'You wait here.'

Chapman took another step and laughed again. 'Not a chance. You're ripping me off, or trying to.'

'I ain't,' said the boy, his tone surprisingly offended. 'He definitely said two.'

Chapman was right up in the boy's face now, her eyes wide. 'We're getting this sorted.'

The boy shrugged and circled his bike, heading back down the path to the flat. 'They ain't gonna let you in,' he called, over his shoulder.

'Let them try and stop me,' Chapman replied.

Liberty balled her fist, so that the boy wouldn't see it was shaking, and stalked after him to the flat. What was she doing, arguing with a drug-dealer? It was a plan with disaster written all over it. Though calling this a plan was an overstatement. Basically, she'd opened her mouth and some words had spilled out. She swallowed hard, trying to dislodge a hard, dry lump in her throat.

The boy knocked at the door. As it was opened, Liberty moved behind him and peered inside.

'What the fuck?' said a voice from inside.

The boy began to mumble, but Liberty spoke up over him. 'I'm getting ripped off here and I want it sorted.'

The man just inside the door stared at her. He was older than the boy, but not by many years. Eighteen tops. The hair on his upper lip was more bum fluff than moustache, and a series of gold chains hung around a skinny neck, still pitted with spots.

'I said, I'm getting ripped off here,' Liberty growled. 'And I'm not happy about it.'

The young man looked first at the boy, then at Liberty. 'What the fuck?' he repeated, and went to close the door, but Liberty skirted around the boy and put her foot in the way.

'I'm not going away,' she said, her voice rising.

The young man scowled at her foot and it occurred to her that if he slammed the door, she might get a broken bone for her trouble. But she left it there and did her best to look angry, rather than terrified.

'Fuck's sake,' he said at last, and opened the door a little wider, so that she could step inside.

Chapter 20

July 1986

It's the last day of term. Everybody's running around, yapping about what they're going to do in the long holidays. Anne-Marie Dobson's told just about anyone prepared to listen that she's going to her nan's caravan in Filey. I sit in the corner of the playground and take out a book and my lunch. I always pack a sandwich and an apple, and Geraldine always makes me bring a slice of cake. Today's offering is lemon drizzle, but the icing's not so much drizzled as slapped on, like plaster. Geraldine likes baking, even if she's not too good at it. She says it helps her deal with stress. And right now she's really stressed. She can't believe the judge said I've got to go and visit Dad and she's furious. I pick off a bit of the icing and suck it.

'Giz a bite.'

I push the lid back over my Tupperware box.

'Don't be tight.'

I look up now and have to cup my eyes against the sun. It's Mark Johnson, a lad from the bottom set, whom everybody calls Jonno.

'Only messing,' he says, and squats next to me. He runs a hand over his fresh skinhead. 'Do you like it?'

I don't know that I do. He had nice thick curly hair before. I can't think why he's chopped it all off.

'Are you going to the fair tonight?' he asks me.

I've not given it any thought so I just shrug.

'It looks a good 'un this time,' he says. 'Speedway, umbrellas, waltzer . . .'

'I'm not that bothered,' I say.

I mean, I like fairs. Last year I went with a couple of mates. We had a laugh and a couple of fair lads took a shine to us, saying they'd give us free rides and that, if we met up with them behind the candyfloss van. We didn't fall for that one. Them girls don't really speak to me now, though. I expect their mams told them not to.

'There's loads of us going,' says Jonno. 'It'll be a right laugh.'

I don't answer. I try to keep myself to myself mostly so I don't have to answer any awkward questions.

'I've got plenty of cash,' he says. 'I've been helping my uncle Barry on his pop van every weekend.'

The back of my neck goes hot and prickly. 'I've got my own cash, thanks for asking.'

He looks at me all embarrassed when I fish in my bag and bring out the emergency money Geraldine insists I carry about.

'I didn't mean anything by it,' says Jonno. 'I just didn't know what happens when you're in care, like. I didn't know if they gave you pocket money.'

'Well, they do,' I say. 'Plenty.'

Jonno laughs. 'Right, then, you can pay for me.' He gets up and wipes the dust from his trousers. 'We're meeting outside Woolie's at half six.'

'I didn't say I was coming, did I?'

He's still laughing, but he seems a bit less cocky now. When one of the other lads kicks a football at him, he heads it away with a big leathery slap. 'You should come,' he calls to me. 'Life's too short as it is.'

The hallway darkened as the front door slammed shut. Liberty knew she was going to have to think fast. In another room, loud hip-hop music played and someone was trying to keep up with the lyrics. A cloud of smoke hung against the ceiling.

'So what's all this about?' the young man asked the boy.

'She says she paid for four grams, but Dax said two, innit.'

'Dax is talking shit,' Liberty piped up. 'I paid for four.'

The young man took off his baseball cap and scratched his forehead. Both front teeth were chipped, which gave him an air of cluelessness. 'My youngers don't make mistakes,' he said.

Liberty shook her head. 'Do I look to you like I'm the one making a mistake? Someone told me to come here, they never said I'd be getting rolled.'

'Ain't nobody rolling you,' he said.

'Looks that way to me, sunshine.' She glanced up the hallway. The flat looked fairly small, only a few rooms where Frankie could be. 'How about we go into your kitchen and get what I'm owed?'

He slid his cap back on, narrowed his eyes and turned to the boy. 'Go find Dax.'

'Serious?'

'Am I smiling, even?'

The boy shuffled out of the door.

'So what now?' Liberty asked.

'Wait for Dax, innit.'

'And how long will that take?'

The drug-dealer didn't answer, but fished in his back pocket and pulled out a half-smoked joint. As he lit it, he screwed up his left eye against the smoke. She needed to move out of the hall-way, check the other rooms.

'Can I use the toilet?' she asked.

'No.'

'Because?'

He brought his smoke to the side of his mouth, took a drag, exhaled through the other side. 'Because this ain't a fucking hotel.'

'Come on,' she said. 'What do you think I'm going to do?'

His mouth parted and the edge of the cigarette paper stuck to the skin of his lower lip. 'You can stand outside the door, if you like.'

Liberty tried a smile but got nothing in return. 'Can I at least sit down? If we stand here much longer, I'll have to pee on your carpet.'

The dealer shook his head. 'Lady, you are some piece of fucking work.'

'It's been said before.' She raised an eyebrow and took one step up the hallway. When he didn't stop her, she felt a fizz of exhilaration in every synapse. She needed to check those other rooms, and if Frankie wasn't there, and her feeling was that he wasn't, she needed to get out before Dax arrived and the guy in the baseball cap realized this whole thing was bullshit.

Sol pulled out his e-cig and tried to fathom what was going on. When Chapman had been given her drugs, she'd started a row with the courier. A proper row. Then she'd virtually pushed her way into the flat. The way she'd shoved her trainer into the door reminded him of Angie. The first time he'd worked with his ex-wife, they'd been on a raid. The birds singing the dawn chorus, a milk float coming down the road in an electric whir. Angie had winked at him in the grey sunrise before the battering ram sent the front door flying off its hinges.

Sol smiled at the thought of it. The way they'd both loved that tension before it all kicked off. The way they'd released the tension later that night; Angie pissed on Bacardi and Coke, swaying in the pub, her sticky lips at his ear whispering, 'See anything you like, pretty boy?' He sighed and took a puff, the sickly sweet taste filling his mouth and lungs, hinting at nicotine but failing to give that hit.

'You're no longer a dirty smoker,' Natasha had told him.

Right.

'You've made a decision to have a healthier life.'

Right.

He took another drag and was watching the door when Hassani called. 'Anything happening at your end?' she asked.

'Not sure,' he said.

'Go on.'

'The lawyer's left the sister in the car and has just disappeared into a drugs house.'

Hassani caught her breath, the excitement almost palpable. 'No way.'

'Way.'

'What do you think she's doing? Buying drugs?'

'Already done that,' Sol replied.

'I don't get it,' said Hassani. 'She's gone all that way to buy drugs? I mean, why? She could get anything she wanted in the Cherry.'

Sol exhaled a cloud of vapour.

'Do you think they're doing a deal?' Hassani asked. 'Something big?'

Sol thought for a second. 'No, it's not that.'

'How can you be sure? I wouldn't be surprised if the Greenwoods wanted to expand into some serious dealing.'

'I've seen enough deals going on in my time,' he said. 'This wasn't one. It's all just too . . . random.'

Hassani snorted. 'I've met Chapman, remember? She does not strike me as someone who does anything random. She is cold and calculating, trust me.'

Sol cocked his head to one side. Calculating was probably a fair description of Chapman. She certainly struck him as someone who analysed every situation. You could almost hear her brain ticking, which was why what was happening right now seemed out of character. But cold? Maybe. He thought back to her in the hotel bar. She'd admitted to having no contact with her family for

239

two decades. Now that was indeed frosty. But there had been something else too. A hint of something behind the ice wall. Or maybe he'd imagined it.

Another younger flashed past on a bike.

'Gotta go,' Sol said, then hung up and melted back into the shadows.

Liberty strode down the hallway, peering through the first open door to a sitting room where two lads lounged on sofas, an iPhone on a coffee-table between them playing the music she'd heard earlier.

No Frankie. No Daisy.

'Who the fuck is that?' one shouted, as she walked to the next door.

'No one,' the dealer in the baseball cap yelled back.

'So what's she doing here, man?'

'Nothing.'

Liberty pushed open the next door. 'Toilet?' She knew full well it wasn't.

'Not that one,' the dealer hissed.

Liberty found a bedroom, where a couple were asleep on the bed, fully clothed, even wearing their trainers. The dealer yanked the door handle and shut it.

'Over there.' He nodded to the door at the end of the corridor. 'Be quick.'

Liberty smiled and set off towards it, checking the other rooms on her way. No sign of Frankie or Daisy, as she'd suspected. The bathroom was pretty much as expected: seat up, rim covered in pubes and no paper. As she closed the door, she knew there was no way she was placing any part of her arse on that toilet. Good job she didn't actually need to go. Instead, she pulled out her mobile and sent Crystal a text: *They're not in here.*

Now all she had to do was get the hell out of there.

She flushed the loo and ran the tap for show. Outside, she could hear that one of the other lads was talking to the dealer with the cap. He sounded angry. Liberty turned off the tap and pressed her ear to the door.

'Chill out, man,' said the man in the cap.

'Don't tell me to chill. I'm vexed and I ain't gonna chill, you understand me?' the other replied.

'It's not a problem.'

'How is it not a problem? There ain't supposed to be nobody in here but us. Nobody. Especially since yesterday.'

Liberty seized the opportunity and opened the door. Both lads looked her up and down. 'You think she's gonna give us any trouble?' asked the lad in the cap.

'That ain't the point,' said the other. 'Nobody inside. No exceptions.'

Liberty put up her hands. 'Whoa there, lads, no need for an argument. If it's a big deal, I'll wait outside.' She took a step in the opposite direction towards the front door.

'It ain't a big deal,' said the one in the cap, and blocked her way.

'It's fine, don't worry about it.' She tried to squeeze past him.

The lad didn't move. 'If I say you can be here, then you can.' He flashed his eyes at his colleague.

Jesus, that was all she needed, a pissing contest between a couple of dealers.

A third lad appeared in the doorway of the sitting room. He was carrying the iPhone, which was still spitting out hip-hop. 'What's going on?' he shouted above the noise.

Liberty put a hand to her head. It was spinning. Any second now the boy on the bike would return with Dax and confirm that she had actually only paid for two grams of coke.

'Nothing's going on,' yelled the lad in the cap. 'Why is everyone getting so fucking stressed?'

241

'You know why,' said the second, and gave him a shove.

'Don't you fucking touch me.'

As the two squared up to each other, the third shot down the hallway and got between them. 'Calm it right down, bruv.' It wasn't clear which one he was talking to but neither listened anyway, screaming around him, trying to take a swing. Liberty knew this was her moment and ran. When she reached the door, she threw it open and rushed out into the glaring sunshine.

As she raced away from the flat, Dax and the other boy turned the corner on their bikes. Shit. She couldn't let them see her. She whipped her head in the opposite direction. If she ran that way, they'd have a clear view of her and would easily catch up. Shit. She scanned the block for anywhere to hide. The only place she could see was a narrow passageway between two flats further up, presumably leading to an area for bins. The boys were almost at the garden gate. She had to do something fast.

'Fuck it,' she said, and vaulted the fence into next door's garden. Someone at the kitchen window looked directly at her, shock on his face. 'Sorry,' she whispered, ran to the next fence and jumped that too, landing with a thump in the third garden. She didn't even speak to the child waiting impatiently in bikini and armbands while her dad huffed, puce-faced, as he blew up a paddling-pool. Instead, she took the last fence like the athlete she most definitely was not, grunting as her hand caught on a nail. At last she was at the passageway and able to dart inside. Out of breath, she leaned against the wall, heaving, her palm stinging. She brought it to her mouth to suck at the ragged skin, but stopped dead. 'What the hell are you doing here?'

Chapter 21

July 1986

When Geraldine stops the car, I don't get out.

'*Don't tell me you've changed your mind.*' *She rolls her eyes.* '*What on earth's wrong with you, Lib?*'

I shrug.

'*Do you want to go back to Langton?*' *she asks.*

I shrug again.

'*Well, make a decision, please. I've already wasted an hour of my time and half a tank of petrol.*'

'*Sorry,*' *I mumble.*

She sighs, turns off the engine. '*You know, you are entitled to have some fun, Lib. Lord knows I wouldn't call being sent around in circles at breakneck speed any fun at all, but then I'm fifty years older than you.*'

'*It's just easier to be on my own,*' *I say.*

'*I'm sure,*' *she says.* '*But not necessarily better.*'

She gives me one of her stares, so I get out of the car. As I'm about to slam the door, she leans over and throws a fiver at me. '*I'll be here at ten. Don't keep me waiting,*' *she shouts, and drives away.*

I immediately wish I'd stayed with Geraldine. It's like she acts as some sort of barrier between me and the world. Not like a brick wall. More like a riot shield. I can see through it and keep up with what's going on but I don't feel so naked.

When I get to Woolie's, Jonno's standing there chatting to Stacey Lamb. She's in the year below us but she's got tits like watermelons, jiggling about under her T-shirt. I thought about stuffing bog roll down my bra but worried it might come loose on one of the rides. Now I wish I'd chanced it.

'Hey oop,' says Jonno, grinning from one jug ear to the other.

Stacey wobbles on her white stilettos and looks me up and down. 'Them pedal pushers new?'

They're not. In fact, they're too tight and I can feel them riding up into the crack of my arse, but I don't know how to go about asking my social worker for money for new clothes. And I can't ask Geraldine. She already gives me so much – I don't want to push my luck.

'C'mon,' says Jonno, and grabs my hand. 'Let's get going. The other lot have already gone up there.'

I let him lead me through town to the fair, listening to him and Stacey warble on about Top of the Pops. When we arrive it takes my breath away. I'd forgotten how mad it all is. Colours crashing towards us. Red and green and yellow and pink. Lights flashing. Swing chairs fly past, a few feet from our faces, the riders screaming their heads off. The smells of chips, candyfloss and diesel hit me in the face.

'Let's get on the speedway,' Jonno shouts, and we run towards it, kicking through the empty pop bottles and polystyrene trays. I have to laugh when Stacey's heel gets caught in a hot dog bun.

Jonno's other mates are already on the ride and wave to us. I don't wave back but I smile and they make room for me on a motorbike. I feel something behind me and realize that Jonno has jumped on the back. He presses against my spine and reaches around me to grab the handlebars. I can't help but laugh.

As the ride whips around and Jonno sings his head off to the music, I feel something I haven't felt in ages. Not happy exactly, but not sad either.

At half nine, I say I've got to head off.

'Past your bedtime, is it?' asks Stacey.

'I'm getting a lift back,' I say.

'From who?' Stacey asks. 'That scruffy old woman?'

'Belt up, Stacey,' Jonno warns.

'What?' Stacey fishes into her pocket for a lip gloss and takes off the top. 'I'm just wondering who she is.' A couple of the other kids laugh and Stacey runs the gloss across her mouth, letting the rollerball smear her lips. 'I don't think I'd want to live with one of them, but maybe you're not bothered, Lib.' She gives an oily pout. 'Maybe you're like that as well.'

Jonno grabs my arm. 'Let's go. I'll walk you back.'

I shake him off and glare at Stacey. 'Like what exactly?'

Stacey glances around at the others, all of them giggling now.

'You're a fucking idiot, Stacey Lamb,' I say.

'At least I'm not a lezza,' she replies.

I ball my fist and smack her hard in the mouth. I feel her lip burst wet against my knuckles. As she screams I hit her again, this time a punch to the stomach. When she doubles over I kick her. And I don't stop until Jonno drags me off.

In the cool of the passageway, the bins stinking of rotten meat, Liberty found herself looking at Sol Connolly. 'I asked what the hell you're doing here.'

He gave a cough. 'I like Brixton. Who doesn't?'

Liberty peered outside to check the boys hadn't followed her. They hadn't and were nowhere to be seen. They must have gone inside the flat. Good luck with that one, she thought. All hell was breaking loose in there. She turned back to Connolly and eyed him coolly. 'I suppose you've got a reasonable explanation?'

'Not really.'

'This is police harassment,' she said.

He ran a hand through his hair. 'I'm sure that's what you'll say in your complaint.'

'You don't seem like you care.'

Connolly gave a lopsided smile. 'What can I say?'

'You're following me,' she said. 'You shouldn't be.'

He shrugged. 'And you shouldn't be buying drugs.'

Liberty felt herself redden and steadfastly avoided looking at her bag where two grams of powder was sitting in a see-through plastic baggie. 'You didn't follow me all the way down here for that,' she said. 'So what's this about?'

'It's about Daisy Clarke and Kyla Anderson and the bullshit alibi you gave your brother,' he said. 'It's about finding out what the fuck's going on.'

She had a sudden urge to tell him everything. That she had lied for Jay because she was crippled by guilt. That anything he had or hadn't done was not his fault but hers. That she was here looking for Frankie and Daisy for the very same reason. That she was trying to make everything right. Would he understand that? Would anyone? 'Nothing's going on,' she said, her voice small.

The front of Daisy's hair had dried into hard strands and her eyelashes were clumped together. She licked her lips and tasted their stickiness. Outside the room, Brixton Dave was raging into his phone. 'So who is she?' he screamed. 'What d'you mean you don't know? I pay you to know these things, arsehole.'

She heard a crash and a thump, presumably from him kicking the wall. Things were moving on to a whole new level. 'Listen to me, you fucking little toerag. Get your crew and find her.' He was panting in fury. 'I want some fucking answers.'

Sol appraised Chapman. He could arrest her right now for possession. In fact, that was what he should do. Arrest her, take her to the nearest nick, let the local plod deal with her. Then he could jump in his car and head to the nearest service station, fill the tank with petrol and buy some fags. He'd be home in time to take Natasha out for dinner. She loved that little Greek place with black-and-white photos on the wall.

'I don't know what you've got yourself into,' he said to her. 'I'd have thought you had too much to lose.' She pressed her lips together. 'But you must realize that things are spiralling out of control now, and that you need to step on the brakes.'

She didn't answer, didn't even look at him, but kept her lips tightly locked.

'Can you at least tell me where Daisy is?' he asked.

'Daisy?' The word tumbled from her mouth.

'Yes,' he replied. 'Daisy Clarke. Whatever you might think about her, she's pretty vulnerable.'

'I know that—'

Chapman was cut off mid-sentence by the arrival of three youngers on bikes who stopped and blocked the entrance to the passageway he and she were in. The sound of spokes and brakes told Sol that the exit behind him was similarly obstructed.

Chapman's eyes widened as she, too, understood their predicament. 'Well, this isn't good.'

One of the boys jumped off his BMX. Sol recognized him as the one Chapman had bought her drugs from. 'Why are you chatting shit about me, bitch?' Spit flew from his mouth. 'Saying I rolled you when I never.'

Chapman put up her hands in surrender. 'Simple mistake.'

The boy shook his head wildly. 'Nah, nah, nah. You didn't make no mistake.'

'Look, I thought I'd paid for four grams,' Chapman said.

'Four grams! Fuck that.'

The boy reached into his waistband and pulled something out. Sol heard Chapman's sharp intake of breath before he saw the gun. 'Come on now.' He kept his voice very calm. 'There's no need for this.'

The boy turned and pointed the gun at Sol. 'Don't tell me what I need. I will tell you what I need.'

'Okay, okay,' said Sol, his eyes locked on the barrel of the gun. 'What do you need?'

'I need to know what this bitch is doing in our area, causing strife to me and my crew.'

Sol nodded slowly. He was outnumbered six to one and at least one of the six had a weapon. Maybe all six did. The odds were not good. 'I think she just came to buy some drugs,' he said.

The boy hawked up a mouthful of snot and spat.

Behind him another younger in a black sweatshirt with a white skull emblazoned on the front laid down his bike. 'And what about you?' He squinted at Sol. 'What you doing out here?'

'I'm here with my friend,' Sol replied. 'That's all.'

'And where you from?' the boy asked. 'Manchester, is it?'

'Leeds,' Sol replied.

'Same thing.'

Even in these most dire circumstances Sol felt the strong desire to explain that that could not be further from the truth.

'Man, this is fucked up,' said the boy with the gun. 'We got people coming from up there acting the Big I Am yesterday, then these two now.' He looked around at the other boys. 'I say we pop them.'

Chapman, who already had her back against the wall, pushed herself even further into the brickwork. Sol took a breath. 'Look, we don't want any trouble,' he said.

'Too late,' the boy spat.

'Right, then.' Sol was surprised when Chapman spoke and was even more surprised by how unruffled she sounded. Her ability to separate her voice from her obvious terror was impressive. Did that come from appearing in court? he wondered. 'How about you take us to who's in charge?

'Chapman,' he warned.

'What? These are just bits of kids.'

Sol groaned. All gangs had youngers. And, yes, they were just bits of kids. But they were bits of kids without any real boundaries. They took all the risks, both in terms of getting nicked, or getting hurt by rivals, and for what? A few quid to buy new trainers and to make a name for themselves. Chapman needed to tread very carefully here.

'Come on, Dax,' she said to the boy with the gun. 'Someone's sent you to come and get me, and I don't think it's Soft Lad in there without any front teeth.'

Sol heard movement behind him. Then the blow came swiftly. A sharp jab to his kidneys. Pain exploded, ricocheting through his body, and he had to fight for breath. Then blackness.

Having her vision removed left Liberty paralysed. Whatever had been pulled over her head seemed to prevent her from moving. It was as if a switch had been flipped and each muscle in her body stiffened. She was half pushed, half carried into a car, then out again. All she could do was try to breathe. Her feet could barely hold her as she was dragged through a door and inside.

When the hood was pulled from her head and the light hit, like battery acid, the switch turned again, flooding her mouth, nose and ears. Every skin cell felt raw. A scream rose in her throat but caught as a man towered over her. 'One sound and I will shut you up with this.' He held up a roll of silver tape. 'Understand?' The scream was suffocating Liberty, but she held it in and nodded.

'All right, then.' He grabbed both her hands, yanked them outstretched in front of her, pressed them together and taped the wrists. Then he dragged her backwards from the middle of the room to the wall. When she was close enough, he moved in front of her and shoved. The back of her skull banged against the wall and she slid down to her knees. The breath left Liberty as a shockwave of pain ran through her neck.

She concentrated on her breathing, while the agony in her shoulders and head subsided and her eyes adjusted to the light. The man ignored her and taped her ankles. He was small in stature, slight even, but he had a wiry energy that frightened her. As he moved away, she saw that she wasn't alone with him, but that there were two more figures: Sol Connolly, face down on the carpet, a rucksack over his head, and Daisy Clarke, also sitting, back against the wall, hair matted, with strands stuck to her cheeks.

Liberty looked around the room wildly for Frankie but there was no one else.

The man bent down, lifted the edge of the bag on Connolly's head and spoke up it. 'I'm gonna take this off, now. Not a word, okay? Not a sound.' He waited, then removed it. Connolly's face was contorted, his lips pulled back from his teeth. He heaved him across to the wall with the window, only one grunt escaping the policeman's mouth when his back knocked against the plaster, then taped his hands and ankles in front of him. The man stepped back. 'Well, ain't this nice?' He gave a grin showing teeth as ugly as his haircut. Liberty glanced at Connolly, but he still had his eyes squeezed shut and was biting his lip, presumably to stop himself crying out.

'Now I'm going to step outside and speak to someone,' said the man. 'And you lot are going to be as good as gold and we can all be friends.' He patted Connolly's head, making him wince. 'If you're not going to be good, then that's where things get tricky. I'd have to tape your mouths up, see.' He waved the roll. 'And that ain't nice, not at all.' He moved from Connolly to Daisy and grabbed her nose, pinching together her nostrils. 'Especially if I do this.'

Daisy's eyes opened wide but she didn't flinch. Liberty wanted to shout out, to tell him to stop.

'Best thing you can hope for is that you pass out.' The man released Daisy's nose in disgust. 'But you might throw up before that and choke on your own vomit, which, I'll be honest, ain't the most pleasant way to go.'

Liberty swallowed hard, already able to taste bile in her throat.

'Now I ain't a monster. I don't want anyone to die here. Do I, Daisy?' He looked at her and she quickly shook her head. 'But I ain't about to let anyone cause me no trouble either, so it's up to you how this goes.'

He grinned at all three of them in turn and left the room.

Chapter 22

August 1986

'Are you my solicitor, then?' I ask.

The woman looks up from the big stack of papers she's reading and smiles at me. Right at me. Not like everyone else who can't face me. 'No,' she says. 'I'm a student, just working here in the holidays.' She's got this mad curly hair that she's tried to rake back into a bun. It reminds me of our Crystal. 'Mr Christian's been held up in court but he'll be back soon.'

There's a pink file on the desk between us with my name written on it in black marker. Next to it there's a toy. Well, I think it's a toy. It's a silver metal stand thing, with four balls hanging from a bar. She sees me frowning at it. 'It's for stress,' she says.

I stare at it. What does she mean? She lifts the first ball, lets it swing so it hits the second, which swings and hits the third, which swings and hits the last. Then they all go backwards. She laughs. 'I don't know either. Give me a bloody punch-bag when things are doing my head in.' She raises an eyebrow. 'Though you've probably done enough punching, lady.'

I feel myself go red and watch the balls hitting one another with a little click until they slow to a stop. 'She called Geraldine a lezza,' I say.

'Your foster-mother?' she asks.

'Not any more,' I say.

'They've moved you again, have they?' she asks.

I nod. 'What's going to happen now? Will I have to go to court?'

She flicks through the papers, running an ink-stained finger down the

252

margins. When she finds what she's looking for, she gives it a tap. 'Well, it didn't help matters when you called the arresting officer a "boz-eyed twat".'

'No,' I say.

'But Mr Christian managed to convince them to offer you a caution. So, providing you keep your boxing gloves to yourself in future, you should be all right. You've been through a lot, and you don't need a criminal record on top of everything else. Not with this thing with your dad hanging over you.' She nods at me. 'It's up to you, though, where you go from here.'

'How do you mean?'

She shrugs. 'You can go the way everyone expects, getting into trouble an' all that. No one would bat an eyelid, would they? Or you can show the likes of Stacey Lamb exactly what you're made of.' She laughs. 'And I don't mean by battering them.'

'How can I do that?'

She puts her hand on the file, pressing down on my name. 'I've seen your school records. You're clever, aren't you?'

'I suppose.'

'How clever do you think Stacey Lamb is?'

'She's virtually backward,' I say.

'Well, then.'

When Mr Christian arrives to take me to the cop shop for my caution, she waves me goodbye. 'Did Miss Chapman explain to you what's going to happen?' he asks.

I nod. 'She explained a lot of things to me.'

Liberty listened intently until she was sure the man was far enough away. 'I'm assuming that's Brixton Dave,' she said.

Daisy didn't react, but stared ahead, eyes heavy-lidded.

'Daisy,' Liberty hissed. 'Daisy, look at me.'

Daisy turned slowly towards her.

'That's Brixton Dave, yeah?' asked Liberty.

Daisy gave a slight nod.

'And where's Frankie?' Daisy didn't react. 'Is he here?'

'I suppose so.'

'But you haven't seen him?'

'No.'

'Heard him?'

Daisy shook her head. Then she looked at Connolly, whose breathing had slowed to a jagged rasp. 'You shouldn't have got the police involved,' she said.

'I didn't,' Liberty replied. 'He bloody well followed me here.'

'When him out there finds out what Sol is . . .' Daisy let her words hang in the air. 'It's not going to end well.'

'He won't find out,' Liberty replied.

Daisy sniffed.

'Well, I'm not going to tell them and I'm bloody certain he's not,' said Liberty. She looked around. Her bag was gone, with her purse and phone and everything else. Presumably Connolly had been searched too and had had his stuff taken. 'Hey,' she whispered to Connolly, as loudly as she dared. 'There's nothing on your phone to say what you are, is there?'

Connolly looked as if he was about to respond but instead leaned forward and threw up, splashing his boots. Liberty wondered why on earth he was wearing boots on such a sunny day, but reasoned that right now he was probably glad. The Parmesan smell of stomach contents filled the room.

Connolly spat and groaned. 'Can someone please tell me what the fuck is going on?'

'Is there anything on your phone?' Liberty repeated.

Connolly shook his head and spat out another gob of vomit and mucus.

'What about your warrant card?' Liberty asked.

'At home,' he said. 'I'm not on duty. Now tell me what's going on.'

Liberty looked at Daisy, her hair in stiff dreadlocks, her top stained orange. 'Do you want to do the honours?'

Daisy sighed. 'That bloke out there is someone Frankie met in Marbella. They kept in touch.'

'Everyone likes a holiday romance that works out,' said Liberty.

Daisy ignored the crack. 'They set up some sort of job together. I was meant to help.'

'I'm assuming it didn't go as planned.'

'I tried to tell Frankie it was dodgy,' said Daisy. 'But you know how it is with him.'

In truth, Liberty didn't know how it was with Frankie. She could try to imagine, but she didn't actually know. It was an unpleasant thought that this woman, with all her problems, knew him better than she, his own flesh and blood, did. 'So he kidnapped you both?' she said.

Daisy nodded. 'Got me to ring Crystal for the money.'

Connolly stared at Liberty. 'And that's why you're in Brixton?' His chin was damp with vomit. 'You should have called the police.'

'Because you've been so accommodating to me and my family thus far,' Liberty snapped.

'You should have just paid up,' Daisy mumbled.

'Jay and Crystal are getting the cash together. In the meantime I figured out you were down here and thought we should try to see what's going on.'

Daisy snorted. 'And how's that working out for you?'

A needle of pain lanced Liberty's shoulder-blades. Right now she had to admit that things were not working out too well. She closed her eyes and tried to think, tried to work out the best way forward.

'We need to stay calm,' said Connolly. 'See what the next move is.'

Daisy raised an eyebrow. 'I like you, Sol, I always have, but your trouble is, you don't think like they do.'

'Don't I?'

'Nah,' she said. 'Which is why you're a good bloke. And why, right now, we're completely fucked.'

Outside the room, Brixton Dave was shouting. 'What do you mean, you don't know who they are? Didn't I say you needed to find that out? I mean, how hard can it fucking be?'

There was a mumbled response before Brixton Dave flew into the room, slamming the door behind him. He immediately went to Connolly and checked the tape on his hands and ankles. 'Jesus,' he roared when he realized there was puke on Connolly's legs and wiped his hand down his jeans. Backing to the other side of the room, he sniffed his fingers. Then he gave the wall a swift kick, leaving a hole in the plaster. Another kick made Liberty's whole body freeze.

'Right,' he said. 'I need to know a few things.'

Liberty and Connolly exchanged a look. They should tell this man absolutely nothing. Given the state he was in, the wrong information could send him over the edge.

'I think we'll start with Daisy here.'

Daisy's head shot up, her eyes wide. 'I don't know anything. How could I?'

Brixton Dave smiled at her, pulled a knife from his back pocket and tapped the blade against his lower lip. The metal caught the light and cast a patch of white on the wall, like a small star.

'I've been here the whole time,' Daisy was gabbling. 'I don't know what's been going on.'

He danced his head from side to side in a maybe–maybe–not gesture and made towards her. When he reached the other side of the room, he slid down the wall so he was seated between her and Liberty. Daisy leaned away from him. 'Now that's not nice, is it?' His words were addressed Liberty. 'And I've been so nice to our Daisy.'

Liberty couldn't take her eyes off the knife. The steel was hard, the edge sharp. She could hear a repeated shushing noise, thought it was the man, then realized it was Daisy quietly crying.

Brixton Dave shook his head. 'See, now on top of puke I'm going to get snot, and that doesn't make me happy. Not one little bit.' He took Liberty's chin in his hand, forced her to look away from the knife and into his face. His breath was like sour milk. 'Why do you think Daisy's behaving like this?'

Liberty's tongue felt thick and dry. It sat in her mouth like a dead thing.

He squeezed tighter, pinching her skin, and brought up the knife so that it was inches from her face. Liberty held her breath, her heart cracking her ribcage. 'She's frightened.' Liberty's voice was a scrape in her throat. 'We're all frightened.'

Brixton Dave nodded and brought the knife flat side down against Liberty's cheek. It was cold. She held impossibly still. Next, the silver of the blade swam through the air like an electric eel and Daisy shrieked as the man brought it down. 'Oh, shut the fuck up,' he said.

Liberty bent forward, expecting to see a gash and crimson blood. Instead, the knife was working through the tape that was holding Daisy's ankles. 'You and me are getting out of here, Daisy,' he said. 'Time for a nice little chat.' He cut the final strip and stood. 'Get up.' He watched as Daisy leaned to her left, pressing her arms into the floor next to Liberty. Then she pushed her knees under her so that she was on all fours, backside in the air.

'Oh, my days,' said Brixton Dave.

Daisy breathed heavily as she used the wall to lever herself to her feet. She shot Liberty a look, her eyes darting downwards. Liberty followed her eye-line and saw a small metal tube.

'Get a move on, girl,' the man shouted.

Daisy grunted and turned, losing her footing slightly so her leg swept out to the side. As she straightened up, Liberty felt the tube being nudged into her thigh.

Brixton Dave threw Daisy into another room. This one was equally bare, without even a carpet. The only difference was that blankets had been fixed across the window so the room was gloomy. 'Kneel down,' he said.

Daisy did as she was told, feeling the cracked floorboards against her shin bones. She was so thin, these days, every bone in her body felt like it could pop through the skin any moment.

'Don't drag this out, Daisy.' He still had the knife, holding it loosely, passing it from one hand to the other. 'Just tell me who they are.'

Daisy let her shoulders sag and her eyes droop as she desperately tried to work out what to say. She couldn't tell him about Sol. God knew how he'd react.

'Help yourself here, Daisy,' he said. 'I wasn't planning on killing you and I still don't wanna. But you know how it goes.'

She had no reason to protect Sol. What had he ever done for her? He'd been half decent to her, but that didn't mean she had to put herself on the line, did it?

'The woman's Frankie's sister,' she said, assuming that he would work this out sooner or later anyway.

He drew back his head. 'You're shitting me?'

Daisy shook her head.

'And what? She came looking for him?'

'I suppose,' Daisy replied.

'What about the guy?' he asked.

'Dunno.' Daisy looked away. 'They have a lot of people work-ing for them.'

He stood over her, eyes narrowed, weighing her up. He put the knife in his back pocket and Daisy breathed a sigh of relief. Then he pulled out his fags and held out the packet. 'Want one?'

'Please.'

He lit one and placed it between her lips, then lit one for him-self. Daisy took a deep drag and watched him through the plume of smoke as he paced around the room. 'People like that,' he said, gesturing to the door with the burning end of his cigarette, 'they think they can do what the fuck they like. They think there'll never be any come-back.' He gave a knowing nod. 'But they're wrong.'

Sol scanned the room. The only exits were the door and the window behind him. He arched his back and turned his head to try to see outside, but the strain sent a juddering pain through his flank that told him he'd be pissing blood for a week. He weighed up their situation. At some point Crystal would realize there was a problem. The same went for Hassani. But what would either of them do? Crystal would not call the police. That much was obvi-ous. And without the police, how could she find them? Hassani would call in back-up eventually, but how long would she leave it? This wasn't an official job and there would be trouble for both of them if she went to a senior officer. She knew that and would avoid involving anyone else for as long as she dared.

In the meantime, Sol was tied up with a nutter breathing down his neck. A nutter who might find out he was a cop at any second. There was no way Daisy wouldn't give him up. Why wouldn't she? 'We have to get out of here,' he said.

Chapman looked up at him. 'Plan?' she asked.

'Fuck knows,' he replied. He brought his wrists to his mouth, tried to bite the tape. It was thick, wound round several times and he couldn't make any headway.

Chapman shuffled over towards him. 'Daisy left this.' She held out a tube that looked like it had been used to smoke heroin. 'Can we use it?'

He checked it. The surface of the tube was dull and smooth but the end had possibilities. As if reading his mind, Chapman ran a finger over it. 'It's not sharp.' She looked around, her gaze resting on the radiator. 'If I rub it against that, I might get somewhere.'

Sol nodded.

Chapman propelled herself to the radiator. 'Tell me if you hear him.' She began to scrape the tube against the side of the radiator, stopped at the noise it made. 'Shit.' She tried again, this time making longer slower swipes in an attempt to keep the sound down.

'Why did you get involved in all this?' he asked.

She kept working. 'Why did you?'

He watched her. Even now, she looked expensive. Hair well cut, teeth white and straight. He imagined a big house with a wardrobe (probably one of those you walked into) full of smart clothes. A boyfriend with a posh name and floppy hair. Nights at the theatre watching complicated plays, with bottles of champagne during the intervals. 'You have a life in London,' he said. 'I bet it's a nice one. You've put all that at risk, for what?'

'You have no idea what my life's like in London.' She finished at the radiator and moved to Sol, indicated for him to put out his hands and began rubbing the now sharpened tube against the tape.

A small crackle told him that it was going to work. A loud succession of thumps told him their captor was coming back. 'Quickly,' he whispered. 'Get back over there.'

Chapman was barely in place when Brixton Dave stamped into

the room. 'Daisy's a good girl,' he said. 'I like Daisy, don't you?' He looked from Sol to Chapman and back again. Neither of them spoke. Sol kept his hands in his lap to hide the damaged shreds of tape. 'Daisy understands the situation in which she finds herself, you see.' He tapped the side of his head with his finger. 'She's worked it out.'

Sol assumed Daisy had given him up. Granted, he and Daisy went back a long way. But what was that worth? At the end of the day, he was police and she was an addict. Why wouldn't she give him up? He wasn't worth taking a kicking over.

'So the price has just gone up,' said the man.

Sol frowned. The Greenwoods weren't about to cough up for his safe return.

'Half a bar for baby Frankie.' Then he leered at Chapman. 'And half for his big sister.'

Daisy strained at the tape around her wrists. No give. Now her legs were free, she thought about hiding behind the door. When Brixton Dave came back, maybe she could surprise him. Knock him out? But it would be hard with her hands still tied. If she messed up, he'd just shank her, wouldn't he?

Shit. He was coming back.

Daisy knelt down again in the same spot and hung her head.

'Right then, Daisy.' He held out Frankie's phone. 'You're on.'

'What?'

Brixton Dave squatted in front of her. 'You're going to tell Crystal Greenwood that we have her sister and we want another five hundred grand.'

'A million quid?' Daisy asked. 'I don't think . . .'

'What? You don't think they've got it?' He laughed. 'Maybe not lying around, no. But they can get it if we give them a bit of time, don't you think?'

Daisy blinked. She had no idea. The Greenwoods had money, yeah, but that much?

Brixton Dave went into recently called numbers, redialled Crystal and put her on speakerphone.

'Daisy?' Crystal sounded out of breath. 'Is that you?'

'Yeah.'

'What's happening?'

'They've got Liberty,' said Daisy.

Crystal didn't speak and only the sound of her panting filled the room.

'They want another five hundred,' said Daisy.

'When and where?' Crystal asked.

'We'll let you know,' Daisy replied. 'Just start getting it together, okay?'

'Yeah, okay.'

Brixton Dave hung up, biting his thumbnail. He wasn't happy. 'Too easy,' he said.

Daisy closed her eyes. He was right. Crystal should have asked more questions. She should at least have asked if Liberty was all right.

'She's here,' he said. 'That bitch came with the other two.'

Daisy wasn't about to say so, but she agreed with him. Jay might even be down here too. And some of their people. 'Crystal won't risk her brother and sister,' said Daisy. 'Family's everything to the Greenwoods. She'll pay up.'

But he was no longer listening.

Chapter 23

September 1986

My new school shoes are slobbing a bit at the back. I tried to shove some cotton wool in the toe, but that made them too tight. Tomorrow I'll wear two pairs of socks and hope that does the trick. This blazer's too big as well. Whoever had it before me must have been a giant.

The other kids stare as I cross the playground. My cheeks burn in shame but I stick out my chin, like Geraldine used to. I do that a lot, when I feel nervous or something. I pretend I'm her. I wish I could tell her that, but the new social worker says I shouldn't get in touch and I need to avoid any more trouble.

Mr Christian says they'll find a new foster placement soon, but I'm all right as I am at the care home. I'm in no rush. I keep myself to myself mostly and I'm near enough to Crystal and Frankie's so I can see them sometimes. Jay's been moved further away so it's trickier to visit him. Mr Christian says he's asked for a travel voucher for me.

I open the door and go down the corridor to the school office. There are a couple of women inside tapping away on typewriters. One of them looks up at me. 'What can I do for you, love?'

'I think I've got some transport arriving,' I say.

'Name?'

'Lib Greenwood.'

She checks down her list. 'Is that short for Liberty?'

'No.'

'Shame,' she says. 'That would be a great name, wouldn't it? Like a film star or summat.' She stabs the list with her thumb. 'Got it. Taxi's outside so I'll sign you out.'

'Thanks,' I say.

She scribbles her name across a sheet of paper. 'Where you skiving off to then, love?'

'Going to see my dad,' I tell her.

Liberty sawed at Connolly's bonds. They were tearing, but so damn slowly. Sweat trickled down her face, into her eyes. She blinked away the salt sting, carried on as fast as she could manage. 'What are you going to do when this is over?' she asked him.

'I'm going to arrest that little prick with his stupid name and make sure he goes on remand in the Mansion.'

Liberty gave a faint smile. 'Sounds like an idea.' She looked up at him. 'What about me? Are you going to arrest me?'

'For what?' asked Sol.

'The coke,' she replied.

'Do you really think that means dick to me?' Connolly asked. 'Anyway, the evidence seems to have gone walkabout.'

The tape came apart and Liberty stopped for a split second to push the hair back from her damp face. Then she passed the tube to Connolly and held out her own wrists. He worked fast, using one hand to cut and the other to hold the tape taut. As soon she was free, Connolly used the tube on his ankles while she attacked hers with her nails.

When they were both loose, Connolly got to his feet and held out a hand to help Liberty to hers. Instinctively they both checked the window. There were no keys to the locks, but the frame looked old, paint peeling from it. 'We can sort that,' said Liberty, and Connolly nodded. 'But we can't leave without Frankie and Daisy.'

'You can,' Connolly replied.

'No.'

'You can get to a phone.'

'No.'

Connolly put a hand on each of her shoulders. 'I can't work you out.'

'I can't work myself out.'

Exasperated, Connolly darted to the door, dragging Liberty with him. He pressed her flat against the wall to the right, then positioned himself similarly to the left. 'When the door opens, I'm going to slam him with it. You move round and kick him in the balls. Hard. Very, very hard.'

'Thank God you said that, or I might have gone easy on him.'

Liberty and Connolly held their breath and waited. It had been a long time since Liberty had hurt anyone, but she knew how easy it was. Kicking this idiot in the balls wouldn't be difficult. It would be a pleasure.

At last they heard Brixton Dave's footsteps, accompanied by his voice as he spoke into his phone. 'I'm telling you,' he said. 'I've got the brother and the sister here now.'

Liberty watched Connolly who held up a finger as if checking the wind. Every muscle in his body was rigid and his eyes were clear and bright. She felt as though she were in freeze-frame as she waited for Connolly's signal. The only noise was the slow but deafening beat of her heart. As Connolly gave a chop with his finger, the air and sound rushed back into the room. He swung the door with force and Liberty heard the crack of wood on bone. She leaped from her hiding position and faced Brixton Dave. His face was a bloody mess, the bridge of his nose split down the middle. When he registered that she was free, his arm moved to his back pocket but Liberty pulled back her knee and kicked out.

The toe of her trainer landed exactly where she wanted and the air left him with a satisfying whoosh. She struck out again and this time he fell to his knees. Her third kick caught him under the chin and his head was thrust backwards in a sickening arc.

He lay on his back in a daze, and Connolly grabbed his feet, dragging him into the room. Blood spilled from his nose and throat. Once inside, Liberty snatched the tape from the window ledge and bound his hands. Together they went through his pockets, seizing phones, lighters, knife.

Outside the room there was a narrow corridor. Connolly stepped into it cautiously, reached out and pushed open the door opposite. The room beyond was empty and he shut the door. He moved down the corridor, beckoning Liberty to follow. She did so, squeezing in closely behind him. He stopped at the threshold to the next door, looked over his shoulder at her and nodded. Again he stretched out his hand and opened the door.

The smell of urine and sweat unfurled towards them and there, in a corner of the room, curled up in a tight ball, was Frankie. Liberty pushed past Connolly and ran to her brother. She ripped off the tape covering his mouth and cupped his face. His eyelashes were matted with salty tears and there was a crust of dried vomit on his T-shirt. He looked like the wide-eyed little boy she'd abandoned a lifetime ago. 'Lib?'

'Yeah.'

'What are you doing here?' he asked.

'I've come for you, Frankie.'

His voice wobbled. 'I fucked up big-time, Lib.'

'Been there, done that,' she replied.

Connolly threw the knife to Liberty. She caught it and quickly freed Frankie.

'Where's Daisy?' he asked, rubbing his wrists. 'We can't leave her.'

'We're not leaving anyone,' Liberty said.

Connolly signalled that they were on the move again. Liberty helped Frankie up and they crept after the policeman.

There was only one door left on the landing, next to the top of the stairs. A little tile was stuck to it, covered with pink flowers and sparkly letters that read 'Thea's Room'. Connolly pushed the door open and revealed Daisy, sitting on the floor, desperately rubbing the tape around her hands against the radiator. She looked up at them. 'Thank God.'

Frankie took the knife from Liberty and cut away the remaining tape securing Daisy's hands. She yanked it from her skin, balled it and threw it into the corner in disgust. 'Where's Mr Fuck Face?' she asked.

'Knocked out and tied up,' Liberty replied.

They moved out of the room and began to make their way down the stairs.

'Quickly,' said Connolly. 'We need to get out of here before any of the youngers get back.'

Liberty took the stairs two at a time. She could almost feel fresh air on her skin. They'd done it. She didn't know exactly what would happen next. Would Crystal and Jay be prepared to leave things? Would Connolly? Right now, she didn't care. All she wanted was to get out of there. The rest could wait.

At the bottom of the stairs there was a small hallway, light pouring in through the glass panels of the front door. Freedom.

Suddenly, a dark shape appeared on the other side of the glass. Then there was a voice. Dread crept through Liberty's chest. As the door opened, she could barely breathe.

'Jesus Christ, Lib,' said Crystal. 'I thought I told you to stay where I could see you.'

Liberty began to laugh.

'It's not funny,' said Crystal.

Liberty moved forward and threw her arms around Crystal's

HELEN BLACK

neck. Her sister's body remained stiff, but Liberty clung on all the same.

'Personal space issues,' said Crystal, patting Liberty's arm.

At last Liberty let her go. 'How did you find us?'

'Jay's contact in Spain came up with the address,' Crystal replied. Then she turned her eyes to Frankie. 'You are dead meat when your brother gets hold of you.'

'Can I have a hug first?' Frankie asked.

'No,' Crystal barked.

'As touching as this family stuff is, can we get out of here?' Sol asked. 'The rest of the crew can't be far and they were definitely packing.'

'And who the fuck are you when you're at home?' asked Crystal.

Back at the Porsche, Crystal hustled Frankie into the back, where he slumped, eyes closed. Chapman stood at the passenger door, both hands on the car roof.

'We'll need to speak about this, Miss Chapman,' Sol said.

She nodded, breathed hard and pulled the band out of her hair. 'I don't know what I'll have to say.'

'I'm sure you'll think of something,' Sol replied, and led Daisy to his car.

He gunned the engine and set off for the nearest petrol station, where he bought a bagful of crap. Daisy fell upon it like it was treasure, scrabbling at the lid of a bottle of Mountain Dew, taking a bite of a Picnic and lighting a Marlboro Red. Sol bit into a Ginster's Cornish pasty, winced and lit a fag instead.

'What's going to happen now, Sol?' Daisy asked.

He exhaled smoke out of his nose in two long flutes. 'I don't know about you, Daisy, but I intend to go and get very drunk indeed.'

268

'Won't your wife have something to say about that?'

'Yep.'

Daisy stubbed out her cigarette in the ashtray. 'Like that, is it?'

Sol didn't answer but took another long drag and turned on the radio.

Chapter 24

September 1986

I used to joke that Geraldine's house was like a castle, but the prison really is a castle. It's got one of them great big archway doors and turrets and everything. I expect a knight on horseback to come charging out any second.

'I think it's this way, Elizabeth,' says my social worker, Darren.

I've never liked that name. It reminds me of a lad in our Jay's class at school. Darren Matthews. He always had a runny nose and had to wear one of them patches for a lazy eye.

We walk around the side of the castle to a much smaller, normal-looking door. Which is a shame: I fancied waiting for the big wooden doors to creak open and walking through like some sort of princess.

There's a bit of a queue forming so we join the back, Darren checking the paperwork for like the hundredth time. He's a bit of a worrier is Darren, which makes me think he won't be in this job too long. In front of us, two women are moaning and smoking cigs. They've got a little boy with them. He's black and is blowing a spit bubble. You don't see too many black people round our way. There's only one in my year at school. She's adopted. What's funny is that she's much better-looking and much cleverer than all her white brothers and sisters who aren't adopted. I bet their mam and dad never saw that one coming.

When we finally get to the front, the guard takes the paperwork from Darren. 'Did no one get in touch?' he says.

'No.' Darren shakes his head so hard it might fall off. 'No, no one got in touch.'

The guard sighs and scratches his chin. 'You'd better come this way.'

Darren gives me a smile that's supposed to say Nothing to Worry About. I don't know why he's bothering cos I'm not especially worried. If the visit's cancelled I'll be perfectly happy. I won't have to see Dad and I'll have missed double maths.

The guard leads us down a corridor to a metal door that he holds open for us. To get inside I have to sort of duck under his arm and get a whiff of his BO. He tells us to sit down while he fetches someone 'more senior' so I take a chair, but Darren paces up and down. 'I honestly don't think there's any need to worry,' he says.

I sigh.

At last the guard comes back with someone else. As far as I can tell it's just another guard in the same uniform, only a bit taller and a bit balder. 'I'm afraid we've got some bad news,' he says.

'Oh dear,' says Darren.

'Mr Greenwood has been involved in an altercation.'

Darren flaps the paperwork around his face, fanning himself as if he might faint.

'You mean a fight?' I ask.

The guard nods.

'Is he all right?'

The guard looks at Darren, quickly works out that he's worse than useless and walks over to me. He puts a big hand on my shoulder. 'I'm sorry, love, but he was stabbed.'

'Is he dead?' I ask.

'Yes, love, he is.'

The Black Cherry was busy when they arrived. A couple of stag parties were in full swing. One group, all in red T-shirts declaring them part of the Pussy Party, ordered pitcher after pitcher of watered-down beer. The girls, sniffing easy money, were circling like vultures.

Jay caught sight of their arrival and strode towards them. He looked at Frankie with relief that soon turned to anger. God, he reminded Liberty of Dad, the way his emotions could turn on a penny. 'You've got a lot of talking to do,' he barked at Frankie.

Mel put a bony hand on Jay's arm. 'Not now, Jay. Not here.'

Jay was still growling, but he allowed himself to be led to the bar.

'What's everybody having?' asked Len.

'I'll sort this, Len,' said Mel, scooting behind the bar. 'You go and clear a few tables. That mob over there are spilling more than they're drinking.'

Len nodded and made himself scarce, while Mel pulled out a bottle of Jack Daniel's and lined up five shot glasses. She filled each one with dark brown liquid. Liberty didn't particularly like bourbon, and she never drank it without ice and Coke, but tonight she picked up her glass and downed it in one. The burn in her throat was shocking but not unpleasant. Mel filled the glasses for a second time.

'This is a mess,' said Jay. 'How likely is it that Brixton Dave will be looking for come-back?'

Liberty knocked back the second shot. 'He's a nutter, so who knows?'

'Then there's the copper,' said Crystal. 'What's he going to do?'

Liberty shrugged. She had no idea how Connolly was going to play this.

'Maybe we can pay him off,' said Jay.

'He doesn't seem that type,' said Liberty.

Mel poured more Jack Daniel's. 'Everyone has a price, love. Though it's not always money.'

The stag party in the red T-shirts roared behind them. Liberty turned to see that a man had jumped up on stage and was dancing around with one of the Lithuanian girls, sloshing beer from his glass down her black-and-pink basque.

'Oh, for fuck's sake,' said Mel. 'If this lot can't behave we need to turf them out, Jay.' She came around the bar. 'Let's all do what we've got to do tonight, get some kip and meet back here first thing.' She gave Frankie a stare. 'And that includes you, so don't even think about taking off to see Daisy the fucking Dog.'

Crystal grabbed Frankie's collar. 'He's coming home with me.'

Mel nodded. Then she and Jay stalked away to control the punters.

Crystal pulled out her phone. 'Do you want a cab, Lib?'

Liberty shook her head.

'Well, you can't drive,' said Crystal. 'We're already in enough shit without you getting nicked for a DUI.'

'I'm not going to drive,' said Liberty. 'I just need a bit of fresh air to clear my head.'

The night was actually hot and humid, the air damp. The street-lights cast a sickly yellow glow. Never mind. Liberty needed to walk. And she needed to be away from Crystal and Frankie. Just for now. It was too far to walk the whole way back to the hotel, so she took the road heading into town. She'd get a cab there.

As she strolled past a pub, she noticed a couple outside. He was young, handsome. The girl was standing very close to him, almost touching but not quite, blonde hair in a messy bun, one escaped tendril falling down her back to meet the zip of her short red dress. She said something to him, which made him smile and kiss her. Liberty tried not to stare, not that it mattered: they were oblivious to her, totally in the moment.

At the next T-junction, Liberty crossed into Carter Street. It had always been a dodgy area, the red-light district, and nothing had changed. Working girls were huddled in groups, chatting, lighting fags, keeping a look-out for clients and cops. At this time of night, the shops were all shut, but light spilled out from an all-night café. Liberty smelt hot fat and bacon and, remembering how hungry she was, she went inside. She took an empty table and checked the plastic-backed menu.

'Be with you in a minute, darling,' called the owner, in a strong Glaswegian accent, as he carried sausage sandwiches over to a couple of skinny rent-boys in the corner.

'No rush,' Liberty called back. She was just weighing up whether she wanted fried eggs on toast or burger and chips, when a man stumbled in, hot and drunk. 'Bloody hell!'

'Well, if it isn't the lovely Miss Chapman,' Connolly slurred back. He staggered towards her table and wobbled in front of her.

'Everything all right, Sol?' the owner shouted.

'Never better, Tony.' Connolly saluted with two fingers. 'I've been punched in the kidney, had a bag put over my head, threatened with a knife and a gun. A pretty good day all told.'

Tony laughed and shook his head. 'You're a funny man for the polis.'

'A compliment indeed,' said Connolly, taking a bow.

'You're also pished, I see.'

'That I can't deny,' Connolly replied.

'I'll bring you a strong coffee,' said Tony.

Connolly gestured to the chair opposite Liberty and she nodded. He sank into it, pushing his hair from his eyes. Liberty noticed that one eye was slightly more oval than the other and had an old scar running under it, like a perfect smile. When he noticed her looking, he shook his head so that his fringe masked him again.

'Been on a bender, then?' she asked.

He shrugged.

'I'm not lecturing,' she said.

Tony came over with tea for Liberty and a coffee for Connolly. 'It'll help you sober up,' he said.

'I'm not sure I want to sober up,' said Connolly, but he took a sip all the same.

Liberty ordered fried eggs on toast. 'And some bacon.'

'Don't ask me what I'm going to do,' said Connolly.

'I wasn't going to.'

'Because I don't know,' he said, putting down his coffee with exaggerated care. 'I need to work it all out.' He tapped the side of his head. 'Process it.' He put his elbow on the table and tried to rest his chin in his palm but missed. 'I need to get everything under control.'

'Control's an illusion,' Liberty told him. 'We try to control things to make ourselves feel better. But we're just in denial.'

'Denial about what?'

Liberty laughed. 'About everything. That the world is spinning in spite of what we do. That our understanding of it is tiny. That we're all just a bunch of needs and wants and urges.' The food arrived and she cut a huge forkful, cramming it into her mouth.

'You remind me of my ex-wife,' said Connolly.

'That doesn't sound good,' she said, through the food.

Connolly patted down his pockets, took out a packet of Marlboro, put one in his mouth. 'Why?'

'I'm assuming there's a reason she's the ex.'

Cigarette between his lips, he searched his pockets again, presumably for a light. When he couldn't find one, he sighed and put the fag behind his ear. 'She's the ex because I'm trying not to be a bunch of needs and wants and the other one . . .'

'Urges.' Liberty picked up a rasher of bacon with her fingers and took a bite.

'Trouble is,' said Connolly. 'I'm fucking rubbish at it.'

★ ★ ★

275

Sol woke with a headache and a sore throat. Natasha had already gone out but had left a bottle of water and a packet of paracetamol on his bedside table. He took two before throwing off the duvet and heading into the shower.

He'd spent hours last night in Scottish Tony's, drinking coffee with Chapman. They'd talked. A lot. She'd told him what had happened to her parents, her brothers and sister. He'd told her all about his mum and Angie, and a whole lot of other things he never even thought about most of the time, if he could help it.

Eventually, when he was virtually sober, she'd stood to leave and given him a slow, sad, secret smile. 'Be kind to yourself, Sol Connolly,' she said.

And he'd stood too, facing her across a greasy table piled with chipped cups and ketchup-smeared plates. He'd wanted to kiss her then, full on the mouth. He didn't think she would have stopped him, but in the end he stopped himself.

He groaned now and poured a huge dollop of shampoo directly onto his head from the bottle – some peppermint stuff Natasha always bought that felt weirdly cold even in hot running water. Why couldn't life be straightforward?

Daisy headed to the Black Cherry in a taxi. It was too early and it wouldn't even be near open yet, but Jay had summoned her and she was in no position to argue. 'Hurry up, would you?' she told the driver, who was watching her through his rear-view mirror. 'And keep your eyes on the bloody road.'

There were some drivers who would knock off the fare for a blow-job. And, yeah, she did it sometimes, when she was skint. But today she was in no mood. She was already in a truckload of trouble with the Greenwoods and the last thing she needed was to be late.

The car park was a mess. Pools of vomit, discarded T-shirts and a blow-up doll tied to a lamppost. Mel was already at the door, face like a dying monkfish. 'Get in,' she said. 'They're all here.'

Once inside, all four Greenwoods turned to look at her. Daisy's hands were already sweating and she wiped them down her top. Crystal glared at her, as if she could cheerfully have killed her on the spot. At least Jay was behind the bar, pouring everyone an orange juice. Though she wouldn't have put it past him to vault over it and knock her head off. At least Frankie looked as nervous as she felt. As for Liberty, well, it was impossible to tell what she was thinking. 'It weren't my idea,' she blurted out. 'Sorry,' she said to Frankie, 'but you know it weren't.'

'We know that,' said Liberty.

'You can't blame me,' Daisy said.

Jay gave a growl in his throat but Liberty spoke again. 'No one's blaming you for anything.'

'Then why am I here?'

'We need to work out what we're going to do now,' said Liberty. 'We need to make a plan.'

Daisy almost laughed. She hadn't made a plan for over ten years. Each day she got up and made herself feel better the best way she could. Then, when she felt worse, she made herself feel better again. Sometimes it was easy. Sometimes it was harder. She just reacted to what came along.

'We think maybe you and Frankie should go away for a bit,' said Liberty.

Daisy's scalp began to itch and she raked it with her nails. The Greenwoods wanted her gone. But where would she go? She didn't have anywhere else to go. She didn't know anyone, except a few junkies and working girls living in a two-mile radius.

'We were thinking that rehab might be a good idea,' said Liberty.

HELEN BLACK

The soundtrack of Daisy's life came to a scratching halt as someone lifted the needle.

'We'd pay,' said Liberty. 'Obviously.'

Daisy glanced at Jay, who was still scowling. This was definitely not his idea and she doubted it was Crystal's either.

Frankie lifted his head to look at her. He seemed tired this morning, his hair a bit dirty, crusts of yellow sleep in the corners of his eyes. 'We both know we need to,' he said.

Daisy blew air through her mouth. Rehab? Obviously, she'd thought about it. Usually when she was up in court and needed to tell the magistrate something. It was easy to think about it when you knew there was no chance in hell of getting funding. 'How long?' she asked.

'Seventy days,' Liberty replied.

Seventy days! Christ, she hadn't been without class-A drugs for seventy hours since she was seventeen. Even in jail she'd always managed to make sure she packed enough in her arse to last her until she got bail. 'Can I think about it?' she asked.

Mel looked at her watch, a big gold face with a leopard-print strap. 'You've got about ten seconds, sweetheart, then the offer's off the table. So I suggest you go back to that shithole you call home, pack your tut and get your arse back here in an hour. Otherwise, you're on your own.'

Liberty watched Daisy leave. 'Do you think she'll come back?'

'Who knows?' said Mel.

'Who cares?' said Jay.

'I do,' Liberty replied.

'And I do,' said Frankie.

Jay rolled his eyes. 'It's a bit late to be coming over all caring and sharing now.' He pointed at Frankie. 'You got her into a heap of shit and now we're having to pay to get her out.'

278

'I said I'd pay,' Liberty muttered. It had been her idea to send Daisy and Frankie to rehab. They needed to be out of the way in case there was any come-back from Brixton Dave. Rehab seemed to kill two birds with one stone and she'd offered to foot the bill numerous times.

'This is a family problem, so the family is paying,' said Crystal. 'End of story. To be honest, we've got bigger fish to fry here.'

Jay nodded from behind the bar. 'The copper. What's his name again?'

'Sol Connolly,' Mel replied, tapping acrylic nails against the granite worktop.

'And we don't have anything on him?' Jay asked.

'Not a thing,' said Mel.

'I say we make him an offer he can't refuse,' said Crystal. 'Put him on the books.'

Liberty shook her head. Sol was not someone who could be bought. She'd known that from the start and last night had only confirmed it. If they offered him cash for his silence, he'd be furious. 'I think that's a bad idea,' she said.

'You would,' Crystal snapped.

'We don't even know if he intends to do anything yet,' said Liberty. 'I mean, he didn't actually speak to Rebecca, did he? And he didn't pursue me for harassing Daisy either. So what makes us think he'll do anything about what happened in Brixton?'

Crystal snorted and Mel leaned over and tapped Liberty on the arm. 'You're worth a bob on, love,' she said.

'What do you mean?'

Jay sighed. 'We're the Greenwoods, Lib. The police will use any leverage they have. Maybe not today, maybe not tomorrow, but one day, trust me, this will come home to roost.'

'But how?' Liberty asked. 'We didn't actually do anything wrong. We were the victims here.'

Jay put up his left hand and touched the thumb with his right index finger. 'First, I got Daisy to retract her statement for you.'

'I didn't ask you to do that.'

He waved that away and went back to his list, touching index finger with index finger. 'Second, I lied to police about visiting Kyla.'

'And I might have lied about her working here,' Mel added.

Jay tapped the middle finger of his left hand. 'Third, there's the small matter of you giving a false alibi.'

'And us paying off your speeding ticket,' said Crystal. 'And all that's before Bonnie and Clyde here went down to London with guns.'

Liberty deflated. 'So what do we do?'

Jay took a sip from his glass of orange juice, winced and opened an ice bucket. Inside there was just a pool of water. 'Let's get him down here and ask him. See what he's after.'

Chapter 25

I was right about Darren. He's put in for a transfer to another team. I'll be allocated a new social worker soon, but in the meantime someone temporary comes with me. Rachel Something. I like the way she's done her eye-liner, all flicky, like Cleopatra.

We pull up outside the mortuary.

Rachel stabs at the bell.

At last a bloke comes and opens the door. He's wearing them white and green overalls you see on the telly. He's even got a pair of thin plastic gloves on his hands. Not the yellow ones for washing-up. 'Can I help you?' he asks.

'We have an appointment,' says Rachel. 'To see a Mr James Greenwood.'

The man looks puzzled. 'No one by that name works here.'

'Mr Greenwood isn't an employee,' says Rachel, with a smile. 'He's dead.'

The man's eyes open wide as if the thought of someone being dead is shocking. Which is a bit weird, considering where he works.

'We've come to view the body,' says Rachel.

'Right.' The man seems flustered. 'Unfortunately no one told me you were coming.'

'Well, that is unfortunate,' says Rachel. 'I believe that, with the court proceedings concluded, this is probably her last chance to see her father's body.'

281

'I see,' says the man, and ushers us inside. 'I'm afraid that, because I wasn't expecting you, the cadaver hasn't been prepared for viewing.'

I wonder what they normally do to make a dead body presentable and if it makes any real difference.

He takes us down a corridor where there are two doors. One's marked 'Preparation Room', the other 'Storage'. When Rachel puts her hand on the first, the man gives a cough. 'Not that one. I was working in there when you arrived.'

We move to Storage and go inside. It's cold. Colder than the kitchen at Langton Manor, which is saying something. One of the walls is metal with handles attached to it and the man pulls at one and it slides towards him. Bloody hell! Dad really is in storage. He's only in a drawer . . .

'Are you sure you want to do this?' the man asks me. 'It can be quite traumatic.'

'I'm fine,' I say, twisting my bangle.

He nods and steps around the drawer. It's obviously a body in there, but it's covered in plastic. The man begins to unroll it at the top end until I make out a tuft of dark hair. I take a step closer and I can see him now. It's Dad, but it's not Dad. His skin is a strange grey. His lips have no colour at all and they look all papery and dry. Mam would say they needed a good dollop of Vaseline. His eyes are closed but his mouth is slightly open and I can see his top teeth, brown from years of smoking. He smells of disinfectant.

Apparently, there was a fight in the prison showers and someone stabbed him. Not with a proper knife, but a toothbrush with a razor blade melted into it. By the time the medics got there, he was already dead.

'These things happen in prison,' Rachel said to me, on the way here.

I look at Dad for one last time and step away.

'Thank you,' I say to the man, and leave the room. I keep walking until I'm outside in the car park where a bit of sun is trying to peep through the clouds.

★ ★ ★

Sol put a Diet Coke in front of Hassani and took a long draught from his pint.

'I can't believe you went all the way to Brixton and then lost them,' she said.

'Ran out of petrol,' he told her.

Hassani looked in pain. 'We've got nothing, Sol. Daisy's still on the missing list so eventually the case against Rance will collapse. And we can't budge Chapman's alibi, so there's nothing doing about Kyla Anderson.'

'You win some, you lose some,' Sol replied.

'I don't know whether I can do this any more.' Hassani closed her eyes and, for a second, Sol thought she might cry. 'I'm trying to do a good job, but it's like I'm stood on an ocean of ice.'

'Very poetic.'

Someone turned the music on and 'Everybody Hurts' by R.E.M. filled the bar. Sol snorted and spat beer onto his trousers.

'You think it's funny?' Hassani asked. She dipped her fingers into her Diet Coke, extracted an ice cube and threw it at him. He just laughed all the harder.

When he received a text, he drained his pint. 'Gotta go.'

'I don't know how you can just walk away from all this,' said Hassani.

'There's more than one way to skin a cat.'

Mel was waiting for Sol at the door of the Black Cherry. He felt surprisingly calm. And he was very curious as to what the Greenwoods would have to say.

They were sitting at a table near the bar. Liberty, Jay and Frankie, like peas in a pod. Only Crystal, with her curly red hair, seemed to jar slightly. There was an empty chair, which he took.

'What can I get you, Sol?' Mel asked.

'I'm fine, thanks,' he replied.

She nodded and sat on a stool at the bar. All four Greenwoods looked at him intently. They were nervous, as well they might be. Sol had to admit he was enjoying that.

'Thanks for coming.' It was Liberty who spoke.

'Why wouldn't I?' he asked.

'I can think of a lot of reasons,' she said.

Sol opened his palms. 'And yet here I am.' He looked at Mel. 'Maybe I will get that drink.'

'Beer?' she asked.

Sol nodded, and no one said anything further until Mel put a bottle of Bud in front of him. He picked it up and brought it to his mouth. He took a sip, wiped his lips and placed the bottle back on the table.

'We'd like to know what you're thinking, Sol,' said Liberty.

'I'm thinking I should probably drink less,' Sol replied. 'Not good for me at my age.'

Liberty pursed her lips.

'Oh, you mean about what happened in Brixton?' said Sol, with a chuckle.

'And the rest.'

He took another swig of beer. Didn't speak.

'Are you going to do anything?' Liberty asked. 'Are you going to take it further?'

He eyed her across the table. If she was tired after their late night, she didn't look it. Her hair was freshly washed, hanging around her face, clean and shiny.

What was he going to do about what had happened in Brixton? Well, he'd already lied to Hassani about it, hadn't he? The fact was, he should never have been there. He'd put himself in a stupid situation and ended up with no perp to show for it. 'I'm assuming that no one in this family wants to report a crime,' he said.

'What crime?' Liberty murmured.

Sol laughed and took another drink. He already knew that Daisy wouldn't corroborate anything he might say about what had taken place. 'Just tell me one thing,' he said. 'For my own peace of mind. What happened to Kyla Anderson?'

Liberty leaned forward, her face serious. 'Jay didn't touch her.'

'He went to the hospital to visit her, though.'

'Yes.'

'Because?'

'Because she's a friend of his and that's what friends do.'

'What about you?' Sol asked. 'Are you okay with the lies you've told?'

Her eyes darkened. 'I've lived with a lot worse.'

Liberty watched Sol Connolly leave with a pang of regret. She shouldn't care what he thought of her, yet she did. Was it possible that he understood? That none of this was about truth and lies, but something much more important?

'Can we trust him?' Crystal said.

'Trust a copper? Are you shitting me?' Jay said.

'He's not going to say anything about Brixton,' said Liberty. 'What's he going to do? Say, "Sorry, I forgot to report a kidnapping, but it slipped my mind. Oh and, by the way, none of the other people involved will give evidence"?'

Mel slid off her stool and took Connolly's empty seat. 'She's right. The time for him to say anything to the powers-that-be has been and gone.'

'So we're in the clear?' Frankie asked.

Jay cuffed him around the back of the head. 'For now, maybe. But something tells me we're going to be hearing from DI Connolly again.'

The door opened behind them and Liberty expected him to

be there with another question. When she saw who it was, her heart raced.

'Well, ain't this nice?' said Brixton Dave. 'We've got the band back together.'

Jay stood, knocking over Connolly's empty beer bottle, but Brixton Dave had a gun aimed at him. Behind him was Dax, also holding a gun, though his was aimed at Liberty.

'Where's my little Daisy, though?' said Brixton Dave. 'It's not the same without her cheeky face, is it?'

If he'd seemed out of control before, today he was almost manic. His nose was swollen, with a large cut across the bridge, and both eyes were black. He moved his jaw up and down mechanically and hopped from side to side in a perpetual motion. Even Dax looked at him with a wary eye.

'What do you want?' Jay asked, his voice impassive.

Brixton Dave laughed. A horrible high-pitched cackle. 'Hear that, Dax? They want to know what we want.' He strode towards the table, yanked it with his free hand, upturning it so glasses and bottles crashed to the floor, shards of glass skittering across the room. The barrel of his gun was now less than a foot from Jay's forehead. If he fired, Jay's skull would hit the door at the back of the bar.

Liberty glanced at Dax. He was still locked onto her own face with his weapon, further away than Brixton Dave, but easily able to kill her with one shot. The fear was like a physical pain in her stomach.

'Nothing to say, Frankie, mate?' said Brixton Dave. 'I mean, you left in such a hurry yesterday.'

'Dave—' Frankie began, but Jay silenced him with a look.

'Oh, yeah, I see what Frankie means now,' said Brixton Dave. 'You think you're the right old big swinging dick, don't you? The top boy, eh? King of the manor?' He looked around the Black Cherry. 'Except your manor's a fucking shithole. So what does that make you? King of a shithole.' He let out another peal of screeched laughter. 'Sit down,' he told Jay.

Jay sat. His face gave nothing away, but a tiny muscle was pulsing at the corner of his mouth.

'Excellent,' said Brixton Dave. 'Look how much happier we all are when we play nicely. Now who's got the keys to this place?'

No one moved. Or spoke. Brixton Dave crunched through the broken glass and pushed the muzzle of his gun into Jay's face. Jay didn't flinch. Then, without warning, Brixton Dave snapped the gun away and pointed it at Frankie. Unlike Jay, Frankie let out a whimper.

'So.' Brixton Dave grinned. 'Keys?'

There was another pause, the silence punctuated only by Frankie's ragged breathing.

'Oh, for God's sake,' said Mel, and reached into the pocket of her leather trousers for a fob of keys. They jangled as she let them dangle from her finger. Brixton Dave winked at her and gestured to Dax to take them. The young lad did as he was told and headed to the door.

Liberty exhaled loudly, relieved that his gun was no longer trained on her.

'Don't get too comfortable, Princess,' said Brixton Dave. 'There's still a lot of work to be done.' He pressed his gun so close to Frankie that the metal touched the skin of his temple. Frankie closed his eyes. 'If I pulled the trigger, there'd be quite a mess here. Serious amounts of claret.' He applied more pressure, forcing Frankie's head sideways. 'And all the other shit. Bone, hair, brains, you'd be surprised how fucking horrible it is.'

Dax came back and stood close to the group.

'Where's the safe?' said Brixton Dave.

Again, no one spoke.

'This is getting boring now,' said Brixton Dave, and Liberty heard the click as he removed the safety catch of his gun. 'I don't wanna hurt anyone but, to be honest, I don't care if I do. Your call.'

Liberty didn't know much about guns. But she knew enough to understand that, once the safety was off, even the smallest pressure on the trigger was dangerous. If Brixton Dave tripped right now, he would blow Frankie's head clean off.

'It's in the office,' said Crystal. 'I'll show you.'

With the gun still glued to Frankie, Brixton Dave flashed a smile at Crystal. 'Well, thank you for your kind offer, but Dax is gonna go with this one.' He jerked his head at Liberty. 'Ain't that right, Dax?'

Dax just grunted and Liberty's heart sank.

'She doesn't know where it is,' said Crystal. 'And she doesn't have the combination.'

Brixton Dave tutted loudly. 'What sort of family business is it where the big sis doesn't get access to the money?'

'She's not part of the business,' said Crystal. 'She doesn't even live round here.'

Brixton Dave nodded as if he understood and dropped his voice to a whisper. 'I get what you're telling me. But here's the thing. She kind of made this her business when she came sniffing around.' He looked at Liberty now, his eyes dead. 'And when she kicked me in the meat and two veg.'

Dax skirted the group, until he was standing at Liberty's shoulder.

'Off you pop,' said Brixton Dave.

'It's behind the mirror,' said Jay, without looking at her.

'Combination?' Liberty asked.

'Jimmy Greenwood's birthday.'

Liberty stared at her brother. He used that as his code? Dad's birthday?

'Move,' said Brixton Dave.

Liberty got up and felt the hardness of steel in her lower back.

She felt unsteady on her feet as she dragged them through the broken glass. A particularly sharp piece glinted up at her. For a second she considered trying to grasp it to defend herself, but she knew that Dax would put a bullet through her spine before she'd even got to the floor.

She walked across the bar to the office and opened the door. Jay had had numerous deliveries and his desk was piled with boxes, one for Leather Bondage Bralettes. The picture on the side was of a woman on a bed wearing a black bra with so many straps and studs she'd have been more comfortable in a strait-jacket.

Liberty moved behind the desk to the huge mirror. When she pushed it to one side, she found a built-in safe. 'Could you help me move this?' she asked.

The boy just glared at her.

'I won't be able to do it on my own,' she told him. 'I might look strong but I'm not bloody Popeye.'

'Who?' the boy asked.

'Never mind. Just take that end, would you?'

The boy stood still for a second, clearly weighing things up. Then he slipped his gun into the back of his waistband and took the left side of the mirror in both hands.

'How old are you?' Liberty asked, grasping her end of the mirror. 'Fourteen? Fifteen?'

The boy didn't answer but took the weight of the mirror and together they lifted it up from its hinge.

'I'll take that as fourteen, then,' said Liberty.

They carried the mirror to the side of the office and propped it against the wall. Dax then removed his gun and waved it first at Liberty, then at the safe.

'Trust me, Dax.' Liberty approached the safe and checked the code pad. 'This isn't going to end well.' Dax gave a snort and Liberty shot him a glance. 'What? You think him out there has got this all under control?'

'Seems like him and me are the ones got the gats.'

'Gats? You've been watching too much telly.' Liberty opened her eyes wide. 'He's going to get you killed.'

Dax's eyes blazed. 'Just shut up and open it.'

Liberty went back to the safe and pressed the date of her father's birthday. There was a bleep and the door unlocked. 'You need to use your brains here, Dax,' she said, opening the door and peering inside. 'You've got your whole life ahead of you and you do not want to make today the day you fucked it all up.'

Dax kissed his teeth. 'Whole life ahead of me? Don't chat so much shit. You don't know nothing.'

'I know a lot more than you think.'

Inside the safe there were piles of notes. Separate ones for tens, twenties, fifties. Over a hundred grand, Liberty estimated. 'You're going to need a bag,' she said.

'What?'

'A bag.' She held out a brick of purple twenty-pound notes. 'You're going to need one to carry this lot.'

Dax looked around the office but there was no bag.

'Try in there,' said Liberty, pointing to the box of bralettes.

Dax ripped open the box and pulled out a plastic bag containing an item of underwear. He tore open the seal and shook out the bralette. It hit the desk with a clatter of studs. 'Fuck me,' he said.

'Yup,' said Liberty. 'Now hold it open.'

Dax attempted to do so one-handed, but the plastic slid together. Sighing, he slipped the gun into the front of his waistband this time and used both hands. Liberty nodded and let the money fall in with a satisfying plop. Then she returned to the safe. She repeated the movement three times, with three more piles of cash. Then, at the back of the safe, she saw what she was expecting to find. A small handgun.

A ripple of fear passed through her, like a shiver. She had never held a gun before.

But she knew she had to put an end to this. She took hold of another stack of notes with her left hand, then reached in with her right for the gun. She lifted it by the handle. It was cold and surprisingly heavy. She slipped her index finger around the trigger. She would need to be very quick.

'How much more is there?' asked Dax.

'A few thousand, give or take,' she replied.

In one smooth motion she turned, dropped the money into the bag, so that Dax's eye-line would inevitably follow, then raised her hand with the gun so that it pointed squarely at Dax's chest. When he saw it, he gave a sound, almost a gurgle in his throat.

'Keep hold of the bag,' she said. 'Arms out in front, like they are now and turn around.'

'Fuck off,' he said.

'I mean it, Dax. Turn around now.'

'Shut up,' he said. 'You ain't gonna do nothing.'

Liberty raised an eyebrow and clicked off the safety. 'Don't tell me what I will or won't do, Dax. By the time I was your age, both my parents were dead and I'd bounced around more children's homes than I can remember. I haven't got this far by not knowing how to survive.'

Something flitted across his face. First shock, then fear. He was just a kid, after all, with a gun shoved at the place where his heart would be. Liberty physically turned him and took possession of his gun, glad that he could no longer see her and notice how violently her hands were shaking.

Daisy humped her bags off the number sixty-three as if she had a knife to her throat. She didn't want to go to rehab. Well, she did. Sort of. Fact was, it had been a shock to the system to realize that all her stuff, the things that were worth keeping at any rate, filled three black bin bags. She knew she needed to change.

But seventy days without any gear. There wasn't anyone alive who would run towards that prospect with a spring in their step.

She tried the door to the Cherry but it was locked. She rattled it hard, hoping Mel would hear, but no one came.

Jay and Liberty's cars were parked nearby so she knew full well that the Greenwoods were still inside. Admittedly, she'd taken longer than the hour Mel had given but she should try dealing with buses on a Sunday.

Her mobile rang and she saw it was Sol. 'Hiya,' she said.

'How are you?' he asked.

'I'm going to rehab, Sol,' she said.

There was a pause. 'Where?'

'Not sure yet,' Daisy said. 'The Greenwoods are sorting it out.'

'That's very nice of them.'

Daisy walked around the side of the building to the door at the back of the bar. 'Well, you know what they're like, Sol. All heart.'

'What about Rance?' Sol asked.

Daisy sighed. 'I told you before all this that I'm dropping it.'

'The officer in the case won't be happy.'

'That ain't my problem, Sol. Anyway, if I'm trying to get clean I don't need the stress. I can't be dealing with weeks in court being called every sort of cunt by his lawyers,' she said. 'Tell the Muslim bird I'm sorry. She seemed all right, but you know how it goes.'

'Indeed.'

She got to the bar door and yanked it open. 'Wish me luck?'

'Good luck, Daisy,' he said. 'I've got everything crossed for you.'

Brixton Dave leered at Dax when the boy entered the bar with the sack of cash. 'Just what the therapist ordered,' he said.

'Not really,' said Liberty, and raised the gun so it was pointing at the young lad's head.

Brixton Dave cocked his own head to one side. 'Ain't you full of surprises, Princess?'

Liberty handed Dax's weapon to Crystal, who cocked it and aimed at Brixton Dave. 'Seems you're outnumbered,' said Liberty.

Brixton Dave's left eye began to wink uncontrollably as he stepped swiftly behind Frankie. He grabbed his chin, forced his head up and pushed the gun into Frankie's mouth. The sound of one of Frankie's teeth breaking filled the room. 'Now here's a thing,' said Brixton Dave. 'If you shoot me, what are the chances of my gun going off?' He shoved the gun further into Frankie's throat, making him gag. 'What odds do you give your baby brother?'

Liberty felt Crystal stiffen beside her. The odds were very poor indeed.

'See, I'm not a gambling man.' Brixton Dave hauled Frankie to his feet. Blood-flecked spittle flew from Frankie's mouth as he choked. 'Frankie here will tell you that I don't even play the slot machines.'

Behind him, at the back of the bar, the door opened and Daisy stuck her head around. She looked about to speak until she saw what was happening.

'We can work this out,' Liberty shouted. 'Sit down like adults and have a drink.'

'She's right,' said Crystal, who had also clocked Daisy. No doubt Jay had too.

'Are you totally mental?' asked Brixton Dave.

'Probably.' Liberty gave the loudest laugh she could muster, while Daisy stood there, eyes wide. 'There's a bottle of Jack Daniel's, though, and I bet it's got your name on it.' She stared at Brixton Dave, willing him to stare back at her while Daisy crept up to the counter. Her hand, so pale and skinny, covered with scars, old and new, picked up the bottle.

'Do it,' Liberty screamed.

As if they were acting as one, Jay pulled Frankie backwards away from the gun and Daisy brought the bottle crashing down on Brixton Dave's head.

'Is he breathing?' Liberty whispered.

No one answered as they all stared at Brixton Dave on the floor, the top half of his body already in a pool of thick blood. Something white protruded through his hair.

'Is that bone?' Daisy asked. 'If it is, that is so rank.'

'We should call an ambulance,' said Liberty.

No one moved.

At last Mel spoke, her voice cool and clear. 'Jay, get everyone out of here, please.' He looked up at her and she nodded at him. 'Lock the doors after you.' She reached behind the bar for her handbag and pulled out two mobiles. 'I'll get the message out to the girls and tell them we're closed today. Gas leak. If any of them still want to work I'll organize transport to one of the other clubs.'

'The place will need cleaning,' said Crystal.

Mel had a phone in each hand. 'I'll get started as soon as you lot are out of here.'

Liberty felt herself being pulled gently by her brother, leading her to the door. She shot a last look at Brixton Dave. Then at Dax, who was still holding the sack of banknotes. 'What about him?' she asked. 'He's just a kid.'

'What do you think I'm gonna do here?' Mel asked. 'Wring his neck with my bare hands? Now fuck off out of it and leave me to get on.' Then she turned away and spoke into one of her phones. 'Danny, it's Mel here. How's the weather out there?' She paused, listened, laughed as if there was nothing wrong. 'Listen, I need a little favour.'

A week later, Liberty crossed the Radisson car park with her suitcase and found Sol Connolly leaning against her car.

'Officer Connolly,' she said. 'What an unexpected pleasure.'

'Miss Chapman, or should I call you Miss Greenwood?'

Liberty laughed. 'I really don't mind.'

'Daisy and Frankie doing okay?' he asked.

'As far as I know,' she said. 'Early days.'

'What about our friend Brixton Dave? Any sign of him?'

'Nope. Jay heard he'd taken off to Spain.'

Connolly nodded and moved the hair out of his eyes. 'I wonder if we could have a quick word about your client Mr Rance?'

'Daisy won't change her mind,' Liberty said.

'I know,' he said. 'It's not about that.'

'What, then?'

'Kyla Anderson's woken up,' he said. 'She's been able to identify the man who attacked her from photographs.'

'And?'

'And I'm afraid it seems to be the handiwork of your client Mr Rance.' Connolly paused. 'There's forensic evidence, too, so we'll be arresting him shortly to take his DNA. I'm pretty sure we'll get a match.'

'He's not my client,' said Liberty.

'No? What about anyone else from your firm?'

'You won't get them on a Sunday,' she said. 'Golf course.'

'He'll just have to get the duty solicitor like everyone else, then,' said Connolly. 'I believe Mr Raj Singh is around today.'

Liberty laughed.

'Right then,' said Connolly, and began to move away. 'I expect you'll be heading back to London.'

Liberty opened the door and wedged her case on the back seat. 'Actually, I'm going to stay with my brother for a bit.'

He nodded and smiled. 'So you're hanging around these parts?'

'Like the proverbial bad penny,' she said.

'Well, if you ever get bored, you could call me,' he said.

'I will,' said Liberty, and got into the car. 'If ever I get bored.'

He gave her his two-fingered salute and she shut the door, gunned the engine and drove away.

Acknowledgements

Thanks as ever to the Buckmans. I appreciate your support in all things and your long-standing tolerance of my poor admin skills.

Thanks also to Krystyna and everyone on the Constable team for giving me the opportunity to bring Liberty to life.

Finally, love and gratitude to my family who are prepared to share me with my imaginary friends.